SECOND SURVIVOR

By Leah Moyes

Second Survivor is a work of fiction. Names characters, places and incidents are either the product of the author's imagination or are used fictitiously. Any resemblance to actual persons, living or dead, events, or locales is entirely coincidental.

Copyright © 2020 Leah Moyes All rights reserved.

This book or any portion thereof may not be reproduced or used in any manner whatsoever without the express written permission of the publisher except for the use of brief quotations in a book review or scholarly journal.

First Printing. ISBN 979-8567188033

Cover Design by Molly Phipps/WGYC Book Design
Map Design by Samantha Thatcher
Published by: SpuCruiser Media
Email: Leahmoyesauthor@gmail.com
Website: https://www.leahmoyes.com/
Facebook @BerlinButterfly
Twitter @authormoyes

Acknowledgements

As always, I feel immensely indebted to an exceptional group of people for their friendship, love, and support of my writing addiction. This page is only a small representation of that appreciation.

To Taylor Brown and Dawne Anderson for your love of the English language and your editing talents. Especially when you catch those small details that make a huge difference in the final product. You're amazing!

To my advance critique team. There is not enough room on this page to convey your value. Every story I have written has benefitted from your suggestions and comments as readers and writers and everything you do plays a larger role in who I have become as an author. Thank you, Diana Allred, Dawne Anderson, Taylor Brown, Maria Carrasco, Wendy Hargrave, Melisa Harker, Irene Hunt, Stacey Johnson, Susan Provost, Lani Taunima, and Lina Taunima.

Thank you to my writing pals, Jennie Durkee and Stacy Johnson, for your friendship, advice, and for our getaways.

A special gràcies to Fernando Contreras, Aida Roman and Sanisera for the opportunity to be part of the Menorcan experience and my Spain buddies, Lydia McDonnell, Chloe Stringer, Elana Manasse-Piha, Ben Watson, Katie Norris, Janice Morrison, Maria Garcia and Johan Wentzel and to the wonderful people in Ciutadella for sharing your lovely town especially the *Convento de San Agustin* where the Général Chanzy story came to life for me.

Thank you, Greg, and my wonderful family for helping me to follow my dreams whether it is writing novels or digging for ancient artifacts. I love you.

Above all, to the descendants of the victims of The Général Chanzy, I wish you peace and strength and hope that I have brought some light to a dark part of history that was unfortunately forgotten.

*To Francisco and Ysabel Carrasco
and your many descendants*

Mediterranean Sea (Général Chanzy route- Marseille to Algiers)

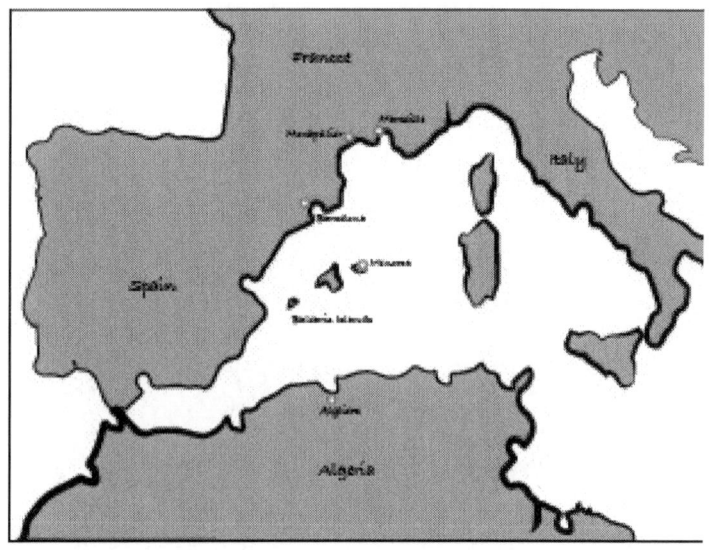

Menorca, Balearic Islands, Spain

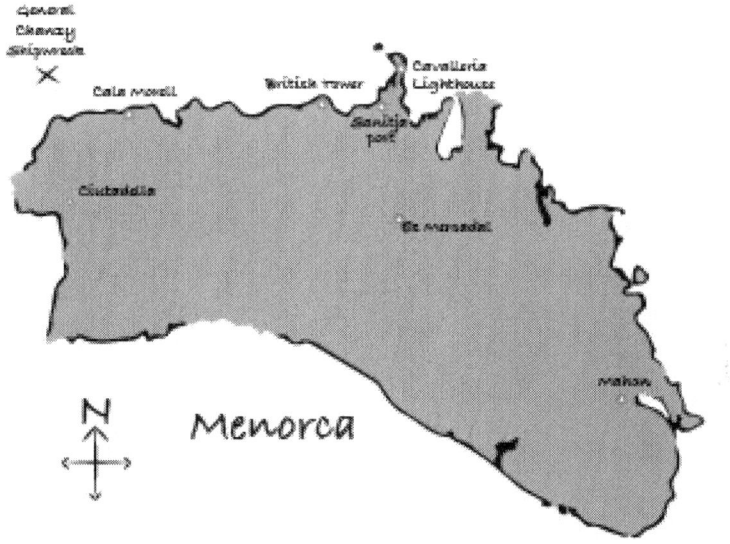

*Map design by Samantha Thatcher

Author's Note

With any historical fiction piece, dedicated research is required into locations, time periods, cultural and language differences. Though I have done my best to stay true to the time period, mistakes can happen, and I apologize in advance.

This novel includes the beautiful languages of French, Arabic and Catalan. Catalan is part of the romance branch of languages. It has similarities to Spanish, French, Italian and Portuguese. The two main languages spoken on Menorca are Spanish and Catalan, however for the purpose of this story, Catalan is used.

In most cases the author intertwines the English meaning within dialogue, but for the reader's convenience, she has included a **Language Glossary** at the end of the book.

Thank you for reading *Second Survivor*.

PROLOGUE

Algiers, Colonial Algeria

April 1909

"*Monsieur* Chastain?" Felipe gripped the rim of his hat tightly in one hand. His silvery head bowed beneath the arched entry like a spineless coward. "I have papers . . . *ton frère* insists."

I squared my shoulders and lifted my chin. This was the third time in a month my brother had sent his man of business here, and I tired of the nuisance. "Tell *mon frère* I will respond in my own time," I huffed, then shoved the pathetic little man backward. The strong scent of garlic and cloves assaulted my nose before he fell to the ground. "And do not come back to my home!" I slammed the door with such force that each of the half dozen lite panels sculpted within rattled in response.

"Arthur!" I bellowed through the vacant foyer. With its dim lighting and barren stone walls, the manor resembled more of a crypt than the fashionable Rococo style from its infancy several centuries ago. "Draft a letter," I demanded.

My manservant, Arthur, had been my father's valet since before my birth. Now he served me with similar loyalties but had grown slow in his old age.

"Today, Arthur!" I poured a glass of *Elixir d'Amorique* from the fully stocked sideboard in my study. Despite some economic shortages, my *liqueur* was never one of them. The old man's feet shuffled around the corner as he entered in his nightshirt. Peering over to the ormolu-mounted mantle clock I muttered with irritation under my breath. The gilt-bronze hour hand pointed barely past the number seven.

Without additional direction, Arthur dutifully moved to the desk and sat down. As he uncorked a bottle of ink and dipped the quill, I paced thoughtfully before him and gathered my words for dictation.

"To whom am I addressing, Monsieur?"

"Monsieur Antoine Fontaine of Bella Vista Estate, Marseille, France." I took a long sip. Even though my earlier consumption had loosened my stride—my mind was well aware of my direction. I had been contemplating this action for weeks.

I began to recite.

12 April 1909

Monsieur Fontaine,
I have the sincerest appreciation for our correspondence these last few months. The discussions we've entertained on merging our business dealings have brought forth such renewed confidence. As you know, our family corporation is expanding throughout Portugal, Morocco, and Tunisia later this year and your industry projects success throughout Northern Spain and Eastern Europe.

Notably, I pose a simple, yet powerful, offer to link our two strong, profitable establishments into one unprecedented European strength. Please consider my proposal of entering into the sacred institution of marriage with your daughter, Isabel Marie.

Bonds created through advantageous marriages have historically proven that such loyalties can become indestructible.

As Isabel is your only daughter, this cannot be a decision you make lightly. However, I pray that you will take into consideration not only my French heritage, but also the superior attributes of our compagnie established by my father twenty years ago and those same characteristics exhibited previously in our family home. You will be pleased to know she will never want for anything.

I took another long sip and smiled before I spoke . . .

I know, my dearly departed mother, a Parisian herself, could not have chosen a more suitable bride for her son had she lived to see it. I await your answer with the utmost respect.

I set the glass down and let the next words slip out casually.

*Monsieur Thomas Chastain
12 rue de Fusillés
16331 Ain Naadja ALGER*

Arthur paused. His eyes peered over his thinly wired reading glasses with a stare that bore through me.

My lip curled with impatience. "Sign it."

His hands shook slightly, but this had occurred more often as his fingers aged. His actions could not be construed otherwise. He knew better than to defy me.

"Must I repeat it?" I studied him from my angle. He irritated me so. Pouring a fresh glass of *whisky*, I waited as he pressed the tip of his utensil to the paper then supped slowly as the honeyed liqueur tingled my tongue. It took him nearly as long to sign the name as it did to pen the entire document. If only my allowance were increased as requested, I could afford a more amenable man for the manor.

"Finished?" I strolled over to him. He lifted the letter up and blew on the wet ink before I snatched it from him to inspect. Reading over the missive, I smirked with satisfaction. Even at seventy-one, he demonstrated pristine penmanship. "This is adequate. See that it is sent first thing tomorrow."

I returned to the sidebar and topped off my glass. Arthur stood to leave with the letter folded carefully in his fingers. "And Arthur . . ." My eyes issued a simple threat. "Not one word."

1

5 September 1909

Bella Vista Estate, Marseille, France

Isabel Fontaine

"Papa, why?" I peered up from the *Confit de canard* on my plate. Despite the compelling scent of bay leaves and thyme, I lost all appetite for the duck—even though it was my favorite dish.

The curl at the end of Papa's mustache went still when he stopped chewing. I knew this look. I'd seen it dozens of times in my youth. "It's your duty to the family."

"I don't know him. I've never met him." I leaned back on my chair and crossed my arms like a toddler, although we were not discussing childish things.

"You will. It's been settled. We leave for Algiers in six months."

Though the sunshine filtered through the crisscrossed lattice in the courtyard, an icy chill spread swiftly across my face. I glanced towards *Maman,* her blonde hair delicately poised in a perfect *chignon du cou* at the nape of her neck. It was her fair family traits from the Northwest of France that I most resembled. One strand of hair loosened and trickled down her cheek, but she did not take her eyes off her roasted potato.

Even the servants turned away from me.

Tears formed at the corners of my eyes. "Maman, please?" The desperation in my voice rang clear. "There are potential suitors here in France. Why must you send me away?"

Papa's jaw grew rigid. Although he had many attributes, patience was never one of them. His complexion bled a darker shade of red. "You have refused every prospective gentleman who has called on you since your sixteenth birthday."

"I will do better, I promise. Please give me another chance."

"No!" The sound rumbled across the table and shook the crystal goblets. "That's enough!"

As I stood up, the metal legs of my chair screeched against the clay tiles in loud protest. Circling my back towards my family, I crossed my arms against my chest. The patter of my fretful heart thumped against my skin. *I need to stop this. How can I stop this?* Maybe I should've been kinder to Monsieur Bisset or danced with Sir Laurent. Now I'm being shipped away . . . away from Marseille and forced to marry a man I'm wholly unacquainted with.

"Will I ever be allowed to return?" I whispered. My chin dipped and my back remained an affront to my parents as I braced for the answer. Inhaling the strong scent of hanging orchids, I worked to keep my lips from trembling. The summer bloom had always brought pleasure to me as we dined in the garden. Only now, my melancholy vanquished any beauty that surrounded me.

Papa's voice leveled, though the softness from my childhood had been absent for years. "When your husband deems it necessary." I flinched as the word *husband* slipped easily from his lips. "In time, you both may return to manage the estate and its affairs. But the decision is his alone."

I wanted to argue and refuse, yet the only word to escape my lips was "why?"

Papa's loud sigh resonated from behind. For a brief moment, my heart hoped he would change his mind, but it was fleeting. "You are eighteen, Isabel. It's time for you to accept your responsibility as the only Fontaine heir. The contract is complete." Crushed, I fled from the veranda, but Papa's thunderous voice echoed in my ears. "You *will* wed Thomas Chastain in February."

That night as I readied for bed and Ines brushed my long waves, it didn't bring forth the comfort it had in the past. Irritation festered beneath my skin. My foot tapped tediously against the leg of my dressing table where a burgundy vase rattled a fresh bouquet of *May Rose*. Even the sweet scent of my favorite flower failed to soothe.

"Settle, dear." Ines stopped brushing and placed one weathered hand on my shoulder. Her gentle touch had calmed me since birth. I leaned my cheek against her warm fingers. She was more of a mother to me than Maman had ever been, though her years would have qualified her to be my grandmother. For every fond memory that meant something to me, Ines was the only face that came to mind. Hers and the curled-up ball of fur on my lap. Rémy, my miniature Pekingese, licked my hand as if he knew my heart fell forlorn.

"My father is selling me to the highest bidder, Ines."

"Hush love, your father would not give you to any man unworthy of your hand."

"How could he possibly know anything about this man, Thomas? He lives so far away."

"Your father is meticulous in his business. I'm sure he scrutinized this gentleman with a fine-toothed comb. I know your father loves you, Isabel."

"He loves his money." I scoffed.

Through the mirror, a crooked line formed between her brows. "I don't hear any complaints about the beautiful gowns or the jeweled gifts he bestows upon you."

I lowered my eyes. My long eyelashes fluttered back tears as I caressed the lace trimming of my silk *négligé*. As the only child of an accomplished *l'homme d'affaires*, Papa's pecuniary associations afforded luxurious indulgences, including endless social invitations and a steady entourage of handsome dance partners. Yet, as silly as it sounded, the only thing I truly longed for was to feel loved. Loved by my father, my mother, and was it too foolish to desire affection with my future husband as well?

"Don't fret any more tonight, *petite fille*." Her nickname "little girl" stayed long after I'd outgrown it. Ines led me to my bed. Hesitantly, my hands brushed the edge of my Napoleon footboard and traced the delicate motifs of cherubs carved into the spiral bedpost as I contemplated the time before I would have to say goodbye. "Come, love." She held open my plush duvet and tucked me inside. Leaning down, she kissed my forehead. "All will be well soon enough—you will see."

2

Six months later-

9 February 1910

Algiers, Algeria

Thomas Chastain

"I have matters to attend to in town." I gestured to Arthur and Felicia, his wife, who served as my housekeeper. Both of whom had one foot in the grave. My days of enduring their dreary company, alone, were finally coming to an end. "I anticipate my return to be quite late." Perfecting the final knot in my *ascot*, I tucked the tail of the silk tie into my waist coat. "Have you prepared the bedchambers for our guests? They arrive tomorrow afternoon."

Felicia retrieved my long coat from the armoire and nodded. "I have completed everything you asked—the fresh linens, the flowers, the meats and cheeses, and hired an additional maid, but . . ." Her voice trailed off.

"*Oui?*" I queried through gritted teeth. "Speak up, woman."

Arthur stepped forward. His behavior suggested his need to protect his wife from my scorn. "The money, Monsieur."

"Didn't my allowance arrive this week?"

"*Non*, Monsieur."

My stare shot flaming arrows through them both. "Pardon me?"

"I gave you the note, sir . . . from Felipe. He bade—"

I brushed the loose hair from my forehead and cut him off. "You know I disregard his posts . . . and his demands." Peering into the looking glass, I studied my reflection. *It has been far too long since my last groom. I must have Elena come over first thing in the morning.* "Take what you need from the reserves, Arthur."

He didn't move, but his wife's hand reached out and touched his arm. My eyes narrowed as he lowered his head. "Th—there is none, s—sir."

"What are you saying?" They both trembled in place. I clenched my hands behind my back, fighting the temptation to strike them where they stood. *If I do so, they will likely perish, then I won't have any staff for my guests tomorrow.* I resisted.

"Y—you t—told me t—to use it for the arrears, Monsieur."

I slammed my fist against the desk. I had forgotten that our taxes came due and meant to retrieve the monies from my brother last week. *My brother, that damn fool, thinks he can play games with my stipend?* I circled back to the two pitiful figures before me. "I will see to it." Then shoved my finger against Arthur's chest. "Make sure this house is presentable."

"Oui, Monsieur."

When I mounted Calypso, the orange-blossomed scent of neroli drifted from my leather gloves, though I didn't stop to enjoy it and rode hastily from the grounds. My majestic mare always sensed my anger *and* my need for relief. If only the people in my life were as loyal or served me in this same manner, life would be less problematic. *Yet, my fate is about to change.* My smile grew steadily as I reflected on the morrow. A wealthy man will be toasting me as his son-to-be and my journey towards monetary freedom will commence.

Twenty minutes passed before I entered the back roads of Algiers. The setting sun left an eerie glow across the pitched tiled roofs, allowing the shadows to creep against the *Kabyle* stone.

My original purpose in coming to town was not to see my brother, yet here I was. Tying Calypso to the nearest post, I peeked through the workshop windows at his radiant lamps. Certainly he would still be here, he hardly ever left the workplace. I pressed the handle, surprised to find it locked.

I knocked. No answer. I knocked harder.

The door opened. A shrewd grin filled his face, the same condescending expression I had despised since adolescence. As blood, we shared distinctive similarities—dark eyes, thin lips, square jaw, and though we both favored a well-trimmed mustache, he preferred a clean-shaven chin to my bristly one.

He smirked, "I knew you'd come if I stopped the money."

My lips flattened. If he weren't essential to the success of the compagnie, I would have dispatched him long ago. Pushing past him, I invited myself in. "You are not allowed to withhold funds. It's written in the will."

"It's also written in the will that you have a duty to the family business. I haven't seen you in a month."

"I've been occupied."

"Yes, I'm quite aware of what keeps you *occupied*."

I snarled at him. "I have other matters to attend to. What is the delay?"

"I have papers for you to sign. The Tunisia and Morocco shipments are ready for departure and, of course, they require both of our signatures. This would've been unnecessary if you'd allowed Felipe in. You need to stop refusing him."

"How can you even find purpose in Felipe?" I brushed a speck of dirt off my collar. "He's an old ruin."

"He was *Père's* solicitor. Why must you be so disrespectful?"

"I'm surrounded by incompetent people," I mumbled. "I have no use for Father's scraps."

He waved me forward. "You might learn something from these so-called *scraps*. They have decades of knowledge."

When I entered Father's office, a glimpse of our youth unexpectedly caught in my throat. We used to hide under the expansive mahogany desk and let Father seek us out. Memories of slipping my feet into Father's patent calf slippers and donning his oversized fedora brought forth a twinge of remorse.

Those simpler times were long buried, but the memory stirred a singular restlessness. I peered down at my boots, unsure if I wanted to venture down a path of forsaken fantasies from times past. I glanced over to him. Repressed words tipped my tongue and emerged with hope. "Remember, brother, when we dreamt of more? Remember when we spoke of novelty and modernization?"

"We were foolish children."

"We had dreams—cultural innovations like the cinema, cabaret halls, and art movements. Don't you believe we can offer more to our countrymen?" I reached for the sleeve of his coat with unexpected enthusiasm. "There are new inventions and advanced ideas, far beyond simple merchandizing. Father held us back with old, narrow mindsets, but as the oldest heir—his executor—you can change all that. You have the power to not only conceive but implement change. We can do it together—precisely how Father wanted it."

A loud sigh escaped his lips before they pulled into a frown. "You speak of new designs and ideas, but you scarcely make an appearance at the one place you can substantiate your devotion. The industry you speak of requires time, effort, and finance, none of which you demonstrate an adeptness for. Have you checked on our associations in Spain and France recently?"

If my brother hoped to silence any further talk of aspirations, he succeeded. "Yes," I grumbled. "All is well."

Turning his back on me, he continued, "Father built this compagnie into a strong competitor in the trading world. I will not allow imprudence or indolence to damage it."

My jaw grew rigid. "I've forgotten how simple-minded you've become, brother," I retorted. "I should've known you would never see our dreams through. Besides . . ." I stalled until he faced me again. "I have plans of my own."

"What plans?"

"None that concern you."

"Everything you do concerns me."

I held my tongue and studied him. There was a time when there were no secrets between us, but that was years ago. I brushed off his feigned interest. "In no time at all, it will be you asking me for counsel and possibly even money."

He barked out loud. "What scheme are you dallying in now?"

"It's not a scheme!" I snapped. "I've made arrangements. I plan to leave this place by the end of the year. You can have that old, decrepit house back and the senile staff as well."

"Father bequeathed it to you. Why would you leave it . . . or Algiers?"

"There's nothing for me here. Greater opportunities are coming."

"What are you up to?" He eyed me warily. "And if it's so great, why are you here begging for your allowance?"

I grimaced. At twenty-eight, he might be a couple of years older, but I had always been stronger. He chose books. I chose sport. If I wanted to, I could have him on his knees in a matter of seconds. His capitulation might not take long but the adverse effects on my apparel would be inconvenient. Though he deserved to be shamed, I'd already been here longer than intended. "My time is more worthwhile elsewhere. Do you want me to sign those papers or not?"

His features pulled so tight he resembled rotten fruit. I matched his glare. A lifetime ago we'd been friends, back when the estate saw happier days. Since Mother's death, any semblance of joy in our family vanished with her.

He pointed to the desk where a small stack of papers laid on top. Handing me the quill, he watched intently as I signed them all, though no words were spoken. It didn't matter what they said. I knew enough about the business to get by but couldn't care less about the particulars. That was his responsibility.

"Here." He handed me a leather pouch of money which I promptly opened.

"You don't trust me?"

"No." I counted the bills and glowered. "It's short."

"Oui." He reached for an open letter. "Here are your latest corollaries from a pub. The compagnie will not be responsible for your temper . . . or your pride."

I ignored the letter and tucked the pouch inside my coat.

"You need to be here more often. Your accounts need attention." He showed me towards the door. "Père's instructions were clear."

"*Ah* yes . . . " My sarcasm driveled. "Father . . . yet *he's* not here either."

"That's not fair, little brother, he was mourning. He wasn't himself."

"He was a coward." I taunted. "He was weak."

A ruddy shade flared up around his ears and spread across his cheeks. He thrust one long finger toward my face. "How dare you speak of the dead in such a manner!"

My lips lifted into a self-satisfying half grin. "What does it matter?"

"Just be here!" He ordered, running one hand down the length of his worn face stopping at his chin. "Any day is preferable; your presence is needed."

"I manage my associates' accounts sufficiently. Besides, I'm busy and if Father hadn't left me that God forsaken property, I would have more time, wouldn't I?"

"It's peculiar how you speak of having such little time yet somehow manage to frequent the pubs and gaming halls in town several nights a week. And—"

"And what?" I shot around to face him, though I kept one hand firmly on the door handle.

"See *her*."

My other hand curled at my side. Eight years of submission—*his* rules, *his* restrictions, and *his* authority. The desire to clobber him arose with such intensity that flames surged through my veins. "That's enough!" My shout rattled the window but did nothing to stop his provocation.

"You still insist on wounding her." He stepped backward as if he anticipated a fight yet kept on. "It wasn't enough that she was young and innocent when she served in our home, you actually made her believe she had a future with you."

Sweat layered my forehead and nose. My knuckles turned white under my grip on the lever.

"Somehow, even now, you keep your claws in her." He must've known my temper flared. "Let her go, mon frère." His voice softened under pleading eyes. "Show some honor. Marry Charlotte or let her go."

"She . . ." I seethed, "is none of your business."

I threw the door open and let it slam against the stone exterior. Without looking back, I untied Calypso in a fury, hoisted myself easily onto her back, and galloped swiftly away. Though my fury peaked over talk of a woman, the real ire came from the resentment I held for my father. It was the same wrath that spilled over against my brother because he spoke of him as if he was an honorable man. Perhaps at one time he was, but he chose death over his two teenage sons. Mother didn't choose to leave us, but he did.

I rode faster, harder. Each time Calypso's hooves connected with the ground, another layer of hatred, rage, or loathing festered within my chest. I needed a release. A drink . . . *no, something else.* Riding past the respectable part of town I reached the squalid end of the city in a matter of minutes.

Winding through the narrow streets atop my horse, I stooped to avoid the wash clothes hung from laced wires. Retrieving my handkerchief, I placed it over my nose in an effort to prevent the gaseous smoke that swirled above metal shafts from penetrating my senses, although nothing could stop the crude scent of a nearby flesher. The raw meat blended contrary to delectable hints of cumin, turmeric, and coriander spices.

"*Marry* her?" I muttered as Calypso slowed to a stop. "She can offer me nothing but a warm bed." I descended and patted the long neck of my beautiful mare. "No, tomorrow my new destiny awaits, and I will never have to bother with my brother again."

I circled around and shook my hands as if I could shake the aggravation off as well. "Who is he to tell me what to do?"

Irritated, I forced his wily face and false accusations from my mind and stepped forward. *I've never harmed Charlotte or forced myself on her. I've never had to.* I tapped her ramshackle door and waited. *Besides, this is it . . . the last time I come. For tomorrow, I will meet my bride.*

3

9 February 1910

Carrasco Ranch, Menorca, Spain

Francisco Carrasco

"Javier?" I glanced across the sprawling knoll toward the sea and the ominous dark clouds as they swallowed what was left of our sunny afternoon.

"Sí, Francisco." My devoted ranch hand followed my focus and in response pulled his hat tighter against his forehead as if the blackened skies would unleash their fury in an instant.

"The storm is heading our direction." I shivered as a cool breeze nipped at my nose and ears. Only an hour ago the balmy rays warmed my back as I unloaded hay bales from the wagon. I flinched when a jagged lightning bolt speared through the angry firmament followed by a roaring cackle of thunder. "Take

Guillermo and Roberto with you to check the tree stakes. I can't take any chances with the crops."

Javier immediately mounted his horse. "Looks like a bad one. I'll have Charles see to the barn and the horses."

"Very well, I'm headed over to the Contreras' farm. See you in an hour."

I jumped onto Diego and galloped to my closest neighbors, still several kilometers away. As I steered down the dirt road, the dark gray clouds that gathered offshore contrasted jarringly against the bright yellow buds of wild honeysuckle that channeled my path.

Both of our properties graced the northern coast and the vehemence that hovered threatened a hostile torrent and forced the waves to swell to triple their normal size. Menorca always had its fair share of blustery weather though nature's wrath generally disturbed more of the Mediterranean than the island itself.

"*Senyor* Contreras," I cried out upon approach. Their humble domicile was tucked serenely within a half dozen almond trees.

Anita's wrinkled face appeared on the porch. Wringing her hands together, she hustled down the steps to meet me. "What's wrong, Cisco?"

"There's a rough storm heading this way. Where's Miguel?"

Both of her fists moved to her hips. "Where do you think he is?" For a woman in her seventies, Anita proved to be quite lively.

I laughed. *Of course, he's down at the cove—fishing pole in hand.*

Childhood sweethearts and married for fifty years, the stories of Miguel and Anita were legendary. As my godparents, most of my twenty-three years of life outside of my home had been spent here on their little farm.

"Should I send Henry for him?" Her tone rose with alarm.

"No, if he's at the cove, he'll see it soon enough. We have a good half hour before the worst hits us."

"Where do you need me?" Anita's sturdy frame grew taut. Retrieving a pair of gloves from a nearby chair, she appeared as though she could take on the storm single handedly.

My smile lifted halfway. I've never known a stronger spirit. "Secure your house and windows. Henry and I will batten down the barn. How's that side door?"

"Henry fixed it last week. That boy is a godsend."

"I'm sure his mother is grateful for the work. That family could sure use the wages."

"Henry?" Anita's hands cupped around her mouth for volume. The strapping sixteen-year-old came flying around the corner. He swiped his straw-colored bangs aside, though he hardly broke a sweat.

"Yes, *senyora?*"

"Bad weather comin', dear. Francisco is here to help you secure the animals."

"*Bé*, Sra. Contreras." He turned to me. "And gràcies to you, Sr. Carrasco."

"I've told you before, Henry, call me Cisco. The honor of senyor belongs to my father."

"Yes, sir."

I chuckled. I only had seven years on the lad, but he never failed to recognize authority. We rushed through the garden and to the chicken pens. I checked their fences, ushered them inside the wooden shelter, and barricaded the doors to keep them safely inside. The pigs hadn't wandered out yet, though they were quite capable of handling the storm and would most likely come out in the rain to relish the mud. Henry, the Contreras' only hired help, worked as hard as three men, therefore Anita never employed more.

A noise drew my attention to the barn door. Miguel suddenly appeared. Gripping his chest, he panted between words. "What—

can—I—do?" He must've run the path from the cove without taking a break. Anita always worried his seventy-two-year-old heart might not make it back one day.

I pointed to the side of the barn. "Ensure the seams of that new door are fastened tight. If it leaks it could ruin your hay."

"Sí."

We rushed around the property with urgency. Out in the country and far from the nearest town, the only warning we had on pending storms was darkened skies and the ache in Miguel's joints. In Ciutadella, the closest town, a relatively new system endeavored to give residents an earlier forecast. Ships in the Mediterranean Sea would use their radios to report inclement weather. It was a luxury that would surely come in handy for the rural farms one day.

"Gràcies, son." Once finished, Miguel stumbled to the porch and picked up his fishing pole where he had tossed it upon his return. "Come inside, boys. Anita would be disappointed if you didn't."

"Gràcies, but no," I replied. "I must see Javier. If we lose the olives, Father will be beside himself. Especially after losing the distributor."

"Unfortunate news following Oscar's death." Miguel sighed. He and Oscar were childhood friends and the loss stung personally, but Miguel referred to what happened *after* he died.

"Sí." The thought boiled the blood beneath my skin. Our families had been partners for over two decades, but when the elder Reyes passed away, his arrogant son went to a bigger label. My thoughts swiftly shifted to my parents and the reason they left abruptly at harvest time. "Father hopes to locate a new distributor on the mainland." I rubbed my chin noting how the stubble poked at my palm. As busy as I had been with Father absent, I'd forgotten to shave. Maybe I would get to it before my mother returned and scolded me for my scruffy façade. That, and my unkempt hair which now competed with Diego's wild mane. Wiping my forehead, I replaced my hat and stepped to the door. "You're all set, senyora."

"Wait, Cisco, wait!" She hollered from the kitchen.

Miguel tilted his head toward me and smiled. "I warned you."

I laughed.

Anita busted through the door with a bulging towel. "Here, take these."

"Sra. Contreras, if you continue to spoil me with your cooking, I will get fat."

Her eyebrow rose as she plopped the warm towel in my hands. "That's hardly possible, Cisco." She grabbed one of my arms and squeezed the muscle. "You get stronger and taller every time I see you."

"Well, gràcies." I bent forward and placed a gentle kiss upon her cheek. "You do spoil me so."

Her hand patted my face. "I try." She winked then eyed me warily. "Let me find you a nice girl, Francisco."

"Oh, no," I chuckled. "No gràcies, senyora. I'm still recovering from the last time."

Anita huffed and threw her hands in the air. "I didn't know she had peculiar tastes."

"Peculiar tastes?" I grinned.

Though she's the niece of Anita's oldest friend, she is also the mayor's daughter. Their position in society affords more luxuries than the average Menorcan but should never permit one to denigrate others.

"Maybe Ana is a tad overindulged." She shrugged her shoulders.

"Overindulged is not the word I have in mind." I snickered. Miguel sat back in his rocking chair and smiled at our banter. "Selfish," I added, "would be more appropriate."

When the Contreras' invited Ana and I to join them for dinner, she refused to remove her shawl and placed her handkerchief on the chair before she sat down. Just thinking about that night aggravated me all over again.

Anita's eyebrows arched. "She was quite beautiful though, wouldn't you say?"

I paused. "Attractive yes, beautiful no. There's a difference." I recalled her pretentiousness over Anita's simple hand sewn tablecloth and napkins, and despite Anita being the best cook on this side of the island, the woman had the audacity to murmur over their modest clay dinnerware as well. That's when I realized beauty would never be enough. The next woman I planned to court would not be a shallow, pampered miss.

"Frida's granddaughter is visiting from Almeria for the summer. I hear she has a lovely singing voice."

"*Adéu*, Sra. Contreras." I hurried down the steps before she could name all the eligible young ladies visiting their elderly relations on Menorca.

I popped a warm biscuit into my mouth the same time a raindrop hit my hand. Glancing up at the sky, I stuffed the rest into my side leather pouch and leveraged myself onto Diego. I gripped his reins, pulled to the left, and kicked him into a dead run. I had dallied too long. Hopefully Javier had everything under control at our place.

As I hit the long stretch leading to our ranch, the rain pelted down, soaking through my clothes and causing my wet hair to cling to my forehead and neck. When the thunder snarled above me, I knew this was going to be one of those nights.

I arrived at the barn where Charles met me immediately. The boy was only fifteen and strong like Henry. Within seconds, he removed the saddle from my horse and laid it over its perch. I led Diego back to his stall. He'd been my lead horse for five years now, tough, and steady. I patted his thick black mane gently. "Thank you for bringing me home, boy."

"Charles, get to the house. I will lock up here."

Charles wiped his brow and nodded. Though the ranch hands had small quarters above the barn, I always insisted they join my sister Susana and I at the main house when these storms rolled through and they readily agreed. The winds howled and tormented much worse out here.

I peeked in on each of our seven horses before fastening the main doors tightly. When lightning crackled across the sky, I ducked as if it intended to strike me down where I stood. The sky's tempestuous games had begun.

Running to the house, Susana waited at the door. "I'm glad you're back, *germà*. I was worried."

"I needed to make sure the Contreras' were okay."

She grabbed some linen and threw it around my drenched shoulders. "You are good to them. Father would be proud."

"He would've done it himself had he been here."

"Sí." She smiled faintly. "Yes, he would."

4

9 February 1910

Mediterranean Sea

Isabel

Heaven isn't supposed to hurt . . . or does it? Maybe it's Hell.

Tossed and thrown like a helpless rag doll, my limbs fought for freedom as I attempted to grasp at reality. *Where am I?* Though my body was weighed down and restricted, a conflicting sense of buoyancy and freedom emerged. *The ship!* I went to sleep on the ship. *Am I dreaming?*

I gasped.

Cold and wet, darkness enveloped me—*I'm in purgatory.*

I argued with Papa last night. My stubbornness had sealed my fate. My iniquity sentenced me to the eternal pit for sinful souls.

My rebellion and repudiation over marrying Thomas collected its final recompense.

An earsplitting crack shattered the air around me. Its lengthened fractures sliced into me as if an actual blade punctured my skin and painstakingly carved. My chest thumped wildly. Ghastly wailings followed as if the walls mourned their own death. Frantic glances—although brief—confirmed my fear that the starboard side of the ship no longer existed. Water spilled from every open cavity into a chamber that once resembled my stateroom. Heavy salt water filled my cheeks, my nostrils, and stifled my throat. The more I tried to force it out the more I swallowed.

"Maman," I gurgled. "*Aidez-moi, Pap*—" My cries for help cut short as waves continuously raged. Blackness enveloped me. *Is it behind my eyelids or are my eyes wide open?*

Fingers grazed my arm then tightly gripped my wrist. Unable to scream, I fought to detach. Once I reached the surface, a woman's dowsed face met mine.

Ines!

Relief filled my soul. Both of my hands grappled for her shoulders and clung tightly. Her wide, frightened eyes and the touch of her flesh confirmed to me the reality of the moment. *I'm not dreaming!*

Ines drew me close, resting her cheek against mine. "Oh, Isabel," she whispered. The familiar scent of bergamot was faint, but the citrus fragrance assured me of her existence and rekindled my faith.

Another ferocious clatter buried us in a violent swell and severed our grasp. Clambering for her touch once more, my body tumbled in a swirl of angry surges which hurled me through the splintered opening and out to an open sea. I thrashed fiercely as I struggled to find the surface again. Within seconds, air penetrated my watery strangulation and when I opened my mouth to unrestricted breaths, I screamed for Ines.

Nothing but blurred confusion surrounded me.

"Ines! Please, God, please?"

The strike came quickly and severely. My flailing hands desperately reached to find the pointed object that struck my head. Though I knew it had injured me, I needed it. Something solid—anything solid to hold on to. I pulled it toward me. My fingers gripped its width barely enough to grant my head an additional moment of leverage.

With each attempt my fingers made to secure my embrace on the splintered piece of timber, slivers sliced easily beneath my wet skin. As painful as the punctures should've been, they failed to suppress the shock of the frigid water. The torrent struck vigorously against my face.

Choking and vomiting, air reached my lungs once more, though exhaustion weakened me. Resting my forehead against the wood, raindrops wove a fluid path down my face and pooled deep red in the crevices of the board. My long strands of hair tangled harshly around my naked arms, while the torn sleeves of my négligé floated effortlessly across the dark surface.

Lightning branched madly above me like skeletal fingers reaching for what were once the proud flags of the *Général Chanzy*. The silhouette of its grand deck, now conquered and fragmented, emerged before a faint sunrise.

Fleeting images of my parents, Ines, and my dog Rémy tore at my heart.

"Even living a life without choice is still living, Isabel." Maman's voice echoed in my ear. Those were her last words before she kissed me goodnight. I stifled a sob. Another wave swallowed my small strip of timber as if consumed by a whale. I clung tightly as additional swells dragged me fiercely away—away from the ship, and away from my family.

Ragged groans materialized from the broken vessel as if it struggled to stay alive. I lifted my head to witness the mighty ship deliver a morbid farewell. Startling steam whistles shrilled in the eerie calm before the catastrophic explosion. Though my distance from the ship protected me from the flying debris, the shuddering enormity of the blast reached deep into my chest and seemingly gouged out my heart. Dreadfully shaken, I scrambled to keep hold of the wood, but failed and slipped into the depths of the shadowy abyss. My weakened body no longer had the strength to fight. I was descending inevitably into a watery grave.

"Petite fille." Ines' wrinkled hand reached for me once more. Her calm voice and gentle touch washed over me like the sun's rays on a balmy afternoon. Though water churned briskly around me, the struggle and anxiety of being submerged once again vanished. It was as if I subsisted in another realm, one in which I conversed and breathed underwater.

"I'm frightened." The words formed in my mind, yet Ines appeared to understand. A familiar peace spread across her face and ended in a smile. "Time to live, my love."

I reached for her, but she faded, consumed by the blackness of the deep. Before I cried out, my body jerked as if pushed, twisting and rolling under additional turmoil, then miraculously propelled to the surface. I coughed. The air came easier than expected.

Although the rain had now slowed to a sprinkle, the winds had doubled in strength. I scrambled in search of a buoy. A thick chunk of something unidentifiable floated a few metres away. With a sudden desire to live, I swam towards it.

After two failed attempts to climb atop, I clutched my night rail tightly in my fist and ripped it from my body. The clingy fabric had restricted my ankles and now with only the lightness of my *chemise* and *voile drawers*, I was able to crawl my way up the level wooden slat. My stomach lay flat, while my arms and legs extended outward in complete fatigue.

A throbbing from my forehead drew my fingers to a deep gash near my hairline. As I hesitantly explored the injury, a new line of blood trickled down my cheek and splattered in drops below my chin. I tore the lace off the collar of my chemise and pressed it against my wound knowing that the holes in the fabric would not do much, but hopefully slow the hemorrhage.

Terrified of being thrown into the water again, I gripped the plank with absolute fortitude. My fingers, riddled in fresh blood, scratched and scraped for survival against the rough sea. Ines told me I was to live, but I'm sure she expected me to do the work.

Though I personally was unaccustomed to manual labor, Ines had been the perfect example of attentiveness and devotion. Up before dawn, she cleaned and pressed my dresses, readied my bath, and always provided a warm croissant with sweet juice next to a fresh bouquet of flowers on my dressing table. Never one to complain, she met my needs as her foremost obligation and the more I considered this, the more I realized I rarely thanked her.

I rubbed my eyes. *Where did she go?* I need to find her and thank her, thank her for everything she had ever done for me.

How odd.

I pondered at the misdirection of my thoughts. I found myself worrying more about my need to show her my gratitude than my need to find her, to save her from peril. Suddenly my focus changed.

"Ines!" I called hoarsely. Surely she could hear me. I saw her, she was here. I leaned over the side of my board and blinked hard, squeezing the excess water from my eyes. The water's murkiness limited my reach. "Ines!" I cried louder and rubbed my arm where she had touched it. She *was* real, yet nowhere to be found. Aside from the seawater that streaked my cheeks, tears sprang easily. I couldn't imagine my life without Ines.

From the corner of my eye, the blue-gray tint of a budding sunrise forced the blackness of night to begin its retreat. My eyelashes fluttered through aggressive bursts of air which tossed my makeshift raft harshly about. I scanned the horizon. Only the smokestacks of the liner were visible above the hostile waves, and even then, they were sinking at a rapid pace. A faint outline of land protruded opposite the ship, offering a dash of hope. *We are not in the middle of the sea!*

A puffy bulk of wool bumped the corner of my "lifeboat". I reached to push it aside and fingered soft swollen flesh. Rippling chills ran the length of my spine as I found myself peering into a pair of ghastly white eyes, gawking upward. *No!* I opened my mouth to scream, but my throat, too dry and tight, refused to make a sound. I shielded my head in naivety. As I peeked through my fingers, my awareness rose with the dawn and a daunting reality haunted me. *The horror is real.* Every floating piece of debris suddenly became a body in my mind, even if it wasn't.

It really is purgatory.

I strained to push the body away with my foot. A part of the clothing snagged on the jagged corner of the wood and my efforts were in vain. I frantically felt for the catch and squeezed my eyes shut as if that would aid in its release. Fighting back the image in my head, I groped the folds to unhinge the form. A sharp pain burned across my shoulder and up my neck. Steeling myself to peek, I watched the body until it disappeared. *Is it a man? A woman? A child?* My weary body fell flat against the board once more, allowing the hypnotic roll of the waves to carry me and my thoughts back to the night before.

"Papa, please, may we discuss this before tomorrow?" I pleaded. For six months I had disputed the betrothal, but here on the eve of our arrival, I became desperate in my supplication.

"Isabel, you should be dressed for dinner by now. Ines, why is Isabel still in her tea gown?"

"I'm sorry, Monsieur, she insisted she speak with you first."

"Papa! Please!" I shrugged away from Ines' attempt to guide me back to my stateroom. "Do not ignore me. We've been on this ship for over a day now and you have disregarded my every concern."

"Isabel." Papa stood stately before me in his black tailcoat and matching top hat. "There will be no further discussion on this matter." He fussed with his cravat without the slightest glance my direction. "You *will* soon wed Thomas and we will *not* speak of this again."

"Papa."

"Isabel! No more!" Clipping on his pearl cufflinks, he waved for his chamberlain. "Victor, please let our guests know we will be dining shortly." This ended our conversation.

Steamed, I slapped my hands against my skirt and rushed out of the room. Tears loomed on my lower lashes and threatened to fall. Slamming the door to my connecting stateroom, I dropped to the bed hopelessly. Ines arrived a moment later, though I turned from her as if she were part of the arrangement.

"Ines, I can't do it," I whimpered. "I can't marry someone I've never met."

"Petite fille, please calm down." She reached for my hand and patted it softly. "We've discussed this. Your father has made his decision. Thomas must be an honorable man. You must believe he wouldn't give away his only daughter to someone who didn't meet his standards."

"Father isn't concerned whether the man is dreadful or not, he's only concerned about his partnership. His business means more to him than I do!"

"That is not so, dear. He loves you." Ines guided me to my feet and unbuttoned my dress. "He simply shows it differently, that's all."

"He doesn't show it at all!" I stepped out of my tea dress while Ines reached for the ivory muslin gown on the bed. I frowned, then shouted, hoping he could still hear me, "He only loves finance. He doesn't even love Maman."

"Shame on you, child. Do not speak unkindly of him," Ines snapped. "I've known him for twenty-two years and he's never been cruel to anyone. He's a proud man, but not heartless." She adjusted my chemise, tightened my corset, then pulled the soft silk dress over my head. It flowed easily along my figure to the floor. My hands caressed the fine lace across my bodice when the ship suddenly rocked roughly to one side. I reached out and steadied myself against the stateroom wall to keep from falling. Glancing at Ines, I perceived my growing alarm in her gray eyes. In our silence, the rain's deluge against the window intensified.

"I fear the weather has turned rather rough." Ines straightened her countenance and motioned for me to sit. "Come, let me arrange your hair. Your chignon du cou has loosened."

The storm rattled with force, but I stubbornly returned to my earlier plight. Crossing both arms at my waist, I kept a rigid stance and fumed. "I shall refuse to join them."

Ines led me by the hand and urged me to sit once more on the *bergère*. Her gentle touch reassured as she gathered and tucked my hair into a fresh bun against my neck. "How can Papa be indifferent to my sentiments?" I whined.

The ship rocked again. My hands shot to the framed armrests on my chair at the same time Ines dropped the pins to the floor.

"Oh my," she cried. "Be careful as you move to the dining lounge."

She scrambled to pick them up as I reached for my silver hand mirror. My fingers brushed the ornate etchings on the backside before I rotated it over to face me. Though my complexion was now free of tears, evidence of sadness reflected from my azure eyes. "I'm sure Papa wishes he had a son and not a daughter."

"Isabel," Ines consoled. "He gave you everything he would've given a son. A fine education and a comfortable living." She put the pearl studs in my ears and latched the diamond bracelet around my wrist. "Not to mention exquisite jewelry, something a son would not receive."

Glancing at my reflection in the mirror once more, I winced at what I saw. "Yes." My heart ached. "He's given me everything but the only thing I truly desire . . . my freedom."

∽

Fighting off the sting of shame, I strained under the brightness of daylight. The sun, partially hidden by gloomy clouds, exploded straight overhead. Every muscle in my body screamed for relief. Stiff and quivering, I wrestled with shock as the chilly February air seeped easily through my wet smallclothes. Lifting my head again, I wanted to cry out, but only brisk wheezes discharged. Nothing in my sights resembled a ship or a shipwreck—only a vast body of unforgiving water and a distant shoreline.

My head fell back to the board. Sobs racked my body until my breath grew shallow and my spirit turned weak. Remnants of the horrendous storm had dissipated to a dry gray sky and any footprint of my terrifying night had vanished, though I was far from feeling safe.

Resigned to a bitter end, I whispered faintly, "I'm sorry, Ines." Then closed my eyes. "I can't."

5

11 February 1910

Port de Sanitja, Menorca, Spain

Miguel Contreras

"Home by noon, husband!"

My jaw squared. The moment I reached for my bucket, my pole slid off my shoulder and hit the ground with a thud. "*Merda!*" I cussed.

"I heard that," Anita piped in from the kitchen.

"Of course you did," I grumbled.

"Noon!" She repeated.

"For heaven's sake," I muttered under my breath. After all these years, she knows fishing is not a timed sport. If we're to dine on bluefish tonight, it takes time to catch one big enough for her taste. *Home by noon!* I droned as I reached for the pole once more and brushed the dirt off the handle. I checked the wire and hook for tangles and set out on the rocky path that led to the cove.

"Take your sweater, Miguel."

"I'm fine."

"You'll catch your death, *Marit*."

"It's sunny and clear, *Dona*." There was a time the words *husband* and *wife* were spoken like terms of endearment. Over time, they distorted to more of a pester.

"There's still a chill and don't argue with me."

"Ugghh, fine, woman." I stomped back up the steps and snagged the wool sweater from its hook. Throwing it over my free shoulder, I complied with a smirk, but had no intention of actually wearing it.

"Aren't you taking Hugo?"

I answered with a long whistle. Within seconds, the hairy sheepdog came bounding from the house and jogged to my side like an excited child on his first adventure—though he had followed me down this path for nearly a decade. "Now don't you go scaring the fish, ole boy!" Hugo peered up at me, his eyes barely peeking through his matted fluff and sneezed on cue as if this was his answer.

The hike to the cove was not arduous, but in the last few years, the strain on my knees and back had become more pronounced. As a younger man, I would run to the cove in two minutes flat, but now if I limited my rest time to one stop each way, I could do it in ten.

The beauty of the bay never ceased to amaze me. Having lived on this part of the island now for over seventy years, I never pictured the Mediterranean as anything but magnificent. The old British tower marked my way. Its decline in the last decade had made it more of an eye sore than a grand stone defensive tower as first commissioned. Despite its decay, I'd spent countless days climbing to the top overlooking the Sanitja Port and the Cavalleria lighthouse to the east and Cala Torta to the west.

Many great memories happened here—I built my first fishing boat... *which sank*, I dove for crawdads and clams with my brother, Jorge, and even asked Anita to be my bride here fifty years ago. Now it had become my daily sanctuary.

I set my bucket against the large boulder that fringed the sea. The water appeared calm today. The storm that blew through two nights ago had cleared out and the Mediterranean shone its clearest blue so far this year. I sat on the rock that was shaped like *un vàter*, having claimed the old stone toilet as my personal throne years ago, and inhaled the pungent scent of seaweed. After untying my boots, I slipped my stockings off one by one. With my pant legs rolled up, I stood and dipped my toes in the frigid water. Each one curled with delight. It was like home for them.

Although Menorca was an island that experienced very little cold aside from seasonal storms, the sea had not yet warmed in February, and it now took longer for my old body to adjust. Stepping back out onto the small beach of white sand, I reached for my pole just as Hugo barked. It was not his normal happy yelp. His cry was strained. *What has that dog gotten into this time?* He seemed to find trouble where there was none. Picturing him tied up in a lobster trap or caught on a prickly bush, I ignored him briefly to see if the moment would pass.

Hugo barked twice this time. I reluctantly put my boots back on, knowing my feet disagreed with the stickers on the pathway. Annoyed, I stomped towards the rocks where all I saw was his bushy tail wagging madly. "Hugo? What are you up to now?"

Two more barks led me to the edge of the water near the point. This particular mass of rocks had been the sight of many lurking dangers. Hugo's focus never wavered, and the urgency in his bark only increased.

I stepped closer.

Thunk! A large wooden panel smacked the rocks with each subsequent wave. "Seriously mutt? Rubbish? You brought me over here for rubbish?"

Then the hand appeared.

A petite palm with slender fingers, nearly the same color as the sand, lying completely still.

"Oh! Holy . . . " I jumped backward. "Th—that's a hand, boy."

I spoke to Hugo as if he could respond. I gripped the edges of the heavy timber. Mustering all the strength possible, I heaved it to the side, hoping desperately the hand was still attached to a body.

My eyes beheld a staggering sight.

A woman, small and broken, curled against the sand in between two rocks with barely a shred of clothing over her. She didn't move, and I hesitated to touch her. *Is she alive?* Hugo barked again and danced around my feet with urgency. "Settle down, boy." I bent forward and tapped her skin. It was ice cold, colder than the sea.

Just leaning over, my back strained in two places. I did not have the strength to lift her. I considered my options carefully. Most of her body rested on the sand, only her toes touched the water. I brushed her matted and twisted hair away from her face. There was little distinction between the torn linen and her flesh, aside from the extensive discoloration of her injuries. I dropped to my knees. I knew a bit about wounded soldiers from my two years in the Spanish military. My *subteniente* insisted all *soldados* should know how to listen for a heartbeat or the hiss of a breath. I leaned in.

Nothing.

Nothing but the waves continually crashing nearby. I pulled my hat off my head and wiped the growing sweat off my brow then tried again. I pressed my ear against her chest. The faint thump could hardly be called a pulse, but its possibility made my own heart soar. Sliding my hands under her arms, I pulled her several inches farther onto dry land. The water no longer reached her, but her skin chilled in my grip. That deplorable sweater my wife insisted I bring lay next to the toilet rock. I retrieved it quickly. After I laid the heavy wool across the woman's body, my aging fingers trembled as I formed the cross of the holy trinity from my forehead to chest and each shoulder. It shouldn't matter that the last time I had done that was years ago...*or would it?* "Oh, please God, save this child." Pushing back up to my feet, I ran back to the farm faster than I had in years.

"Henry! Anita!" I hollered the moment our clay tiled roof came into view. "Help! Help, I need help!"

"Heavens, what on earth..." Anita appeared at the door drained of color. "Marit, what is the matter?"

"Quick, I need help. Where's Henry?" I bent over with both my hands on my knees, struggling to catch my breath. Anita retrieved a glass of water. There were many things this woman understood before I did and for that I was grateful.

"He's around back. You look as though you've seen a ghost."

"I may have."

Anita's brows met in the middle, but she didn't hesitate. "Henry?" She cried out as she hustled to the side of the house. "Henry, come quick."

Within seconds he appeared, his youthfulness apparent in the ease and swiftness with which he arrived.

"¿Sí, senyora?"

"Miguel needs you."

My hand was permanently stuck to my chest as if that aided in bringing more oxygen in. I inhaled deeply. "There's a girl . . . a woman . . . washed up at the cove. She might still be alive."

Henry took off in a full sprint before I even finished my sentence. *Bless that boy.* Anita disappeared briefly into the house to make ready for Henry's return.

"Sit down, Miguel," she chastised upon her return. "Pacing won't help a thing," Yet she, herself, began shuffling nervously around the porch as we waited.

Just then, Henry's golden locks bounced above the stone wall. As he made the turn into the garden, I rushed towards him. The petite form lay lifeless in his arms. "Quick! This way. Anita has prepared a bed."

The kettle whistled from the stove where Anita warmed water. "Here, Henry, put her here." She pointed to the mattress in our spare bedroom. "Please, go to the Carrasco's and bring Susana. Take the wagon."

"Sí, senyora."

"What can I do to help?" I stood over the girl. She looked young in some ways, and not in others, but quite frail.

"Here, tear this linen into strips. Her skin is ice cold, we need to warm her up." Anita poured the scalding water into a bowl with cold water to create a warmish temperature and submerged the strips. She then placed them on her head, chest, arms, and legs.

"Warm her feet, Miguel."

I took turns enveloping each foot with my ungainly hands while she massaged her arms. We rubbed until we could no longer feel the frost in our palms.

"Look, she has some color in her cheeks," I said as Anita rewarmed the towels and placed them over her again. She pressed her own head down to listen as Susana burst through the door.

"Is she alive?"

"I believe she has a heartbeat. It's quite faint." Anita stepped back as Susana moved to her side. Francisco stood motionless in the doorway.

"What can I do, Sus?" His eyes teemed with shock.

"Open my kit, please, and hand me the stethoscope."

"Stethoscope?"

"Yes, the listening tubes."

"Oh, sí."

Susana placed the device on the woman's chest. I watched her work with fascination until she stopped abruptly.

Tossing the tubes aside, she ripped the top of the woman's camisole apart.

I shielded my sight and turned. "Perhaps Cisco and I should wait outside."

Anita nodded. As we motioned to leave, Susana pounded on the woman's chest.

In the kitchen, I slid to a chair at the table and motioned for Francisco to take the other one.

"Gràcies for coming, Son." I removed my hat and set it down on the table. Anita would be too distracted to scold me for my poor manners at a time like this. I pinched the bridge of my nose and exhaled. "And we are grateful Susana has been studying medicine with us being quite far from a doctor. Although—" I chuckled softly. "I always believed Anita or myself would be her first patient."

Francisco grinned back. "You're as strong as an ox. You'll probably live to be 100."

I shook with laughter. *Heaven forbid!*

"Would you like me to make you some tea, Sr. Contreras?" Francisco looked over to me. His light brown eyes clearly conveyed concern for my welfare.

"You can make tea?" My hands moved to my knees where they tapped nervously. I always burned everything... even water. "That would be fine, son, and one day, I might get you to call me Miguel."

This time when Francisco smiled, a deep dimple appeared only on one side of his cheek. He chuckled. "I doubt it." As a child, I would coax him to giggle simply to see it.

He jumped to his feet and hustled around our small kitchen. He was a strapping man, nearly a head taller than me, although it seemed only yesterday his parents invited us over to meet the bouncing baby boy born on Patron Saint *Joan de Missa* day.

I glanced at the door where Anita and Susana worked. I needed to get my mind off of what was happening in there. "How are your *pares*, Cisco?"

"I believe my parents are well. According to their last correspondence, they departed Barcelona four days ago. Their next stop was France."

"They find that partner they were looking for?"

"One possibility in Barcelona—the Delgado Familia."

"How certain is that?"

"They didn't say."

"Well, maybe something more will come from France."

"Knowing them... " Francisco chuckled. "Their jaunt to France is more for leisure."

"Shame that business fell through with Oscar. He was an honest man." Muffled movement emerged from the room again. I shifted awkwardly in my seat with one ear angled the women's direction and the other towards Francisco. *I sure hope that girl hasn't died.*

"Yeah," Francisco whispered. The same discouraging tone from our last conversation materialized. "Oscar's son went with a larger farm."

"Did he taste the fruit? Did he actually come and taste the crop?"

"No. He sent another man, but it appeared he only came out of obligation."

The whistle blew on the kettle and Francisco filled four mugs. After finding Anita's spices, he added equal amounts of ginger and turmeric, and a pinch of cinnamon.

"I don't think the women will be thinking about tea, even though it is kind of you to offer."

"No matter what happens in there, tea will be waiting." He flashed his smile. The dent in his right cheek deepened again. It wasn't long ago this lad was barely old enough to run and climb and now he's a grown man and making tea!

"Gràcies, Cisco and thank you for your help before the storm. It could've been disastrous had you not come."

"*Benvingut,* senyor. I will always come."

I never doubted he meant it. His father had taught him well. The room grew quiet. Rustlings continued in the other room to the sounds of us sipping our tea.

"Did Susana finish her studies?"

"Sí, she practices full-time now. She no longer works the farm. Between house calls and delivering babies, the country keeps her quite busy. We are most grateful Dr. Garcia agreed to teach her. She is quite determined, like my mother, for most men would not even consider tutoring a woman in the medical field."

I nodded in agreement. "I'm certain Dr. Garcia has welcomed the help if it means he no longer has to travel the half day from Ciutadella."

"Yes, her assistance has offered him much relief. Unless its surgery, Susana doesn't operate."

"No marriage prospects?" I inquired, knowing views were harsh on an unmarried woman of twenty-five. Susana, however, a bright-eyed, lovely brunette, could hardly have a lack of suitors.

"There have been several." Francisco peeked to the door as if he feared having this conversation overheard. "But they always want her to leave for the mainland. Susana says she will never leave Menorca."

"Sí, I can't blame her for staying. I could never leave either." Wrapping my fingers around the warm cup, I steadied my tremble. I hadn't even noticed the quiver until I lifted it to my lips. After a nice long sip, I paused. "What about you, son?"

Francisco smiled again. Caution flashed humbly across his face, then he quickly changed the subject. "How did you find her? The girl from the water?"

"I was fishing at the cove and she was caught under debris. Actually, Hugo found her first. Quite a sight I must say. I wasn't sure she was going to make it."

"Yes, but if she has any chance, Susana will find it."

"I believe so, that's why Anita sent for her."

"Where do you suppose she came from?"

"*No ho sé*, possibly an overturned sloop or a troubled swim?"

"In February?"

I shrugged. It wasn't uncommon to have boat mishaps here.

"I can send Javier into town, maybe there's news." Francisco stood and glanced out the window. He scanned the sky as it darkened a bit.

"That's a half day's journey, Cisco. Unless you have business in Ciutadella, it's unnecessary." I took another long sip and let the prickly taste of turmeric tingle on my tongue. "If something happened in the sea, we'll be sure to hear of it within the week. Besides, I'm certain you need Javier at the ranch."

"Sí, but we want to help with anything you need."

"I appreciate that." I peered over the rim of my mug at him and marveled at his manners. His father must be quite proud. The Carrascos had owned the ranch next door for three generations. The olives were known to be some of the best on this side of the island, nevertheless the twenty acres they farmed, unfortunately, branded them trivial to the larger ranches. That's most likely why Oscar Reyes' son took his business elsewhere.

Within the hour, Anita stepped out of the room and called us back in.

When I stepped in, I felt my breath catch in my throat. "Oh my." She looked as if she could've been an angel were it not for the bruising. Her skin shone practically translucent. The women had put her in a dry nightdress and cleaned her up as best they could.

"We stitched the cut on her head and the longer one on her stomach. Thankfully most of the cuts on her hands, arms, and legs were just scratches so no additional stitches were necessary. She has a broken clavicle and ankle as well." Susana spoke as she used nippers to pull the slivers out of the girl's slender fingers and from under her fingernails. The young woman didn't budge although several of the shards looked like they should hurt.

"That's some serious bruising on her face and neck." I leaned over the bed.

"Sí." Susana confirmed.

The woman's long blonde hair fell softly against the pillow, shrouding portions of her injuries. In a way, she appeared peaceful and serene.

"But she is . . . definitely alive?" Francisco asked what I was wondering.

"For now." Susana placed another warm rag on her forehead. "But I'm unsure it will stay that way. Her breathing is quite unsteady."

"Y—you saved her though," I stuttered.

"No, Sr. Contreras." Susana's voice did not offer much confidence. "You found her, I only helped. But don't feel at ease quite yet, if she has internal bleeding, she might not even make it through the night. Who knows how long she was out there, exposed to the water and cold."

"What do we do now?" I questioned.

"She really should be in the infirmary, but if we move her, she will surely die." Susana reached for her wrist. "We will need to watch her and keep her warm. Above all, we need to keep her heart beating."

"Can you stay the night, Susana?" I feared for the woman's life if left solely in our hands.

She glanced over to Francisco.

"Yes, we will stay."

"Anita?" Susana tucked the blanket tight against the patient's legs. "Are you able to take some time watching her?"

"Of course, dear."

"I will help, Sus." Francisco offered.

"Me, too." I rubbed my forehead again, feeling the crucial weight of the next twelve hours.

6

12 February 1910

Menorca, Spain

Isabel

My head hurts.
My body hurts.
What happened?

The ship. I recalled my first sight of the Général Chanzy at *Le Vieux Port*. Though the weather was rather gray and my parasol slanted my view, its majestic size nearly took my breath away. A handful of automobiles were intermixed with carriages as travelers prepared to embark on our two-day journey to Algiers. Father hired a half dozen attendants to transport our luggage. Naturally, my four trunks comprised the bulk of our cargo. Maman insisted I pack for a year. *One year away from France!* My breath caught in my throat, and I remembered why each step I took on the accommodation ladder towards the Main Deck felt like a final walk to the guillotine.

The argument. I recalled the last words I exchanged with my father. We didn't speak at supper. From the opposite end of the dining table, he easily conversed with newly formed acquaintances, but declined to acknowledge me. Only his eyes reproached from afar. At bedtime, Maman came to my bedside, yet I barely looked at her. Her final words of accepting my new life were delivered like a dagger to my heart.

The jolt out of bed. I recalled the crash that brought me to the floor of my stateroom, and before I stood to my feet, the side of the ship cracked open. I remember now . . . clutching Ines, then being whipped into the sea.

The water. The fight for my life against the wild waves. Struggling for breath, I grappled to stay above the surface. Then I sank. *Ines.* She came to me . . . spoke to me. *Is she here? Is she dead?*

I willed my eyes to open, just a sliver at first. Finally, I glanced around the strange room I found myself in. A simple bed beneath me faced a colorful cross on the wall. It centered two mismatched picture frames. I couldn't make out what they held. Red curtains with yellow flowers hung above a modest desk in the corner and a small bedside table sat beside me.

Where am I?

A young woman toiled at my side. Her expression conveyed alarm though she did not respond to my pleas. The linen she dabbed on my skin left a putrid odor of vinegar behind.

Who are you? I begged again. *Please help me.* I attempted to lift my arms but couldn't. *Hello?* Why can't she hear me? Why doesn't she answer me?

"Rub her feet, Francisco. They're cold again." She spoke, but not to me. A man entered the room. He's looking right at me.

Help me, Monsieur! Help me, please? I tried to get his attention, but he didn't respond either. Why can't they hear me?

"Remove the slippers," she said. "Let the warmth of your hands transfer through her skin."

"Of course." He rushed forward. They are speaking to each other, why can't they hear me?

Wait . . . their language, it's Catalan! They must not understand French. I can speak Catalan. It's one of the languages my father insisted I learn as a young girl. His business often took us to Andorra and different parts of Spain.

Hola, si us plau? They still didn't respond to my greeting.

I trembled at the caress on my feet. It was gentle and soothing. The warmth immediately soaked in. *Wait, don't touch me.* Although his hands comforted, he was a stranger to me. *Stop!* I cried. *Get away from me!* Why isn't he listening? *Don't touch me!*

An elderly woman appeared.

"Come, Anita . . ." The first woman called. "Her heartbeat has weakened again. Please warm some more linens." The urgency in their movements and touch flowed through me. "Keep the blood going, Francisco. Don't stop."

Francisco. The man's name is Francisco.

7

Contreras Farm, Menorca, Spain

Same night

Francisco

"Can you help me, brother?"

I'd fallen asleep on the floor next to the stove. The darkness outside crept eerily through the half-covered windows. The moonshine accented the bold colors on Anita's simple curtains and matching tablecloth. When Susana appeared, only her silhouette was seen, and though she whispered, an urgency arose with unmistaken clarity.

"Yes, certainly." Rubbing my eyes, I jumped up quickly.

"I need you to warm her feet." She led me into the lowly lit room. A lone candlestick flickered in the corner. "They're cold again."

"Her feet?" I glanced at the woman who remained still on the bed. The peace that draped across her visage contrasted greatly to the trauma which surely occurred in her body. She appeared as though she slept comfortably, but the reality of a more permanent sleep hovered quite close.

"Yes, remove the slippers," she said. "Let the warmth of your hands transfer through her skin."

The first touch confirmed to me why Susana spoke with desperation. Her skin resembled the cold, hard coating of my leather saddle. I enveloped them carefully. The heat from my hands sank into her frigid flesh. Massaging them with tenderness and determination, I envisioned a happier time for her. The blonde hair that surrounded her bruised cheeks may have bounced in curls. Her eyes, although I didn't know their color, must've sparkled a time or two, and though her lips rested in a straight line, I was sure there was a moment when they curved upward in amusement. *What pain she must've endured before she came under our care.*

"What do you think happened to her, Sus?"

"Boat overturned, I suspect. Probably caught in the storm."

I tried to picture her without all the injuries. The swelling made it difficult.

"How old do you think she is?"

"I'm not sure. She has breasts."

Heat tinged my cheeks. I was grateful Susana couldn't see it in the shadows.

"Oh, I'm sorry, brother."

"It's fine, Sus." I brushed off her directness. "It's not like I don't know what they are."

"Yes, but I tend to speak too clinically sometimes. She may be in her late teens, early twenties."

"Do you think she's from Ciutadella?"

"Not sure."

"I wonder where her family is or why she was alone?"

"Keep going, Cisco, it's working. Her heartbeat is stronger."

"I hope she makes it."

"Me too."

After two hours of continuous care, my hands ached, but the warmth that radiated from her feet made the pain worth it.

"Okay, Cisco, I think she's safe for now. She's breathing normally and her heartbeat is much stronger. Go ahead and rest, I will let you know if I need you again."

I stepped over to the sleeping patient. A long strand of hair had fallen across her face. Lifting it, pieces of sand and dirt stuck to my fingers. *What horror it must've been.* Did she have a mother pacing in a kitchen somewhere, worrying, or a father who'd taken to the seas in a sloop searching for any trace of his daughter? If this were Susana, there would be no question on either one. Papa and I would never have come home until we found her.

"She will make it germà. I feel it in my heart. She's resilient but needs us—needs time." Susana patted me on the shoulder and gently nudged me to the door. Her amber eyes, usually bright and engaged, now reflected pure exhaustion. "Get some sleep. I may need your strength in the morning."

As I moved to the living room once more, the light of the moon shone barely enough to highlight the objects on the Contreras' counter. I sat on a nearby stool. The outline of a familiar shape caught my eye. I picked up the tapered bottle and inspected it as closely as I could in the shadows. *Alcón Enterprises...* I read from the label. If only our distributor hadn't deserted us. Then Mother and Father wouldn't have had to travel in search of another partner for our product and they would be home with us now.

I popped the cork and brushed the bottle under my nose. The rich aroma of ginger and lime filled my cavities. Olive oil was one of my greatest pleasures in life. I never tired of the smell. Give me a baguette and a nice *oli de romaní i all*, and it was quite as close to heaven as I imagined.

Moving to the floor, I pulled the quilt to my chin and my thoughts drifted back to the ranch. Our twenty acres of olive trees had been in the family for over a century. They produced beautiful, healthy olives, but our ranch was small in comparison to others. It would never be large enough for someone like Alcón to invest in.

I shivered. The night had become much colder in the early hours. I rested my head on the cushion Anita provided and imagined my parents in their travels. I grinned as I envisioned them walking, hand in hand, along the streets of Barcelona in search of mouth-watering tapas or a melodic plaza. Maybe mother painted another Gaudí original or a magnificent façade in the *Barri Gòtic*. They were both romantics at heart and often traveled the mainland in search of new places to cherish. Though this was a business trip seeking a new distributor, I was sure they had turned it into a lovely holiday.

Closing my eyes, I let the sounds of the night lull me to sleep, but inexplicably, a part of me grieved for the mysterious woman and her foreboding circumstances in the room nearby.

8

15 February 1910

Contreras Farm, Menorca, Spain

Isabel

"*Hola, amor.*" A woman's kind voice filled my ears. My eyelashes flickered repeatedly. "Susana, come quickly! She's waking up."

Another woman rushed into the room. "Sí, she is! Oh Anita, this is wonderful news."

I stared. They actually engaged me this time.

"Can you speak?" The younger woman at my bedside leaned in.

I understood her perfectly, but my mouth moved too slowly to respond. Instead of words, strange utterances emerged.

"It's alright, dear, don't push yourself."

Wait . . . you can hear me now?

The older woman squeezed my hand.

"B—bon—j." *Why is it difficult to speak?* "Bon—"

"Take it slow." The young woman spoke gently.

"S—salut—"

Her brows crinkled. My attempts were frustrating. *Oh, yes, they speak Catalan.*

"H—hola."

"Hola!" The older woman clapped her hands. I flinched at her outburst.

"Oh, dear, I'm sorry to frighten you. What's your name, love, can you tell us your name?"

"Slow down, senyora. I'm sure this is all shocking for her." The young woman pressed her hand against my forehead and reached for my wrist.

"I—" My mind whirled dazed and confused. I wanted to trust them. I believed they helped me, but fear restrained me. Licking my chapped lips, I pleaded. "*Aigua, si—us plau—*"

"Oh, yes. Water, of course. We've only placed a cold cloth on your lips and tongue. You must be parched." The older woman ran out of the room and quickly returned with a glass of water. I tasted it before it even touched my lips.

"G—*gràcies.*"

The younger woman pulled a chair up close to the bed. "My name is Susana Carrasco. This is Anita Contreras, and this is her home." I nodded as she continued, "her husband Miguel found you at the cove. You were in the water, but we don't know for how long. Can you tell me if your body hurts anywhere precisely?"

I thought hard about it, but even thinking hurt. It would've been easier to tell her where I didn't ache. I attempted to lift my right arm, but it was confined by a fabric band. My shoulder burned until I rested it back down to my side. My left hand went to my head. A bulky pad prevented me from touching the injury. It ran the course of my hairline to my right temple. I gasped.

"Yes, that wound was quite severe. This one as well." She pulled the covers down tenderly and lifted my nightdress. Exposing my stomach, she pointed to where the stitches ran a good hand-length long.

I bit the inside of my cheek. *Am I dreaming? Am I dead?*

"I believe the worst is over." The woman replaced the covers. You have other wounds, bruises, and cuts, but if you aren't in serious pain, I'm sure you will recover."

I couldn't be dead if she spoke to me this way.

"What's your name?"

Again, I cringed. My mind spun anxiously.

"Do you remember anything? An accident or why you were in the water?"

I hesitated. *In the water?* My thoughts flashed back to my last memories. The side of the ship cracked open. Water suffocated me . . . I drowned. *Didn't I drown?* The shipwreck! Don't they know about the shipwreck?

My head shook. The tremor in my hands matched it. What if they already knew all this? What if they were fixing me only to deliver me to Thomas? My breathing escalated.

"It's alright." The woman who introduced herself as Susana assured. "Please remain calm. You don't need to say anything."

The older woman, Anita, moved to my side. Her fingers brushed my arm and tapped gently. "Please listen to her, love. Susana saved your life. There is nothing to fear here." My eyes shot to hers. The kindness in them was unmistakable. "You are safe here."

I blinked. Their assurances brought an element of comfort. *Maybe they don't know about Thomas. Maybe I don't have to tell.*

Anita tucked a sprig of lavender over one of my ears. I recognized the piney floral scent from my garden. "This will help you sleep."

She reminded me of Grand-mère, my sweet grandmother who remained in Marseille. She refused to board the ship after she made inquiries about the upcoming weather predictions. Papa brushed it aside and called her superstitious. "A little rain would do no harm to a ship as grand as the Chanzy," he bellowed as he instructed a *serviteur* to return Grand-mère's luggage to her bedchamber. *Does she know of the tragedy?* I imagined her receiving the news. She was a strong woman, but to learn the fate of your only son and his family must've been devastating.

Anita lifted my hand and caressed the tips of my fingers. "You had many splinters in your fingertips and nails. They will be tender for some time."

I peered down at my chipped and jagged nails, which had been perfectly manicured for the voyage. I looked back up to her kind countenance and whispered in a strained voice, "*on sóc?*"

The women stopped what they were doing and peeked at each other. Susana spoke first. "You don't know where you are?"

I shook my head slowly.

"You are on the island of Menorca."

Anita inserted, "Spain, love."

Relief washed over me. *I'm not in Algeria.* Tears broke through the corners of my eyes. I couldn't stop them. Though the women showed concern for my growing emotion, they were clearly unaware they were tears of joy.

Anita dabbed a handkerchief on my face. "Please don't cry, sweet. You will get home soon enough. We only need to help you recover first."

I tried to smile in return, but the way my face ached, I'm sure it appeared awkward. "*Maria. El meu nom és Maria.*"

"Maria." Anita placed her hand over her heart. "What a beautiful name."

Susana came to the other side and touched my cheeks. "Your temperature has reduced." She seemed quite invested in my care. She must be the *infirmière*. "Rest now, Maria. We can speak later."

The two women left the room but remained near the door. I leaned towards their whisperings, and my heart thumped a half-second faster. *What if they know I'm lying?*

"Her Catalan is excellent, but with an accent unfamiliar to Menorca."

"From the mainland?"

"Possibly, but there's something else . . ." Their voices faded. I tried to lean forward to hear, but the tender pain on my stomach protested the move. Then they disappeared.

Maybe I should try and leave before they come back. Maybe they are testing me and know all about the shipwreck, Thomas, and my deception.

With my free arm, I removed the covers, but that was as far as I got. Every part of me screamed in agony, from a simple twitch of a finger down to my toes. I glanced at the wooden contraption that imprisoned my leg from the knee down. *I will go nowhere with that device attached.* Searing pain shot steadily from both my stomach and my bound shoulder. I pulled the quilt back over me.

Impossible. I won't be leaving anytime soon . . . at least not before I'm stronger. And until that happens, I need to be extra careful about what comes out of my mouth.

9

17 February 1910

Algiers, Algeria

Thomas

The tighter my fingers clasped the glass, the more my knuckles flared from bright red to white.

"I'm sorry, Monsieur." The voice next to me repeated the same sentence multiple times. I lost count after five.

I lifted the snifter and swallowed the contents in three gulps. Numb, the sting of the hard liqueur barely nipped anymore.

"I'm sorry, Monsieur."

I threw the short-stemmed tumbler at the wall, shattering it into hundreds of pieces. "Stop saying that!" I shouted.

Arthur stooped as quickly as his dated legs allowed and picked up the shards. I wanted to smash all of the glasses before me.

Felicia hustled towards me.

"Oh, dear." She rested her hands on her hips, standing only to my shoulders. For a brief moment, her countenance resembled my grandmother's exasperated brow when at the infantile age of five, I refused to stop sliding down the iron handrail of our grand staircase. "This behavior will not bring her back, Monsieur." She exhaled.

Anger stirred heatedly in my chest.

I didn't hesitate this time, and with both hands, wiped the bar from all its contents. Crashing a half-dozen bottles to the floor in my rage, I watched the liquid splatter the walls, the furnishings, and the tiled floor.

"*Oh, doux, Saint Laziosi.*" Felicia always summoned her Catholic Saints. "Pray for her." She laid a hand on my arm. "Pray for her family, son. Do not let your anger consume you."

"Pray?" I shook her hand free. "It was God who took her!" I rubbed my hands through my thick black hair. The room spun, and I stumbled imbalanced. Maybe it was the drink. Maybe it was the incomprehensible news.

"A dreadful tragedy." She pointed to her forehead, chest, and shoulders in the sign of the cross. "May they rest in peace."

"Peace? What about my peace, *Femme*?" I watched Arthur attempt to clean up the mess. Several pieces of glass were scattered within his white hair.

"I'm leaving. Tell Gabriel to prepare Calypso. I ride to town. Do not expect me home tonight."

"Monsieur, you shouldn't go in such—"

My finger pointed fiercely at Felicia. She stopped mid-sentence. "Enough!" I commanded.

"Oui, Monsieur."

I wiped the sweat from my brow and returned to my bedchamber. On my bureau was the photograph of an enchanting young woman with long flaxen curls that draped across her open-necked frock. The lace concealed her *décolletage*, but her feminine curves descended attractively downward. She held a parasol in one hand and a book in the other. She was posing, but her laugh made the photograph appear unrehearsed. The look in her bright blue eyes was playful and enticing at the same time.

It was hard to believe this had been taken a year ago when she was only seventeen. Imagine how much more beautiful and womanlier she would've become in a year. I reached for the picture and stared. My hands shook. This was to be my lot—my destiny. I tore the image in half and threw the pieces at the mirror.

I changed into my jodhpurs and paddock boots before I mounted Calypso. She seemed as antsy as me, trotting restlessly in circles. Immediately upon the saddle, we took to a powerful run. I needed to get to Algiers. I needed more information, but deliberately chose the longest way to get there.

I headed over the hills. My estate was six kilometers from the harbor, but I went to the river first. It was where I went as a child every time Mother scolded me. It was where I retreated to when I received news of her death and then later—after Papa's suicide.

I reached the water quickly and jumped off as if my breeches were on fire. I led Calypso to drink. She had raced hard, harder than I normally drive her. I gazed at the water as it danced around the rocks and lifted my face to the sway of a light breeze, though none of this natural tranquility brought the comfort I had hoped for.

I put my hands in the water and filled them with the cool liquid then splashed it across my face. Some lingered in the scruff on my chin and dripped casually on my shirt. *What am I going to do now?* I pounded the clay, but it didn't break as easily as the bottles. I pounded harder. The tear in my knuckles was hardly noticeable until blood trickled down my fingers. I stuck them back in the water and peered up as Calypso stared back. She observed my every movement with intensity. Surely, she knew something was wrong. She'd been my truest companion over the years. I reached up and patted her neck. "What am I to do now, Calypso?" Her neigh answered for me. *Yes . . .we ride.* Ride until the raw sting of disappointment and anguish dulled.

I arrived in the city after dusk. The streets hummed with activity. Men, women, and children rushed the cobblestone from house to shanty, café to shop. All were whispering, gossiping, even crying. *So, the news has infiltrated the port.*

I tied Calypso up next to a tavern and went inside.

"Whisky," I mumbled as I approached the bar and sat down. The overpowering odor of tobacco and oakmoss lingered nearby. Though the room was reasonably empty, two additional men occupied the stools on the far end.

The barman placed my drink in front of me, and in return, I dropped a centime down.

"What do you know of the shipwreck?" I attempted to whisper, but the word shipwreck brought the attention of anyone within earshot. One of the patrons spoke straightaway.

"Week 'go, at sunrise, storm sank the Chanzy."

This was knowledge I'd already received from an earlier messenger. I needed more details. I glanced his way with a cocked brow. "*Et . . .*"

"And what?" He gulped his liquor, half of the contents splashed down his chin.

"What else?" I barked at the imbecile.

He stammered, "w—well, I . . ."

"Yes, precisely what I thought. You know nothing." My eyes returned to the barman, who was drying some drinking glasses.

His head lowered to his task as he spoke. "Only one survivor, a French chap. He swam to shore near Ciutadella, Menorca."

"And they're sure no one else survived?" My head already knew the answer to this.

"No. Bodies and debris everywhere. Ciutadella sent for help. The bulk of the ship is at the bottom of the sea, but a lot of rubbish washed ashore."

The useless man interrupted again. "Comin' from Marseille, 'eard there was some fine fortune aboard," he scoffed. "Maybe I should lent a dinghy and search myself."

It took everything I had to keep my pistol concealed under my coat. I rotated back to the barman. "How can I be certain no one else survived?"

"No one else has been found alive, Monsieur."

My grip tightened around the glass. I watched the barman's eyes drop to it.

"Your family on that ship?" He set his rag down and paid full attention to me now.

My jaw tightened. "More whisky." I placed another coin on the bar as he considered this.

"Now." I tapped my glass then glanced up at him. He hesitated before he poured.

Out of the corner of my eye, I watched the other men slink from the bar. Maybe they assumed, like the barman, that something might happen.

I considered this. *Why not go out with a bang?* My father did, and he had more to live for than me. Isabel was my way out . . . my providence. Now it's all gone—the assets, the estate, the fortune. I released my stranglehold on the glass. The barman's exhale was slightly louder than expected.

"Where can I find more information?"

"About the ship?"

"Oui." I hissed. *What else would I be referring to?*

"Down at the docks, son."

I scowled. Though I doubted the elderly man had any knowledge of my twenty-six years, I was no *son* of his.

He continued, "I believe they are assembling a list. 'Lot of foreign names. Can barely pronounce 'em." He chuckled, then stiffened at my glare and walked away.

Once again, I scanned the room in search of something to break. Tempted to reach over the bar for the long-necked bottles, I refrained. The local *Sûreté*, here, would be all too happy to see my face behind bars again.

Instead, I left without a fight and sauntered down to the harbor. The calmness of the waters contradicted the weather the day Isabel was due to arrive. I reflected on that day and the anticipation that swelled within. I met my hired carriage in the rain, but no ship docked. Hours later, we retired with the assumption it had slowed in the storm. When I returned the next day, the Chanzy still had not arrived. Locals and crews carried the same confused look for days. Where had this ship, with 156 *personnes*, vanished? The barge stretched over 100 metres long and had made the trek between Marseille and Algiers dozens of times.

The messenger from this particular morning, brought the fateful news from France:

Le Temps, n° 17.761, 16 Févier 1910

Naufrage du Paquebot (Général Chanzy)

156 victimes

La France, déjà si éprouvée par les désastres des inondations, vient d'être frappe par un deuil tragique. Un des paquebots de la Compagnie transatlantique qui font le service entre Marseille et Alger, le Général Chanzy, s'est perdu corps et biens sur la côte nord de

Majorque, aux îles Baléares. Des 156 personnes, passagers et hommes d'équipage, qui se trouvaient à son bord, une seule, un passager du nom de Marcel Badez, a été sauvée.

The news press detailed how the Général Chanzy ran aground off the Northwest coast of Menorca near Point Llosa. All passengers and cargo were lost to the Mediterranean Sea. All, but one. A Monsieur Marcel Badez from France. *The wrong bloody Frenchman.* I disparaged.

I stood transfixed at the dock. The rank stench of fish and seawater suspended in the air. A merchant ship slowed into port, much smaller than the Chanzy, but arrived in one piece no less. A stir of jealousy surged beneath my coat. It was generated from the eager expectations upon receiving Isabel here, and aggravated by the dire circumstances I now found myself in with the loss.

I watched a sailor disembark and envisioned a lady instead. One who glided down the plank with little effort, where all eyes would be cast her direction. Dressed in the latest fashion, she'd greet me with an enchanting smile. Her father would have reached for my hand and given me the nod of approval. Her mother, pleased with both my appearance and vigor, would've shown subtle delight for her daughter. Pleasantries would have commenced at the manor surrounding the nuptials. Then in two days' time, to my great relief, they would've returned to Marseille, leaving Isabel and her sizeable dowry with me. That is, until we joined them in Marseille, where my plan was to reach full fruition.

Tension amplified beneath my collar as an entirely different outcome hovered before me. I studied the crowd that gathered with disgust. Mobs of French Algerians, Europeans, and Arabs were pushing their way through to the fish house to catch a glimpse of papers posted to the wall outside. Few were crying, most were not. I suspect many just had a morbid desire to leer at the names of the deceased.

I pushed forward. A nauseating mixture of sweat, and the fecal smell of *oudh* assaulted me as I channeled my way through the crowd. Blocked short of my intentions, I retrieved my pistol and waved it slightly back and forth in front of me. The crowd submissively dispersed. I never had my finger on the trigger, but women gasped in fear anyway. I reached the post easily now and scanned the list of the passenger's names who had boarded the Général Chanzy eight days ago in Marseilles. A note at the top had been scribbled to warn the reader the contents were incomplete. It didn't matter. There was only one name I searched for. I swiftly scanned the document. The letters started small but grew with each passing second.

Billot (Marie-Pierre-Gabriel)

Henry (Léon-Paul)

Savin (Marguerite-Victorine-Marie-Anne)

Gros- (André)

Fontaine- (Antoine -Harriet-Isabel)

Isabel.

My mustache tingled as my lips pulled tight. I knew people were watching me. I tugged my hat low, barely above my brows, and puffed out my chest. The only emotion to mount was anger. I hadn't cried for years. In fact, the moment I left my mother's bedside the night before she drew her last breath, I swore I'd never shed another tear. Though Isabel's loss was devastating—the financial forfeiture alone would bring a weak man to his knees—I was not weak.

I rode Calypso to a different pub. Slipping inside, I had no intent to surface for hours. Next to my horse—drinks and cards had become my most fervent diversions. Sizzling my belly and fogging my mind, the easy swill of liqueur doused any threat of sentiment to flourish. I refused to sanction grief of any kind and drank until I no longer recalled the name of the ship or the face of my betrothed.

Three hours later, I surfaced at Charlotte's door, unaware of how I arrived. Pounding with one hand, I wiped my eyes with the other. The dizzying effects of my *état irve,* fatigued me. I pounded again. The sound reverberated down the narrow corridor and through the connecting doors of the sullied neighborhood. Several flames flickered to life, while the familiar smell of onion and fried egg from *bourak* drifted from a nearby window. I lifted my boots from an endless pile of refuse and stepped closer to her door.

"What is your purpose at this late hour?" A man, two flats down, stuck his head out. His hair in a matted mess, apparent he'd been awakened.

"None of your concern." My eyes narrowed him to silence.

A wide-eyed face appeared in the small pane before me. The door latch unlocked. I spied her bare shoulder through the crack.

"Why are you here?" Charlotte whispered.

"I need you," A heavy breath released from my lips. My gaze lingered on her smooth skin.

"But, I thought . . ."

"No, open up."

Her hesitation was brief. I knew she couldn't resist. The gap expanded, and I stepped inside.

10

24 February 1910

Contreras Farm, Menorca, Spain

Isabel

Anita clapped her hands together at the foot of my bed. "*Meravellós,* Maria! You could barely move that arm a week ago."

"It still pains me."

"Sí," Anita sighed. "Susana said since that bone cannot be properly braced, it might take longer to heal."

"Will she call on me today?" I pushed my body up into a seated position while Anita tucked an extra pillow behind my back. "I'd like to ask her a question."

"Yes, she's going to check your stitches this afternoon. She might be able to remove them."

"Oh." The idea thrilled me. They itched relentlessly. "Gràcies for helping me."

"Benvingut, dear." Anita paused at the doorway. "Are you certain there isn't anyone we can notify of your welfare? Maybe someone at the home you were calling on?"

I shook my head vigorously then slowed. "No, senyora. I wasn't visiting family here, just on holiday."

"Where is home again?"

I bit my lower lip. "Northern Spain."

"There must be someone we can notify of your condition."

Lowering my head, I mumbled, "no, there's not."

Anita stepped back over to me and gently tugged my chin upward. "I'm sorry, dear."

"It's alright."

"Oh, I nearly forgot." Anita's face lit up. "I have something for you."

"For me?" I questioned. *Why me?*

She moved to the corner desk and retrieved an object from the drawer. When she returned, she placed it onto my lap. I gasped. It was a palm-size wooden box. My fingers grazed over the skillfully decorated lid covered entirely in seashells. "This is lovely." I lifted the lid to find it empty but instantly fell in love with it. "Are you sure it's for me?"

Anita's smile filled most of her face. "Yes, it was something I made years ago. All the shells were collected from the cove you were found in. I would be pleased if you'd accept it."

"I'm truly honored. Thank you."

She sat down at the end of the bed. "I hope it will bring you some happiness. I can't imagine the misfortune you've faced since your accident." Patting my leg tenderly over the quilt, she sighed.

"Until you woke up and told us how the waves dragged you from the rocks, we were certain you were part of that large shipwreck off the Nati Headland."

"Th—there was a shipwreck?" I squeaked out. Lying did not come easy. "H—how frightful."

"Oh, yes, dear. From what we've read, it was disastrous. There was only one survivor."

"Only one?" I bit my inner cheek.

That makes me a second survivor.

Images of Ines and my dog Remý came to mind first. Naturally, the loss of my parents was horrifying, but Ines was more of a mother to me than Maman. I cringed at her suffering. "Do you know if the survivor was a passenger or a crew member?" Anita stopped and peered at me oddly. "I—I'm only c—curious," I stuttered. "It would be a dreadful experience for either one."

"Yes, it would be. I believe he was a young Frenchman. He was hospitalized in Palma. Miguel read about it in the newspaper, but I'm sure he has since put it in the coop.

"The coop?"

"With the chickens. He places the paper under the hay to reduce the smell."

"Oh." I wasn't quite sure what a *coop* was but considered retrieving the paper to find out more information on the wreck.

"I can't recall much else on the details only that it came as quite a relief to know you weren't a part of that horror."

My cheeks warmed. I quickly glanced towards the window, afraid she realized my pretenses. "Many loved ones are suffering today," I mumbled and fought the tears that so desperately ached to spill. Glimpses of faces materialized. Some I passed on the dock in Marseille, others on the various decks. A group of lively cabaret performers erupted in song twice during tea. Though at the time, my contemplations centered on my pending betrothal, I can still see their spirited expressions in my dreams. Then I thought of their families, much like Grand-mère, anxiously awaiting news and then learning of their fate.

"Those waves have no mercy," Anita added. "They can be both beautiful and deadly."

I peered back to her for elaboration.

She shook her head solemnly. "Many ships have taken their last turn in the sea here near Menorca."

"You've had *many* shipwrecks?"

"Too many to count. In the bay alone where Miguel found you, there's been at least a dozen that I know of. It was a Roman port at one time. I suspect even more would be found if someone ventured under water."

Did my father know this? Did he understand the risk of leaving France?

Anita's voice interrupted my thoughts. "With the construction of the Cavalleria lighthouse back in '57, shipwrecks reduced significantly in this area. Unfortunately, the part of the island where the Chanzy sank remains unprotected."

My mind recalled a faint beam in the darkness. "I saw a light. Was that Cavalleria?"

"Possibly, it's not too far from where Miguel found you." Her lips pulled tight before she exhaled loudly. "Oh Maria, I can't imagine your fear. Standing on the rocks one moment and fighting for your life in the next." Sorrow deepened the lines around her eyes. "*Ho sento, amor.*"

"You have nothing to be sorry for," I muttered, "but thank you." These strangers had saved me. They brought me into their home, healed me, and cared for me. I didn't deserve their kindness. The guilt of my deception stung deep, yet I justified my reasons for anonymity. My untruths, though illogical, were essential to my secrecy.

Once Anita left the room, I replayed the last night on the ship over and over in my mind. I had never been that cruel to my father. He only wanted what was best for me, and I cursed him, and now I questioned his decision to take us aboard a ship bound for misfortune. Grand-mère knew. Why didn't she try harder to stop him? I gazed upward. If there was a heaven, as I'd been taught, would he be there? Is he looking down on me now, waiting... hoping for my apology or forgiveness? Tears balanced at the edges of my eyes. I squeezed my eyelids and let them glide down my cheeks.

"Are you well?" My eyes flashed open to Anita, who had entered once more. She held a vase filled with fresh yellow flowers.

Each horn-shaped bud was two-lipped, with additional delicate stems protruding. The sweet aroma of the wild arrangement drew me in. I inhaled deeply. "I'm fine."

After she set it on the bedside table, she cupped my cheek. "It might do you some good to start moving about if Susana gives her approval."

I nodded.

She opened the curtains wide. "I think we all need a bit of sunshine today, don't you?" She peered back over to me though I said nothing. "Maybe a stroll in the garden, or a visit on the porch? I could even write a letter for you—to a friend?"

"No." I snapped unfairly. "I—I mean not now, maybe another time." I rolled my back towards her indicating my desire to be alone. Anita and Miguel had been nothing but kind to me. I had no reason not to trust them. Nonetheless, I knew if I intended on beginning a new life—a new *anonymous* life—I needed to tell no one of my association to the Chanzy, Marseille, or Thomas Chastain.

Anita left without another word. I cringed at the thought of shutting her out. She was right. There *is* someone at home. My greatest regret was imagining the heartache my Grand-mère Fontaine presently faced.

She was all alone at the Marseille estate learning the news of her only son, his wife, and her granddaughter—dead at sea, never to return. She was not a frail woman by any means, being the wife of the man who started the Fontaine industry back in 1878. She was the sole reason my grandfather had the confidence to pursue his bold endeavors in the first place, but this distressing news would surely age her unlike anything else.

There was no doubt, Grand-mère loved me dearly. Aside from Ines, she was an ally, though she never argued with Papa. Even when I cried night after night in her bedchamber, she remained silent. For she knew upon my marriage, our companies would've been connected, and our families united. If she didn't dispute the arrangement back then, she might still honor Papa's wish and force me now to wed this man for the security of our future. *I can't let that happen.* As selfish as it seemed, I could not bring myself to submit to the original course. And as painful as her image was, I defended my reasons. Knowing this—a return to France could never happen.

Tugging my quilt up to my chin, I relaxed in the knowledge of my decision. For the first time in my entire life, I had made a significant choice utterly alone. No Father to silence me. No Mother to urge submission, not even Ines, here to rationalize. It was me, and me alone, and while I should've taken lengthy satisfaction in this moment, a second-most alarming thought emerged.

With my refusal to surface as Isabel Fontaine, I had no foresight to where and how I might live. I had no means and no skills beyond refinements. A sudden stirring erupted in my chest as my alarm grew. I have *nothing* to offer this world beyond needlepoint, propriety, and the pianoforte. What could I possibly do to help me earn a living in the country?

"Maria, how do you feel today?" Susana appeared in the doorway. Startled, my intake was short. "You look a bit flushed. Are you feeling well?" She stepped over to the side of my bed.

"Sí," I squeaked out. She visited nearly every day since I awoke. Anita reminded me often of Susana's healing hands and my near-death recovery. I was grateful, but there were times I wondered if the consequence of death would surpass captivity. I had no foreknowledge that my marriage meant bondage, I only assumed if a man was willing to circumvent any approval from the woman herself, he might take those afforded liberties a step further after the vows.

As Susana unpacked her instruments, I allowed my wandering thoughts to continue. My refusal to marry a stranger began with my self-seeking childhood fantasies that I would be swept off my feet by a man who I'd fallen hopelessly in love with—not a man who bartered for me like cattle. I'd never met Thomas. I knew nothing of him other than his capabilities in business. Maman assured me of the careful list Papa had covered in qualifying my husband, though Papa himself had never met the man or traveled to Algeria.

"Chastain *L'Industrie* is highly admired throughout Europe." I remember Papa doing his best to influence my regard last December. "And according to my informers, Thomas Chastain is recognized as an upstanding gentleman amongst his peers."

"Is he kind and compassionate?" I questioned.

"He maintains his father's legacy and endorses the family name."

"Is he charitable and good?" I provoked.

"He's proper and respectable, and that is all you should concern yourself with. He will make a fine husband, and you will uphold your duty as his wife."

I hated being the pawn in this negotiation. Papa could only see a fiscally beneficial alliance. His motives went against everything any young woman could want, and my tender heart yearned for romance. Ines could be partly to blame. She'd read me the fairy tales from the moment I held a book—stories of chivalry, devotion, and enduring love. The prince saving the princess, the knight fighting the beast for his one true love. Even Romeo and Juliet, as tragically as their young love ended, they were still bound together.

Susana leaned in. "May I check your injuries?" She pointed to my stomach. I nodded as she peeled back the bandage. A week ago, it looked as though it was going to be infected, but under Susana's direction, Anita applied an ointment regularly to prevent that.

"I'm sore. I haven't stood up for more than a few minutes each day, and even then, I still need help because of my ankle."

"Yes, I imagine so, Maria. It's only been two weeks. Your recovery will take quite some time."

"I'm sorry to be a burden." Guilt washed over me for the time and attention I required, and still lied about my life.

"No burden at all, darling." Anita entered the room. "Before you, all I did was knit and chase chickens." She chuckled, but I'm sure she spoke the truth. I hardly saw her without yarn in her hands . . . even when she chased the chickens.

"Do you have children or grandchildren, Anita?" I asked, wondering why I hadn't seen anyone but the two of them living here.

"Uh," Anita uttered a strange laugh, and Susana peered her direction.

"Oh," I gasped. "Pardon me, that was quite forward of me to ask."

"No, love, it wasn't. No, Miguel and I, we—we don't have any children." Her smile only lifted part way. "We couldn't bear them."

My cheeks singed. I shouldn't have been so meddlesome. Anita appeared to notice and patted my arm gently. "Don't fret, love, we came to terms with it long ago. Though since your arrival—" she paused, "—it doesn't quite feel as empty here."

My eyelashes fluttered. "I'm eternally indebted to you, Anita. I don't know if I could ever repay you for your kindness."

"Well, there is no repayment required, dear. Your recovery will be thanks enough."

I peered up to a genuinely kind face and shared a smile back. In the short time I'd been here, Anita had filled a void in my very hollow heart. It was as if she was both my grand-mère and Ines rolled into one.

"So, Maria, your accent doesn't sound Menorcan," Susana said as she clipped each stitch and pulled the string. I winced under the tender pressure.

"No, I—I'm not from here." *I must keep to the story I started.* "My family originates in Northern Spain. I speak Catalan, Spanish, French, and Latin."

Both women stared at me. Their expressions conveyed astonishment.

"Multiple languages are quite a gift," Anita spoke first. "You must've had a fine education growing up."

I swallowed hard. I had practiced several answers over and over in my head for days now.

"Yes, I was amply educated before I lost my parents."

"No parents?" Anita pulled up a chair and sat close to the bed. Her motherly instincts immediately sprang to high alert.

"No, I lost them recently. And I have no brothers or sisters." My throat seared as I wrestled my emotions. "As the only child, I left my home to see different parts of Europe before I became established. I had only arrived on the morning of the accident. I hadn't even checked into my inn." *It wasn't entirely a lie.*

"What a dreadful situation, my dear. I'm sorry you've had many difficulties. I have some tea ready. Would you like some?" She jumped to her feet and was in the kitchen before I responded. Anita blended the best tea flavors. In my opinion, hers were better than the finest *brasseries* in France. My own personal favorite was her *mélange* of honey, lemon, and rosemary.

"How long did you plan to visit Menorca?" Susana queried as she removed the stitches from my head.

I flinched at the discomfort. "A week maybe."

"Where were you headed to next?" Anita caught the last of my words as she handed me a warm mug. When the last stitch was released, I exhaled loudly.

Susana smiled. "You were very brave."

My hand slid to the jagged line on my forehead now that the stitches were absent. I frowned as my fingers found the raised mark. *This must look awful.*

Susana must've read my mind. "Your hair will cover it nicely." She placed her hand over mine and brought it back to my lap. "And over time, it will be so faint, hardly anyone will notice."

"Thank you." I turned my head to Anita to answer her question. "Maybe Seville is where I'd like to go next." I'd been there once before with my parents and fell in love with the city and the old tower square.

"Well, dear." Anita smiled. "You are welcome to stay here as long as you want..." Her hesitation brought my eyes to meet hers. "Even permanently if you'd consider it." She slipped that last part in casually.

"Thank you," I whispered. Her offer came with an overwhelming desire to accept. The love that flowed freely about instilled a hope that such joy was within my reach. Something I hadn't allowed myself to imagine for many months.

Anita's words should've been reassuring, but the warning in my head pointed out the plain reality. Since my arrival here, there was little I'd been honest about. They knew me under false pretenses. Even a *faux* name. I was not the woman they'd grown fond of. *I'm a deceptive liar.*

"I should move on," I mumbled. "I've been quite the burden already."

"Nonsense!" Anita insisted. "Not the least bit of a burden, but we won't pressure you, love. Right now, you must continue to heal."

I smiled in response as if Ines stood before me. An affectionate ping in my chest reminded me of how much I missed her. "Oh, Susana," I babbled her direction as she examined my ankle. "I meant to inquire something of you. Who was the young man with you the first night?"

Susana stopped what she was doing. "The first night we found you or the first night you woke up?"

"I guess it would be the night you found me. He was in the room here."

"Oh, you must mean Henry, my farmhand," Anita chimed in. "He was the one who carried you from the cove."

"He was gentle with me." I reflected on how alarmed I was but calmed under his tender touch. "And most kind to rub my feet that night."

Both women faced me abruptly.

"Rub your feet?" Susana questioned.

"Y—yes." I hesitated. "He rubbed my feet until blood started to flow through them." I brushed my cheek. "Actually . . . it was the strangest feeling. My spirit wanted to slip away, but when he touched me, he brought me back."

The women exchanged peculiar looks, then Susana patted her forehead. "Oh, my goodness, how could I forget. My brother, Francisco, was here. I woke him up that first night to help me." Her eyes narrowed, "... but you were unconscious, how do you remember that?"

"I—I don't know." I studied my hands then followed the outline of my body towards my feet. "It was odd." *Francisco* ... I mouthed silently. *Somehow that name sounds familiar.*

"Tell me more," Susana urged. She appeared quite engaged in this.

"I'm not sure I can explain it." I paused for a second. "It was as if I was like one of those *Hargrave* kites." I had seen the box kite presented at the *Exposition Universelle* in Paris, ten years ago. "My body floated up and away, but your brother held on to the string and brought me back down." I regarded their expressions. "I know that sounds strange, but something inside me was trying to leave. Then he touched my feet. When he rubbed them, it brought me back together."

"Interesting." She tapped her finger against her chin. "I've heard of this before. In the clinic over a year ago, a man was unconscious, but relayed everything that happened in the room. Every touch, every visitor, and every conversation; nearly word for word. He too described feeling outside of his body."

I marveled at the whole experience. Her brother, a stranger, helped save me.

"What else do you remember?"

"Not much, really."

"That's how it happened, Maria." Susana's countenance conveyed her astonishment. "We *were* losing you. Your body tried to shut down, but you came back."

"Well . . ." I grinned. "I was angry at first, offended almost. No man other than my Papa had touched my feet before, and that was when I was a child." I chuckled. "I kept telling him to stop touching me."

Anita laughed. "I think the experience was a first for Francisco, too."

"I'm surprised you remember that." Susana continued, "you didn't wake up for several days afterward."

"I kept trying to speak to you all. I thought it was because I was speaking in French, and you didn't understand me." I giggled partly out loud and partly to myself for my foolishness. "Will you thank Francisco for me?"

"Of course. He would have returned himself, but the ranch keeps him quite occupied, especially since our father, who handles most of the business side of things, has not yet returned from abroad."

"Where is he?"

"He and our mother went to Valencia, Barcelona, and I believe parts of France to secure associations with businesses for our olives. That's what we produce—*Carrasco Olives*."

"I *love* Spanish olives," I blurted out, forgetting that I'm *supposed* to be from Spain. "I mean—" I recovered swiftly. "Compared to other countries, they're wonderful."

"We lost our distributor four months ago, and this is our livelihood, so Mother and Father ventured to the mainland in search of new prospects. Francisco has had to manage the farm himself, and of course, I'm of no help either since I started working as a nurse full time."

"I'm grateful to you for that, Susana. You saved my life. You, Anita, Miguel, and Francisco; you all saved me."

"Happy to do so, love." Anita stood up and left the room.

Susana peered towards the door Anita exited and pulled a small leather pouch from her pocket. "I believe this belongs to you, Maria." She handed it to me. The way she whispered led me to believe this was a conversation only the two of us would have. I opened it. It was a sole pearl earring and my bracelet. *How did this survive the shipwreck?* I didn't even recall seeing it on my wrist while I fought to stay on that board. My fingers fondly brushed over the braided gold chains. Six diamond studs wound its length fringed by two stunning emeralds near the clasp. These were now my only possessions.

"How did you find these?"

"The earring was still in your ear, I'm sorry, but the other must've been lost. The bracelet was tangled in your hair. I actually had to cut a small strand in order to free it. You won't notice it though." She smiled, then added, "the bracelet is quite exquisite. Was it a gift?"

She may have assumed it came from a lover, but it was the bracelet my father gave to me when I turned fifteen. I only wore it on special occasions, but I did that night at dinner, and as angry as I was when I readied for bed, I must've forgotten to put it in my jewelry chest. I held it tightly in my hands and drew it to my heart, grateful for this small miracle. "My father gave it to me. It's the only thing I have now."

"Oh, Maria." Susana patted my arm. "I'm pleased we found it."

"Yes, I am too."

When Susana left the room, I reached for the newly gifted seashell box from Anita and slipped the pouch inside. My attention whirled back to the shipwreck once again, and what little I knew about it other than what I had witnessed. The events of that fateful night replayed often in my mind. So much, that sometimes I imagined an alternate outcome for my family—the possibility of their heroic rescue and remarkable retreat to an exotic location. One where they found everlasting happiness and peace. No doubt, wherever they may be, regardless of our strained relationship, they were greatly missed.

11

27 Feb 1910

Algiers, Algeria

Thomas

"There must be a way!" My hand slammed the desk, and the scrawny form before me jumped. His glasses slid down his shiny nose. He pushed them up with trembling fingers as I bellowed out another expletive, "Merde! Your firm was recommended by my creditor. Did you hear me . . . recommended?"

"I, uh, we welcome your business, Sayed—"

"Monsieur," I interrupted. "I am French, not Algerian."

"Oui, Monsieur." The man stumbled over his words. "But, uh, we cannot begin an acquisition until you can produce a certificate of marriage."

"Are you not listening?" My patience ran thin and blood boiled hotly in my veins. "I was to wed her upon arrival. I have a contract of marriage signed by her father. I have every right to her possessions. Her entire family perished in the shipwreck."

"Have they identified her body?" A tall, confident man entered the room. I shifted my stare from the puny, fainting man before me to the newest victim. Only he did not cower in the same way.

"She could be at the bottom of the ocean, *cul*." I sneered, though he didn't flinch at being called an ass. "The names of her family are on the manifest."

"That was not my question, *Monsieur*." His eyebrows met in the middle, and his chest rose slightly under his pressed suit coat. He was not as easy to intimidate. I already designed his demise in my head.

"They are still retrieving bodies from the ocean," I scoffed. "The identification process is ongoing and complicated. It was a shipwreck, remember?"

"What proof do you have that she perished?"

My lips formed a tight line. "Everyone perished." My temper flared, but this man was unyielding.

"Not so, Monsieur. There is a rumor of a survivor. A Frenchman on his way to employment here. What's to say there aren't more?"

"If there were other survivors they would have come forth by now. It's been over two weeks." I glowered with revulsion. "What *proof* do you need?"

The man raised his chin in thought. "The Ministry of Justice would require something more than a contract. A body, to be sure, would be the most logical. Certification from Spain confirming her death, or a proven possession from the salvaged ship goods might suffice."

I grumbled under my breath. *Impossible.*

"I suggest you go to Ciutadella personally and see if you can acquire substantial confirmation of the subject's mortality, and only then—" He frowned. "—can we begin the acquisition process."

"And to think," I barked. "I was led to believe that your office furnishes the finest solicitors in Algiers." I snatched the contract from the desk and stuffed it inside my coat. My eyes blurred with rage as I slammed the chair to the floor and stomped out. "Unbelievable!" I muttered. "The Chanzy runs aground, killing everyone aboard . . . except one bloody Frenchman!" Heat swelled in my cheeks and sweat built on my nose. "My future, my prosperity is lying on the bottom of the Mediterranean Sea, and now I must provide proof?"

Anger ran wild as I glowered and paced outside of the Maître' Bureau. I pumped my fists to keep them from breaking a window. The outcome festered irritatingly under my skin. I chose this establishment intentionally. They had no prior relationship with my father's business. I slammed my fist against a nearby post. *This was my chance!*

Without question, Calypso allowed me to lead her to the *dark district* in a familiar part of town. The pub I often frequented came into sight. The desire to drown my displeasures in a *boisson* arose with equal fervor to bury myself in a game of cards.

Maisîr was strictly forbidden for those who followed the Islamic Quran, but the gambling sport could still be found in the backrooms of some taverns. And since the colonial regime taxed the Arabs excessively in the open, many found ways to supplement an income behind closed doors. This was one of those places. I entered seeking a drink, diversion, and if permitted, the affection of a willing lady. Anything to ease my irritation—or at least numb it.

"M—monnsssieur!" A man declared upon sight of me. His head hung low over the bar, where his hat draped carelessly to the side. "'Ere be your *jolie* bride?"

I glared at Domingo, the drunken local who squatted here more than the owner himself. I was hardly in the mood for his amusements tonight and instantly regretted the time I boasted of my pending marriage in inebriated decadence.

Hakim took one glance at my demeanor and shushed him from behind the bar. "*Kun hadiana*, Dom." He glanced back to me and held both hands up near his chest. "I don't want any trouble tonight, Chastain. What would you like? My courtesy."

"Whisky." I sat on the stool far from the others, my mind spinning with the day's events. The Maître office had come recommended by a local banker, Monsieur Peron. He insisted they could help with "my rather delicate circumstance." I, of course, refused to show him the particulars of the contact, but if all worked out the way I intended, few would know of its marginal ruse.

Hakim placed a glass in front of me. Pouring from the bottle, his hand shook slightly. I grabbed his wrist. "Leave it."

His lips pursed, but he obeyed and set the bottle down next to my glass. I had no intention of causing trouble but never turned it down if it came looking for me. Hakim knew this.

I lifted my chin to the closed door behind him. "Are there games tonight?"

He stilled. It should've been an easy answer. *Yes or no.* Hakim's stare shifted between me and the other patrons in the room. Granted, his memory never allowed him to forget an earlier incident which nearly burned his pub to the ground, but in my defense, the foreign bloke *was* cheating at cards.

Hakim wiped his brow. "I—"

"Da dun dun da dun . . . " The sloppy hum of a bridal chorus cut off his answer. I glared at the direction in which the sound came. Domingo's smug head bounced back and forth as he continued to drone with drunken delight. Then ended in a crude belch. My jaw squared. He picked the wrong night to be a ragger.

Hakim moved swiftly from behind the bar and hustled towards Domingo. "Not tonight, Dom. Leave, take a walk."

"Wh—why me?" He slurred. "I was 'ere first."

"*Adhhab,*" Hakim insisted. "Go!"

Domingo struggled to his feet. I poured another glass and emptied it by the time the lush took his first step. Barely a sip remained in the decanter once Domingo reached my side. I kept my eyes forward but ached to reach out and strangle him. When he paused behind me, I set my glass down and waited. His foul breath wafted over my shoulder as he garbled, "refused you, didn't she?" My fingers slid from the tumbler and up to the narrow neck of the bottle. One flick of my wrist and he would be silenced. Hakim jumped between us and hustled Domingo out the door.

Quickly behind the bar once more as if nothing had interrupted him, Hakim handed me a fresh bottle. "One to go."

My lips twisted in forced self-control. I hated this town. I hated the pubs and lowlifes that filled them. My fingers tingled with the knowledge of how close I had come to being rid of it all. The Fontaine's wealth ensured me a prosperous future away from the sludge of the earth. I reached for the weighty bottle and slid off the stool. Tipping my hat, I sneered. "Until next time, Hakim."

Stepping back into the cool night, I inhaled the fresh air. Though I occasionally enjoyed a cigar, the hookah smoke that swirled about Hakim's place, annoyed me. Many times, only the stale scent of unflavored tobacco leaves reeked, but occasionally other customary fumes wafted about like opium or molasses sugar.

Neither appealed to me, yet as one of few gaming establishments that hadn't prohibited my patronage, I tolerated the nuisance.

I took a long, drawn-out drink from the bottle. The sharp liquid slid down my thirsty throat and left a sting that could not be satisfied with drink alone. I needed the touch of soft flesh.

Isabel's picture came to mind. Our wedding day would have come and gone. A small ceremony at the *Notre-Dame d'Afrique*, something her father insisted on. I wasn't a religious man of any sort but agreed to the Cathedral as a means to please. And the wedding night... I couldn't help but visualize it. I would have taken Isabel to a private suite on the upper floor of *Et Hotel Excelsior on Rue Michelet*. Beads of sweat formed on my forehead as I fantasized the pleasure of her. Another long swig filled my belly, but the more I imagined what would never be, the more the taste regurgitated sour and unpleasant. My mind undressed her from her bridal gown, exposing her perfectly white, soft skin—*Merde! The bottle is empty*.

"Oy, good Mademoiselle..." A familiar irritating cheerfulness arose from across the street. I watched as the drunkard attempted to tip his hat to a woman strolling on the arm of a passing gentleman.

My grip on the whisky bottle tightened and my aggravation magnified as I replayed Domingo's offenses in my head—the wedding chorus, his references to my bride, his overall filth. My stomach churned. All the liquid contents within me rattled with provocation.

I took a step off the curb, and my eyes darted his direction with one purpose only. It wasn't until I was halfway across the road that Domingo caught sight of me. When he did, he scrambled with all the energy he could muster, but his legs jiggled weakly underneath. I sauntered. Watching my pathetic victim squirm, I relished in the high that alcohol couldn't match. With the neighborhood smothered in blackness, a sole streetlamp was the only source of light Domingo could hope for, yet he clambered clumsily towards the darkest alley nearby. It could not have been more perfect.

Twenty minutes later, when I arrived at Charlotte's door, my heightened breath had finally calmed to a hum. My eager knock signaled my rush, though I feared nothing. Glancing at my hand resting against the wood, blood splattered across my knuckles and trailed down my fingers. I quickly wiped them against my dark trousers. It was more for her benefit than mine.

Once again, she answered in her thin night rail. I struggled to find her eyes.

"Monsieur." Her voice melted in my ears. "You said no more. Remember, you told me—" I held my newly cleaned finger against her lips, her soft supple lips.

"I know what I said." I nudged the door open, which forced her grasp on the nightdress to release. I entered and slammed the door shut with my foot.

12

2 March 1910

Contreras Farm, Menorca, Spain

Isabel

Sitting next to the stove, I moved my hands back and forth across the coals. I'd been given a knitted shawl by Anita to keep warm, but I missed the warmth of my fur-lined coats and thick *pettis* I wore back in France. Though the comforts were longed for, most everything else wasn't . . . except for Ines and Remý.

Hugo, the Contreras' sheepdog, curled at my feet. His long hair hid his eyes, and only the cold end of his nose was seen pressed against my skin. Sometimes his sloppy tongue licked my toes and tickled me relentlessly, causing me to miss my little fur pile even more. Remý was small enough to go almost everywhere I did, thus the horrid result of his absence. Visions of his helpless little form being flung into the water tore my heart to shreds.

"Why so sad?" Anita questioned in the rocking chair across from me.

I shook my head and smiled. "I miss my dog."

"You own a dog?"

"Sí, a little brown Pekingese named Remý."

"Remý. That's an unusual name."

I smiled. "He was sweet."

"Was?"

My grin faded. "He's gone now."

"I'm sorry, love." Anita patted my knee.

Today was the second day in a row I had managed to move from the bed to the kitchen and to this chair. While I still limped, it was minimal, and even though my shoulder ached, I no longer wore the band. These were small successes that should've been celebrated, but instead, I planned my recovery as a means to leave and live my fraudulent life where I couldn't cause harm.

"Anita, do you manage this home all alone?" Glancing around the small space, I recalled no introduction to a maid or a manservant.

"Oh, heavens no," she chortled. "Miguel does his share, and Henry, he manages the barn and the animals."

"No, I mean, um, servants? Do you have any help like that?"

"Servants? Why on earth would I need servants?"

"Uh," I fidgeted in the chair. "Um, people often need assistance, that's all."

"Oh love, we've managed this place for decades and well, if you can't get it done yourself, then it wasn't meant to be done." She tittered. "Besides, it's a tiny thing. No need to trip over someone else in the kitchen."

I thought about this. I had servants my entire life—cooks and maids, even a groom for a horse I never rode. Bridgette cared for my quarters, but Ines bathed me, dressed me, and met all of my personal needs. I hadn't imagined people living any other way.

Anita had the makings of a blanket in her lap, and the knitting needles flew furiously in her hands. The pale pink and yellow shades together created such a bright energy that merely watching her made me happy.

"Would you teach me how to knit?" I was exceptional at needlepoint, but knitting was not a skill *Mesdames* in France were taught.

"Certainly, love. I would be delighted to teach you anything you like."

Though Anita never pushed, she made it abundantly clear that I was more than welcome to remain here well after my recovery. There was no doubt in my mind this was the kind of home I yearned for. The sort I would've loved as a child. I didn't have the fancy dresses, jewels, or *fêtes*, but it abounded in warmth and compassion—like when Ines was near.

"I recalled something last night as I was falling asleep." I folded my hands underneath my shawl. I feared their tremble would expose my dishonesty. "When I was at the point watching the—the water . . ." I sputtered, fabricating the story as I spoke. "B—before I fell in . . ."

"Take your time, love." Anita watched me. "I know this must be difficult to speak of."

I took a deep breath. The greater challenge at the moment was lying, but I had to get information somehow. I licked my lips. "I noticed a great ship off in the distance. It had a couple of large columns and a long deck—possibly a pleasure, or shipping barge. Do you suppose it could've been the ship that had that horrible wreck, the one you thought I might've been a part of?"

"Perhaps, both occurred around the same time, but we have many ships that travel through here." Anita went back to knitting.

"I can't stop thinking about that terrible tragedy," I whispered. "You mentioned there was only one survivor? Do you know anything more?" I bit my lip.

"Only a little, dear. He was a young man from France. He must've been a strong swimmer because all the others perished. All those men, women, and children. Over 150, I believe."

I covered my mouth with my hand and fought the tears that wanted to fall. "No other survivors?"

"Not that I've heard. Javier, the Carrasco's ranch hand, told me that when he was in town for supplies, he heard the poor chap clung to rocks and sheltered in a cave for over a day. After the storm ceased, he climbed a cliff and was found by a fisherman. It wasn't until that young man reached Ciutadella two days later that they even realized the ship had sank." She continued knitting in a frenzy. "They were pulling bodies from the rocks and water for weeks. Several even got as far as the coastline near Susana and Francisco's home. Javier found a man and a child. It was quite devastating, you know. A body in the sea that long doesn't look well."

I turned my head slightly and closed my eyes. My breakfast lodged in my throat.

"Oh, Maria, there I go again, I'm sorry." Her hands stopped moving. "This news must be quite distressing with you almost drowning yourself. Forgive me, dear, I should be less frank. Would you like some tea? Your cheeks are pale."

"Yes, please," I mumbled. Anita's tea had become a healing restorative, and always offered at just the right moment. "What a sad turn of events."

"Certainly, most horrific." She went to the stove and filled a kettle with water.

"Do you suppose personal belongings washed ashore?"

"Oh, I'm certain of it. Miguel read a recent article to me. It mentioned that much of the cargo was burned from the explosion, but anything found was being stored in a fish house near the harbor. I suppose that's the most fitting choice. It allows the family to at least lay claim to it. Although, I presume some have been pilfered, and most are beyond recognition."

"Do they have a list of the dead?"

"The press described an initial manifest of the crew members and half of the seventy-five passengers who purchased tickets through appropriate means, but it's incomplete. There's also the exchange of tickets on the docks without a record of who bought them. This impetuous endeavor has created a vast discrepancy of those who were on board."

"Where would one find such a list?"

Anita circled around to face me. She stared until I lowered my head. "Why, dear?"

"I—I have many friends from Marseille. I visited often. I fear some may have been traveling."

"Of course, love, that makes sense."

Anita stopped again. "How do you know the ship came from Marseille?"

"I, uh—" My cheeks heated. "I just assumed it did. From the surviving Frenchman and I'm aware that the port in Marseille is widely utilized from France." My story grew thinner by the moment. I only wanted to see my family names in writing. I knew they were dead, but a morbid privation haunted me.

"Do you really believe you might have had friends on the ship?" Anita asked.

I bit my bottom lip and nodded.

"That's awful."

We sat in silence for several minutes until Anita spoke up. "Did you come from wealth, Maria?"

I paused and stole a deep breath. "Yes, when I was younger." My hands continued to tremble beneath the blanket. "I no longer have money. I lost everything."

"I'm sorry." She stood before me now. "I imagine it's hard to endure such loss."

I nodded again but didn't look at her. Her fingers tugged my chin upward. "God must've preserved you for a higher purpose, love."

I considered her words. Why wouldn't God save Father? His business employed hundreds of men. What would happen to them now? And Mother? She oversaw the needs of two orphan institutions. What about the children? Or Ines? Her heart was pure gold—the most loving woman I had ever known. I attempted to think of all the reasons why God would keep me, but nothing came to mind. Surely it was a mistake somehow.

Anita must've seen my expression. Her thumb rubbed my cheek. "Sometimes our purpose is hidden from us and we must seek it out. Your survival is sure to bring happiness to others." With her other hand, she offered me a cup of tea then smiled, "It has to me."

I pulled my hands out to receive the warm mug. "Happiness?" *What exactly is that?* I questioned. I recalled what made me smile over the years. *The Salon de Vente* in Paris and a season of new *House of Worth* gowns, my emerald teardrop earrings, beaded pearl handbag, and rose-colored boutis quilt . . .

When Anita sat back down, she eyed me carefully before she picked up her knitting again. Then as if she knew exactly what occupied my mind, she added, "When I was a little girl, my mother died, and my father worked long hours as a butcher. It was then that I learned to find joy in simple things. A sunrise, a newborn colt, a rope swing in my favorite tree and Miguel's poetry."

"Poetry?"

"Oh, sí. He wrote me the most beautiful poems."

I watched as her eyes took on a far-away look. No doubt reciting one of those poems in her head. I tried to picture an obstinate Miguel spouting sonnets of love and romance. I wrinkled my nose and chuckled. It was difficult.

Anita glanced back to me. "Happiness is different for everyone. I'm certain you will find yours. Not just what puts a smile on your face, Maria, but what melts your heart."

We exchanged meaningful looks.

Her needles twirled with yarn once again. "When you are feeling up to it, dear, I can have Henry, or Javier take you into town. Any information you want on the shipwreck, you'll find there."

The shipwreck. Yes, I had nearly forgotten our original conversation. "How soon do you think I could go?"

"It's an arduous journey, dear, half-day to Ciutadella and a full day to Mahón." She continued to watch me. "Mahón has a port. That's where you would go to board a ship, but the recovery took place closer to Ciutadella."

"No. Not Mahón." I had no intention of getting on a ship anytime soon. "Ciutadella will be fine."

Anita settled back in her chair and sighed as if she found relief in my answer. "Good to hear that." She smiled. "But all that jostling in a wagon to town may do your poor body more harm than good. You must continue to rest and get stronger before you go."

"Yes, you're right." I glanced down at my ankle. It needed more time. "Thank you, Anita. I will wait a bit longer."

13

10 March 1910

Contreras Farm, Menorca, Spain

Francisco

"*Bon dia,* Sra. Contreras."

"Good morning to you too, Francisco. What brings you to our home this morning?"

"I have the freshest reap of olives. I'm taking some to Maduro's market in Es Mercadal, but of course, you get the first pick." I kissed her on the cheek. She laughed. Her laugh reminded me of my own mother's giggle. Then brought a frown to my face.

"Are you well, Cisco?"

"Sí," I assured. "I think of Mother when I see you, that's all."

"You still haven't heard from them? How long has it been now?"

"It's been over a month. Our last telegram came on the eighth of February saying they were leaving Spain to France, but according to their original plan, they should've been home a week ago."

"Dear, you know communication is slow. They probably chose to take a voyage over to Italy or Greece. Haven't they done that on previous trips?"

"Santorini." I smiled in recollection.

"They are quite the romantics, aren't they?" Anita laughed again.

"Very much so." Then reminisced the story of how they met. Mother was only fifteen and father twenty, but from that moment on, they loved no other. These trips they would take for business had become an excuse for them to lose themselves together.

"See, they have always enjoyed lovely surprises. We will have much to hear about upon their return, you will see, Cisco."

"Yes, I guess with this harvest being our largest yet, I'm concerned about moving the product quickly. The greatest collection will begin shortly, and I need to know where to send it."

She inspected the basket with a smile. "How can anyone not love these?"

I returned her smile. "The local merchants are no problem, but if Papa had secured something more substantial in Spain, I would need to ship by the end of the month."

"Your father will be successful. He always is." She patted my arm. "Would you like to come in, Francisco? Maybe for breakfast or tea?"

"I must be off. I have several families to visit before town."

"Well, you must have time to say hi to Maria before you go."

"Maria . . . that's right. With all the work at the ranch, I had nearly forgotten her plight."

"She would be delighted to see you." Anita winked and pointed inside.

"Sra. Contreras . . ." I gave her a stern brow.

"What?" She threw her hands up, feigning innocence. "Just come say hello," she huffed.

"She doesn't know me, Anita, don't be conjuring up any tricks."

"Yet, she somehow remembers you." Anita's mouth twisted up in satisfaction as she led me through the front door.

"Of course, I will say hi. It would be rude if I didn't." I entered the kitchen. A young woman sat near the stove with her back towards me. It was nice to see she was no longer bound to her bed. She must be recovering well.

"Hello, Maria."

She swung around and faced me, although her tiny nose pulled into a wrinkle. "Ugghh," she groaned delicately. Her fingers fighting the long-pointed tips of knitting needles. Yarn lay tangled in her lap while strings wound all through her fingers. The ball rolled off her knees and thumped to the floor. I chuckled, but when she glanced up, my mouth fell open.

Her eyebrows bent in anger. "Are you laughing at me?" Her tone was sharp, but I barely heard her. My mind whirled at the transformation before me. Images of the swollen, bruised, and broken woman I'd seen a month ago vanished into something else.

I couldn't form words. The large cut on her forehead was now a faint, jagged line, pink tinged her cheeks, and her blonde waves flowed easily and cleanly down her back. She wore a simple oversized dress that most likely had been Anita's at one time, and a torn shawl around her shoulders, but she was the most beautiful woman I'd ever seen.

"No," I choked apologetically. "I'm not laughing . . . I know nothing of knitting."

Her face softened. "I have no idea why I even try it myself. I'm awful."

"At least you are trying. I couldn't even get that far." I kneeled and picked up the wayward ball. When I handed it back to her, I found myself staring.

Her shining blue eyes met mine easily, then grew bashful under long black eyelashes. When she smiled, the timid curve of her full lips launched my heart from my chest, and I couldn't pull my eyes away as she spoke. "That's kind of you to say."

Captivated, a greater desire had never surfaced before to reach out and take a woman into my arms. Flashes between seeing her now and the night she was found, stirred my soul and an unexpected need to protect her arose. *What just happened?* One minute I'm picking up runaway yarn, and the next, I'm paralyzed in her presence. I shook my head and took two steps back.

Her eyes widened. "Did I—" The quiver in her voice was unmistaken. "Did I offend?"

"Sit down, Francisco!" Anita barked from the stove. "I will bring your tea."

I stumbled to the closest chair, trying not to gape, and failing all the while.

"No, I—I uh, how are you feeling?" I asked, forgetting I had refused to fall for Anita's matchmaking game.

"Much improved, thanks to all of you," she whispered.

"You look, you look . . ." I couldn't even find the words.

"Beautiful." Anita finished my sentence. "She looks beautiful." She set the tea down in front of me.

I nodded. Maria's cheeks flared a bright shade of pink, and those black eyelashes that stunned me before fluttered downward as if embarrassed.

"I don't mean to stare. You just look so much better than that first night."

"I feel much better." She sighed. "I'm indebted to you . . . for your help."

Entranced by her charming disposition, I forced myself to look away when Anita took a seat across from us. Anita winked. I struggled to find composure over this sudden pounding in my chest. I glanced back to Maria. "No, you don't owe me anything. It was the right thing to do. Anybody would've done it."

"You helped save me," she persisted.

"Susana told me you remembered me rubbing your feet. I'm glad it helped."

She tilted her head and found my eyes. "It might sound silly, but I believe that was what kept me alive."

Unable to break her stare, I exhaled subtly. "I don't know if that was the reason, but I'm quite grateful it helped," I said this before I realized how appreciative I *really* was and how awkward it sounded. I gulped the tea. The heat singed my tongue, but I ignored it and jumped to my feet. "I must go. Thank you, Sra. Contreras, for the tea, and thank you, Maria, for the visit." I headed towards the door and glanced back. Maria's chin dipped low.

Her whisper bordered sadness. "You're welcome." I must've made her feel bad, though it was not my intention. I had little experience with women and much less with beautiful women.

"Francisco, you should visit more often." Anita spoke quite loudly for the small house. Her chin jutted slyly towards Maria.

I smiled. "I will. I promise." Then hustled out of the house and jumped on the wagon.

Although I visited another ten families that day, I couldn't recall what I said to any of them. The only thing I saw in my mind was the curves of Maria's face, the glow of her skin, and the rapture in her eyes. I nearly tumbled the wagon off the road twice and once almost walked away without the wagon all together.

At the end of the day, I knew one thing was for sure—I needed to visit her again soon, or I would lose my mind, my wagon, or both.

14

12 March 1910

Contreras Farm, Menorca, Spain

Isabel

"Maria?" Miguel placed his fishing pole next to the front door and lifted the large fish from the bucket. "Francisco asked if he could visit you tomorrow?"

"Francisco?" The image of him the day he stopped by sent a curious tingling through my body. It wasn't for a lack of masculine attention. I'd been around handsome men before, even some who were primed for royalty, but there was something about Francisco's rugged appeal and unintended charm that intrigued me.

"Are you sure he wants to visit me, Sr. Contreras?" I leaned forward from the sitting room with clear sight to the front porch. A certain scowl covered his countenance.

"Not you too!" Miguel huffed. "Call me Miguel." He kicked his waders off and splashed droplets of water all over the entryway.

"Marit! Take those out back immediately. How many times have I told you I don't want it to smell like the sea in here!"

"I just got home, woman, I thought you might like to see the catch. There's a special grouper especially for you." Miguel winked and pulled the hanging fish closer to Anita as she tried to shoo him out.

"Go!" She squealed as he chased her farther into the kitchen.

I smiled at their playful banter. I never witnessed my parents this relaxed with each other and even though, that night on the ship, I accused my father of not loving my mother, I knew he did. He just showed it differently.

"Well?" Miguel re-entered the front room.

"Pardon me?" I blinked with bewilderment.

"Is it alright for Francisco to stop by . . . tomorrow? Maybe take you for a ride?"

"Oh, yes, of course." I shrugged my shoulders. I didn't want to appear too anxious but admittedly I was thrilled. My only real interaction with Francisco was brief. It was the day he brought the olives over and though his words were few, the kindness he exuded was unmistakable. I imagined him entering the kitchen again, his eyes solely on me. I brushed my hands across my skirt. Two grease stains stared back at me. This would be my first social call as Maria, so yes, there was no doubt of my apprehension.

"Are Basilio and Cristina home now?" Anita called from the kitchen. Miguel moved back to the doorway.

"No, and no word. Francisco sent telegrams to his family friends on the mainland and to the potential associates in Barcelona. He's considering a trip to town to make telephone calls, like to the hotel they stay at in Paris. No need to worry. They've always found their way home."

My ears perked up at the possibility of him making a trip into town. Maybe I could convince him to take me along, I really wanted to see it. Well, specifically to see the manifest.

"Dear, they've never been gone this long without a word," Anita added. A rise of concern filled her tone.

"Nothing to worry about. Now, how's Maria doing?" I'm sure he meant to whisper but it certainly didn't come out that way.

"Ask her yourself, she's not deaf." Anita chortled and pointed to my chair. Which conveniently hadn't moved since he spoke to me upon his arrival. I grinned. Their lively interaction each day supplied me with endless smiles.

"I'm asking you," he protested.

"Ask her!"

"Fine, I will." He stomped my direction and stood in front of me. I pulled my lips tight to prevent myself from laughing out loud. He placed his thumbs inside his suspenders and hung them there. "So, Maria, you okay?"

I chuckled. It was too hard to fight it. "Yes, Sr. Contreras, I'm getting stronger every day."

"Miguel, call me Miguel . . . why does everyone feel the need to call my name like I'm an old man or something?"

Anita yelled from the kitchen, "Because you are, Marit."

He grumbled but his stare remained in my direction. "So, when do you think you'll be all better?"

My mouth suddenly pulled into a frown. *He wants me to leave.* Surely that's why he asked Anita first. "Um, I—I should be quite improved soon enough."

"Good!"

"D—do you want m—me to leave soon?" My stutter came out with a squeak.

"Oh, heaven's no, child!" The laugh started in his belly but got louder by the time it reached his mouth. "I want you to stay on here forever if you wish. Anita really enjoys your companionship. Goodness sake, Maria, why would you think I want you gone?"

I exhaled quietly. I wasn't sure of my plans once I healed. Part of me hoped I could stay, but part of me feared the consequences of my deception. "Thank you, Miguel." When I said his given name, he beamed, and his chin lifted higher. "I—I truly appreciate your kindness. I really love it here."

"Well, there, it's settled." He picked up the smelly fish bucket.

Before he turned away, I added, "and maybe you could share more stories of Menorca with me."

"Oh yes," he snickered. "I have some good ones about Anita."

"I heard that," Anita called from the kitchen as he scurried out of the house.

The next morning, Francisco arrived early. He held a small package in his hands when he stepped inside the house. I studied him as he made his greetings to Anita. He towered over her. I hadn't noticed this before, but his stature reflected the rigorous work he attended to in the fields—strong arms, broad shoulders, and a tinted glow of color on his neck and cheeks. He was far less polished than the men who visited Bella Vista, or the ones who begged for my attention at the soirées I attended. Even his hair fell carelessly across his forehead, over his ears and down the back of his neck as if he didn't know how to tame it, but when he smiled my direction, my breath caught in my throat. A deep dimple appeared only on one cheek. A sudden warmth crept up my face. I'd never been nervous around a man before.

As Francisco approached, he did so with the care of a gentleman, though his boots were scuffed, and his shirt hung loose and untucked. I met his eyes. The golden brown flickered brightly and his attentiveness never wavered. I'd never suffered such transparency. My hands quickly smoothed out the frock I wore, another oversized jumper from Anita. Discolorations dotted the skirt, and the hem was torn, but the fresh aroma of soap confirmed its cleanliness. My cheeks flushed. This was one of those rare times, I wished I stood before him in a dazzling gown, one that would take his breath away.

"Here." His smile grew the closer he moved. I found myself riveted by his dimple again, until the earthy scent that emitted from his proximity distracted me. "This is from Susana."

I exhaled, not realizing at first that my breath had stilled.

"She, uh . . ." Francisco stumbled boyishly over his words. "She thought you might like some dresses." He held out the package.

"Oh!" I clapped my hands together. "That is very kind of her." My excitement boiled over as if I'd been presented a precious gem. Susana was much closer to my size and I had tired of wearing the same two bulky dresses around the house.

"Do you mind if I put one on before we leave?"

"That would actually make Susana happy. She wasn't sure how you would feel."

"About what?"

"Getting dresses from someone else."

"Oh." I realized with Susana finding my bracelet, she had to have known I came from money. The bracelet she found was lavish, the most expensive piece in my collection. I frowned. "I don't mind. Excuse me."

I need to convince Susana and Francisco I'm poor. I entered my bedroom and stopped before the small, cracked mirror. Examining my image, I paused . . . but I *am* poor. I have nothing. I'm Maria with no family, no future, and no prospects—and it's okay.

I set the package on my bed and pulled the two dresses from the paper. One was made of a bright blue fabric and revealed a mid-calf sweeping skirt . . . something that might be considered scandalous in my home. Especially since I never saw Anita or Susana wearing stockings. Their bare ankles were commonplace with no consequential negativity. I traced the small red flowers that had been delicately embroidered on the bodice and the hem. The garment was stunning. The second one was entirely white, breezy, and cool.

I chose the blue one for today and quickly put it on. Glancing back at my appearance in the small glass, my hands swept over the fabric. I emerged feminine again. An element I didn't realize I was missing, until now. My wounds had healed well, and only a few parts of my body still ached, but usually only at the end of the day. The scar on my forehead stayed hidden under my wayward wisps and I was growing stronger. I reached for a thin ribbon on the desk and tied it around my hair.

I stepped out of my room with hesitation. This seemed harder than descending our grand staircase into the entry hall before arriving in the ballroom. I lacked that usual air of confidence as I moved towards the kitchen and into Anita and Francisco's presence.

When I entered, Francisco stood high atop a chair. His arms reached above his head, hammering a nail into the plaster wall. Anita's face found me first. Her hands clapped together softly, and a modest smile appeared. "Oh, Maria, you look lovely. That color matches your eyes." The hammering stopped. I peered up slowly. Francisco's arms remained frozen in place while he tipped his head my direction and smiled. I blushed and returned my sight to Anita.

The hammering resumed.

"Thank you, Cisco." Anita handed him a picture frame. "Though Miguel won't admit it, his skivvying days are coming to an end." She chuckled as Francisco placed a picture of the Virgin Mary on the wall.

As he handed the hammer back to Anita, her eyes danced. Then her head tilted and bobbed my direction with mischievous motive. Francisco, not following the path of her eyes, leaned in and kissed her on the cheek. Anita pressed one fist against her hip and grunted, while her other hand waved openly my direction. I put one hand over my mouth to muffle my laugh, but Francisco's chuckle came out loud and playful.

Anita smacked him on the arm. "You are such a tease."

He snickered again then casually turned my direction. "Oh, Maria," he spoke loud enough for Anita to hear. I blushed having witnessed their spirited tête à tête. His eyes warmed over me. I shifted nervously when he spoke. "You look—" His words no longer carried a teasing tone. "You look beautiful." When he stepped closer, he grinned widely. "I'm positive that dress never looked as good on Susana." My lips parted in surprise, then we both laughed. I'm sure he didn't intend to insult his sister by complimenting me.

I placed a hand on his arm. It came so naturally. "Thank you, Francisco." Then I swiftly pulled it back. It had been ages since I flirted. "Please tell Susana how grateful I am for her kindness."

"I will. She will be pleased you like them."

"I do, very much."

Francisco pointed to my leg. Below the hem, a thin bandage appeared around my ankle. The splint had been removed three days ago and now I bore only a slight limp. "You seem to be healing quite well."

"Sí, every day is one day closer to being myself."

"Are you sure you're up for a wagon ride?"

My smile broadened. "Yes, please!" I reached for my shawl. My walks had only taken me to the garden and the barn. I was more than anxious to see anything beyond the property. The stories Miguel regaled me with every evening, sparked a curious desire within to know more about this mystical island.

Francisco chuckled at my anxious response. "You'll love it here in the spring. It's the island's most beautiful time of year." He reached for my hand tenderly and led me to the wagon. His touch tingled my fingers. It surprised me how comfortable I felt around him in such a short time. His easy smile and simple laugh most certainly contributed to that.

Amusement and lightheartedness weren't common characteristics of the Fontaine Estate. Papa and Maman exhibited a seriousness I grew accustomed to. Occasionally, in my youth, I roused Ines merely to get a reaction from her. She, in turn, would giggle joyfully and provide that much needed gaiety.

Standing before the wagon, I realized I couldn't make my way up to the seat without help. I circled towards Francisco, but he had already moved to my side.

"May I?" He asked. I nodded. As he placed his hands around my waist, his calloused skin breached the thin fabric, and the strength of his fingers made my ascent swift and easy. Once I arrived at the bench, he immediately let go. I stole a much-needed inhale as he made his way around to the other side. Placing my hand on my chest, I attempted to slow the unbridled sprint of my heart.

"Wait!" Anita came running out to meet us, a small basket gripped tightly in her fist. "You forgot this, Cisco." She placed the basket in the back of his wagon and covered it with a blanket. I watched her curiously. *What is she up to?*

Francisco hopped up next to me and grabbed the reins, but before we left, he turned to me. "Ready?"

"More than ready," I assured. A flutter of butterflies tickled my stomach. To finally be outdoors and away from the bed or the rocking chair brought forth a variety of emotion. Much like the first time I visited Chateau d'if in Marseille, the lure of a riveting adventure piqued my curiosity.

"Hyah!" He whipped the reins and his two beautiful black steeds jerked forward in motion. As we made our way down the dirt road, my eyes flashed in every possible direction.

Francisco pointed past me. "Over there past that hill is our ranch."

"I can see the olive trees from here." I scanned with excitement. Everything in my view was like unwrapping a pretty gift on Noël. It had been thirty-two days since the shipwreck, and my only knowledge of the island of Menorca outside the Contreras' farm, had been filled with darkness and violence.

"How many trees do you have?"

"A little over 7,000."

My mouth gaped open. I was under the impression his family had a *small* farm. "That's quite a lot."

"Yes, every generation has built upon the last. My father added the last 1,000 a couple of years ago."

"So, with that many olives, how can you not find a distributor?"

"Spain is filled with many farms our size. Menorca has quite a few itself. The competition is challenging."

"Why not distribute them yourselves?"

Francisco removed his hat and wiped the sweat from his brow. The day had grown warmer. His bangs stuck to the right side of his forehead and I found myself staring at him and his coarse attractiveness.

"That would require more workers, more connections. I only have five hired hands and can't afford to take on more at the moment. I have to hope my parents have found success on the mainland first."

"I hope so, too." I settled in my seat and continued to enjoy the sights before me.

With each passing tree and lovely flower seen, I quivered with excitement. Even the clouds as they floated above us, gave me cause to cry in delight. Everything was beautiful. When I caught Francisco watching me, he shared my enthusiasm. "This isn't even the best part." He chuckled.

"I love it here. It reminds me of home."

"Where is home?"

My smile doused a bit. I had created this false image of who I was and where I came from with Anita and Miguel, even Susana, but little pricks stung as I considered the depth of my deceit, especially with him. *It shouldn't be any different.* I rebuked myself. I didn't understand why this seemed harder.

"L'Escala."

"Oh . . ." He sighed. "What a beautiful place."

"You've heard of it?" I steadied my voice. I was a bit surprised by his answer, hoping I had chosen a little-known destination.

"Northeast Spain." The dimple in his cheek deepened. "My parents have been there. They travel the coast often. I've seen a painting of it. It's breathtaking."

"It is," I concurred. My parents had taken me there twice on holiday. It was near the border of France. It was a delightful seaside community and seemed like the best place to reinvent my life.

"Why did you leave?"

I cringed, wishing Susana had mentioned all this to him from an earlier conversation with her. Apparently, she hadn't. "I—I just needed to leave." That was it. That's all I wanted to say.

"Where were you staying before your accident?"

I stared straight ahead. "I arrived in Menorca that same morning. I was going to find an inn."

"The cove is pretty far off from traditional roads, Maria. We're quite remote from any lodging."

"I must've traveled far in the water." This was probably the only truth to my fabrication. Anita said two bodies from the shipwreck had been found near Francisco's ranch, but nobody besides me came close to the Contreras cove. "It wasn't long after I arrived that I wanted to explore the sights. I was drawn to the view of the water. I don't know exactly where I was, but I imagine after the waves overtook me, I could've traveled some distance." I hoped the turn in my voice would stop the questions. The raw gnawing in my stomach reminded me of the hole I continued to dig.

"Does your family know where you are?"

"I have none." I wanted this to end now. "I—I don't want to talk about it." My response was curt. If I had turned my head sideways, I would've surely seen shock in his eyes. He was only being polite.

"I'm sorry. I didn't mean to pry."

I glanced out to the surroundings, though they didn't hold the same amount of fervor. My guilt cast an ugly gloom over a perfectly pleasant setting and soiled it. Then almost as quickly as before, the idea of running away as soon as my limbs allowed surfaced again.

Several minutes of silence passed. I knew I needed to speak, anything to fix the awkwardness that now prevailed between us. He was doing this for me, after all.

"You're right Francisco, it's quite beautiful here."

"Sí." His response was simple.

"Have you lived here your whole life?"

"Yes, it will always be my home. I can't imagine going anywhere else." I was thankful his tone did not seem to carry resentment.

"It reminds me of Marseille."

"France?"

I exhaled. "It's one of the prettiest places on earth."

"How often did you go?"

"To Marseille?" Once again, I'd let my emotions tangle with the truth.

He nodded.

"I went quite often. My father's business took us to France. Sometimes for a season or more."

"What did your father do . . . or is that something you don't want to share?"

"No, it's fine." I shook my head. "I'm sorry I snapped at you. I—I lost them recently and it's all still new."

He pulled the reins and brought the team to an abrupt stop. Then faced me directly. My cheeks heated at his complete attention. "I'm sorry, Maria. I didn't know. It must be devastating without them."

My eyes wandered past him and towards the wild reeds that swayed on the side of the road. I'd had a lot of time to think about my parents during my recovery. A lot of lonely thoughts when all I did was lay in bed. I missed them. It was strange to say that after the tumultuous last year, but I could say without any hint of deception that I truly missed them, despite our differences.

Francisco's hand covered mine. "I lost my grandparents only a year ago, both within a month." I drew my sight to where his touch warmed my fingers. "I know it's not the same as losing your parents, but I'm no stranger to grief." The way he bit his bottom lip led me to believe he chose his next words carefully. "If you don't want to talk about it, I promise I will never push you, but if you do—I'm a good listener."

The honey-colored flecks in his brown eyes simmered as he beheld me. The tingling commenced. "Thank you," I whispered.

Francisco drove us along the countryside for nearly an hour before he wheeled off onto a narrow, vacant road. It was less used and moderately rough.

I tried not to sound anxious when I asked. "Are we coming to our destination soon?" My body had started to feel the consequence of the unforgiving terrain.

"Are you in pain?" Francisco pulled his team to a slow walk. He placed one hand on my shoulder. "We can return. I'm sorry, maybe this is too soon."

"Where are we headed?" My eyes shifted to where his hand rested. He noticed my gaze and let go, grabbing the loose strap again.

"There is this place I want to show you. I think you'll love it."

"What is it?" My lips curved curiously.

"It would be an injustice to even describe it to you. Do you still want to see it?"

"Certainly."

Though he kept the team at a slower pace, we still bounced along. The pain subsided the moment we cleared the last bend and came face to face with the most amazing and terrifying sight I had ever seen.

I gasped.

When Francisco stopped the wagon, I stood up. The cliffs that bordered the wagon were breathtaking drops—a shear plummet to the water below. Francisco jumped out and came to my side. When I reached for his outstretched hand, mine trembled unabashedly. He held my fingers tenderly on the descent from the wagon but the closer we inched to the edge, my grip tightened.

The water appeared fragmented—angry and wild against the rocks, yet calm and still the farther I scanned the open sea. This was not how I remembered it a month ago. I stared hard. The emotion that built was both alarming and spellbinding at the same time. My eyes glossed over. I tried to hide my sniffle.

"Are you well?" Francisco turned towards me. I dared not look at his eyes, afraid my tears would cascade. Mesmerized with the roll of the waves, my chest burned and constricted desperate for air. Every part of my body recalled the fight it took for me to stay on the wooden plank the night of the shipwreck. Unable to stop myself, I began to cry.

"Oh no." Francisco slapped his forehead with his free hand. I jumped as he spoke, "how insensitive of me." I shook at his outburst. "How could I have not remembered your ordeal and the traumatic incident in the water." He guided me away from the edge and towards a large rock that flanked the wagon.

I moved obediently still shaken by the sight.

"Maria, forgive me." His voice seeped with remorse. He helped me settle to the perch and then paced in apparent irritation. "What could I have been thinking?"

"Francisco, please don't." I whimpered. My arms crossed over my chest. I tried to minimize how hard my breath heaved. "Don't blame yourself."

He moved back over to me and bent down. When he placed his hands softly on my arms, his touch brought all my attention back to him. The sorrow in his eyes tugged at my heart. "I should not have brought you out this soon." His hands squeezed gently. "And of all the places I take you, it's to the water."

He stood up and resumed his pacing with no intent to forgive himself.

Although I was stunned at the sight of the sea—both beautiful and deadly—I acknowledged its existence, having lived near the water my entire life.

I took a deep breath and reached for his arm to stop him from moving. "Please Francisco don't feel bad. I *want* to be here."

He watched me carefully. This was one of the few times I comfortably faced him knowing what I said was the truth. "I love *and* hate the sea." I confronted the massive creation before me. It was the watery grave of my loved ones, and yet I survived because of its actions as well. For some reason, it chose not to keep me that day.

"The sea is ambiguous," Francisco cautioned. "Its secrets lie beneath the surface."

My chest physically rose to the reckless beat of my heart. *The sea and I are one and the same.*

A line from one of my favorite authors came to mind. I quoted the verse, "In the nature, in the trees and in the plants, there is a vague shade of justice and of kindness, in the sea, not the sea smiles us, caresses us, threatens us, squashes us capricious . . ."

Francisco stared at me.

"Pio Baroja." I added. "He speaks of our desire to know the sea, but because she's an incomprehensible sphinx, we are unable to decipher her mystery."

"He speaks the truth."

"That he does."

"Maria, we can go someplace else," he reasoned. "This should be a good day for you, your first day out."

My grin came naturally. I wanted to be away from the house, it had become confining. "No, I want to stay here. I want to see what you have to show me."

"Are you sure?"

"Yes."

He grinned and reached for my hand once again, I let him lift me to my feet and this time the touch came confidently. We walked away from the water and towards large boulders behind us. The steps up the hill had been roughly carved. Francisco held my elbow as we took one step at a time. He seemed vigilant, checking my face for any traces of pain. I held it well. I really wanted to see what was ahead of us. We crossed a narrow wooden bridge that had been loosely constructed over a deep ravine. On the other side, we ascended a slanted slope and arrived at an overwhelming sight.

"This is the *Necropolis de Cala Morell*." Francisco announced with a hint of excitement in his voice.

"Necropolis?" I whispered. Though I had a personal tutor most of my childhood, my parents allowed me to attend special courses last year at the University of Provence, *Aix-Marseille 1*. This was where I studied languages and attended lectures on Ancient Civilizations. Nonetheless, I never imagined exploring a crypt in person. "I, um—"

"There's no more skeletons." Francisco swiftly assured with bright eyes. "Though hundreds of people were buried in these hills, many of the tombs have since been looted and an excavation team removed most everything else." I bit my lip. "But..." he grinned wide, "I want to show you the hidden one."

"Hidden what?"

"Cave."

Drawn to his enthusiasm and tempted by the mystery, I agreed, but reiterated, "no skeletons, right?"

"No, but there is something interesting left behind. Do you want to see it?"

"Very much so." The closest I had come to an ancient burial site was the *Abbaye Saint-Victor* in Marseille. Though the 11th century abbey housed a crypt with medieval tombs and sarcophagi, I never ventured past the entry into the first catacombs. Normally scenes involving death or bones intrigued me, but since the shipwreck and the floating bodies, I hardly had the strength for it, though I couldn't say this to Francisco.

He held out his hand and I met it. Then focused on the path ahead to distract me from the resulting tingle in his touch. Maneuvering past another set of massive boulders, I shivered in anticipation of what was to come.

After we hiked up another set of carved steps, we came to a small pond surrounded by thick brush. By now my ankle ached something fierce, but nothing was going to stop me from continuing, except that our trail came to an abrupt stop. I glanced at Francisco. He raised one eyebrow and shot me that stirring half smile from before. I wrinkled my nose. "Where is it?"

"Over there." He pointed to a small partially hidden opening past the pond and against the rocks.

My lips separated. *Impossible.* I had already pushed my limits too far. I frowned in disappointment.

"Hey..." One of his hands went to my chin. He gently nudged it up. "What's wrong?"

"I don't know if I can do it." I glanced down at my foot then back to the narrow rocky path around the pond that led to the door.

"I can help you." His fingers had not left my skin and his touch cluttered my thoughts. "But I don't want to make you go."

I paused.

For some strange reason, my mind flickered to my parents. How they never let me do anything adventurous or risky. Everything I participated in was always proper and controlled, never dangerous. Climbing bluffs and discovering artifacts in a necropolis would have been forbidden. I peered up into Francisco's eyes. He didn't have to say anything, I knew he wouldn't let me fall. "I want to try."

He squeezed my hand and led me forward, blocking the tall wild reeds with his body. This allowed me access to the corridor against the rock wall. At the edge of the water, small frogs rested on scattered stones, making the only sounds in the area louder than my irregular breath. I stood against the stone. When Francisco brushed past me to put himself in front, I gasped lightly. The moment was fleeting, but the sensation left me breathless.

I peered down; the trail thinned more than I anticipated. Francisco glanced back with confidence. "This looks harder than it really is," he reassured. "Follow me and put your hands and feet exactly where I put mine. It will be simple."

I bit my lip. Maybe I was trying too hard. He stepped up onto the rocky ledge and gripped a crevice above him with his left hand. He stepped forward pressing his chest against the wall, then moved his left hand slowly for another crack and let his right hand go where his left had been. He took several steps like this then waited for me. I took a deep breath and stepped onto the same ledge. Francisco talked me through each step. I went much slower than him, but he was patient. He allowed me as much time as I needed before my hands moved on. My entire body shook. It was thrilling and frightening and something I never believed I would or could do.

The path on the ledge was approximately five metres in length but daunted as if it were fifty. When Francisco hopped down to the opening, he waited. Holding onto the frame of the entry with one hand, he extended his other one towards me. I shuffled my feet slowly and reached for my final grip. I overshot the crack and as my hand slipped down the slick rock, my feet lost balance. My body wobbled awkwardly towards the water.

"Francisco!" I cried out and closed my eyes, unable to witness my fall into the muddy swamp. Two hands reached around my waist and swiftly pulled me onto the landing. The move came so quickly I didn't entirely fathom the rescue until I found myself safely in Francisco's arms. If I hadn't been so frightened, the idea of being held by him would have been thrilling, but I trembled madly.

"You're safe now." His smooth voice enveloped me.

A reverent silence hung as my eyes regarded him at this closeness. I scanned over the angular lines of his jaw where new stubble emerged, skimmed across his lips, and to his cheek just as his dimple slowly appeared. He returned my gaze with one of his own. "Th—thank you." Even my words stumbled. Francisco's proximity overshadowed any sensibility I might've had. I attempted composure and quickly took a step away to where breath transpired easier.

"Are you okay?" Francisco's strong physique blocked the sunlight from shining through the cavern opening. As I scanned his profile with appreciation, I hoped the shadow hid any color that might've tinged my cheeks. He was magnificent. "Maria, are you alright?" He repeated his question and the way he said it, teetered between confidence and concern.

"Yes." I brushed my skirt and wiggled my head out from my stupor. "I would've fallen if you hadn't caught me." This we both knew to be true.

I glanced deeper inside the cavern. Only steps away, the space immersed in total darkness. "I don't think we'll be able to see anything back there."

A sly smile emerged. "I've been here before, remember." Francisco teased. The wider his mouth curved, the deeper his dimple hollowed, and each time it did, my eyes were drawn to it. He reached for a wooden stick against the wall. It had been wrapped with a tight linen and when he picked it up, a strange musty smell transpired. He reached into his pocket and retrieved a piece of flint and steel. This, I recognized from my father's workshop.

With only a couple of strokes, Francisco had a decent flame and transferred it to his torch. It instantly lit up the gloomy space. He held it out in front of us and reached for my hand again. Only this time, I pulled myself closer to him than before, genuinely anxious of what lay ahead. As we took a few steps inward, Francisco flashed his torch towards the sides. "Amphora." He pointed to the clay cylindrical pots with pointed bottoms leaning against the walls, some the length of my leg, others the size of my palm.

We continued to creep. It didn't take long before we reached the back of the cave. There, Francisco's touch tightened at the same time he flashed the light towards a pile of rubbish. I inched closer. My heart pounded rapidly as the outline of an unusual piece came into focus within a pile of shattered ceramics.

"Look." Francisco tilted the flame towards the find. "Do you see what that is?"

I squinted. "Can I pick it up?"

He nodded. I reached out and cupped it gently as I drew it closer for inspection.

"It's beautiful," I whispered, allowing my fingers to explore the unique shape and detail. "What is it?"

"An earthen oil lamp."

"Oh . . ." I breathed, rotating it around to see the wide body and thin spout. "There's something on the top surrounding these two small holes. A peculiar design."

"Yes." Once again, Francisco dipped the light closer. "See that? They're lions. And this," he pointed to some odd angles. "This is a man."

The image came through much clearer now that he had explained it. Fully focused, there was no doubt of the carving. A man with two lions. As I went to lay it back in its resting place something crawled underneath. I screamed and flew to Francisco's side. Had he not been holding a flame; I would've jumped into his arms.

"What happened?"

"It moved, something moved."

Francisco placed one arm around my waist and stretched out the torch. Sure enough, a black spider scurried along the ground.

Hopping from one foot to the other as if that would halt its approach, I whimpered. "Okay, I think I've seen enough."

"There's more to see down there." He pointed to a narrow enclave.

"No, I'm ready to leave."

"Alright, Maria. We can go." Francisco kept me close as he led me cautiously back to the entrance, and though I scanned the ground for further insects, his nearness wasn't far from my thoughts. Once again at the opening, we used the same exact method as before to climb out, only he stayed much closer to me this time.

On dry land and back on the main path, I located a rock to sit upon. Catching my breath, I rubbed the tender side of my ankle as Francisco approached. Leaning down on one knee he pointed to my injury. "May I see?"

I nodded as he unraveled the bandage and placed his hands carefully around my bare ankle. I winced.

"It's swollen. I pushed you too hard today." Disappointment clouded his countenance.

I shook my head. "No, I wanted to come." I tugged at his sleeve to get him to look at me again. "I've never seen anything like this. It's wonderful."

He laughed out loud. "I don't think I've ever heard someone describe a necropolis as wonderful except for me."

I smiled back. His laugh tickled my heart.

After he replaced the bandage, he held out his hand once more. We hiked slowly down the stone steps, over the bridge and towards the wagon. "Wait here." He pulled out Anita's secret bucket and laid the blanket across the flat edge on the end of the wagon.

"Do you mind if I help you up again?"

"I don't mind," I replied. Then waited for my insides to somersault again at his grip on my waist. He didn't let go until he was assured I sat securely on the boards.

He opened the bucket and spread the food out, then hopped up next to me. "Anita makes the best potato tortillas."

"I know." I confirmed with a chuckle. "I live there. She makes the best everything, actually."

"I don't know what I'd do without Miguel and Anita." Francisco poured two glasses of Hibiscus lemonade and set them next to the plates. "They are more like family than friends."

"How long have you lived next to them?"

"My whole life. I don't have many childhood memories without them."

I took a sip then paused, "They are the kindest people I've ever met." Speaking the truth felt good.

"Sí," Francisco handed me a plate. "You will love my parents, too. I can't wait for you to meet them."

"When do they return?"

"Soon," he said. But when I peered closer, a sliver of doubt slipped through his countenance. He met my gaze and continued, "May I ask you something?"

I braced for more lies to tell. I hated fibbing but could not refuse him. "Yes."

"Do you have happy memories from your childhood?"

I hesitated at his question and placed my plate down on the wagon. My mind whirled past the last seven months, the months I had cried nearly every night and back to kinder days. When my parents traveled, it was Ines' duty to remain with me. I beamed in remembrance of our escapades. "When I was twelve, Ines, my companion, took me to the Santa Maria Del Pi."

"Where?" Francisco's eyes lifted.

"A church, in Barcelona."

"Are you religious?"

"A little, but this was not just a church, this was a monument. It had massive Gothic arches that led to a glorious circular glass window. I stared at that window for almost an hour. I'd never seen anything like it. Now, whenever I travel, I visit the cathedrals. The ones that are rather old and could probably topple on top of you." I chuckled.

"Well, you are in for a treat, *senyoreta*... wait, I don't even know your family name?"

He caught me off guard. "It's—" *What name? What name do I give? Grand-mère's birth name, that's it.* "It's Caron."

"Srta. Caron." The words slipped off his tongue pleasantly, but they didn't belong to me. I peeked down at my hands as he continued, "Ciutadella happens to have one of the most beautiful, *old*," he emphasized, "and unique cathedrals I've ever known. Would you like to see it?"

"Yes." I glanced back up. "Very much so."

Francisco placed a cluster of grapes on my plate then opened a jar of olives. "These are from our ranch. Taste them and tell me what you think."

"You don't have to convince me that they are wonderful. I had some at Miguel and Anita's." I laughed and popped one in my mouth. "They are truly delicious." I devoured a handful before I spoke again. "Tell me more about your parents, Francisco."

"Mother is from the Canary Islands. Father met her on holiday. They fell in love instantly, but Mother couldn't marry him until he proved himself worthy in my grandfather's eyes. It took him three years."

"Three years?" Amazed at the devotion, I marveled. "He must've truly loved her."

"She is his one and only."

I considered this. What a beautiful example of commitment. "Did your father always want to be part of his family's olive ranch?"

"Yes, as long as I can remember. Menorca is our home. He loves its soil, fruits, plants, the sea, and Mother, of course. I don't have a single memory where my father didn't show overwhelming adoration for my mother."

A twinge of jealousy burst. This was precisely what I hoped for in a husband and precisely what my father was willing to deprive me of. My body trembled lightly as I thought of Thomas. How can something as precious as love emerge from an arranged marriage?

"What does your mother do while he's in the field?"

"Oh, she's an artist. I will show you her paintings sometime. She's quite talented." He tore a piece of the tortilla apart, the scent of sweet corn floated towards me as he chewed. "Anita could sell these, right from her home, they are incredibly tasty."

"You must miss your mother's cooking." I observed him as he savored every bite.

"Oh, I miss her, but not her cooking." He laughed. "We have a cook, though nobody is as good as Anita."

"I had a cook also," I spoke before thinking. "Actually, we had three."

"Three?" He held a grape near his mouth but didn't eat. "Three?"

"Uh, yes . . ." *I'm terrible at this.* "Not all at once though." I fibbed . . . again.

"What business was your father in? Do you mind me asking?"

So much for keeping the questions off of me. I hesitated. A feathery breeze swept over me and I inhaled the hint of salt from the sea. I wanted Francisco to know parts of me were real. That everything I felt and experienced when I was with him was genuine. "Papa was a merchant. He brought goods from all over the world to France then sent things back all over the world."

"Why France?"

I bit my lip. *Drat I keep messing up.* In my efforts to keep my association away from France or the shipwreck, I failed mercilessly.

"We were close to the border. Papa's business kept him busy in both countries. Marseille is a world port, and he was rarely home. I was mostly raised by Ines."

"Why not your mother?" Francisco's forehead wrinkled. "Wasn't she there in your home?"

I swallowed a sip of the lemonade. My throat had gone dry. "She was there. It just wasn't her way."

Francisco's face revealed confusion. Having a nurse and *au pair* raise children in affluent families was quite common in France. From his reaction, it must not be common here.

"Were you close to Ines?"

"Oh, yes, more than my parents actually. She was good to me."

"You speak of her as if she's no longer with you."

"She's not." My nose stung and a tear balanced on my lower lash. When I blinked, it trickled down my cheek. Francisco reached up and caught it before it dropped off my jaw. His countenance softened while he watched me.

How can I keep lying to him? I matched his stare. *He's so kind and gentle with me.*

"Maria, how long do you plan to stay with the Contreras'?" He paused as if he wanted to say more but didn't.

"I'm not sure. They invited me to stay as long as I want."

"They did?" His voice lifted.

"But I can't." I gazed back towards the water. "I should be on my way soon. I don't really belong here."

"Where is it you belong?"

"I don't know." I sipped my lemonade and kept the cup to my lips. Talking led to more trouble. I couldn't entertain the idea of living a lie for the rest of my life. It could hurt me and destroy them.

We finished the food in silence. It wasn't intentional, but with the lingering questions, the awe-inspiring scenery and being out of the house, exhaustion consumed me.

Francisco packed up the picnic and placed it back in the wagon. Once again, he helped me to the seat and guided his beautiful team towards home. When we arrived at the Contreras', he helped me down.

"I'm sorry I got you dirty." He chuckled as he pointed out the dirt that had covered parts of my dress. This made me smile as well. An offense that would have surely caused a quandary in Marseille but remained a lighthearted joke here.

"I don't mind getting dirty sometimes," I said without reservation.

Francisco's hand remained at the small of my back as he led me to the door. "Maria, may I visit you again?"

I stopped and faced him. My eyes skimmed the arresting features across his handsome face while he waited for my answer. I was tempted, *very tempted*. Would it be so hard to take on this new identity and live here, happily away from my past and my fears? But the reality of my fictitious façade nipped at me. I knew the closer I got to anyone, the more my lies could surface and cause undue pain. For heaven's sake, I could barely keep track of it all in a simple conversation.

Then before I stopped myself, I answered, "yes."

15

Carrasco Ranch, Menorca, Spain

Francisco

    The moment I drove the team from the Contreras' to our property, I wanted to jump, yell, even kick my heels if that was something an ordinary guy would do. But these feelings were far from ordinary.

    My mind relived our goodbye merely minutes ago. *She said yes!* For one small moment I feared she would refuse me, but she didn't. Everything about today generated a new and exciting sensation. I could hardly put the experience to words.

    I unhitched the horses and Javier met me to take them inside the stable, but I couldn't go inside the house just yet. All of this pent-up energy had to go somewhere. *The olives, I will check the trees.* I yelled back to Javier, "Saddle Diego please, I'm heading out."

    "To the fields, senyor?"

"Sí."

Javier never questioned me, but his eyes flicked towards the setting sun.

"It's fine. I want to ride."

He relented and prepared my horse. I hopped on and took him to a full gallop. Darting through the trees, I intended to check their status, but my mind flew far from the crop. Every image that materialized in my head was of Maria. The way her blue eyes dazzled, her charming smile, the scent of lavender when the breeze caught her hair, even the tremble in her touch. My thoughts lingered on her skin . . . the very skin I had grazed when I checked her ankle. And her waist, where my hands clung to keep her from falling or lifting her to the wagon. Even the way she slid next to me when she was frightened at sight of the spider. How many times did I fight the desire to get closer . . .tempted to hold her tight and never let go?

I kicked Diego. The faster we went—the faster I cleared my head.

I cringed at the idea I had pushed her too hard physically, but she was strong. I would have offered to carry her down from the caves if she had allowed me, but I knew that to be impossible. She conducts herself like a lady. One moment she exhibits a sense of pride, and the next, alluring insecurity. Everything about her fascinates me, though I hardly know her.

I replayed our conversations in my head. She hides her sadness well, but anyone who has faced that much loss must suffer to some degree. She attempted to conceal her pain, but instead exposed genuine vulnerability. I'm nearly driven mad with a mysterious desire to care for her.

I slowed my horse to a stop at the border of our properties. The Contreras' little home glowed by firelight the short distance away. My heart thumped in rhythm. I placed my palm against my chest as assumptions crept through my mind like malicious thieves. What if she leaves? She said she needed to leave. What if there is another? What if someone else holds her heart and she's too polite to disclose? Sweat built upon my forehead and neck. Never before had my heart stirred this way, and if I didn't do something about it, it may never again.

I will take her to Ciutadella. That would make her happy. This I knew for sure. I'll show her the fresh produce at *Plaza del Mercat*, the *fleques* with the most indulgent pastries, the *Plaça d'es Born*, and the place she wants to see the most, the Cathedral Basilica of Ciutadella.

I will give Isabel a reason to stay.

I nodded goodbye to the house down below and kicked Diego forward. The energy drawn from my decision pumped wildly through my veins. There would be no sleeping tonight. Tonight, there are plans to make.

Rounding the corner to the stables, I nearly knocked Susana over. Barefoot and in her nightdress, she shouted my name, "Cisco! Oh, Cisco!"

I flew off Diego even before he came to a stop and ran to her side. Tears streamed effortlessly down her cheeks. She held up her hand where something was tightly gripped within her fingers.

"What is it, Sus?" The invigorating pleasure flowing through my limbs moments ago dissipated at the sight of seeing her completely distraught.

She passed a post to me. I grabbed her with one arm to keep her from falling to the ground. I quickly read over the contents. "It's from our friends in Zaragoza." She sniffled.

Dear Sr. and Srta. Carrasco,

We sincerely apologize for this unremitting correspondence. We have exhausted all avenues in locating your parents. They departed Barcelona on the morning of February 6th and arrived in Montpellier, France on Feb 8th. The *Domaine de Verchant* where they took lodging had no further information as to what their plans were upon departure. This is the last date that we have verifiable knowledge of their whereabouts. We sent word as far as Paris, Rome, and Athens, and riders along the coast as far as Genoa. None of their familial contacts have seen or heard from them. We received notice today that they haven't been sighted in any of those previously suggested cities. As of this moment, with no further knowledge of their location, please send word on our next course of action. With deepest sympathy,

Sr. Pedro Velasquez.

Heat surged through my veins. I crumpled the paper and realized my sister still wilted at my side. I lifted her up and carried her inside. She wasn't crying as frantically as before, but her soft whimpers tore at my chest nearly as much.

"Wh—what d—do we do?" she muttered. Her head fell weakly against my shoulder.

I didn't have an answer for her. For the last month I had sent money and resources to the mainland for help. Now, from this correspondence, I found that nothing we'd done had yielded answers.

"Could they have been the victims of highway crime?" Susana whimpered as I tucked her into bed. I knew there were some territories where gypsies attacked carriages or coaches, but Father wouldn't risk Mother's life that way. They often traveled by train whenever possible.

"I believe if there had been any foul play, we would know." I pulled the quilt up to her chin. Some sort of evidence left behind . . . .even a body perhaps, although I didn't say this out loud. I shuddered at the thought. The very idea of Mother, breathless and still, caused a cold chill to ripple my skin. "Do you need anything, Susana, tea maybe?"

Her tears slowed but she remained in a haze. "No, brother. Thank you."

"We'll find them, Sus." I kissed her on the forehead and closed her door.

I went to the fireplace and added a log. As I watched the flame grow larger and brighter, I settled into my father's favorite wingback chair nearby, a glass of brandy in my hand. I didn't drink often, but tonight called for something more than tea.

As today's events swirled chaotically in my mind, a hint of clove buds from my father's hand-rolled cigarettes leaked from the velvet headrest and instantly my attentions went to him. My elation over Maria quickly doused with the reality of my parent's disappearance. I had no right to engage in selfish desires when my family suffered. Whether it was locating my mother and father, or comforting my sister, my mind needed to stay focused on them—only them.

16

17 March 1910

Contreras Farm, Menorca, Spain

Miguel

Throwing on my boots, I entered the kitchen to what was sure to be a hint of disaster. Anita and Maria wore matching aprons, each layered with flour from nearly top to bottom.

"What is that smell?"

Both women glanced up at me with varying degrees of shock. Maria's appeared to be near tears and Anita's scowl could've sliced me to ribbons.

"You—you think it smells?" Maria's timid voice sailed through the air. Then I realized why my wife sent daggers my direction.

"Oh," I grimaced. "Whatever it is, it smells . . .wonderful."

Two blackened crusts cooled on the counter. I leaned forward and poked one out of curiosity then stepped backward when Anita sent a quick warning.

"What are you making, Maria?" I downplayed my unease.

Her lips quivered. "Anita is teaching me how to make her potato tortillas. I'm afraid I don't have her skill."

"You are doing fine, dear." Anita patted her arm. "We simply have to be mindful of the time it's in the fire. You are trying to learn too much all at once."

Tears bubbled on the girl's lashes. I wrung my hands together roughly. I'm not good at this crying thing. I should've headed straight for my pole and the door and avoided the kitchen all together.

"I'm sure it's fine," I mumbled. "In fact, I will take some with me fishing. How's that?"

"You will?" Her pretty, blue eyes lit up.

I knew that once I reached the water, the fishes might gobble them up. It might make decent bait. "Of course, wrap me up some and I'll be on my way."

"Wait!" Those same eyes, now layered between excitement and apprehension, studied me. "May I go with you?"

"What?" My voice cracked. I blinked twice at Maria and double that number Anita's direction.

"You're going fishing, correct?"

"Uh, yes, it's uh, a man's leisure." I emphasized *man*.

Out of the corner of my eye, my wife attempted to stifle a laugh. She placed her hand over her mouth and glanced away.

"But might I go with you?" Maria waited.

"It's a dirty place, dear. There's mud and rocks, and what about your ankle? It's been swollen since you returned from your outing with Francisco."

"That was days ago and it's fine now. Please? May I go?"

My heart wilted. If she had been my daughter, there is no doubt I would've taken her fishing the moment she could hold a pole. In fact, I would've given her *anything* she asked. And though Maria was not my daughter by blood, she had me right near wrapped around her finger since she arrived.

I pulled my hat off my head and scratched my hair. My fishing time was just that, *my time*. No nagging, no labor, no nothing, not even talking, except to Hugo or the fishes. "Okay," I relented.

Maria squealed and ripped off her apron. "I'll prepare double the tortillas. We can have a picnic."

My mouth bowed. Anita's form shook with laughter in the corner. She best be careful I didn't point this out to Maria. "Yes, pack for two, but you're going to have to wear sensible clothes and boots!" I shouted as she dashed towards her room.

Anita met me with a wide smile and a kiss on the cheek. This startled me, until I noticed she continued to giggle on her way to Maria's room. I had been ambushed.

Outside, I whistled for Hugo. He came bounding around the corner as I retrieved an additional pole. "Girls' got no business fishing . . . that's a man's sport," I grumbled to the dog who tilted his head as if he understood.

Moments later, I had to suppress my own laugh as Maria stepped out to the porch. Not only had Anita found her some fishing clothes . . . it was *my* fishing clothes and they nearly drowned the poor girl! Maria bent over and tucked her pant legs into a pair of large rubber boots then pushed the long sleeves up to her elbows. A small piece of rope had been tied around her waist to keep the overalls from falling to the ground. The only thing natural about this image was her smile.

"I'm ready!" With one hand she picked up the basket with the tortillas, the burnt ones for sure, and in the other hand she lifted a bucket.

I shook my head and sighed. Well, this would be a first. Not even Anita dared to interrupt my sanctuary with the fishes. "Come on," I muttered, and she quickly fell behind me where Hugo trotted side by side next to her. "Traitor," I blurted his direction.

When we approached the bay a good fifteen minutes later, Maria's steps slowed to a trickle. "Come on girl. If you're going to do this, you're going to do it right, hook and all."

She came to a complete stop.

Her whisper was so slight I had to ask her to speak up. When she did, it occurred to me why she really wanted to come.

"Wh—where did you find me?"

I set the poles down and moved over to her. I had never been one for much affection, but I immediately placed an arm around her shoulders. She curled into me as if she'd been denied this basic need. I patted her back until her tears ceased. Then led her to the rocks I'd not forgotten changed both our lives. "There." I pointed. "You were covered with debris and partially in the water. I didn't know if you were alive or dead."

She stepped forward and knelt at the edge of the sea. When her fingers dipped in, her shoulders quivered. I moved towards her again. This comforting thing was not my forte. I placed a hand on her head, and patted softly, allowing her strands to curl in my fingers. "There, there, Maria." I watched her. Her form appeared smaller than I had noticed before. She's somebody's daughter and she is in pain. But at that very moment, I had never wanted her to be mine more than ever before. I urged her to her feet and pulled her in for a deeply needed hug. I told myself it was for her, but knew it was for me all along.

After several minutes, she separated and held a small hand to my scratchy jaw. "You are the kindest man I know." She kissed my cheek and stepped over to the poles. "Okay, I'm ready for my lesson."

I chuckled and wiped my chin. This might not be so bad after all.

Later that afternoon as we packed up and headed back, I reflected on this most unusual day. It didn't take long for Maria to learn how to hook a worm, and surprisingly she didn't cringe like most girls might. She dug right in. She also didn't squirm over the slimy scales from the two groupers I caught. But best of all, once we settled into fishing, she didn't force me to talk which seemed right comfortable for us both. With only a nibble for her efforts, she seemed discouraged when she didn't hook a fish, but I reminded her it took time and practice. I'd been doing it for over sixty years now.

Although I wasn't too keen on taking her in the first place, I really didn't mind if she chose to come along again—without the burnt tortillas, of course.

Back at home, she helped me put the gear away and at the top of the porch she flung her arms around me one last time. "Thank you for today, Miguel." She grinned as she pulled away. "I have never done anything like that before." I wasn't quite sure what she referred to . . . the fishing? The getaway? Maybe it was the assurance she needed? Whatever it was, there was no way I would be fine if she left us now.

17

18 Mar 1910

Algiers, Algeria

Thomas

I led Calypso to an obscure part of the port that I rarely visited. Glancing down, I reread the numbers on the scratchy vellum in my hand. Once the location was identified, I realized it was the only building without broken windows, or fissures in the stone exterior. Unique for this neighborhood, the edifice displayed characteristics to the Baroque revival seen only in the wealthier parts of the city. A metallic sign near the door revealed "Moreau Antiquities". I tied Calypso to a nearby post, brushed out my wrinkled coat, and knocked.

A woman opened the door. Underneath unruly auburn curls, her dark eyes pierced me with petulance, but it was the way her lace chemise had slipped down one shoulder leaving it completely bare that drew the most attention. That, and the bright red corset that squeezed her slim waist, exposing a considerable amount of her décolletage. I grinned. *If I didn't have pressing matters...*

"What's your business?" Her tantalizing lips pulled into a scowl.

Issuing my most gentlemanly nod, I removed my hat and offered the smile that brought many women to my bed. "Milady, I'm here to see Monsieur Moreau."

One eyebrow lifted, and her stance held tight as if unaffected by my charm. "I am unaware of any appointments this afternoon. Has the Monsieur been notified of your call?" She didn't move aside to allow me passage.

Ah, a feisty one. My smile grew. *They are the best kind.* "Yes, he's expecting me." I brushed past her and entered a dim foyer.

With both fists resting on her curvaceous hips, she glared. "I did not invite you in."

"That's irrelevant," I countered. "I'm expected." Then issued my own piercing threat. "Now notify Monsieur Moreau, that I am here, Mademoiselle ... posthaste."

She wrinkled her nose and though her mouth dangled as if she had more to say, she closed the front door. I waited for another round of sparring, but she only pointed to a chair and left the room.

The decor within was unusual in taste—a burgundy Moroccan rug with black fringe, matching velvet curtains, a nearly empty sideboard, and two luxurious wingback chairs facing one another. A hint of myrrh released from the upholstery as I took my seat.

"Ah, Monsieur Chastain, I presume?" The man who entered was older than I expected. A speckled gray covered his crown and he walked with a cane, though it appeared more for style than medical. His dress, however, a high button-stance behind a four-button coat with slim lapels could not be mistaken as one of the finest suits I had ever laid eyes upon. I studied him with intrigue. He must be in his fifties. *Was the woman his daughter or his lover?*

"Monsieur Moreau, *merci* for your time." I stood to shake his hand although he did not meet mine.

"Oui, the correspondence indicated it was rather urgent. Who should I thank for our acquaintance, good sir?" Moreau eyed me skeptically. I glanced past him to find another man standing in an arched doorway. Though he didn't move or speak, the man watched me with hawk-like attention. One hand rested in his pocket. I grinned. I wasn't intimidated by Moreau's henchman. My own hand patted my jacket where the contour of my pistol protruded. I hoped its use was unnecessary.

I faced the gentleman again. "I was referred by a client of yours, a Monsieur Boucher. He speaks highly of your *special* skills and advised me to seek you out for assistance."

He sat down and waved one hand my direction. "Please, be seated." He retrieved a cigar from an ornately crafted humidor on the table nearby. After clipping the tip, he handed it to me. "Elaborate, Monsieur."

I accepted his gift and waited for him to ignite the smoke with a silver lighter fashioned after a dragon. I admired his taste. Sitting back, I drew a decent inhale before I spoke. "I have a rather delicate conundrum involving a woman."

His head rolled back, and a loud laugh erupted. "Don't we all."

I eased at his humor and set the cigar on a cast iron tray before I retrieved the two ripped pieces of Isabel's photograph from my inside pocket. Placing them on table next to his chair, I pointed. "This woman."

He pushed them together to make a complete image. "She's beautiful."

"She perished in the Chanzy shipwreck."

He tilted his head. "And you want me to bring her back?" His chuckle began in his chest but by the time it reached his throat it was noisy and grating. "I am very good at what I do, but I cannot raise the dead."

"I understand that." Impatience surfaced in my tone. "I need proof that she is dead to claim her estate."

Monsieur Moreau leaned forward and studied me. "Even with evidence of her death, what qualifies you to her estate."

"A marriage of contract between her father and myself."

"Interesting." His hands clasped in front of him, steepling his fingers against his upper lip. "And what of her father?"

"Deceased and there are no other children.

"You mentioned in your letter that you met with the Maître' Bureau. Why would they not accept her death from the ship's records?"

"Since there was one survivor, they believe there is a possibility of more."

"Improbable," he barked. "It's been over a month. Any additional survivors would have come forth by this time. Her name was clearly on the manifest, correct?"

"Oui. Though they require additional proof."

The sultry woman entered and handed a goblet to each of us. The strong herbal scent of an Algerian wine filled my nostrils. Superior ones are hard to come by, but I assumed nothing was beyond Moreau's reach. I thanked her and watched her leave as I waited for my host. He seemed to be contemplating much in that short time.

I swallowed the contents quickly and set the empty glass on the table next to my smoldering cigar. "I'm off to Ciutadella soon in search of anything to prove her demise, but if I'm unable to, I need a document fabricated enough to pacify the Bureau." I leaned forward. "Is that possible?"

Monsieur glanced from the photograph back to me. He rubbed his beard slowly. "Now, *that* is more my expertise." A sly smile emerged. "But can you afford me?"

My jaw grew rigid. I was a well-dressed gentleman despite my limited resources.

"How much?"

"One hundred Francs."

Heat grew beneath my collar though I kept my countenance clear of emotion. One hundred Francs were nothing to the Fontaine Estate, but for me in my current position it would be nearly impossible. I offered an alternative. "If it brings the desired results, you will be handsomely rewarded."

"My charge is paid directly, regardless of the results."

I took a silent breath. My mind considered all the options. I'm already selling the silver for passage and travel expenses, but even that could not cover this fee. The silence grew thick between us while my mind spun with possibilities. *I can sell the Degas paintings.* I know they would fetch a decent coin, but the process to find a buyer could take weeks. *My brother must never know.* I cleared my throat. "I will go to Ciutadella first and see what I can locate. As her betrothed, they should not give me any trouble."

"It is unlikely you will find what you are looking for in Ciutadella." He swirled the wine in his glass and sniffed it before he took a long sip. "Unless something personalized is identified to belong to her. A monogramed case or the clothing or parasol from this photograph was found in the collection," He stared hard. He was not a dim man. "Even then it does not prove her demise, only that she was a passenger. No, I suspect you will need adequate confirmation involving a body."

"But I read only a portion of the bodies were found." A hint of desperation leaked out when I spoke.

He nodded. "That is my understanding as well. Have you received notification that *she* was recovered?"

"No, I have written to the solicitors in Ciutadella, but received no reply as of yet." I wiped the sweat from my brow. "I intend to send a man at once to Menorca for that purpose and join him myself by the end of the week."

"The odds are slim but that is the best course of action for someone... without immediate means. Especially if the procurement is confirmed through the authorities."

"And if she hasn't been recovered?"

Again, Monsieur Moreau hesitated with a lengthy stare my direction, most likely assessing my ability to keep confidences. "My reproductions, Monsieur, specifically documentation of the deceased, exceed authenticity requirements. I can assure you nobody would know the certificate's origin didn't come from the proper authorities."

I silently damned my brother. If only I had free access to my inheritance and he didn't control the allotments, I could pay for this straightaway and be done. "Monsieur Moreau, if nothing is resolved in Menorca, do we have an arrangement upon my return?"

He smiled wryly once more. "Leave a detailed description of the woman and what you know of her family with Madeleine, my assistant." He pointed to the woman who had just re-entered the room, "If you have the means when we reconvene, consider it resolved."

Assistant? The same shrewd grin from before, spread across my lips. So, she *is* his lover.

"Madeleine, dear, take note of his specifics then kindly show him out."

I bowed his direction. "Thank you, Monsieur."

"Like I said," he stood to his feet. "I am very good at what I do."

Thirty minutes later I entered the old Moorish coffee shop. I had only been here once before with my father, fifteen years ago. I cringed at the memory. An older man with an indigo-colored turban welcomed me. His stare led me to believe my father frequented the place. It was not far from our compagnie and though I wouldn't admit it, there were similarities in our appearances.

"May I help you?" He set aside his glass hookah pipe and bowed slightly my direction.

Peering around, I located the reason I had come. "No."

He tipped his head again and went back to his pipe.

"Jacque?" I motioned towards the tallest man in the room. His curly black hair easily a head above the rest.

"Monsieur Chastain?" He stood quickly and hustled to greet me. Jacque was a trusted employee of our company for over five years. After a recent disagreement with my brother and a humiliating reprimand, it was I who convinced my brother not to dismiss him. Since then, Jacque became an ally of mine. Several times in the last couple of months he arrived at the manor with information my brother sought to withhold from me. This behavior proved him to be a loyal mate. Precisely the man I needed for this job.

"I must speak with you," I demanded. "Do you have a moment?"

"Yes, of course."

He led me over to a small private table. "What can I do for you, Monsieur?"

"I have a pressing task." I glanced around to make sure our conversation remained confidential. "I have business in Menorca but can't be there for a few days. I need you to go ahead of me and take care of some rather private matters."

"Menorca, Spain?"

I glanced at him warily as if there was another Menorca. "I will pay your passage and all expenses if you will depart shortly. Unfortunately, I can't join you yet. I have a situation that requires me to remain here, momentarily."

"Is this about our cargo?"

"Non. This has nothing to do with the company nor should it be disclosed."

He shifted nervously. "What about your brother? He expects me to square the ledgers."

"Leave him to me. We have a meeting tomorrow and I will take care of it. Leave as soon as you are ready." I placed a leather coin purse before him.

"What do you need me to do while I'm there?"

I showed him the torn picture of Isabel. "This woman perished in the Général Chanzy shipwreck. I need you to find out anything you can of her in Ciutadella."

He stared at the picture. "Is she your family?"

"Not exactly." I tucked the picture in a folded letter and handed it to him. "All of the details of your duty are listed within. Do not read this until you are on a ship." Though I provided substantial information for Jacque to begin a search, I did not include anything about the betrothal or my reasons.

"Oui, Monsieur. I am in your debt and will gladly see this through." His allegiance reassured me.

"One more thing, Jacque. It is imperative that you do not mention the reason for your departure to anyone." I pointed to his chums in the corner. "Above all, my involvement or the name Chastain must not be disclosed."

We shook hands. Jacque swiftly said his goodbyes and mounted his horse. If everything goes as planned, one way or another, it won't be long before the Fontaine fortune will be in my possession.

18

21 March 1910

Carrasco Ranch, Menorca, Spain

Francisco

    Plucking the fruit off an olive tree was something I'd done since I was three years old. Over time, I no longer needed to climb up inside the thick trunk to reach the bright green branches and burrs. Parting the tapered leaves, I maneuvered my hand deep inside the thick foliage and retrieved a cluster of the plump fruit. When I drew the raw produce to my face, the bitter scent skimmed through my nose and settled in my throat.

    Normally, on harvest days, I found a comfortable balance between the pleasant atmosphere and the speed of the reap. Only today, nothing I did brought forth the aforementioned outcome.

My mind bounced haphazardly between my parent's current state, their whereabouts, and the woman who had managed to drive me near madness with intrigue. What was it about Maria that was unlike previous courtships? Though they weren't numerous, I was no stranger to affection. Yet, something about her stirred my soul with a restlessness to which I was unaccustomed. My jaw tightened. I couldn't seem to focus. Whether I was with her or away from her, a curious yearning burrowed within me. A reckless desire to be near her amplified and drove me to forgo all other duties.

"Senyor!" Javier called me from behind. "Are you going to bring that bag here or keep praying over it?"

"I'm not praying over it!" I tucked the fruit from my hands into the heaping canvas bag slung around my neck.

"You're doing something over it." Javier teased. "I've moved three bags to your one."

"I'm coming." I lifted the strap over my head and placed the bag in the wagon. Then stopped to fill a cup of water from a nearby jug.

"You are getting old and slow." Javier quipped as he too poured himself a cup.

"Old?" I retorted. "You're five years my senior, Javier. If I'm old, you're ancient."

"Then it's that girl isn't it?"

"What girl?" I feigned innocence, but he knew me too well.

"The woman that has you all tied up in knots. You can't focus, you can't work. Susana said you even had trouble with the ledgers yesterday. She had to correct three different entries. You've never done that before."

"It's nothing."

Javier's eyebrows rose. Though my father employed him, he was always more like a brother to me.

He stared until I relented. "Maybe—maybe she's on my mind a bit."

"A bit?" He scoffed.

I grew silent. This was a conversation I would've had with my father. Knowing how much he loved my mother; he would've known exactly what to say when I told him about the unrelenting fervor I faced when Maria was near. He would've listened and offered advice and above all, he would've insisted I bring her home to meet them.

"What's the matter, Cisco?" Javier himself turned serious.

"I wish I could talk to my parents about her."

He nodded. "You will."

"There's a great deal I want to ask." I removed my hat and raked my hands through my sweaty bangs. "What was it like for you and Lupe?"

Javier was newly married as of six months ago and when he smiled wide, I sensed the excitement in his eyes. "It's. . ." He chuckled lightly. "It's wonderful."

"Did your heart practically beat out of your chest every time you were near her?"

Javier chortled aloud now and patted me on the shoulder, "Oh boy, yes, little brother, you are in trouble now."

"What do you mean?"

"That's exactly what happened and look where it led me . . . to the alter." He laughed again. My pulse raced. I wasn't ready for that . . . or was I?

Javier threw an empty bag at me. "But these olives won't pick themselves. The sooner you finish, the sooner you can ride over to see your sweetheart."

I grinned. I liked the sound of that. Would *she* like the sound of that? I gripped the bag and watched Javier retrieve his own empty pouch. I was surrounded by examples of true love—Mother and

Father, Anita and Miguel, and now Javier and Lupe, but what if it's not meant for everyone. What if it's not meant for me? There really was only one way for me to find out. I needed to see Maria today. I needed to know. But as much as I wanted to jump on Diego and ride to the Contreras' at that very moment, I knew that my responsibility was here and if I weren't careful, I could make things worse for the ranch—even though, in the absence of my father, it didn't seem like it could get any worse.

Javier stopped me before I left the wagon and placed one hand on my arm. "Don't worry, Cisco, you know your parents would adore anyone you brought home. Because if she loved you, they would only love her that much more."

19

21 March 1910

Contreras Farm, Menorca, Spain

Miguel

"Why the long face, Maria?" I entered the kitchen after working in the barn with Henry. For decades, I labored outside from dawn to dusk, yet now could barely toil an hour before I required rest. Maria sat on a stool with her hands propped below her chin. A look of discouragement swept across her face.

"No reason." She sighed.

Now I don't claim to know much about women, but one thing I knew from my marriage with Anita was that their words hardly ever matched their feelings. I sat on the stool next to her. "Did you and Anita cook today?" I lifted my nose upward. A lingering whiff of sausage and cheese moistened my mouth.

"Sí."

"What did you make?"

"Empanadas."

I licked my lips scanning the kitchen for the evidence of such a delicacy. In the last week, Anita had spent the entirety of three days teaching Maria how to make her delicious baking dough. The first day had been a complete disaster, much like the tortillas, but every day since, Maria's skills in the kitchen had improved. "So where are these said empanadas?" I clasped my hands together.

"Wash first, Marit." Anita entered from behind. "You are a walking sandbag." Though I had removed my boots at the door, my breeches were caked in mud and when I lifted my palms, dirt lined the creases.

"Fine," I grumbled. Anita patted my arm as I stepped to the wash basin in the corner.

"So, Maria was about to tell me why she has a frown on her face." Scrubbing each nail with a bristled brush I glanced at her with a sly smile.

Her eyes widened. "I was?" No grin came forth. My face scrunched. I could always get her to smile.

Anita glanced between us both. "What's going on?"

Maria shrugged her shoulders.

"Well, look at her Anita!" I scowled, "she looks like she fell off a horse."

"Or maybe wants to get on one?" Anita winked my direction. Maria had asked me to teach her how to ride since the brace had been removed. I wrinkled my nose knowing I had just stumbled into a hornet's nest.

"Yes!" Maria jumped from her stool. "Yes, I would love to ride today. Maybe we could ride around the property and, well, maybe," she stuttered, "m—maybe over to the Carrasco's?"

My brows curved inward. "Why there?"

Anita shot me a disapproving grimace. "Oh . . ." Something clicked. "Francisco," I muttered.

"Oh, no," Maria peered down to her feet. "I miss Susana is all."

I wiped my hands dry with the small towel and circled around to see Anita drape an arm around Maria's shoulders. "Susana, huh?" I snickered only to get the full wrath of Anita in a matter of seconds.

Anita's hand brushed across Maria's hair and down her back. "I'm sure Francisco is very busy."

Maria bit her lip. "But he asked if he could come see me and then I don't hear from him for almost a week."

"Don't fret, love," Anita assured. "With his father absent, he must run the ranch himself."

"Do you think it's me? That maybe he doesn't like me?"

"Oh, from the expression on his face when he said goodbye the other day, I quite doubt that should be your concern."

I smirked at the talk of mushy things and took my place back on the stool. "Alright, and what about those empanadas?"

"Is that all you can think of husband? Your stomach?"

"No." I scratched my head. "I think of fishing too."

Anita smacked me on the shoulder with her towel. Maria laughed out loud. It was good to see that smile again. She flung her arms around my neck and rested her head on my shoulder. "I love being here."

Anita's eyes welled up.

I glanced between them both. "Empanadas?"

Anita glowered and pulled the plate from the oven. They were warm and ready. The aroma of sausage and potatoes, onions, and carrots forced my mouth to water immediately. She held them barely outside of my reach.

"Are you teaching Maria to ride today?" She lifted her chin.

"What?" My gawk went from the plate to her face. "Ride?"

She pulled the food back towards her, farther out of my reach. "Well, are you?" I peeked over to Maria as she stepped away. Her hand covered her mouth, but her eyes were smiling.

"For heaven's sake, woman."

Her eyebrows rose as she waited.

"Sí," I retorted. "Give me the darn food."

"Well, see how well it works when everyone gets what they want." Anita placed the steaming plate before me. Her smile was meant for me, but the wink was entirely for Maria.

An hour later, Maria stood before me in the barn wearing those same large overalls from before when she went fishing, with the same rope tied around her tiny waist in the attempt to keep them upright. I chuckled at the sight of her. From the neck up, she was as primped as a princess. I recognized one of Anita's combs pulled her lengthy blonde hair away from her face and behind her shoulders.

"Thank you for teaching me, Miguel." She smiled though she wasn't good at hiding her apprehension.

"Henry has saddled Penelope for you. She's a gentle horse."

"Okay." She brushed her hand along the neck of one of my oldest mares.

"I've owned her for over a decade," I added. Penelope lowered her snout to nibble at Maria's sleeve. She seemed to enjoy her touch.

"Alright, this is much like fishing. If you do as I tell you, it'll be fine." I pointed to the stirrup. "Place one foot there and swing your other up and over the horse." Maria was a tiny little thing. She tried three times and slumped with a frown next to the saddle. I wasn't sure myself if I would be strong enough to help her. "Henry, come over here." The boy took two easy strides to my side. "Will you help Maria to the top?"

His smile answered for me. *Of course*, I chortled. *The boy's not blind*. A woman with features like Maria's was hardly missed. He moved to her side and explained how he would help. Then asked permission to touch her. *Lord, for working on a farm, that boy sure knows his manners*.

In an instant Maria was on top. Her hands trembled as Henry handed her the reins. I moved over to Paco. He was anxious to go. It had been several weeks since I'd ridden him last. I heaved myself up and guided him next to Penelope.

"We won't go far. Nice and slow and stay on the property." Her chin dipped, but she said nothing. This must be about her earlier comment and going to the Carrasco's. I quickly added, "then maybe we can see how our neighbors are faring." Her face lifted to mine as if the sparkle in her eyes had never been absent.

I pulled on the straps and nudged my heel into Paco's side to move him forward. I knew Penelope was intelligent enough to follow Paco, but I kept a steady eye on her. As we trotted past the house. Anita stood on the porch and waved. Maria, too afraid to let go of the ropes, only grinned in return. We went past the garden and through the gate which led to the wide-open acreage we now let run wild.

Many years ago, this land had been the site of a bounteous harvest of grape vines. Over time, the years had taken its toll and our crops reduced from ten acres to one. Henry still managed it on his own. Enough to cover our basic needs and pay his wages, but many times I'd considered selling the rest of it to the Carrasco's. Francisco had a strong team of hired help and with the careful attention they placed on their olive trees, my land would be in good hands.

"How's it going?" I forced Paco to move side by side with Penelope. Though he was anxious to fly into a dead run, he was obedient.

"Good, I think." Her eyes never left the horse. She was stiff as a board.

"Relax, Maria. It's supposed to be enjoyable."

"It is, I promise it is. I only fear falling."

"You won't fall, she's not going fast enough for you to even slip from the saddle." She tore her eyes from the mane and glanced at me. A look of panic flashed across her face when I mentioned slipping from the saddle. "You will be more comfortable the next time."

Did I just commit to a next time? I swatted a fly away and shook my head. *This girl is getting under my skin.*

"Do you make your own wine?" She asked as we passed the leafy green plants spread across the lengthy wires.

"Well, I wouldn't exactly call it wine." I chuckled. "We've made our own version of the fruity liqueur for years."

"They're beautiful. When I was younger, my parents took me to many fine wineries in Northwest France and these could stand with the best of them."

Her comment swelled my chest. This was a source of pride for me. If only I'd been blessed with someone to pass them down to. I quickly swept any sadness aside. Anita and I had accepted our childless lives long ago.

"Look who it is, Maria." I pointed out the horse approaching us from the west. Francisco rode confidently in our direction.

Uncertainty flashed across her cheeks. Her grip tightened on the ropes as she glanced down to her disheveled wardrobe. My nose wrinkled. *I thought she wanted to see him.* "Women," I mumbled.

"Sr. Contreras?" Francisco slowed to a trot before he arrived next to us. "Maria." He removed his hat but held it tight in his hands. "I was just on my way over."

I might as well have not even been present for his eyes never actually reached me. A rosy shade crept across Maria's cheeks when she smiled. "Hello Francisco. How are you?"

"I'm doing well, and you?"

"Yes, I'm well too."

"Oh my," I groaned. "I'm good too."

Francisco laughed. "Susana will be pleased to hear it. About both of you." He shot me a knowing look. Susana had been telling me for years I needed to be more active. I suppose riding a horse counted.

"How's your crop, Cisco?"

"Strong and healthy, senyor. Javier oversees it nicely."

"We both know Javier doesn't do a thing without the okay from your father or you. You have managed well, son."

"Gràcies." He exhaled as if he'd been holding his breath.

"Well, well," I patted Paco's side. "It's been a long day for Paco here." Maria shot me a worried glance. I practically heard her plea for us to stay longer. I smiled partway and turned to Francisco. "Do you mind leading Maria and Penelope back to the farm after the old girl has stretched her legs a bit more?"

Francisco's wide grin was the answer. Maria herself could hardly fight the smile that replaced the concern.

"Yes, sir, I'd be happy to do that."

I reached for Maria's hand and patted it. "Francisco knows Penelope's conduct almost as much as me. You're in good hands." And I swung Paco around and with a swift kick we darted into the full run he'd been waiting for.

20

Menorca, Spain

Isabel

When Miguel first mentioned returning, only a minute after seeing Francisco, my mind went into a panic trying desperately to find a reason to stay, but in the end that lovely old man gave me more than that—an afternoon with Francisco.

"It's nice to see you on a horse, Maria."

"Yes." I grinned awkwardly as our horses walked side by side towards his ranch. "I have only ridden once before, and it didn't end well."

"Oh really?" He chuckled. "How did it end?"

"With me in a mud puddle." I laughed. "I was ten years old and my father thought it was time I learned to ride. I feared the beasts though and fought vigorously to stay away from them. When I showed up for my first riding lesson in a pink chiffon dress instead of my riding habit, my father was furious, but he made me ride anyway. When I returned to the house an hour later, with a torn skirt and not one patch of skin showing through the dirt, my mother forbade me from trying again." I smiled at the memory.

"Did Miguel coerce you to ride today?"

"Oh, no, I begged him. Actually, Anita bribed him."

"Bribed him?"

"With the empanadas we made this morning."

"Oh, an empanada sounds delicious right about now."

"You're welcome to join us for supper." I hesitated to ask, unsure of why he had avoided me this week. "Unless you're too busy."

Francisco stopped his horse. The magnificent black hair glistened in the sunlight. I had seen beautiful animals before, but Francisco's horses were unmatched. "I'm not too busy." He reached for my hand which I willingly offered. "I'm sorry, I haven't come by."

When he let go, he hopped down from his horse and stepped over to mine. "Would you like to walk a bit?" With my consent, he reached up and helped me to the ground.

"Whose property is this? Yours or the Contreras'?"

"Ours now. That's the boundary line." He pointed to the line of trees we passed.

As we walked, Francisco remained by my side. His hands casually clasped behind his back while mine toyed with the buckles and buttons on the overalls. Thankfully, Francisco said nothing about my odd attire. Winding around the trees, we brushed shoulders several times. Francisco apologized, but I rather enjoyed it.

"What would you say is your favorite diversion?" My smile teased. "Besides exploring caves?"

Francisco's lips curled slightly. "Does discovering Roman ruins fall under that title as well?"

I laughed. "Yes, besides your adventures, what do you like to do at home?"

He seemed to contemplate my question with seriousness now. "I would have to say my horses." He pointed back to where our horses nibbled the grass beneath a tree and when he spoke his voice asserted conviction. "When I mount Diego, there is a sense of freedom that surges through me. An intense mixture of energy drives my desire to become one with him." My body went still as I watched him describe this. "I can confront any emotion on the back of a horse."

Something rebellious, almost defiant flashed within his eyes. Instantly drawn to it, my breath caught in my throat. For as much as Francisco was a gentleman, it was clear to me, a deep passion blazed beneath his skin. Then almost as quickly as it arose, it vanished. In my miniscule experience with men, there was one thing I learned for certain—the lengths they went, to keep any vulnerability hidden. I allowed my mind to wander. *Was passion Francisco's limitation or temptation?*

"What about you? What pleases you, Maria?"

Drawn to the sound of a small stream trickling nearby, I strolled towards the water. "There was this place near my home that I would go when I wanted to be alone." Beneath the boughs of a giant shade tree, I sat down on a rock and continued, "I was rarely alone. Bridgette and Ines hovered often. It was their duty to remain with me throughout the course of the day, but occasionally I found the means to sneak away."

"I like the idea of sneaking away." Francisco chuckled and sat on the ground next to me.

"This particular place was filled with wildflowers in every direction, but in the center, a small barren space had been carved out as if it had been made only for me. A hiding place of sorts. I'd take a coverlet and a novel and would lie there for hours, reading and watching the clouds move across the sky."

"Do you miss it? Your home?"

I nodded. "There are some things I do and others I don't, but being here especially in this place, it reminds of my field and my books." When he smiled, his dimple deepened. Tender pulsing tickled my heart. I missed seeing him this week.

"Who is your favorite author?"

There were many I enjoyed, but only one I could say was my favorite. "Tolstoy." I grinned. It had been months since my fingers grazed the pages of *Anna Karenina*.

"Tolstoy?" Francisco's eyes warmed over me. "My mother adores him. I believe she has several of his works in her library. Maybe I can borrow one."

My spirit leapt at the idea. I had already read—twice—the only literature Anita and Miguel owned. One was Miguel de Cervantes' novel of *Don Quixote* and the other, a collection of fables by Félix María Samaniego. "Thank you, I would like that very much."

Francisco glanced over the surroundings then picked up a small stone. "I used to come here with my grandmother." His fingers rubbed the smooth edges of it before he flicked it into the water. "We'd pack a picnic lunch and spend the whole day here. She loved to tell me stories of her youth. You know she trained to be a bullfighter in Almeria."

"She did?"

"Yes, before she met my grandfather. Of course, women were not allowed in the ring, but that didn't stop her from trying." He laughed.

"You must miss her so."

"I do, but I have many fond memories." Francisco's eyes met mine. "You must have some good memories of your parents."

Unlike the warmth that embraced me when Francisco spoke of his family, I hesitated, unsure if I could even share *one*. Though desired, the longing for similar affection could not be summoned. When I glanced back at him, the tears that settled in the corners of my eyes threatened to fall.

Met only with a look of compassion, he knelt at my side. When his hand brushed my cheek, I leaned my head into his palm. The gentleness of his touch awakened me, and I allowed its intensity to run wild. His fingers then trailed my jaw, and his thumb held my chin. When he lifted it up to face him, my lips parted. I had never been alone with a man long enough for him to kiss me, but here alone with Francisco, I had never wanted it more.

When he leaned in, a raw woodsy aroma intensified. His brown eyes darkened, and his breath slowed. "May I kiss you?" he whispered.

My nod came with no resistance, but only a moment before his lips met mine. When they melted against me, the sweetness of his taste lured me in. He pressed gently, though his hands moved to my arms and gripped with a loving urgency. The pulsating in my chest compounded to the depth of his kiss. I wanted it to last forever.

He leaned back, smiling. My eyelashes fluttered, stunned. "Is that—" I inhaled deeply. All I saw were his lips. "Is that how all kisses are?"

He chuckled and kissed my forehead. "No. That one was exceptional."

When he reached for me, I stood weakly. My legs wobbled and he was quick to wrap his arm around my waist. "Are you alright?"

My mind still focused on the kiss. "I think so."

"Can you ride?"

"Hmmm."

Francisco held me next to him as if that helped me gain composure. *It didn't.* Both of his arms now wound around my back. I inhaled the earthy scent that emanated off his skin. Resting my head against his chest, the steady rise and fall of his own breath lulled me. It had a quickness to it much like my own.

"May I still come for dinner tonight?" His words reverberated against my ear.

"Please do. I've missed you."

He held me out from him long enough to meet my eyes. "I'm sorry Maria, I meant to come over sooner. I really did. A lot has happened since Cala Morrell. My parents are still missing and I'm afraid something awful has happened."

A hint of fear tinged his tone when he spoke, and guilt immersed me for being selfish. How could I have presumed he had abandoned me when his duties to his family and ranch were so much greater? "Please don't apologize. It is I who should be sorry. Is there anything I can do to assist?"

"No, but thank you." He led me to my horse. I had found strength in my limbs once again. His hands reached around me and lifted me up as if I weighed nothing at all. The muscularity in his arms pushed against his sleeves. I watched with admiration then placed my feet in the stirrups.

He easily jumped to his horse and guided us back the way Miguel and I had come.

"Francisco, I have resources on the mainland, and in France. Maybe they could help you," I said this without thinking it through first. It seemed as though my desire to help, outweighed my desire to stay anonymous. I marveled at this thought. Up until now, my only consideration had been over my own fears and needs.

"I appreciate the suggestion." He smiled but it didn't bring forth the dimple I desperately wanted to see. "I have some associates searching over there now. If nothing transpires soon, I will go there myself."

"You'll leave Menorca?" Slight alarm arose in my voice. I wasn't even sure why, but his presence made me feel safe. The thought of him being gone for weeks or a month brought a sadness to my countenance. His horse stopped next to Penelope. His hand reached over and rubbed my hand. "It won't be for long, but I need answers."

I understood his longing for answers. I had not been able to get my own. Though I was certain my family perished in the shipwreck, I yearned to see their names on the manifest—to know they really were gone.

"Yes," I agreed. "Yes, you do." My hand relished his touch. The spark that triggered was undeniable and assured my heart that the sensation was shared.

After he released my hand, we trotted in near silence to the Contreras'. A peaceful tranquility drifted naturally between us.

Once in the barn. Francisco quickly descended his mount to assist. "What time would you like me to be here tonight?"

Once he brought me down, his hands remained on the sides of my lumpy breeches, again with no mention of my awkward attire. "As soon as you can." I smiled.

He grinned and kissed my cheek. "I will check the ranch and clean up." He rubbed his chin. "I should probably shave too." I laughed, though his scruff didn't interfere with our earlier kiss one bit. I doubt it would tonight either, hoping for a repeat.

"And bring Susana," I added. "I would love to see her again."

"I will." He hopped back up and tipped his hat leading Diego from the barn. By the time I reached the porch Francisco launched into a swift run. The idea that he was rushing home only to return, thrilled me beyond words. After all the times I had interacted with properly attired gentlemen and starched titles at the many social events I attended, not one touch, not one glance brought about the frenzy of butterflies that seized my chest at this moment.

When I entered the house, I paused. I was a woman who had just stepped over the threshold of adulthood. My fingers grazed the surface of my lips as a tingle trailed through my body. My first kiss was everything I had hoped it would be. This man and his charming dimple raptured me to no end.

Later that night, Miguel and Anita regaled us with stories of Francisco and Susana as children. Most of them were harmless, only the occasional tale brought forth unending humiliation in which either one or both emphatically denied.

"Is Javier going to town this week, Francisco? Anita asked as she cleared the table.

"No, actually..." He glanced over to me and grinned. "I was hoping to ask Maria if she would join me on a jaunt to Ciutadella on Friday?"

"Truly?" My enthusiasm came strong.

He nodded.

"Oh, yes, I would love to go."

"Cisco, she's still recovering." Susana scolded. "Don't make her walk all over town."

"I'm getting stronger." I assured her. "I even went riding today."

Her mouth fell open. "On a horse."

"Well what else do you think she would ride?" Miguel quipped, "a pig?"

"You two." Susana shook her finger at both men. "You better hope all the work we've done to heal her doesn't get undone with your foolish exploits."

Everyone laughed. Especially after the stories switched to me and my determination to learn as much as I could about the farm and the kitchen. Between cooking, fishing, and milking the cow, there wasn't much I had left to learn or be humiliated by.

"I promise, Susana, I will take care of her." My cheeks heated at the way Francisco gazed at me. "I would never let anything bad happen to her."

Anita clapped from the corner, though nobody knew for sure what she was celebrating. She whirled back around with the largest smile I'd ever seen grace her lips, though she said nothing.

"What are you grinning about, Dona?" Miguel eyed her curiously.

She continued to smile as she brought a freshly baked *Imperial* to the table, though I was sure it wasn't the dessert that had her all aglow.

Francisco winked my direction. "I'll make the trip eventful and not painful, dear sister."

My thoughts went to the kiss once more. It was all I thought about during our brief separation. Would we have the chance to do it again?

"Maria wants to see the Cathedral, senyora." Francisco stood to help Anita cut the spongy custard cake and dish it out.

"Oh, you will love it, dear," she hummed. "It was built in the sixteenth century. Very elegant. Such a lovely place. If you have time, go to the convent as well."

"There's a convent?" My pulse raced. I'd been to one in Paris. I absolutely loved it.

"Oh, yes, both the courtyard and the chapel should be open to visitors, although the other rooms I'm not sure."

"I would truly love that." The meringue frosting dissolved on my tongue.

"And Cisco do you mind picking up a few supplies for us while you're there?" Anita inquired.

"I'd be happy to, anything you need."

After the kitchen was cleaned and it was time for Francisco and Susana to leave, I offered to walk them out. Susana deliberately walked ahead to the wagon as Francisco remained on the porch with me. He took both of my hands in his.

"I'm not pushing you too quickly, am I?" His face went smooth except for the small crease above his nose.

"Oh, not at all," I assured. "I'm anxious to go to town. Gràcies for offering to take me."

Francisco's pause was longer than normal before he spoke. "I couldn't imagine going with anyone else."

We were finally alone, and the memory of his earlier kiss lingered fresh on my lips. As my mind predicted, I couldn't deny the compelling lure that mounted between us. The physical ache that arose reminded me of how much I belonged in Francisco's arms.

He lifted my hand to his mouth. Though his own hands were rough and calloused, his touch emerged tender and light. He grinned harmlessly, but his stare revealed cryptic intentions. He turned my hand over, and the moment his lips touched my palm, a shudder seized my chest. I closed my eyes and from the amount of pressure he used, the trail he blazed along my skin was easy to follow. When his lips reached the tender part of my inner wrist, the warmth of his breath swept through me like a burning ember.

"Oh, my . . ." I breathed. I had no idea a kiss like this could be as powerful as one on the lips. My body may never be the same.

I opened my eyes to his smile. He had to have known the effect of what he'd done. I struggled to control the pulsating of my heart. "Goodnight, Maria," he whispered. Then let go of my hands and stepped away.

I watched until they were completely out of sight before I ambled dizzily back to my bedroom, praying for God to speed up the next three days as swiftly as possible.

21

23 March 1910

Algiers, Algeria

Thomas

"Are my bags packed, Arthur?"

"Oui, Monsieur."

"Did you make the proper arrangements for travel?"

"I did. Here is the money from the silver." He handed me a leather pouch swollen with bills.

"What about the paintings?"

"*Le peinture apparaiser* is coming tomorrow to inspect them."

"Very well, don't let him take advantage of you. The two Degas dance paintings are worth a substantial price."

"Oui, Monsieur . . ."

The hesitation in Arthur's voice and his taut stance indicated he had more to say.

"Speak, Arthur," I groaned.

"The paintings, Monsieur . . ."

"What about them?"

"They were your maman's."

My fist tightened and released twice before I found the strength to keep my voice level. "And?"

Arthur took a couple of steps back though it had been over a month since I had physically touched him. "I'm not certain your brother would agree."

I gritted my teeth and hissed, "My brother has nothing to do with this. They belong to the house. *My* house. Understood?"

"Oui, Monsieur."

"Anything else?"

Arthur's trembling hands extended. "Here are your documents for the ship. Sr. Diaz is the man who will meet you at the dock."

I snatched the papers. "And he has arranged my lodging in Mahón?"

"Oui, in addition to a transport to Ciutadella once your business in Mahón is complete."

When I met with my brother two days ago, I informed him that Jacque would be accompanying me as my valet to Menorca since Arthur was too old to travel. In exchange for my use of Jacque, my brother insisted I meet with a newly acquainted textile manufacturer in Mahón. I never disclosed that Jacque had already departed for the island or my true reason for traveling there, other than pursuing leisure, but I agreed to his request to keep him from prodding.

"Very well, Arthur." I tucked the money into my waist coat. "I should return in a fortnight. If I intend to stay longer, I will send word."

Felicia handed me my hat and stepped out of the way as I made for the door. "And Arthur, I have advised my brother that Felipe can leave the allowance with you." I glared one last time at the bent man. "Make sure you are fiscal with the funds. There should be plenty upon my return."

I went outside to the wagon. Calypso neighed restlessly at the idea of being restrained. I wished there was a way I could've taken her. She most certainly sensed my abandonment the moment we arrived at the port. I patted her chocolate mane and consoled in her ear. "I will see you soon, my love."

As my groom unloaded my bags, I silently protested my reasons to depart for Menorca. If only I had direct access to my full coffers. I could've paid Moreau immediately, allowing the process of acquisition to proceed without delay.

Going to Ciutadella seemed unnecessary and most unwanted. Monsieur Moreau already confirmed his ability to secure the necessary documentation needed to obtain the Fontaine Estate and its holdings, so to have to be inconvenienced with travel frustrated me. I scowled at my predicament. I could've been on a ship to France at this very moment instead of Spain. Nonetheless, the quicker this was remedied the better.

"Monsieur? Your name?"

"Fabron," I reached for a cigar inside my vest as the duty stamped my entry document. "Luc Fabron," I added. It wasn't the first time I used my grandmother's surname.

"Thank you, Monsieur Fabron. The serviteur will show you to your station and your luggage will be tagged for retrieval in Mahón."

"Is there a lounge on board, good sir?"

"Yes, you will find one on your deck."

Though this was not an overnight journey, I paid the price to travel in luxury with a personal stateroom. Once inside, I inspected the accommodations. I imagined traveling aboard many grand ocean liners once the finances are assigned. I have always wanted to visit Greece and Italy. I peeked through the porthole as the ship kicked away from the dock. The desire to never return to Algiers materialized easily within my soul. Though I knew it to be currently impossible, I fantasized about the day I would leave it permanently behind.

"Is it to your satisfaction, Monsieur?" The young man who led me here could not be more than sixteen. Though he fashioned a uniform for the position, his creased trousers and frayed hems revealed his lesser status.

"Oui." I faced the looking glass on the dressing table and tucked a wayward strand of hair behind my ear. "Would you direct me to the lounge?"

"Of course. Do you prefer the smoking room or the palm court, Monsieur?" He glanced down to the cigar I still held in my fingers though I had yet to light it.

I tucked it back into my waist coat pocket. "I'm in want of a nip. To the lounge please."

The young man led me towards a wide set of stairs. The lavish detail increased with each level of ascent. By the time I reached the highest deck, a starlight glass covered the room he referred to as the Palm Court. Appropriately named, miniature palm trees dotted the room between luxuriously decorated tables. Most of them occupied by fashionably dressed travelers. The lad led me to an empty table near the center and retrieved my chair, whereupon he immediately called for a *garçon* to address me.

I reached into my pocket and retrieved a generous tip.

"Oh, Merci, Monsieur." His enthusiastic response to the amount did precisely what I hoped. Now everyone within earshot peered my direction. I smiled casually and directed my attention to the garçon who now eagerly awaited my order.

"Brandy." Though its tang was no more than diluted *limonade*, I had an image to foster and whisky did not fall within the standards of this lofty decorum.

"Oui, Monsieur." He rushed from my side.

I glanced around the room and met several curious stares, none of which enticed me to linger long, until my sight fell upon a handsome young woman. Though her companions no longer gawked my direction, she did. I grinned and tipped my hat. She teasingly lifted her painted fan to cover her mouth, but her eyes pierced me from beneath dark lashes.

My drink arrived. I lifted it her direction and sipped slowly. Her fan lowered just enough to expose her lips. The light tinted pink curved gradually in response. I chuckled to myself. I had grown used to the women back in Algeria throwing themselves at me. Of course, it was always in a tavern or a brothel. I had forgotten how much more work it took to seduce a cultured lady.

I turned away and scanned the intricacies of the room. Colorful frescos and crystal sconces favored each column, and a lowly lit lamp created an unusual ambiance for an afternoon cruise. *I could get used to these luxuries.* I leaned back in my chair and continued to romanticize how to spend my future income.

"Another brandy, please." I waved my garçon over. "And send a plate of *Profiteroles* to the young lady's party over there." I pointed to the table where the woman continued to play hide 'n seek with her hand fan.

If I were to travel abroad, the idea of docking at a different port weekly, enticed me. My mind aroused with anticipation of exotic maidens, superior fare, and grand adventures.

I smiled at the woman the moment the garçon departed her table. She seemed pleased with the succulent crème puffs but once again teased from behind her propriety. I set my glass down. This childish flirting vexed me, and I strode deliberately over to her table.

Several hours later, I departed my stateroom having changed from my traveling clothes to my formal attire. The scent of Mademoiselle Dupont's perfume still lingered about me. It had not taken much for me to convince the French Miss to take a stroll about the deck on my arm and within a moment's time, I managed to steal kisses in a darkened corridor—an action she fervently accepted. While only a kiss remained innocent enough, had we been on a longer voyage, there was no doubt in my mind the sweet Parisian Mademoiselle would have bedded me by nightfall.

I smirked at the thought and tugged on my jacket sleeves. "I believe the affluent lifestyle suits me." I concluded as I strode down the empty corridor. "I need only to show patience." I stepped outside and off the ship ready to meet Sr. Diaz.

22

24 March 1910

Ciutadella, Menorca, Spain

Isabel

My smile grew as we wound through several narrow streets with high windows and iron gate balconies. Shop owners were only beginning to open their doors and the smell of cured meats and aged cheeses floated through their arched entryways. I stopped at one window. A photograph revealed a magnificent black horse decorated with ribbons and flowers. The words *Festes Sant Joan. 23-24 Junio* appeared in black lettering below.

"What is the Festes Sant Joan?" I turned to see Francisco peruse over a peddler's wares. He held up an item and examined it, though I couldn't make out its shape from where I stood.

"It's a local festivity honoring their patron saint." He strode to my side. "But the real attraction is the horses—as you can see." His smile broadened.

"They are identical to yours." I pointed to the advertisement once more.

"Yes, they are a distinctive breed on the island. Though not common outside of older families."

When Francisco stood behind me, the weight of his proximity tingled the hair on the back of my neck. "Would you bring me back for the festival in June?" I asked with hope in my voice.

He paused. "Will you be here in June?" I caught his expression through the reflection of the glass. It mirrored my longing and for a brief second my heart titillated. Then I fretted. *How long can I keep this guise up? He doesn't even know my real name.*

As my guilt continued to surge, I faced him. "Francisco, I need to—" A lump caught in my throat at the very sight of him. Though we had ridden together in the wagon and even walked for several streets, the way he appeared before me now took my breath away. He wore a white button-down shirt that accentuated his bronze skin, black trousers and though his hair was still ruggedly wild, his jaw was clean-shaven. When his engaging eyes met mine, they revealed a desire I recognized similar to my own. My chest stirred madly under his gaze.

Can I tell him the truth? I measured my risks then faltered as I willed him to hold me first—to take me in his arms and tell me everything would be okay, but I feared it would not be. For the moment my confession surfaced, everything would change.

In the quiet moment of my contemplation, his hand reached over and slipped a bracelet onto my wrist. I peered down. My fingers grazed the metal band while tears ensued. It was fashioned from simple copper, but as I peered closer, delicate floral etchings lined the edges. Though it didn't dazzle with gems or precious stones, it was the most endearing gift I had ever received. I threw my arms around his neck. When my cheek brushed his, Francisco's masculine aroma filled my senses and soothed me. Wrapping his arms around my waist, he held me against his chest in an intimate embrace. Though reluctant to release, I did and whispered my gratitude, "thank you, Francisco. It's beautiful."

His dimple deepened to his wide smile and he easily slipped his fingers into mine. "On to the Basilica?"

I nodded with hesitation. My courage to confess was fleeting, then shadowed by the enticement of the church. Persuasion came easily as I deferred the task to a later hour . . . or day. I brushed any guilt aside and squeezed my body next to Francisco, knowing his nearness would lighten my mind.

As the majestic cathedral tower came into view, its distinctive cast iron bell hovered above only a street away. Ignoring the merchant's trinkets that would have called to me any other time, my bosom swelled with excitement and anticipation the closer we got.

Barely inside the grand entrance, I held my breath and scanned the expansive room before my sights settled upon the vaulted ceiling. I have never been overly religious or moved with a need to enter a church for repentance, but the draw I had to these aged structures could not be helped.

I brushed my fingers along the backside of the closest bench for stability. My entire body tingled with giddiness. I stepped to the center of the room and slowly circled about, admiring the exquisite details of the tombs. The rich reds, golds, and silvers sparkled under the dramatic candelabras. Elongated panes depicting Heavenly beings circled the space allowing barely enough natural light to pour in and distinguish the colossal cross found before me. I took a deep breath as if the very oxygen in the room satisfied a long deprivation.

Though my eyes never wavered from the splendor, I slipped around to the front of a wooden bench and sank to the seat. Francisco joined me but said nothing.

After spending quite some time within, we emerged back to the quaint streets of a now bustling town.

"Did you enjoy it?" Francisco reached for my hand again. Though the move became more natural, my skin still tickled with delight.

"It was breathtaking," I said, enchanted.

"I haven't been in there for years, but I must agree with you, it was beautiful."

We wandered the tapered alleys for several minutes until we reached a wide-open Plaza. My heart leapt for joy. Its picturesque and charming ambiance reminded me of *Place de Lenche*, a square near the port in the older section of Marseille.

"I thought we could eat before we go to the convent."

I smiled. A handful of cafes dotted its borders with family and friends leisurely drinking and conversing, but the real joy came from the center of the square.

A small crowd had gathered around a band of musicians who played eagerly and cheerfully. We drew closer out of curiosity. A tall man with a horseshoe mustache strummed on the guitar, a much shorter version of the first played a violin, and a man with a belly as round as his tambourine danced in circles as he struck the instrument as if unaware of watchful eyes.

Several couples spontaneously started dancing in front of the musicians and the longer they played the more people joined in. Infected by the energy, I clapped my hands together excitedly. The only time I'd seen an outdoor dance festival before, was when my friend Irène and I passed one near the opera house one night. I had never participated in one since all the dances I was accustomed to were held in grand halls or ballrooms.

Francisco grinned wide, his dimple profound and engaging. Since our ride to Ciutadella this morning, I had successfully brought the dimple out nearly a dozen times. He extended his hand. I glanced back at him nervously. I used to be a fantastic dancer, but I feared the weakness of my ankle changed everything.

"I don't know if I can."

"We can go slow." The gold flecks in his eyes smoldered, and when he leaned in his lips brushed my ear. "It will be fun."

Impossible to resist, I met his hand and he led me to the edge of the dancers. When he released and placed it gently around the lower part of my back, the touch nearly paralyzed me. He held his other hand out for mine.

"How did you get this scar?" I pointed to a long, jagged mark on the inside of his hand.

Francisco snickered. "I was holding wire down during a windstorm." He rolled it over for a better view. "The force caused the wire to slice through my flesh. It was quite foolish actually," his laugh grew. "But it was the first tree I had planted on my own and I feared losing it, so I defended it with my life."

I marveled at his devotion. "Did you save it?" I ran one finger the length of his palm and recognized its similarities to my own scars.

He closed his eyes to my touch and let out a simple exhale. "Sí." Then drew me close and opened his eyes. "And it was worth it."

With his proximity, I had difficulty focusing. *Dancing, yes, we're here to dance.* I met his hand without further hesitation. I wouldn't have minded just standing and staring at his remarkable lips but as more people joined around us, we would've been an obstacle.

Francisco guided me slowly. I sensed he didn't want to push me, but the more comfortable I was the faster we moved. Everything came back and astonishingly, Francisco, himself, met the challenge well. For a *farm* boy, his skill in dance was quite impressive. By the end of the song, we were only getting started and without a word, we casually enjoyed another two before we stepped aside.

"You surprise me, Francisco. Where exactly do you practice on your ranch?" I laughed as we took two seats in the patio of a nearby cafe.

"I had a mother who insisted her son know how to sweep a woman off her feet . . . on the dance floor."

I grinned. "How many women have you swept off?"

Francisco bit his lower lip and glanced down at the menu, but it didn't seem as though he read it. "You would be the first who matters, Maria." He peered back up with an intensity. "That is . . . if I actually *have* swept you off your feet."

My cheeks warmed, and I smiled. There was no doubt in my mind of what he had accomplished.

"But it is my father's example that taught me how to love a woman." Still gazing upon me with those penetrating eyes, my lips separated in awe. I was unsure whether I heard him correctly.

"*Bon dia amics meus.*" The waiter appeared.

Francisco's lips curved devilishly. Then directed his attention to the man who had welcomed us and greeted him back. "Bon dia, senyor."

"*Què puc aconseguir per tu?*" The waiter inquired after our order.

"Do you love seafood, Maria?"

"Uh, um." I was a driveling fool. I shook my head attempting to come back to reason. "I'm sorry. Yes, anything."

"*Arroz caldos amb peix con langosta si us plau.*" Francisco ordered. I beamed. Lobster and rice were a favorite of mine. "Oh, and please add *Buñuelos* to the meal." He turned to me, "You'll love Mahón cheese."

We continued to watch the musicians and the dancers. I could not think of a single day in Marseille that I enjoyed more than this very one.

"Any news on your parents yet?" The mood swung dark. I instantly missed his smile.

"No."

Two days ago, we walked the orchards together and he told me about the letter they received. It was heartbreaking. I knew how he felt. His parents could've perished and that is an awful, awful outcome, but not knowing seemed even worse than that.

"I know someone in Marseille." I offered again. "That's not far from Montpellier."

"No, but thank you." He sipped his coffee.

"They can't disappear, Francisco." I placed my hand on his arm. "There must be a trace, a trail or something." When he regarded me, he appeared as though he might break. I'd never seen that look before.

He took two deep breaths before he spoke. "I appreciate your concern, Maria, but I don't want to discuss it anymore."

I understood that more than anyone. In fact, I had said those very same words to him several weeks ago at the necropolis.

The meal was consumed quietly. Discouraged, I berated myself silently for being solely responsible for shifting the mood. Maybe he will lighten up at the convent. I also hadn't had a chance yet to visit the docks. According to the paper Anita read, any information about the Chanzy would be found there. I was sure the manifest would be, but how could I suggest this without sounding suspicious?

"We must leave," Francisco announced suddenly.

"To the Convent or home?" Slight alarm arose in my voice fearing I may have shortened our visit with my careless words.

When he didn't answer, I spoke up. "Are we going to the convent?"

Francisco laid his money for the meal on the table and arose. When he took my arm there was an urgency in his touch—an uncharacteristic coarseness transpired. I must've upset him when I brought up his parents.

"Forgive me, Francisco. I'm truly sorry I asked about your family." I implored understanding.

He gently guided me forward. His steps were quick. Not only did I struggle to fight the tears as we moved farther away from the plaza, but I had to nearly run to keep up with him.

"Slow down please," I cried.

Francisco ducked into an alcove and pulled me close. His cheek brushed mine while his breath warmed my neck. *Will he kiss me?* I wanted him to kiss me, but his behavior was strange. His lips brushed my ear again and tingled my skin until his words propelled the tingle to terror. "I think a man is following us."

I inhaled a short breath and tried to look back, but he held me into him. "He was staring at you while we were dancing but I didn't think much of it until I noticed him looming nearby at the café as well. He left when we did."

I was thankful Francisco didn't see my eyes when he held me. They would've betrayed me.

He held tight. "I don't know who he is or what he wants, but there is no mistake, Maria, his sights are set entirely on you."

Oh, please no. I pled in my mind as Francisco swiftly guided me into a nearby *passtissería*. Tears flowed easily down my cheeks. *Has he found me? Has Thomas found me?* This should've been impossible to believe. *He's not in Ciutadella! He's in Algiers!* Yet, we are being followed. I wanted to disappear.

My chin lowered as Francisco maneuvered behind a bread rack with clear view of the front window. My breath amplified in my ears. I peeked as a man with black hair, dressed in white trousers and a dark blue sweater passed by then stopped. His head jerked all around as if he were searching . . . searching for me.

"That's him, isn't it?" I cried out with a shudder.

"Have you seen him before?"

"No, never."

Francisco's hand cupped my cheek. His thumb wiped my tears. "I won't let anything happen to you, Maria, I promise."

I clung to him. I wanted to believe he would still feel the same way if he knew my secrets. If he knew who I really was or why I ended up at his neighbors, or even why this man might be looking for me . . . would he keep that promise?

"One baguette please." Francisco did not let go of me as he paid the woman then handed it to me. "Keep this near your face," he suggested. The aromatic scent of a fresh loaf of bread didn't soothe my shaking torso as we stepped outside.

My thoughts spun madly. I didn't know what to think. I knew no one in Menorca or even Ciutadella, but Thomas could've easily come to Ciutadella upon news of the shipwreck. How likely is it that he would even recognize me in a crowd of people? Yet, I knew he had my photograph. I never received one from him since Papa refused to let it affect the decision. He told me I would learn to love him no matter how he appeared, but right now at this very moment I wished with all my might that I knew what Thomas looked like.

Cutting through several alleyways, we meandered closer to the water. Every turn we made, I searched for the man in the blue sweater.

"We're almost back to the *estable* and the horses," Francisco said. "I'm sorry we cut the day short." The sadness in his eyes replaced any regret I owned. He was more concerned about my safety and for that I could never fault him. "We can get to the wagon down this way, but I want to be sure again we aren't being followed." Francisco pointed to a nearby tavern. "If the man is nearby, I would see him from inside." My mouth fell open. I had never been in a pub before, though he seemed too preoccupied with the surroundings to see my reaction. I quickly closed my lips. He's trying to keep me safe. I will go wherever he wants me to.

Inside the dark room, only a handful of people resided. Our hurried entry shot a few glances our way but were swiftly unheeded. Francisco scanned the street. The man in the blue sweater was nowhere to be seen.

With an obvious sigh, Francisco relaxed, and we were outside in a matter of minutes. We stepped down to the docks and hustled past the fishing boats tied up along the waterway. As the sun began its descent, its reflection cast a golden glow off the water. If we weren't running from a stranger, this would have been a powerfully romantic setting.

Once we reached the stable, the line in Francisco's forehead had finally disappeared. He handed the stable boy a coin for watching the wagon and reached for the bread. When he met me, he lingered on my face for several seconds. "Are you afraid?" he asked.

Tears and perspiration moistened my skin but there was no doubt I felt safe with him. "Not anymore." He reached around me and helped me step up and onto the wagon seat. I exhaled. The sooner we left, the better. As Francisco moved to the back to secure the goods he had purchased for Anita and his ranch, my thoughts went astray. *I will tell Francisco the truth on the way home.* It's time he knew the truth.

Francisco switched to the front and checked his team. They were well rested and ready to go. The moment Francisco placed his hands on the wagon boards to ascend, he stopped cold. The man in the blue sweater appeared to the left side of the horses. My gasp was the only sound heard.

The man stared for an uncomfortable amount of time, but only at me.

Francisco stepped away from the wagon and moved forward. "What is your business, senyor?" He attempted to draw the man's attention to him, but his eyes did not budge. I hid my shaking hands in the folds of my dress. Francisco stepped closer again, his hand went to his pocket where I knew he kept his knife. The one he told me he always carried, and I was grateful for that.

The man pointed towards me with a fervor. "You were there."

My eyes widened. He spoke in broken Spanish, but there was no mistaking his French accent. Thomas was French though he resided in Algeria.

Francisco deliberately stood in his line of sight and forced the man to face him. "To what do you refer?"

"It's her." He seemed almost trancelike when he spoke and tried to jockey around Francisco for another look. "I can't believe it. She's here."

My breaths escaped in short bursts. *It's Thomas, I know it is. How did he find me? If I flee, he might outrun me. Where can I go? Where can I hide?* He's found me and now everything will come crashing down.

"Senyor, explain yourself!" Francisco's voice exuded anger.

The man's hands lifted chest high. "I have no quarrel with you, either of you," he said, then repeated with equal astonishment. "I'm only surprised to see her here . . . alive."

"Alive? What are you referring to?" Francisco's tone hinted he was losing patience.

"She was on the ship."

Francisco's feet remained planted but when his body twisted back, his cheeks drained all color.

My mouth fell open. *How can he know that?* I swallowed hard.

"What ship?" Francisco questioned, although I was sure he already knew the answer when he asked.

I lowered my head. The shaking in my torso now matched my hands. I folded my arms across my chest to try and stop it but failed.

"The Général Chanzy," the man recounted.

Francisco moved to where he could see both of us at the same time. When he glanced towards me, his jaw turned rigid.

"No." My voice quivered. "No, you have the wrong person."

"Mademoiselle, forgive me, but I never forget a face." The man shifted his weight uncomfortably, "and yours . . . yours is one, men do not forget."

Tears sprung from my eyes. Francisco watched me intently.

"What is your name, sir?" The anger had left Francisco's voice. *He believes him.*

"My name is Marcel Badez I was the only survivor of the Chanzy . . . or so I thought."

"How is it you believe you know this woman?"

"Her family had the uppermost staterooms. I served them."

"Can we go please?" I whimpered to Francisco. "Please?" I refused to acknowledge the possibility. If I scrutinized closer, he perhaps could've been our garçon.

"I believe you are mistaken, sir." Francisco spoke up. "This woman has been a guest of my neighbors for nearly six months. It could not be her."

My lips parted in awe. Francisco lied for me. I'd only been there six *weeks*.

The man shook his head and wiped his brow. "With due respect, senyor, I am sure she is Isabel Fontaine—the daughter of Monsieur Antoine Fontaine."

Francisco urged his departure. "Bon dia to you." Then spun his back on the man. I peered up to see Marcel Badez, watching us, but he said nothing more. Francisco made a final check on the horses then jumped up to drive.

"Hyah!" He yanked the reins and kept his chin straight forward. The muscles in his arms and shoulders bulged with tension. Those same arms that held me only minutes ago lacked all warmth. My heart physically strained under the pressure. My chance to set things right was stripped from me and now the consequences were grave.

No words were spoken on the ride home, despite the hours. I feared any words from my mouth would make things tragically worse. Francisco knew I had lied. He knew I had lied to everyone.

When we reached Anita's, he helped me down as expected, but the tenderness in his touch had vanished. He didn't even look me in the eyes. Pulling the supplies from the wagon, he dutifully went inside and paid his respects to the Contreras'.

I remained next to the wagon. When Francisco returned, he tipped his hat formally then jumped up to his seat. I faced him, frozen in place. My heart lagged the heaviest it had been since the shipwreck. How could I ever explain my reasoning? Would he even understand or care?

"Francisco," I begged. "Please let me explain."

He relaxed the reins but didn't turn my direction.

"Please don't go. Stay and talk to me." Tears simmered at the corners of my eyes and threatened to fall with the slightest movement.

A light breeze blew Francisco's bangs across his eyes, but he made no attempt to brush them away. "Is it true?" The sharpness in his voice cut through me. "Is everything he said true?"

I held my breath. Sharp pains pierced my chest as if a knife stabbed me repeatedly. Words teased at the tip of my tongue but when he faced me and the betrayal in his eyes emerged, I choked.

"Hyah." Francisco shook the reins. I stepped backward only to avoid being run over. The dirt the wagon kicked up as it passed hit me directly. The result was a muddy mix on my nose and cheeks. I was a mess.

I stood there completely still until the sobs racked my body to the ground.

"Dear, oh dear, what is it?" Anita came running out and to my side. I curled like an infant. My cries prevented me from speaking.

"Miguel," Anita called to the house. "Miguel, please come help."

Between the two of them, they assisted me inside. Anita helped me undress and into bed and brought me a cup of tea, but I didn't reach for the cup and continued to cry.

"Did something happen?" She inquired. Then added with very obvious doubt, "did . . . did Francisco do something?"

"No, never." Was all I mustered. No matter what, he could not be blamed for my suffering.

The night was long. My eyes closed for mere moments to imagine how this could have all gone differently. I hurt him and I was about to hurt the others. Francisco could've told Anita and Miguel, but it seemed he chose not to . . . not yet anyway. I should've told the truth from the beginning. I knew my risks, but nothing, not even my own selfish interests was worth the treachery I now inflicted.

I sighed in relief the moment the morning light spooked the blackness away hoping the sun's rays would provide an element of peace, but the reality of the situation only brought more sadness. Unsure I could confront what surely awaited me, I remained in bed with no intent to move.

A soft knock shook my spinning mind to a halt. I knew it was Anita. "May I come in?" She had one foot in by the time she asked but I nodded anyway. The moment her hand touched my cheek, new tears trickled from my eyes. She sat at the side of my bed and wiped them gently with her palm.

"Darling, we can only help if you tell us what happened."

I covered my face with the blanket. I feared her disappointment.

I thought about Francisco. He trusted me, and I destroyed that trust. My mind shifted to the survivor, Marcel Badez. I could only imagine his trauma of being the sole survivor then learning of another. He was not intending harm, but it happened. He was not responsible for my lies, but his affirmation changed everything. I cried for Papa, Maman, and Ines, and my sweet puppy Remý. I cried for my grand-mère who mourned me in France. I cried for my life.

Anita tugged the blanket down and brushed her wrinkled hand across my hair. "Please love, let me help you."

My throat swelled with the words that choked me. I wrestled them back while they fought to come forth. I took a deep breath and forced it forward. "I lied."

Anita's hand stopped with a finger intertwined around a strand. "What do you mean, you lied?"

I sniffled hard and wiped my nose on the sleeve of my nightdress. "I didn't tell you the truth of who I really am."

"Oh Maria, not everyone is honest all the time." Her chuckle should have eased the tension, but it didn't. "I believed Miguel was a rich Portuguese fisherman in the beginning. When I found out he was a poor Spanish farmer, I was already in love."

My eyes met hers. They were filled with the greatest love I had ever known. "I wasn't honest at all," I mumbled and glanced down to my trembling hands. "My name is Isabel Marie Fontaine. My family is from Marseille."

"Isabel?"

I nodded and buried my head in my hands.

"It's only a name, dear."

I peeked through my fingers. "I was on the Général Chanzy ship. My family was killed in the shipwreck."

I almost heard her heart stop beating.

"Oh my, oh my, Maria—Isabel." The lines across her forehead deepened. "You lost your family that night?"

My tears came faster. "Yes, I lost them all. Everyone but my grand-mère who remains in France."

Her hands shook nearly as hard, but she wrapped them warmly over mine. "Oh, my dear sweet girl, you must feel such sorrow." She stood up quickly. "I need to get you some tea. This is a moment for tea."

My lips forced a slight grin. She hesitated as though she awaited permission to leave. I tapped her hand. "Thank you." She rushed into the kitchen. She frantically clanked pots around. When she returned, she asked the one question I feared. "Why? Why did you not tell us?"

I couldn't hide it now. Everything needed to come out.

"I was frightened."

"Frightened of us?" Tears gathered in her eyes.

"No, oh never," I assured. "My father promised me to a man, a prospective business partner."

"Marriage?"

"Sí."

"Where is this man?"

"Algiers. We were on our way for me to be delivered to him."

"Oh . . ." She gasped. "Delivered? You'd never met him before?"

"No. My father made all the arrangements."

"Is he a wicked man?"

"I don't know. I know nothing about him. I begged my father to not go through with it."

"Were you in love with another?"

My thoughts instantly went to Francisco. The tearing in my chest amplified. "No, not at the time." I hesitated. Anita seemed to understand more than I divulged. "I believed I had a right to my own choice, not his."

"I see."

"I imagined if I kept my survival a secret, I could be someone else. I could change my fate."

She dwelled on my words for several seconds. "Does Francisco know?"

I nodded yes—then no. She tilted her head.

"A man, that man, Monsieur Badez, the only survivor from the ship recognized me in Ciutadella yesterday."

Her eyes widened.

"I was with Francisco when he confronted me." My voice squeaked. I barely got the words out. "Francisco knows I didn't tell the truth. I have injured him."

"Did you tell him *why* you did what you did?"

"No, Anita, you didn't see his face. He was crushed. I lied to him. It didn't matter what I would have said, he wouldn't have listened."

"Well, you're wrong there, dear. Francisco is a good man. He deserves to hear the truth . . . from you."

"I betrayed him." I sobbed into the blanket. "I've betrayed you all."

"Maria, Isabel, love, you were scared. Nobody can blame you for being scared. You were about to be married to a man you'd never met, then suddenly your whole world disappeared in a tragic, horrible way. It must be terribly painful." The kettle whistled in the kitchen and she rushed to retrieve it. I waited for her return in silence. The memory of the confrontation haunted me. I wasn't sure if I could ever forget the look in Francisco's eyes when he realized I had lied to him.

"I will send for Francisco immediately." Anita held a mug of steaming tea in her hands when she entered again. "He needs to hear the truth."

I reached for her arm, but it slipped through my grasp. "No, I don't think I can face him."

She handed me the cup and kissed my cheek. "He deserves to know."

Anita rushed outside. Her voice sailed through my window. "Henry, quick, go to the ranch and retrieve Francisco immediately."

My stomach simmered, threatening to revolt. I rushed to the basin and leaned over. Though my gut growled, nothing came forth. I wet a cloth from the pitcher and wiped my chin and forehead. What if Francisco listens but decides I'm not worth the trouble? What if he no longer wishes to be around me because I'm betrothed? Am I still betrothed with my father dead? What if they all believe I should return to my appointed responsibility and send me to Algiers?

I failed to move. Anita retrieved me and helped me clean up. She held my shoulders and pulled me close, though I shuddered under her touch. "Francisco will understand. Do not fear him."

"I don't fear *him*, Anita. I fear what he thinks of me . . of what you all think of me."

She leaned me back and cradled both my cheeks. "My dear, there is nothing you could do or say that would change how I feel about you. You have brought a wonderful warmth to our little home and our lonely childless hearts." She hugged me tighter and as the sound of horses approached, my body trembled all over again.

Anita and I moved towards the door, but it was Susana who entered my room.

"Francisco has left," she announced as she caught her breath.

"Where to?" Anita cried out.

"He told me last night he needed to find answers about our parents. He left this morning before dawn."

I slipped to the floor and buried my face in my hands.

Susana rushed to my side. "Are you ill?"

I didn't answer.

Anita reached for me, "Please help me get her into bed."

Each woman took an arm and guided me tenderly back to bed. Susana immediately went into nurse mode. The back of her hand pressed against my forehead. "You don't have a fever. What are your symptoms?"

"I suspect her ailment is more internal," Anita said and pointed to a chair. "Have a seat Susana, Maria has something to tell you."

23

27 March 1910

Ciutadella, Menorca, Spain

Thomas

"Monsieur?"

"Jacque."

"How was your travel and accommodations?"

"Sufficient."

"And your business in Mahón?"

"Concluded," I retorted with an edginess. The meeting with the manufacturer was lengthy and dull. A waste of time if I had any say on it. "What did you find here?"

"I think you will be pleased."

"They found her body?" I spoke low enough to not be overheard. "Has she been identified?"

"No."

I blinked. I wanted to rip the smug expression off Jacque's face. I knew he didn't know the extent of this bad news, but I despised games.

"Then what?" I gritted my teeth.

"There is no body . . . because she's not dead."

My mind tried to comprehend his words. *Can this truly be possible?* "What do you mean she's not dead?"

"There is a man, the one known survivor of the Chanzy. Over the last couple of days in my inquiries, witnesses have claimed he is boasting openly of another survivor. He speaks of a beautiful woman." Jacque narrowed his stare. "The daughter of a Monsieur Antoine Fontaine. He declared ardently that she is alive and living here on the island!"

I reached for the lapels on his coat and clutched them. "Are you certain? Could this be some cruel joke?"

"I have located a man who knows where we can find the survivor, Monsieur Badez. I have transportation arranged. Did you want to go to your lodging or to the residence first?"

My mind calculated this good fortune. There would no longer be a need to prove her death for our betrothal would resume and the estate and Isabel would be mine. "The residence," I said with renewed confidence. "At once!"

As we navigated the narrow roads to a far side of town, I noticed the living conditions were not unlike those I was familiar with in Algiers. The only difference was that the cracked plaster was whitewashed paint versus the dark gray stone I was accustomed to. The stench of rotten foodstuff, however, did not change. I lifted my handkerchief to my nose and stepped over a pile of unknown refuse on the way to the door.

Jacque reached for the knocker but before he lifted it, I placed my hand on his arm to stop him. I retrieved my pistol and held it in my hand but allowed my coat sleeve to keep it hidden. Jacque's eyes grew wide.

"In case he needs motivation," I declared.

He knocked.

When the door was cracked, only a thatch of white hair could be seen through the break. "Who are you? What do you want?"

"I'm searching for Marcel Badez. Do you know of him?"

"Who's asking?" The man allowed a bit more space and squinted an eye at both of us. We were fashionably dressed as gentleman. He could hardly assume us to be a threat. "What do you want him for?" he mumbled.

My patience grew thin. I could've easily knocked him over with a slight push of the door, but I held my temper. "I am a man who pays handsomely for answers." I held up a silver coin.

The man straightened up and eyed the coin. Then reached out to grab it.

I pulled it back. "Answer the question first."

"Yes, I know of him. I can take you right to him for *two* of those."

My jaw tightened. I despised greed—outside of myself, of course.

I reached in and grabbed his shirt tightly in my fist and pulled his weak form through the opening. "You will show me for *one* or you won't be walking straight tomorrow." I exposed the hidden pistol in my other hand.

"Yes, sir, I will." He staggered backward. "This way." He stumbled behind the house and towards a smaller domicile in the rear. The green shutters exposing a front window were wide open, though one hung by a broken screw. The door was cracked an inch. The man's urgent knock pushed it open.

"Monsieur Badez?" He shouted. "Monsieur?"

"*Qué?* What's the problem Gabe?" A thin lanky man with an unkempt mustache opened the door. He appeared annoyed at the interruption. "What is your haste—" Then he spied me standing next to his lessee.

"Oh, my apologies." He scanned my clothing from my striking hat to my fine Hessians. He must've known I was not from this neighborhood. I held out the coin to the older man. He grabbed it and ran away.

The young man opened the door fully and motioned us inside. "Please, come in." His Spanish was terrible. "How may I be of service to you, senyor?

"Monsieur."

"Monsieur?" A sly smile crossed his lips. "You are from France?"

"Algeria."

"*Bienvenue en Espagne mon ami.*"

"I'm not here for pleasantries," I snapped. "And we are not friends, but if you are more comfortable speaking French, by all means do it."

His expression showed slight surprise, but I advanced past it.

"I have come from Algiers. I am searching for answers about the Chanzy."

"To what purpose?"

"The purpose is my own, but I can make this conversation most rewarding for you."

The man pointed to a lumpy couch. I placed the pistol back in my pocket.

"Please sit." He prompted again.

"I'm not here on a social call. Where is Isabel Fontaine?"

His lips curled into a shrewd grin. "So, news of her survival has reached Algiers?"

This man underestimated my tolerance for amusement. "I need to know of her whereabouts."

"You and a hundred other men, the moment I mentioned her undeniable beauty." His comment was haughty. I restrained myself . . . for now.

"I am not *any* man." My bellow came with authority. "I am her betrothed."

He beamed confidently and sat on top of a nearby barrel. "Her betrothed, huh?" He rubbed his chin. "Interesting."

"Why?" I barked.

"I do recall an argument the night of the wreck between her and her father." His lips curved with a clever smile. "Something concerning a pending marriage."

"Argument?" I questioned cautiously, "what argument?"

"It seemed Isabel did not wish to marry."

I contemplated this new information. I shared a glance with Jacque. He knew only what I shared with him concerning the arrangements. And I intended to keep it that way.

The man carefully watched me. He seemed to get some sort of satisfaction out of my ignorance.

"She had not yet met me." I disregarded his comment. "Had she, I assure you she would not have been disappointed in the least."

"Why didn't she inform you of her survival?"

Now he teetered on tenuous ground. Heat simmered beneath my skin. "Where is she?"

He smiled again. I wanted to claw that smile off his face. "Why should I tell you anything?" He sneered. "She obviously doesn't want you to know."

"Because it appears your circumstances could benefit greatly from your cooperation." He seemed offended before I placed the small leather pouch of coins on the table before us. His eyes glinted as he reached for it. My hand beat him to it and slammed down over the opening. He recoiled in fear. "It's silver I promise you but will not be awarded until I feel your information is adequate enough for payment." He sat back down on the barrel and rubbed his hand although I never touched it.

"She was with a man."

My lips pulled tight. "A man?"

"He was most likely from the outer areas. I have lived here since the accident and have learned much about Ciutadella. He's not a local from town."

"Are you certain?" I listened intently.

"Likely a farmer. I could tell from the boots he wore and the team he drove, he was not poor, but he was careful about showing any wealth. He was tall, strong, seemed to handle himself well and unquestionably took a protective stance before her when I approached. I might guess why, but I'm sure you don't need me to speculate."

My teeth pressed weightily together. This man was enjoying this intrigue too much.

"The woman, Isabel," he continued, "she seemed especially scared I had discovered her. When I revealed my assumptions, she denied it. Even the man tried to insist she had been in his neighbor's home prior to the shipwreck, but I knew. You don't see that kind of woman every day." Badez licked his lips while they curled into a half grin.

"That is my wife you are speaking about," I growled lowly.

"Wife? Future wife . . . possibly if she hasn't already married or been with another man."

That's it. I couldn't listen to his banter anymore. I yanked my pistol out of my pocket, flipped it around and whipped the handle across his face. He hit the ground with a thud and scrambled backwards on the floor to get out of my reach. Jacque stepped forward. I shot him a fiery look until he backed up.

I leaned over the man as he cowered back some more. I pointed my finger roughly into his chest. "Now we can have a civil conversation between two men that will likely make you a hefty reward or I can beat you silly and leave you penniless."

The man waved his hands. "Okay, okay I will tell you everything I know. Then you must leave."

"I have no intention of remaining in this rat-infested swamp any longer than is necessary." I moved back near the couch. "Describe the man to me."

"I—I told you he was strong. He must labor in a field of some sort from his tanned skin. His preparation of the horses led me to believe he is quite comfortable around them. He had light brown hair past his ears and neck. Brown eyes I believe. He was polite though guarded. He seemed surprised when I confronted her. It was if she had not told him of the shipwreck."

"What else did you notice about the wagon or its contents?"

"It was filled with supplies, something you only see from someone who comes to town occasionally. He had a decent number of terra cotta jars stacked in the back of his wagon, like those that would be used for production. Which, on the island could primarily mean one of two things.

"What two?"

"Grapes or olives."

"Continue."

"He had two striking black horses. Like the ones that are used in the festivals. Not your typical farm horses."

"The festivals?"

"The Patron Saint festivals. Ciutadella's is in June."

"Anything else?

"He had a long scar on his left palm, visible when he held me back."

"Alright, describe Isabel... and be cautious in your description." My face issued a stern warning. He nodded, to indicate he understood me quite clearly now.

"*Oui*, Monsieur. Her hair was long, blonde, and straight. Though on the ship she pinned her curls back. She wore a simple white dress, nothing like the silk gown from before and a modest band graced her wrist, unlike the diamond bracelet I had seen on the Chanzy. If I hadn't noticed her very blue eyes and—" he spoke carefully, "—her attractive figure, she could've passed as a simple farmgirl."

I contemplated all he had said.

"Wait, she called the man Francisco."

"Good." I pumped my fist. A name is an excellent start. I paced the small space for a moment to gather my thoughts. So, I would be looking for someone who most likely comes to Ciutadella for supplies. I wondered how often. I could have Jacque do more digging. Whatever it takes.

"My name is Monsieur Fabron and I'm lodging at the *Mar Blava* if you need to reach me. Do not—" I stood and hovered over him again. "Do not tell anyone of my search. Only come to me if you learn something new." I walked out.

After I checked into my room at the Inn, I went below to the garden that led to the inner waterway. I sat at one of the tables they provided and contemplated a plan. If I find her, how do I convince her that it was her father's wish that she should return with me. Of course, if she's been touched... I barely tolerated the thought.

I swallowed my drink slowly and watched the water curl up and break over the rocky edge. Isabel couldn't possibly find happiness in a barn, not after the life she has led. What could conceivably be keeping her here?

24

2 April 1910

Domaine de Verchant, Montpellier, France

Francisco

"Thank you for meeting with me Monsieur Vernier." I was grateful that he spoke Catalan for my French was quite poor. "I was informed Sr. and Sra. Carrasco stayed here on the night of the 8th of February."

"Yes, sir. That is correct, I checked the ledger prior to your arrival. They only stayed one night."

"Did they mention anything at all about their travels beyond your Inn?"

"I already told Sr. Velasquez the answer to this."

"I understand, but I am their son, and we haven't heard from them since they visited this establishment. You can understand why it is imperative I ask again."

The man glanced down his long, pointed nose. Almost to the point that his thick rimmed glasses slid off. "They were here, and they checked out the next morning. In the ledger it states they settled their debt at half past 11 and arranged their own transportation."

"And you don't know where to?"

"No."

"By any chance is the porter who assisted them available to speak to me."

"Hmmm." The man glanced back at the register. "It would have been Francois Leroy. He will be here tomorrow."

"Thank you, and might I rent a room for the night?"

Once my luggage was placed in my accommodations, I wandered the public spaces of the most exquisite hotel I had ever seen. It did not surprise me in the least that my parents chose to stay here. Though not easy to find in the middle of a countryside surrounded by grapevines, the unique stone structure was worth the challenge.

Walking through an enormous arched doorway, I passed a black iron gate that led me to a quaint courtyard filled with varying rustics. The strong scent of the concord grapes soared freely about the grounds, tempting one to engage in the local wine-tasting. I took a seat in a wicker chair and scanned my surroundings, beginning with the large shade tree above me. Its leafy vines twisted uniquely around the enormous trunk from top to bottom. I had never seen anything like it.

With only a handful of other guests this was precisely the place I would have pictured my father wooing my mother. He would've arranged for flowers, a secluded meal, and a romantic walk under the stars. It's precisely what I would've done for Maria, had she been here.

In the first few days of my departure, she had monopolized my every thought—on the ship to Barcelona, the travels around town and especially when I passed by the Santa Maria Del Pi, the Cathedral that she spoke fondly of. It angered me that when my focus should've been on the reason for my arrival, it lingered on her.

However, I could not quite identify my frustration. Confusion tangled with betrayal over the events in Ciutadella. *Why would she have to lie?* Even as we faced a man who clearly knew her and identified her, she still claimed innocence. Everything I believed about her was questioned—her name, her arrival, her family. *Is she really without family?* When she told me her parents were dead, is that the truth? Is she really from Spain? What else have I not been told?

As I sat here reflecting on the last two months, I couldn't deny the sensations that arose when I was with her, and the spell I unquestionably fell under. Even now, her charm surfaced in my mind—from the way her nose wrinkled from frustration, her sea blue eyes fluctuating between fear to excitement, her attempt to knit, the silly overalls that buried her petite frame, the spark and thrill of her touch, and the kiss. I *know* that kiss was real, but why on earth would she lie? Why lie about the shipwreck? Why lie to Miguel and Anita who took her in . . . and Susana who healed her? And to me? None of this made sense and the more I pondered it the more irritated I became. *How did I fall so easily for someone I truly know little about?*

"Gah." I raked my hands through my hair. "I have to stop thinking about her," I groaned. "I need to concentrate on my parents."

"Are you well, Monsieur?" A porter approached me from the inner hallway. He must've seen the emotional battle I fought in my solitude.

"Yes, yes I am, thank you."

He bowed his head and motioned to leave.

"One moment, sir."

He turned around.

"Might I have my supper brought to my room?"

"Oui, Monsieur."

I stood up. I couldn't take any more of the amorous environment. I tried hard to enjoy the image of my parents here, but a different picture continuously invaded my head. The one of a beautiful senyoreta back in Menorca.

The next morning, I found Francois Leroy at the porter's desk. He was an elderly man with thick gray hair and bushy eyebrows. He moved slower than most of the porters but as I waited my turn to approach him, he appeared to be by far the friendliest of all the staff.

"Monsieur Francois Leroy?"

He rotated slowly but his smile broadened quickly. "Oui, Monsieur, how may I help you."

"My name is Francisco Carrasco. I was told that you may have been the porter to assist my parents who stayed here a little over seven weeks ago."

"How long was their visit?"

"One night."

His brow furrowed heavily. "My dear boy . . ." His lips pulled into a tight line. "I can't say I would know someone from only one night's stay. Many travelers cross my path and—."

I reached for his arm in desperation. "There must be something that you remember."

He shook his head, "I'm afraid in my old age, I'm quite forgetful."

"Their names were Carrasco. A tall man with broad shoulders, light brown hair, and a well-trimmed beard. My mother always wore bright colored dresses and a shawl across her shoulders. Her brown hair would've reached to her waist by then, but she often pulled it back with hand-painted combs." I spoke swiftly hoping anything descriptive might help him remember. "Oh, and she was an artist, maybe she painted the courtyard."

"An artist you say?" He rubbed his chin. "Now let me think . . . there was someone like that. They offered me a jar of olives."

"Yes! Yes, they would have." My heart leapt from my chest. I clutched both his arms now. "We own an olive ranch in Menorca, Spain."

"I remember they spoke of it and oh, yes, the olives were most delicious."

I smiled. "Did they happen to mention where they were going after they stayed here. The concierge said they arranged their own transportation."

"They did," he recalled. "They departed for Marseille."

"Marseille!" I kissed the old man on the cheek. "Do you know how they traveled to Marseille?"

"By carriage. They were acquainted with the driver."

"Thank you, I must ready for Marseille."

"Might I arrange transportation for you, Monsieur?"

"Yes, please. To leave as soon as possible." I thanked him for his time and his assistance. The surge of renewed hope filled my soul. Finally, finally something that could lead me beyond what little we knew. I rushed to retrieve my luggage and sent word to Susana on the recent success. It could be entirely possible that their latest posts didn't reach us, and I would find them happily lounging in a guesthouse somewhere.

25

3 April 1910

Ciutadella, Menorca, Spain

Thomas

"*Més*, Dammit!" I slammed the glass back down on the bar for more. "*Ya lbn el sharmouta!*" I insulted. The education my parents afforded me, included multiple languages—Catalan and Arabic were several I honed for business, but often times when my tongue loosened overtly, the dialects intertwined with crude results.

The barman approached with caution. "No more, Frenchman. I think you've had your fill. Go home and sleep it off."

I took silent satisfaction that the man was ignorant to my profane insult. "I w—will inform you when I'm f—finished!" I picked up the glass and threw it at the wall behind him.

The barman pulled a rifle from underneath his bar. "Get out or I will drag you out, dead or alive."

I stared at the outmoded shooter and from deep within my belly a coarse chuckle found its way to the surface. "Riveting antique, s—senyor. You might want to load it f—first." My hand slid to the butt of the *Browning* underneath my coat. Not only was my weapon more accurate, but I was sure to be faster than him.

"Senyor, release your firearm and remove yourself straightaway." This time the voice came from behind me. A different man had his pistol aimed at my head. *Merde!* I would only get one of them and surely get shot in the process.

I lifted both my hands and mumbled, "fine." I tumbled off the stool but caught myself before I hit the floor.

"Don't ever come back here," the barman added.

My lips rolled into a sly grin as I stumbled towards the door and kicked a chair on my way out. It flew across the tile floor and clanked into another. "Th—this is a worthless pub anyway!" I opened the door and stepped to the walk. My light boot caught on the corner of a stone, and I skidded along the ground. Both my palms were scraped from my attempt to keep my face from hitting the ground.

"Damn C—Ciutadella!" I slurred.

For five days I'd been waiting for news as Jacque continued his search. After we met with Marcel Badez and learned with a surety that Isabel survived the Général Chanzy shipwreck and was somewhere on this island, I had found my reason and purpose to pursue. I no longer needed proof of her death but only to find *her*. Once accomplished, I should have no trouble convincing her that her father's intentions were reasonable and that I was a most suitable match.

Three days ago, I hired men to walk the town, day and night, watching and waiting for a wagon with jet black horses and this grape or olive farmer to appear. But nothing came of it.

I pulled myself upright and wiped my forehead. Dirt covered my trousers. "Damn Ciutadella filth." I stepped forward and a horse neighed fretfully. Its load came to a swift stop in front of me.

"Miscreant!" a man yelled and pulled the horse to avoid a collision. "Be off with you!"

I lifted my hand in protest though he was long gone by the time I found words. "Damn townssspeople," I muttered and shuffled down the lowly lit road.

I reached my hotel, though stood outside for an indefinite amount of time questioning whether I wanted to enter or locate another pub.

A young porter opened the door. "Monsieur Fabron, A post has arrived for you."

"Give it ttto mmeee," I slurred and tried to reach for it. The porter appeared to have multiplied. I struggled to focus on the numerous hands and envelopes that appeared before me. "Pput it innn my hand," I bellowed. The moment the paper hit my palm; I clutched my fingers tightly around it.

Unfolding the paper, I struggled to interpret the scribbles. All the letters blurred together. I swiftly found my way to Jacque's door and pounded until he answered.

He appeared in his nightclothes. "Monsieur? Are you well?"

"Read thisss to me." I shoved the note against his chest.

He glanced over it quickly. "It's from Monsieur Badez."

I focused long enough to hear his words.

Monsieur Fabron,
I believe I have found the man you are looking
for. I have an approximate location of his home

> *in the country. From what I have gathered he's in desperate need of services. I will come to Mar Blava tomorrow morning to explain.*
> *-Marcel Badez*

"Let me help you to your room, Monsieur." Jacque held one of my arms up as I leaned against his door.

"This is it, Jacque. All of our grueling work will pay off in the end."

"Monsieur Chastain."

"Shhhhh," I growled. "You are not to call me that here."

"Monsieur, I must insist that you expose the complexity of this arrangement."

"You insist?" I spit as he struggled to guide me to my quarters. He was taller than me, but I was broader and stronger. Even through drunkenness, I was sure I could best him.

"Monsieur, I have done everything you have asked. I believe I have a right to know of your true intentions."

My head hurt too much to argue and though I meant to keep the particulars to myself, Jacque had proved to be a trusted companion.

"Very well. I will disclose it all tomorrow."

26

4 April 1910

Contreras Farm, Menorca, Spain

Miguel

"Excuse me, sir." A chestnut-colored steed trotted towards me. The rider was a tall, thin man with black curly hair that spilled out from under his hat and bordered dark inset eyes. I'd never seen him before.

"Sí?" I waited. He scanned my property meticulously. "How can I help you?" I urged a response. Then leaned my shovel up against the tree and removed my gloves.

"Pardon me." His accent was not Spanish, and his Catalan was fair at best. I narrowed my gaze as he fumbled inside a side bag and pulled out a small bottle. "Is this your label? Are you Sr. Carrasco?" I stepped closer to get a better look at what he held. It was one of the Reyes' older bottles, but no doubt contained the *verde partida* olives from the Carrasco Ranch.

I studied the man who wore a long tan coat in perfect sunshine. His equally heavy hat pulled tight across his forehead. "Why do you ask?"

His lips curved into a slight smile. "My apologies. This must appear rude, but I have travelled from Ciutadella with the understanding that the Carrasco farm is in search of a distributor. My name is Jacque Roman, and I'm associated with such a business. If it pleases you, I would like to discuss this with the owner."

"Hmmm . . ." I removed my hat and wiped my brow with my sleeve. I glanced back up wondering how he could possibly be comfortable in that many layers. "Who sent you?"

The man's hands fumbled with his reins, but nothing in his expression wavered. Even his mustache remained still, and he never took his eyes off mine. "I was sent by Sr. Rafael Ochoa from Ciutadella. Are you the elder Sr. Carrasco?"

"I'm unaware of a Sr. Rafael Ochoa from Ciutadella," I mumbled. Though I was well aware of previous attempts to acquire the Carrasco ranch through less than honorable means and something didn't quite sit right about this man.

He stared at me for several seconds. "Sr. Ochoa is a respected businessman. He mentioned to both me, and my employer, the loss of Sr. Carrasco's recent distributor and with the harvest season coming to an end, the fruit can't stay profitable much longer. It would be a shame to lose an entire crop over pride."

The man spoke the truth. Though I believed Francisco was still on the mainland, it might benefit to know there is a possibility to move the product here on the island. I exhaled. "The Carrasco's are my neighbors. They own the ranch next to mine."

The man stretched his neck and peered the direction I pointed. When he circled back around his focus fell upon the house. "You're the neighbor?"

"Sí. If you go back the way you came, turn to the right at the fork in the road. It will lead you to their property."

"What is your name, good senyor?" He gaped inquisitively towards the house.

"Contreras." I did not like the way he stared. "Anything else?"

His eyes dropped back to me. "Nothing more at the moment. I will see to... the maker of this fine product, Sr. Carrasco, correct?"

"Francisco, the son."

"Son? How old is Francisco?"

His questions were strange, odd for a businessman. "Old enough to run his family business." I snapped a bit terse.

"Pardon me, I meant no offense. I was only surprised." The man clicked to get his horse to turn around then stopped. "Gràcies for your time."

I watched him until I no longer saw the behind of his horse, but out of curiosity I saddled my own. With Francisco away, it would be proper to check on his sister while this stranger loomed about.

"Let's go Paco." My faithful horse turned out and followed my commands to my neighbors. When I arrived, no trace of the man or his horse appeared. I released a quick breath with some relief. Knocking hard, I waited only seconds before I opened the thick door and called. "Susana?" I stepped inside as she came around the corner.

"Miguel? Hello." She smiled her sweetest smile. It was good to see that again. "Is everyone well?"

"Sí, u—uh," I stuttered. It was awkward for me to be here and have entered without waiting. "Is Francisco home?"

"No, but I did receive word that he was headed to Marseille. It seems our parents decided to travel there after Montpellier."

"Well, that's good news, isn't it?"

Her smile faltered a bit. "It's news. Hopefully, we will find more answers there. Did you need him for something? I can retrieve Javier, though he's occupied at the moment. I sent a man to the barn to speak with him."

"A man?" *The stranger is here after all.*

"Yes. A gentleman arrived right before you to see Francisco about the ranch. A possible distributor. Javier is handling it."

"That's good." I let out a long sigh and hoped my doubt didn't creep through. She seemed pleased with the possibility of a business opportunity. I rubbed the back of my neck and wondered if I should make an excuse to remain on property while the stranger did. In the end, Javier was more than capable to handle anything, being both younger and stronger.

"Can I get you a drink?"

"Oh no, I uh . . . I'll go. Gràcies."

"Send my love to Anita." She grinned again then closed the door behind me. As I mounted Paco once more, I glanced towards the barn. I couldn't see what transpired within but for some perplexing reason, I struggled to shake the warning. Trotting slowly down their lane towards my home I couldn't help but hope the sooner the elder Carrasco returns, the better all will be for everyone.

27

4 April 1910

Ciutadella, Menorca, Spain

Thomas

"Monsieur, I have located the ranch." Jacque appeared breathless as if he had run the distance from his horse to the water's edge where I sipped my beer in the hotel's garden.

I straightened to his news. "You've found Isabel?"

"I believe I have. It's a half day's ride from here, near the Northern coast." Jacque waved a man down for a drink. Then slid into the chair next to mine. "It was by mistake that I took the first turn instead of the second and stumbled upon an elderly man with the family name of Contreras."

"Elderly? That is not who Monsieur Badez spoke of. Who is Francisco then?"

"Sr. Contreras and Francisco Carrasco are neighbors. Remember Marcel said that Francisco claimed Isabel resided with his neighbor. Sr. Contreras is the only one within ten kilometers."

"Are you certain?"

"Certain of the area, yes, but I did not see her at the home. I inquired of the olive ranch and Sr. Contreras directed me to the Carrasco's next door."

"So, you believe Isabel is living at the Contreras'?" I rubbed my scratchy chin. "Did anything or anyone give you the impression Isabel and this Francisco Carrasco are courting?"

"I didn't see her or him, Monsieur. I'm uncertain of their relationship other than what Marcel suggested."

"Uncertain?" I launched to my feet. My hands curled into fists at my side. "You traveled a half day's journey there and back to inform me you're uncertain?"

"This is what I know." He tugged on his collar uncomfortably. "Francisco Carrasco is the man who Isabel was with in Ciutadella. Isabel resides with Francisco's neighbor, who I believe to be Sr. Contreras. We also know from the way Francisco behaved around Isabel, that they were—" Jacque let a sigh out before he continued, "they were familiar with each other."

I slammed both fists against the table. The fire that blazed within my chest burned ravenous. "I will kill him if he's touched her. Saddle my horse!"

"Monsieur..." Jacque raised his hands chest high. "Please, one moment."

I paced the small space with agitation and glanced warily at him. "Why wait? I have waited long enough in this dreadful town."

"Please sit and listen to my recommendations."

Jacque had been my voice of reason for a couple of weeks now. I owed him that much. I huffed and returned to my chair.

"Now, if you go charging in there like a mad bull, any number of things can happen—"

"Yes, I could retrieve Isabel!"

"Or you could be arrested . . .or shot."

"We won't be on this island long enough to be arrested. I can outride any old man and be on a ship by sundown."

"Please listen, Monsieur. Since you have revealed to me the full extent of this subterfuge—"

"Subterfuge?" My eyes sent a stern warning.

"Forgive me, that is the wrong word. I meant to say—this arrangement. Since you revealed the arrangement with me concerning Isabel's betrothal contract, I spent a great deal of time on my ride back here contemplating a strategy on how best to approach this—without bloodshed."

"The way I see it." I hissed through gritted teeth. "There's only one person who deserves to pay for his indiscretions. There will be no remorse from me if Francisco happens to meet an untimely fate."

"Monsieur," Jacque leaned closer and whispered, "what would be the purpose of retrieving your bride and acquiring the estate if you risk the opportunity to enjoy them. Why do something foolish and endanger your life and possibly Isabel's?"

"What are you suggesting?"

"Remember what Monsieur Badez said about the Carrasco's needing a distributor?"

"Oui."

"In my visit, I confirmed this to be true. They are desperate to move their olives by the first of May. This presents a unique opportunity for you to engage in business, learn of your enemy and ultimately interact with Isabel without her even knowing your true intent.

My fingers locked and rested against my chin. "A ruse then."

Jacque nodded. "Yes, as Luc Fabron. And there will be no need for constables or mayhem."

"What if they are more than friends."

"I have never known you to be in short supply of charm, Monsieur. How many women have you enticed from another?"

I smiled. He spoke the truth. I mulled over his words for several seconds. "Why not go into this business association as Monsieur Chastain then? If you believe she won't resist me, why hide who I am?"

"Well that's the mystery, Monsieur. Why didn't she come forth as a survivor? She must've known per the contract you would've taken care of her needs, yet she chose to stay hidden in the backcountry of a foreign land."

The very pretense boiled my blood. *Who does she think she is? She doesn't know me.*

Jacque accepted his drink and gulped quickly before he added, "even when she was approached by Monsieur Badez, she emphatically denied her involvement. I believe being cautious is the best course of action at this time."

I sighed with agreement. "Very well. You believe, if I go into business with the Carrasco's as Luc Fabron, I will have ample opportunity to persuade Isabel to join me voluntarily with no reason to elicit force."

"Precisely."

"I can't promise you I won't harm Francisco."

Jacque stretched out his legs and relaxed for the first time since he arrived. "If all goes well, you will bewitch Isabel with your irresistible ways, she will return to Algiers with you, and though Francisco will be vexed, he will be powerless."

I claimed a deep inhale as I contemplated his proposal. It offered a passive alternative, though I rarely resisted a violent solution in the past.

"And," Jacque tilted his pointed chin my direction, "if you must bestow additional consequence upon the poor chap, any decision you make concerning his olives could cause ruinous harm to his ranch. I'm sure you'll have no trouble ensuring a suitable farewell."

This intimation brought a wide smile to my face. Now that was more my style . . . not this ridiculous cavorting. These games were driving me senseless. I didn't particularly like the idea of extending my time on Menorca, but Jacque spoke the truth. When it came down to it, a willing bride was much more appealing than the alternative.

The simple fact was, I needed Isabel long enough to claim the estate and this would not be a swift transition. If I forced her to come, she could at the very least kill me in my sleep.

"Very well, Jacque," I acquiesced, "set up the meeting."

28

8 April 1910
Contreras Farm, Menorca, Spain
Isabel

"Maria?"

"In here, Susana." I called from the bedroom.

"How are you feeling today?"

"I'm getting stronger, thank you."

"Here is some more of the ointment I promised. It appears to be healing your scars nicely."

"Gràcies." I pointed to the chair opposite of my bed. "Come, sit and visit."

"Oh, I'm sorry. Francisco has a meeting with a distributor at the house today, but I wanted to stop in and give you this first."

"Francisco is home?" My voice quivered. I had awaited this answer yet struggled to find comfort in it.

"Sí, he arrived yesterday."

"Was he successful?"

"No." Her voice dipped sadly. "After Montpellier, our parents went to Marseille, but he had no luck from there, so he returned."

"He was in Marseille?"

"Oh, yes, I forget that's your home isn't it?"

"It was."

The room grew quiet. "I'm sorry, Susana. I hoped Francisco would have located them or at least more information about their whereabouts."

She whimpered, "I know I must assume the worst, but I'm not ready to. I want to hold out every possible hope."

"You should." My thoughts immediately went to Grand-mère. No doubt she held out hope until she learned of our fate. Now that I had confessed to the Contreras', maybe it was time for me to let her know as well. Maybe she would ask me home and not require the marriage to proceed.

"How is the farm, Susana?"

"Bé. We have two possible partnerships. Francisco located the one in Barcelona that mother and father contacted and another one reached out to us. It was quite a blessing. With the harvest wrapping up, and our preservation facilities full, Francisco has been beside himself."

"What, um, what are the company names? My father did a lot of business, maybe I might recognize them."

"I'm unsure. Francisco only told me to be prepared for an afternoon visit. The other is due to arrive next week."

"H—how is Francisco doing? Is he well?" I clasped my trembling hands behind my back. He was practically all I thought about these last two weeks. Though I functioned passably around the house, I was miserable over the way things ended. I missed him . . . I missed everything about him.

"He's withstanding. We've never been this long on our own. Papa always managed, and I fear the burden is weighing on Cisco. He hasn't been himself for quite some time."

"I can only imagine."

Her face suddenly lit up. "Maybe after the gentleman has departed, you could come over." A flutter that divvied between my nerves and eyelashes, forced me to take a step backward. "You've always cheered him up, Maria. Come for dinner."

I yearned to see him. I wanted my eyes to fall upon the real Francisco and not the mirage of a man I conjured in my mind, only I questioned whether *he* wanted to see me.

"Oh, no." I waved my hands defensively. "I couldn't. I, uh, I promised Anita and Miguel I would cook for them tonight."

"Cook?" Her expression clearly remembered my last attempt. It took two days for the smoke to clear out of the house.

"I'm sorry Sus, maybe another time."

"Please do." She kissed me on the cheek and departed. I slipped to the chair and let my head fall to my hands. When I removed them, Anita was standing before me with her arms folded across her chest.

"Oh." I jumped to my feet. "Can I get you something, senyora?"

"Not now, Maria, sit down. Rest yourself."

I sat back down but Anita didn't turn away from me. "How long will you let this go?"

I realized she had overheard our conversation. I sighed heavily. "Anita, they have bigger problems without me adding to it. Their parents, the farm. It would not be right for me to bring my troubles into their lives as well."

"I think it's more of a solution than a problem." She hinted.

"Francisco is hurt and betrayed, and I can't ask him to worry about me when he needs to worry about his family and their livelihood. Besides, he just got home and has a distributor coming over."

"I understand, but promise me, Maria, you'll go soon. You need to correct this."

I groaned. I missed the joy Francisco brought to my life in the short time we spent together. "Even if I tell him the truth, Anita, he may never forgive me for lying to him."

"And if he doesn't, he's a fool." She kissed my forehead then added, "if you insist on cooking tonight, please let me help this time."

I grinned in response and met Anita's outstretched hand to join her in the kitchen.

29

Same Day

Carrasco Ranch, Menorca, Spain

Thomas

"Please, come in." The woman who answered the door had a spirited smile. Though her brown curls and comely appearance would appeal to me any other time, I glanced past her and into the comfort of their ranch house. "Francisco will be here shortly, senyor—"

I tipped my hat as she offered me a seat. "Monsieur Fabron, if you please. Gràcies Srta. Carrasco."

"May I offer you some tea?"

"Yes, anything is fine." I flipped the tails of my long coat up as I sat on the nearest chair. Glancing around the interior, I found it to be more impressive than what had been presented outside. Most assuredly, to be the mixture of a significant income and the genteel touch of a woman.

"Tea will be ready in a moment," she said upon her return. A plate of pastries in her hands. "Your Catalan is superb, but you are French?"

"I am. My business necessitates use of multiple languages." One eyebrow lifted. "You know France?"

"Me, very little." She laughed easily. "My parents, however, are quite familiar with it."

"Are they here? I would love to speak the language with another."

"No, I'm sorry, they're not." Her countenance dipped momentarily then she briskly brushed her sadness away. "But I have a neighbor who is fluent. I'm sure she would be delighted to visit with you if you find yourself in need of native conversation."

"A neighbor?" My heart raced. She must be referring to Isabel. "That would be delightful. What might her name—"

"*Bona Tarda*, Monsieur Fabron. I am Francisco Carrasco." A man swiftly entered the room, wishing me a good afternoon. Though he could be considered handsome, a portion of his shirt hung outside of his belt and his tie angled crookedly to the side. *This can't be the man Isabel finds more appealing than me.* I pulled my lips tight and had to remind myself that Isabel had not yet met me. The advantage was all mine.

I stood as we shook hands. He fit Marcel's exact description, from his broad shoulders and longer hair, all the way down to the scar on his hand. It took every ounce of effort to hide my true feelings. Even his smile chafed my insides.

"Thank you for coming out today. After tea, I would like to give you a tour of the grounds and a taste of our products, if that is suitable to you."

"That is why I am here, Sr. Carrasco." Pulling my hands behind my back, the restlessness in my fingers fought to keep them from forming into fists. *I need something stronger than tea to get me through this miserable visit.*

When Srta. Carrasco returned with the beverage, I found myself admiring her figure. She must be in her early twenties and sure to have a number of suitors. I accepted the tea and focused on Francisco. "My associate mentioned that you are responsible for the family business?"

"Yes, Monsieur."

"And it's only the two of you running this farm?"

"No, we have hired hands. During the season, we have upwards of ten. Javier, my manager, and a few others stay on permanently."

"And you—Srta?"

She glanced at me. A pink glow filled her cheeks, a trait I have come to enjoy in my pursuits. "No husband to care for you?" I once again allowed my eyes to take pleasure in her appearance. If my priority was anything but Isabel, she would be a delightful distraction.

"U—uh," she stammered while I gave her my most charming, charismatic smile.

"No!" The young man snapped a bit curtly for our circumstances.

I stared his direction and waited.

He adjusted himself carefully. "No, my sister's nursing occupation is currently her utmost priority." Francisco motioned towards Susana. "Thank you for the tea. Please allow Monsieur Fabron and I to see to business now." He nodded for her to leave. She peered back at him with confusing eyes. I chuckled faintly to myself. He's quite the protective one. Nonetheless, in his desperation, he shows limitations and weakness. This might be easier than I expected. I sipped my tea slowly.

"And you, Sr. Carrasco?"

"Francisco is fine."

"Francisco. No woman to keep you warm at night?"

"No." Another quick response.

This buffoon intrigued me. I was sure Marcel insinuated an obvious closeness between him and Isabel. No matter—I will know soon enough, and he will pay.

"Thank you for sending over your business documents. I have studied the necessary information about the company. I do have one question though, this Monsieur Chastain, the owner, he approves of the endeavor?"

"He trusts me explicitly." I had forgotten in my rush that the Chastain name would be attached. In my effort for anonymity I needed to modulate his involvement. "I handle the accounts in Spain. My decisions are final."

"I see. Would you like to see the grounds now?"

"Certainly." I placed the half-empty teacup on the table and followed his lead to the horses out front.

"What a beautiful stallion." I admired. "I don't believe I've seen a black beauty such as this anywhere."

"Yes, these are my father's . . . they are his pride and joy."

"And where is your father? His, is the name I have crossed with my inquiries of the farm, not yours."

"He is currently unavailable."

"Unavailable?"

"Please don't be alarmed, Monsieur. He taught me well. You are in good hands I assure you." We mounted our horses and trotted around back towards the grove.

My own steed, purchased by Jacque outside Ciutadella, was every bit satisfactory, but next to his magnificent horse, appeared as a pony at best. I scowled as his back fronted me. He even handled the mount with an exactness only a man who has spent much time around the animals could. I vowed this to be the only time Francisco will come out in front as I continued to mull over the details of my scheme in my head.

"These branches are strong and healthy, Francisco. I see you use the stone terraces for the uneven terrain. I have seen this done in many parts of the country and believe it to be the best way to produce a sound product." Though my deceit was thoroughly in motion, I could not risk him questioning my intellect.

"Thank you, Monsieur."

I glanced at the sky and the position of the sun. Time stretched agonizingly long. Especially when we stopped every few minutes and inspected another olive tree. After an hour of repetitive consideration, I had reached my limit. *I can't eat another damn olive, or I will vomit in place.* Francisco explained that much of the Manzanilla fruit had been harvested and was packed underground, but I recognized the taste of the ripe Cacereña olives.

Once again, I feigned interest. "The produce is unmatched. You have more than proven your quality and value to me."

Francisco beamed to my compliment and a deep dimple formed on one side of his face. For the first time in his presence, I deemed him dangerous. There was nothing about him that I believed a prosperous Mademoiselle from France would find appealing, but this miniscule feature was sure to charm someone. Has it charmed Isabel? My knuckles turned white under my grip of the reins.

"Is there anything else you would like to see, the storage, the barn?"

"I would like to ride the boundaries, to see the extent of the land."

"Yes, of course, follow me."

Blah blah blah. As we rode over his expansive acreage, Francisco spoke incessantly about nothing. Even the tone of his voice became bile in my throat. It didn't matter what he said, nothing mattered. I allowed my mind to toy with the prospect of his destruction.

"Well that is a quaint farmhouse over there." I pointed to the nearest structure to the border.

"Yes, the Contreras', approximately ten acres."

"Do they produce also?"

"Oh no, they have a few trees and vines for personal consumption, but they are simple farmers."

"They have a beautiful piece of property. Have they considered selling it to you so you might expand?"

"They have offered it to my father in the past, but no I haven't pursued that course yet. Right now, I have my hands full."

"Well, Francisco, I like to dream big. I want to know that if we plan to work together that there is a possibility of growth."

"Yes, Monsieur, I understand."

I practically had him eating out of my hands. This pathetic bloke didn't have a chance. I may not even have to proceed with my original plan. Once Isabel and I are introduced, she will see how tempting I can be . . . she would be a fool not to accept me over this nonsense.

"I would like to meet Sr. Contreras." I scanned the property hoping for the slightest glimpse of her. "If he has offered this in the past, I would like to discuss the possibility of acquiring it in the future."

"I'm not sure the timing of this is appropriate. We have a lot to attend to."

I stared at Francisco. Though I knew of the desperate circumstances he found himself in, he held an unusual air of confidence. "Maybe you aren't prepared to be involved with my company." I wanted to see him sweat.

"That is not the case, Monsieur. With all due respect, I only believe that the harvest and distribution are our primary concern. We could entertain the idea of expansion next season."

He has courage. Another nail in his coffin. "Well, I'm sure at the very least we could enjoy a pleasant meal together when I return."

"Of course, I can arrange to have Miguel come over the next time you visit."

"No." My refusal came sharp. I took a deep breath and reminded myself that the key to all of this was patience. "If it be acceptable to him, I would like to see his property myself. Arrange for us to meet at his home. Meet his wife, his family. I assure you the visit will be casual."

"You're right. I think he would be more comfortable there as well, though I believe we are speaking ahead of ourselves. When might I expect an answer on your decision?"

"Within the week. I have some items I would like to consider. I do, however, have certain stipulations if we go into business."

"Stipulations?"

"I require to be on site for the collection and transference."

"On site?"

My jaw grew rigid. My request was clear, I didn't understand why he repeated everything I said. "Yes. Will that be an issue?"

"No, uh." His face clearly struggled with something. "I must inform you I'm meeting with another distributor from Barcelona Wednesday next. This was prearranged before you contacted me."

I eyed him carefully. *Another distributor? Unacceptable.* "What is the name of this other company, maybe I have affiliations with them."

"*Delgado Familia.*"

The muscles in my jaw tightened further. I won't allow anything to get in my way. "Inform me of your decision after your visit and I will inform you of mine. Gràcies for your time, Sr. Carrasco."

"Thank you for coming, Monsieur Fabron." Francisco extended his hand once more as the horses came to a stop at the front entrance. I fought my desire to glare. *Must I touch him again?* His courtesies were irritating. I smiled at the vision of sliding Isabel right out from under his nose and into my arms.

As I trotted away. I made mental notes in my head. First, take care of the competition. Second, reach out to him with fabricated concerns. Ones, that will have him eating out of my hands once more. By next weekend, I will make an offer, one that he cannot refuse under his dire circumstances and proceed forward. Since I no longer needed the services of Monsieur Moreau, with the money from the paintings Arthur sold, I can transport the Carrasco's harvest without my brother actually getting involved.

I will, of course, insist on staying on at his home to oversee the investment—a week maybe two. I must notify Arthur of my delay and have the funds sent directly to me. If I plan this correctly, Isabel will join me when I depart, and I will have set the events in motion to destroy Francisco for his role in keeping her from me *and* for something far less significant . . . his ludicrous dimple.

30

9 April 1910

Carrasco Ranch. Menorca, Spain

Isabel

Susana opened the door and met me with a gentle smile. "Hello Maria, please come inside. Or do you prefer to be called Isabel?"

"Maria is fine." I had not only grown used to the name, but many good memories occurred while I was Maria.

"I can see the ointment is working well." She pointed to my forehead. "The scar is beginning to fade."

"Yes, it is, thank you again. How did things go with the distributor yesterday?"

"He's an interesting man. Quite handsome, but somewhat stiff and mysterious. Francisco told me the tour of the trees went well and honestly we don't have much of a choice, we have few options left."

"I hope it succeeds." I stepped inside. I had never been inside their home and though I feared what awaited me, Anita was right. I needed to speak to Francisco.

In his absence, the heavy weight of guilt crushed my shoulders. I spent my days seeking diversion, but my thoughts always pivoted back to Francisco and my unintended deception. Now that he has returned, the same jarring sensation ate at me like a mouse nibbling on cheese, though I'm sure even the cheese fared better than me.

I paused in the entryway stunned by the simple elegance that met me. From the Tuscan tiles to the thick wood beams overhead, the presentation resembled a grand hall with Provincial styled furniture. Even the red plush Victorian chaise in the corner bordered similarities to one of my own. I gasped at the sight. I had seen impeccable style in many a mansion in France, but never imagined its place inside a country ranch house.

"Your house, Susana." I exclaimed. "I—its lovely."

She smiled. "I forget that you have never been here. Our mother shipped many beautiful and fashionable pieces back with her often from their excursions to Spain, Italy, and France. She loved to decorate."

"She has wonderful taste." Inside the great room I moved towards a stunning portrait near the back wall. "Oh my," I uttered with shock. "The Casa Batlló in Barcelona." I wanted to touch every glorious splash of color. It was one of Gaudí's recent designs. My grandfather who passed shortly after my birth was an admirer. "Did your mother paint this?" I remembered Francisco told me their mother was an artist.

"Sí." Susana stood next to me and admired it as if she too were seeing it for the first time. "She's quite talented."

"It's absolutely breathtaking. This is exactly how I remember seeing the house."

"She was always drawn to unusual places. I can't wait to see what she's done on this last trip." Her comment exhibited hope, but she quickly buried it with a trained expression. "How can I help you, Maria?"

I fidgeted with the hem of my skirt. My nerves hovered close to the surface of my skin. "I'm here to see Francisco."

Her eyes brightened, and the typical Susana smile spread across her face. "Thank you for coming. I'll go get him for you."

I nodded and glanced back at the painting. I needed all the strength and beauty I could muster to see him today.

"Maria?"

I circled around to face him. It had been two weeks. The memory of his face when he asked me if the accusation was true could not be erased. I studied him. Something was different. Still handsome as always, but his hair was longer, and he hadn't shaved, just like when we first met. Yet his ruggedness only confirmed his appeal. My heart ached. *I miss him so.*

"Hello Francisco."

His grin appeared forced. Its unnatural curve kept his dimple at bay. *I miss that dimple.* I glanced down at my trembling hands and gripped the sides of my skirt.

"Please . . ." He motioned to the leather braided couch. "Please sit."

I moved to the sofa while he sat in an ornately decorated wingback chair opposite of me.

"What brings you here?" His tone remained flat, nothing high or low, leaving his inquiry as simple as an acquaintance stopping over for coffee. No hint of the way things began or ended with us.

I wasn't sure how to proceed. I had rehearsed this visit and my speech for days in his absence but wrestled to bring forth words.

"Might I get you something to drink?" He was being polite.

I stopped squirming and took a deep breath. "I need to talk about what happened, Francisco."

He hesitated. "I'm not sure there's anything to say."

"I need to tell you the truth."

"What is the truth to you, Maria . . . or whatever your name may be?" His words did not come out bitter, but they lacked kindness.

"It's Isabel Marie," I whispered.

He shook his head. "I'm not certain anything you say, can change what happened."

"I need to tell you why I lied."

He stood up and retrieved a glass from the side bar. "Are you certain I can't get you anything?" I told him no as he poured his own. When he sat back down, he waved for me to proceed, but the gesture conveyed more of an obligation than anything else.

I bit my lip and forced myself to keep going. I needed to make things right even if it didn't matter to him. I fought my tears. I compelled myself to forget the times he had held my hand or touched my waist or danced with me. It would only make this more difficult. I swallowed hard.

"My name is Isabel Marie Fontaine. I am the only child of Antoine and Harriet Fontaine from Marseille, France. My father is the owner and operator of a vast import and export company in Europe. My mother is the daughter of Clair Tisseur, the renowned architect, and poet among other things. They were with me on the Général Chanzy." I heard his breath hitch but stared at my lap. "Last September, my father informed me that we would be traveling to Algiers in February." I lifted my eyes but feared his contempt and glanced past him to the painting once more. "My father insisted . . . he, uh, required . . ." I stumbled on the words. My eyes flickered away from the painting now and towards the nearby fireplace. "um, he told me I must—" I blinked rapidly. On the mantle, next to the gilded candlesticks were a pair of gold trimmed picture frames. My heart stirred then bolted into varying degrees of alarm. I stood to my feet and walked to the fireplace.

"What's wrong Mar—um, Isabel?" Francisco rose to join me. "I'm not sure what to call you now." My sudden shift generated compassion in his tone.

My hands reached for one of the lavishly decorated frames. Inside, a photograph of a handsome couple appeared. My fingers stiffened as I studied the image. An exquisite woman in a fashionable dress sat before her dashing husband. My stomach lurched into my throat. I gasped.

"What's the matter?" Francisco caught the frame before I dropped it. My warm cheeks turned cold, and a numbness spread throughout my body. What started out as a simple tremble in the beginning graduated to a full shake.

Francisco reached for my arms and spun me around to face him. "What is going on?" he questioned.

"Wh—who, who are these people?" Tears formed in my eyes as I pointed to the photograph he set back on the mantle.

Francisco's squeeze tightened, though I barely felt it. "They are my parents, why?"

All the air in the room evaporated, I couldn't breathe. My knees buckled underneath me and the only thing that stopped me from collapsing was his hold. His hands quickly slid from my shoulders to my waist in an effort to keep me upright. But when my body fell lifeless, he scooped me up and carried me to the couch.

Fragmented images flashed through my mind—boarding the Chanzy, fleeting introductions, drinks, a beautiful woman at the railing, the dining table where a devoted couple dallied. Her infectious laugh, his kind words, and though they were amiable, my interaction with them remained brief as I stewed in rebellion over the latest argument with my father.

"Why, Maria?" Francisco's voice buzzed next to my ear. He was close, but I couldn't see or think clearly.

"Maria!" he demanded.

My eyes lifted to his with the most painful of gazes, "because they too were on the ship."

Francisco's hands fell limp. "No," he mumbled. "Impossible." His countenance dimmed and he grew distant. "The ship was going to Algiers, not Mahón." He backed up. "No!" The force of his shout startled me. "It can't be. Maybe they only look familiar."

Through glossy eyes, I whimpered, "I *know* it was them."

"How?"

"They spoke of seeking business in Algiers . . . for their olives."

"No, it can't be." He dropped to his knees. His fingers raked through his hair as he wilted. I reached over to touch him, though my hands did nothing to ease his pain. "It can't be true," he said. "It can't be."

"I'm sorry."

Francisco shot to his feet. "I don't believe it. Why would they go to Algiers?"

I didn't have an answer for him.

"Are you certain?" He held up the frame again.

My chin dipped. Without a doubt, his mother stood next to me when I tarried by the railing saying goodbye to Marseille. Though she hardly knew me, her kind words came at a time I needed them most.

"Your mother," I relented.

He stopped and viewed me from the other side of the room.

"She wore her hair in a chignon with two painted combs holding back the wayward strands. Her evening gown glowed like the color of sunset and the edge of her black shawl was embroidered with pale pink orchids." I pulled my lips together and fought the tears that loomed. Then whispered, "and she was an excellent dancer."

He fled out of the room.

My head fell to my hands where tears flooded them.

"Susana!" Francisco's shouts shook the walls. His voice, thick with strain, made his words nearly unrecognizable. Within seconds, the familiar high pitch of a woman's scream slashed through the air. Susana's cries filled the morbid hollowness that surrounded me.

Though I did not cause their parent's demise, I felt responsible for the suffering that now permeated from this home. How is it that I could lie from the moment I arrived here but resorted to the truth this one terrifying moment.

Even after the recognizable sound of a wagon's departure, my limbs refused to move. The eerie silence that now remained should have alarmed me, but instead, the numbness that crept in, left me without sensation.

"Srta. Maria?" I glanced up to see Javier tapping my shoulder. His eyes were tinged with a ruddy hue. "Francisco and Susana have left for Ciutadella."

Fresh tears flowed as I attempted to speak, but nothing logical came out.

His concern was sincere. "Let me help you home?"

31

Ciutadella, Menorca, Spain

Francisco

"They're not on the manifest, son." The same sentence was repeated three times from the man whose thick white mustache covered his entire mouth and joined jagged layers down his chin.

"May I see it, please?"

He huffed, but only a second before he handed me the papers. Susana, my strong-willed sister who assisted many people through grief, loss, and suffering, cowered weakly by my side. Her continuous tears resulted from our perplexing torment.

I moved my finger meticulously down the alphabetized list and across each letter and number.

Berger (Auguste-Eugéne), garçon, Marseille, nº 1326

Constantini (Charles), chauffeur Bastia n° 289

Cotte (Joseph-Mathieu), premier garçon, Marseille n° 164

Durante (Barthélemy), matelot, Bastia n° 4808

Grimalvi (don Joseph), soutier, Marseille n° 3449

"No, son," The man waved his hand. "Those are the names of the *d'équipage*, the *passagers* are below."

Again, I ran my finger across, this time they were not found in any particular order.

Reynaud (dame), née Paoli (Louise-Cornélie)

Reynaud (Claude-Mathilde)

Jaquet (Rémi-Marius)

Bufor (François-Auguste)

Henry (Elise-Joséphine)

Duraz (Georges-Pierre-Marie-François)

Aussenac (Marius-Benjamin)

Clément (Auguste-Louis)

Billot (Marie-Pierre-Gabriel)

Henry (Léon-Paul)

Nothing I saw resembled Carrasco.

Savin (Marguerite-Victorine-Marie-Anne)

Gros- (André)

Fontaine- (Antoine -Harriet-Isabel)

I stopped.

Fontaine- (Antoine -Harriet-Isabel)

I caught sight of this recently introduced name, and a pinch nipped in the center of my chest. *Isabel Fontaine.*

"Are they on there, Cisco?" Susana's weak voice drew me from my diversion.

"No, Sus." I handed the list back to the man and put my arm around her shoulders. Her form wilted into me. The quakes that racked her body intensified.

"Gràcies for your time, senyor."

His fingers tangled through his unkempt whiskers as if he contemplated something. "Incidentally, you're not the first to believe your loved ones were aboard. Happens frequently."

"It does?"

"Certainly. The list is deficient."

"Why is that?"

"Well, quite often, tickets are sold at the docks, off the books."

"They are?" Susana pulled her handkerchief from her nose. "How?"

"Oh, simple actually. When a ship's hold might be full, speculators abound. A chance to make a profit from those most determined to sail. Marseille is no different than any other port. Especially if the ticket could not be acquired in advance, such as a traveler arriving posthaste from another location."

I glanced down at Susana. Her eyes met mine. Our parents were exactly the sort of travelers to purchase a ticket in a moment's notice.

"Would it be possible to meet with the *Procuradors* who retrieved and documented the items that were collected from the ship?"

"Not a pretty sight if you ask me. It's a boathouse full of damaged, unmarked, unclaimed goods. I doubt you'd find what you're looking for, boy."

"All the same. How do I find the officer in charge?"

"I will get you a name."

I realized this endeavor would most likely be impossible but for both our sakes, we needed to do everything we could before we returned home.

It was barely five hours ago when Maria sat across from me. My mind betrayed my intent to remain aloof and I chastised myself severely for regaling cares on this woman that I hardly knew—yet desired all the same. When I caught sight of the bracelet on her wrist, the one I had given her in Ciutadella, my defenses nearly toppled, but I held true until her body stilled.

At first, I wasn't alarmed when she approached the mantle, but when she retrieved the photograph of my parents and trembled as though the ground shook, angst apprehended me. Then to hear the words from her mouth, of my mother and father's fate aboard the Chanzy, I couldn't stop the rage that engulfed me.

The whole event was scarcely conceivable. Travel to Algiers had been mentioned only once as a brief afterthought if nothing transpired in Spain or France. I couldn't believe they would alter course without so much as a post. Although, at the same time, it wasn't entirely surprising since they did something similar several years ago. A spur of the moment jaunt to Greece from Italy without a word.

The shipwreck would also account for their sudden disappearance with no trace.

My thoughts shifted once again to Maria's face when she described mother down to the precise detail. The impact of the blow propelled as accurately as if I'd been struck in the chest by a whaler's harpoon. It was I who gave her that shawl decorated with the orchids last year for her 45th birthday.

An hour later, Susana and I were directed inside a damp and dusty warehouse. The smell alone drove one to turn and run. A man dressed far to fine to set foot in this establishment stood at the door with a thick stack of papers in his hands.

"Every item has been marked in this dossier. Anything that hasn't been claimed by family or has no identifiers remains here. We don't plan on retaining the lot much longer. The owner requires his roof back.

"The odor is horrific," Susana muttered. "Are you certain there are no body parts in here?"

"None that we know of."

Her eyebrow raised. I tried to read her thoughts. She understood more about rotting human flesh than I did. I imagined the task of collecting anything related to the shipwreck must've incurred a great deal of blight and most burdensome for all involved.

"Most bodies or parts that weren't claimed for private burial were put in a mass grave end of February outside of town."

"How did the items get sorted?"

"Not particularly well, although there were some identifying factors such as monogrammed cases, engraved jewelry or fashion items due to the wealth aboard. Many items of value, I presume, were never returned by those who found them or went down with the ship. Anything that would fetch a coin would've been kept. Most everything recovered was damaged by the elements. Even now the decay proliferates."

"Our parents did have monogrammed personal effects, and they also had items of worth. Do you have a specific list for those?"

The man flipped through several pages before he removed a small stack. Here are the ones we documented with engravings that could be identified. Each was given a number. You can match the corresponding number with the item if you believe it belonged to your family. We generally require some evidence as next of kin, but since we are ceasing operations soon, it won't matter much. Truly just take it.

Susana's sniffle warned me of her proximity as we leaned over the list and once again followed the text methodically row by row.

"There." Her voice cracked with a weakness that rarely escaped her lips. "*C. Carrasco* valise. Contents: 3 articles of clothing, 1 pair of half boots, 1 silver hairbrush and matching hand mirror, 3 handkerchiefs, rectangle box comprised of 13 various sized paintbrushes." Susana glanced up to me with tears lining her bottom lashes. The redness that formed earlier beneath her eyes, intensified. "It's hers."

"And this," I pointed to the line below. "A boxed shaving kit, one razor, one brush, one set of scissors and one pocket watch engraved. "To Basilio, my greatest love, Cristina."

I clasped Susana's hand and pointed to the two lines and back to the man. "We believe these are their possessions, will you help us retrieve them?"

"Of course."

Francisco glanced between Susana and the gentleman and inhaled deeply. "And since the belongings are being discarded shortly, might I check for the property of a friend as well?"

32

10 April 1910

Contreras Farm, Menorca, Spain

Isabel

I dipped the quill into the ink and paused.

Contemplating my actions over the last two months, I mocked the dreadful mess I created through selfish motivations. My intent to remain anonymous—though it did not come without reason or fear—also came with an incalculable cost.

Dearest Grand-mère,
10 April 1910

I frowned. If only I could relate the news personally. She deserved to know of my survival through different means.

> I am alive.
> I survived the shipwreck. It was a treacherous ordeal. Papa, Maman, Ines and Rémy did not, which you must know by now. My heart aches tremendously with their loss. Something I'm sure you comprehend all too well.
> I know this news will come as a colossal shock. Please pardon the dreadful way it's disclosed. I wish I had found a way to deliver it to you personally, but please allow me to share my reasons.
> After being at sea for over a day, I was discovered by a loving couple, Miguel and Anita Contreras, on a beach near their home. Through their genuine kindness and care and the assistance of their neighbors, my health was restored. I'm in Menorca. They have offered me a place in their home, and I am well cared for, though I do miss you and France tremendously.
> Please Grand-mère, forgive me for not coming forward earlier. It was both childish and foolish to conceal my identity. Truthfully, I feared being wed. I know that Papa needed to secure the business and made his decision out of love for our family but leaving Marseille and marrying a stranger, terrified me. I saw this as the means to keep myself hidden from that future. However, I am ashamed, Grand-mère, ashamed of not showing more courage like you and Papa and above all, what you might think of me. I pray that you may understand my reasons. Please come as

soon as you can to Spain. I await your arrival.
L'amour Isabel
Contreras Farm
Port de Sanitja, Menorca, Spain

I studied my words. Although my grandmother recognized my father as the patriarch of the home, she loved me dearly and I hoped with all my heart she would respect my decision not to wed Thomas. I didn't care about the wealth or the estate. I wanted to find happiness on my own and I hoped that future somehow involved the man I loved.

Once I folded the letter and addressed the envelope, my thoughts slipped to Francisco. Even with my resolution to not follow my parent's wishes, I had no assurances Francisco would be pleased or even consider me to be part of his future.

I crossed my arms and laid my head down upon them. The heaviness in my heart amplified as I relived the day I went to his house to confess. When I recognized the image of his mother and father, something inside me broke. Not only did I cause horrendous sorrow—in the end I never got the chance to tell Francisco the truth. Consequently, the pain I brought upon him stands to be the very thing that binds us together. We both lost our parents in the tragic misfortune of the Général Chanzy.

I stepped outside and into the garden. The mixed aroma of various flowers embraced me, cleared my thoughts, and shifted my reflections back to the 9th of February. I sat down on the stone bench near the bougainvillea and elicited the events that led to a blessed introduction.

Shortly upon arrival aboard the Chanzy, my family settled into our staterooms and dressed for a reception in one of the lounges. That is where I met the woman now known to be Francisco's mother for the first time. She must've seen my low spirits. I found no reason to smile. My presence aboard the Chanzy was just one more step towards my perceived execution.

I withdrew from the company and retreated to the deck and the outer railing. A light rain had begun and despite Maman's dissents, I remained outside. A beautiful woman in a vibrant orange muslin gown joined me. A finely knitted shawl draped delicately across her shoulders, matching her black hair which was twisted into a loose bun behind one ear. She stepped to my side. The fresh scent of jasmine drifted over me.

"Look at that commanding fortification." She pointed to the Fort Saint-Jean, the fort which guarded the older section of the Marseille port. Her French was sound but intermixed with a slight Spanish accent. "I wonder what stories it could tell," she whispered but did not draw her eyes from it. "Perhaps tales of piracy, brave legionnaires or damsels in distress. Maybe daring escapes similar to the Château d'if."

I glanced at her. She had just mentioned one of my favorite places in all of Marseille. "Yes." I managed a small grin. "Château d'if, is rather tragic *and* beautiful."

She returned my stare. "What an unusual thing to say about a prison. You've been there?"

I nodded. "My companion took me there a year ago." I peered around to assure our conversation was private. "My parents would've never approved, but Ines understood my curiosity. After I explored the grounds, I entered the depths of the dungeons." My skin grew clammy from the memory. "The scent of pain and death still lingered within its stones."

Her head flew back in a full laugh. "A woman after my own heart." She winked. "You desire adventure and mystery, much like me."

"Oui." My grin curved into a frown. "Yet, it remains outside of my reach."

The woman studied me for a few seconds. Her gaze came softly without criticism. "My dear . . ." She reached for my hand. Her clasp was gentle. "You might not be able to command your world, but you can *always* own your response."

My eyes lifted, captivated with her intellect and charm. When she smiled, two lovely dimples appeared. One of which most assuredly was passed on to her handsome son. Though I didn't know it at the moment, he would be the very man to steal my heart.

She squeezed my fingers. "My name is Cristina."

"Pleased to meet you, I'm Isabel."

Though Francisco's mother had not been informed of my pending betrothal, she read my mind. She peered through me and understood my soul unlike anyone ever had before. Our interaction was brief, but her influence remains and now that I know who she is, I hold that exchange dear to my heart. She was the reason for Francisco's strength, his kindness, and his zest for life. My soul ached for his tremendous loss.

"Maria?"

I glanced up to see Henry standing before me. His hands tucked into the front pockets of his trousers.

"Are you well?"

I brushed away the wetness that had built upon my cheeks and smiled his direction. "Yes, Henry. I was just enjoying the day and well, thinking."

He pointed to the other end of the bench. "May I sit?"

I nodded. Henry pushed the long dark blond locks behind his ears and wiped his brow. When he glanced over to me, I couldn't even discern the edges of his pupils in his deep brown eyes.

Though I often crossed paths with Henry throughout the day, whether in the barn or on the property, he showed confidence in his labors, only here next to me now, an element of shyness arose.

"Anita told me you were on the ship when it wrecked. The one at the Headlands."

"I was." A stir from my chest confirmed my longing to tell the truth and though a slight sting remained from my previous lies, a sense of freedom soared within me.

"It must've been awful. I'm sorry."

"It was." I exhaled. "I recall falling asleep in my stateroom and then being flung into the frigid water." The lump in my throat grew. The recent realization of the Carrasco's suffering the same fate as my family, hung thick. "I don't know why it was me who survived the terrible tragedy."

He bit his bottom lip and I watched as he contemplated his next words. Though his size would suggest he was more mature for his years, the freckles that dotted his nose exposed a juvenile trait. "I believe you survived because of all the people here." I followed his hand as it gestured towards the house. "When I picked you up from the beach, I really thought you were dead and here you are, talking, smiling, and alive."

An encouraging grin formed on his lips. He was right, there were so many people responsible for my survival—beginning with Ines, Miguel and Anita, Susana, Francisco, and this pleasant young man before me, Henry. Was my recovery a miracle—like those I had learned of at church? The same query that had pestered my thoughts since February surfaced. *Why me?*

"May I ask you a question, Maria?"

I nodded again.

"You seem unsettled, like you're not yourself this week. Are you well?"

My eyelashes fluttered rapidly. I wondered if he was perceptive or if this was something he'd heard others mention. "I—I am a bit ill at ease."

"May I ask why?"

"I lied to everyone about how I arrived here, but I never intended on hurting anyone. I—I did it to stay hidden."

"Hidden, why?"

"From a future I was being forced into."

Henry's fingers tapped his knees. "Now that you've told the truth, isn't everything okay now?"

"I wish it were that simple," I mumbled. "I hurt someone I care for, quite deeply."

Henry's grin curved slowly. "He will forgive you."

My head shot up quicky.

His smile flourished until it filled half his face. "Everyone knows Francisco is sweet on you."

I frowned. "Before I lied."

"No." He shook his head. "You have to know Francisco's not like that. He's a good man. He will understand."

"I wish I could turn back time and start over."

"Do you still feel like you must hide?"

I wasn't sure how to answer this. I knew that after I had been sighted by Monsieur Badez, my survival could very well be known, but what that meant for me or my future I still didn't know. "I'm unsure of what to do. I'm healed, but no longer want to be a burden."

"You're not a burden. Why not stay here?" Henry's eyes lit up as I met them. "You belong here."

My heart warmed. There was no doubt in my mind that my soul found a home here, but the restlessness over my dishonesty and deceit resonated.

He continued, "Miguel and Anita love you. Francisco is—well I believe he's *in* love with you and I—" He stopped short.

My voice caught in my throat. "You think Francisco is in love with me?"

He laughed. "I don't think there's a person around who *doesn't* believe that."

I lowered my head. *I don't doubt the kindness that Francisco has shown...but love?* "What about you, Henry? How do you feel about me being here?"

He stared at me. "I like it. I know it's only happened a few times, but I really enjoyed when you read aloud, under the tree." He tilted his head towards his favorite almond tree.

"I thought you were taking a *migdiada?*" I chuckled, recalling his hat covering his face while I read from *Don Quixote* in the quiet afternoons.

"No, I wasn't asleep, I listened."

"Well I'm glad you enjoyed it."

Henry's eyes darted to his dusty boots. "Nobody has ever done that before, senyoreta."

"Done what?"

"Read to me."

"Nobody?" The very thought unnerved me. How could a person have gone sixteen years without an introduction to a book?

He shook his head. "No. Mother never had time, what with four younger siblings and the village laundry for wages."

I reached over for his hand. "Henry, would you like to learn how to read? I could teach you."

His mouth curved into a wide smile. "You would do that for me?"

I squeezed his fingers. "Certainly. I would love to."

"Then you'll stay?" He grinned slyly now as if he accomplished some great hoodwink. In a way he might've fooled me into admitting I would remain here, but in truth, it wasn't a trick. I *wanted* to stay.

"Yes," I surrendered. "For now."

33

15 April 1910

Carrasco Ranch, Menorca, Spain

Miguel

"Walk with me, Maria," I said as I pulled her arm through mine.

She nodded, but her sight lowered to the ground. I had not seen her smile in a week. That was the day we learned of the Carrasco's fate.

"That was a fine service, wouldn't you say?" I grappled for any conversation. Up until now, my mumblings had centered mostly on nonsense. I tried in vain to get Maria's mind off the situation. The last few days alone, I invited her to go fishing, to ride Penelope, hell, I even tried to tempt her with shooting my shotgun, though I wasn't even sure that was ever an attraction. She refused it all. Even Anita tried with knitting, baking, walks, but nothing drew that girl from her isolation. She did venture out to the garden occasionally, but her melancholy was more than I could bear.

"The uh, *vicari* shared some nice remarks." I patted her hand.

"Sí." She spoke so light I had to lean in to hear her answer.

I didn't attend church much, occasionally Mass, and I always left uplifted, but it was Anita who believed more in the Doctrine. Thank goodness too, she's most likely the only reason I'd make it to Heaven.

The memorial this afternoon was held in the Carrasco's garden. There were no bodies to bury but Francisco and Susana had a stone carved with their names.

Basilio and Cristina Carrasco
One in life, one in death.

Nothing could be closer to the truth.

"Watch your step." I stopped Maria before she tripped over a tree root in our path. "Only a bit further."

The family had invited all those who attended the observance to a gathering in their home. Though not requested, many people brought food. It was a long-standing tradition in celebration of the life of the deceased. Anita herself held a pot of *Arroz de la Tierra*. The sausages mixed within came fresh from a recently slaughtered pig.

As we walked, the memory of Javier arriving to our home with a stunned and confused Maria a week ago, remained fresh. At the time her cheeks were absent of tears, but her swollen eyes indicated that she had been crying...a good deal. Javier was the one to tell us what happened. Had I been given a thousand guesses to her distress, I would've undoubtedly never speculated correctly. To learn our dear friends perished on that ship—the very same ship that claimed the lives of Maria's family—well nothing could be put to words.

Susana came to our home two days later to confirm the worst. Their parent's names were never found on the manifest, therefore no next of kin had ever been explored or questioned by the Procuradors. As by pure chance, a small collection of their belongings had been preserved and documented. It helped that the Carrasco's travel cases were marked though only one was located. Susana said that most of her mother's contents within had been spoiled beyond recognition. Only her hand brush, mirror, and paintbrushes, though marred, were identifiable. Her father's shaving case survived as well, though the pocket watch found within was severely damaged. Regardless of their condition, the belongings held more value in their existence than anything else.

"My dear Maria..." We stood near the entrance for an undetermined amount of time. "You don't have to come in if you don't want to." My heart wilted for this precious girl stricken with sorrow. I patted the hand that was looped over my elbow. "It's not your fault." I reiterated for the hundredth time. Her tiny body shook as she laid her head against my shoulder and wept. I moved my hand to her hair and brushed it as tenderly as an awkward oaf possibly could.

If not for her tears, Maria appeared as though she attended one of her soirées, she told us about. She owned nothing in black. The best she could do was the blue dress she had been given from Susana, though its brightness suggested beauty and happiness versus sadness and death.

"If you want to go home, the Carrasco's will understand," Anita said as she appeared at our side. Setting the dish down on a porch chair, she wrapped her arms around the both of us.

"I should stay," Maria mumbled. "I need to tell them how sorry I am."

Anita nudged her chin upward. "It's because of you, they have answers. Nobody knew they had gotten on that ship, love, and nobody would still know if you hadn't recognized them."

I smiled at my wife. She was wise in her years. Of course, having to put up with me all this time, she had to be. I glanced back at Maria and used one hand to wipe her tears. Her cheeks flushed a rosier shade next to her attempted smile. This led me to believe she would be okay.

She peered at the open doorway and continued, "I didn't know their parents for long, but somehow I feel connected to them, especially Cristina."

I intertwined her fingers with mine and held her hand up. "Well then, let's do this together." Anita handed the pot to a serving girl and grabbed Maria's other hand and squeezed. When the three of us entered the home, we did so like a family.

The place was filled with many paying their respects. Friends, acquaintances, the ranch hands and their families, even the pastor and his wife. Many brought food for the occasion and several tables were filled with the delicacies to alleviate the gloom. My mouth watered as I surveyed the goods. I wanted to fill a plate immediately but caught sight of Anita's severe brow. "How does she know?" I grumbled. On our way to where Francisco and Susana stood, Javier and Lupe greeted us.

"Good afternoon, Sr. Contreras." Javier shook hands with me.

"It's good to see you both," I grinned. Then glanced to make sure our hosts were engaged with others before I spoke.

"How are they managing, Javier?"

He shrugged. "Best I can see." Then sighed. "To have to face this and the problems with the farm at the same time. It's a lot to handle."

"Anything I can do?"

"Not really."

"What about the farm, should I send Henry to help with your final reap?"

"No, I believe we have it covered. Francisco hired a few more hands for the last two weeks. The distributor arrives Monday. Between us all, we should be able to patch this season together."

"So, an arrangement was met with a distributor?"

"Yes, but not the one from Barcelona."

"Why not?" My nose scrunched. "Wasn't that the one Basilio obtained. What happened?"

"We don't know actually. They sent word a couple of days ago that they had other interests in mind and stepped away. The distributor who remains insists on living at the home during the harvest. Francisco's actions suggest he's uneasy about this."

I recalled the visit from the strange man, weeks ago. "Is it that man who came by when Francisco was gone to the mainland? The one you met with?"

"Not the same man, no, but his employer."

Similar concerns that swept over me then, returned. "If it feels wrong, Javier, he shouldn't do it. We'll figure it out."

"Senyor, if he doesn't move this product, it will, no doubt, put him and the ranch in a daunting situation. He has no choice."

I inhaled deeply. We all knew this to be true. "Very well, make sure you stay alert. You have been good for him and this place."

"Thank you, Sr. Contreras. They are good to me too."

"Excuse me, Javier, Lupe." I nodded at his beautiful wife. "We must pay our respects."

We shook hands once more and he moved aside. Though Maria remained nearby during my conversation with Javier, she never spoke up and almost instantly pulled behind as Anita and I moved towards the Carrasco's.

"Francisco." I shook his hand once Anita released him from her embrace. My other hand pulled him in to pat his back. "I'm truly sorry for your loss, son. I can't imagine your grief."

"Thank you, senyor. I can honestly say it has been the worst week of my life." He exhaled profoundly. Then continued, "but if that's true, it can only improve, correct?" His lips lifted to one side. It was a faint attempt to lighten the mood. Something he seemed sorely in need of.

I glanced at him warily wondering if I should continue down the path my thoughts toyed with. I pulled him towards me again, having never let go of his hand and brought his ear close to my face. "Francisco, I must implore something of you."

He whispered back, "anything, Sr. Contreras."

"I have grown rather fond of a young woman in my charge." Francisco's breath seized. "Maria needs to know she's not responsible for your grief."

His body stilled under my touch. "She's not." He leaned back and stared at me. "She's the only reason I have knowledge of my parent's fate."

I proceeded to whisper again, "yes, but she has taken this on as if she personally steered the ship herself. Not to forget this event, no doubt, has churned up the pain of her own loss. Please don't hold it against her."

"I would never, senyor." He pulled his lips tight and rubbed his forehead with his free hand. "When she told me, I didn't know how to react. I didn't want to believe her. It was shocking to say the least."

"Of course, of course." I patted his back. "I can imagine the news being most alarming. Please, son, take your time in your grief. Your parents will be sorely missed." I paused and took a full breath myself. "Just know there are a great many people who care for you and are willing to bear this burden alongside you. If you have need of anything, please let us know."

He nodded and I released my grip. When I turned around, I found Maria still positioned a good distance behind. Her behavior suggested she hoped for the room to clear before she approached.

I moved to the side and allowed Francisco to view her fully. She glanced up and in that one instant when their eyes met, my own heart sensed the jolt. There was no denying something drew them together, but whether this tragedy would bring them close or tear them apart, I did not know.

"Excuse me, Cisco. I believe the mushrooms and asparagus in the *oliaigua soup* are calling for me."

He smiled as I excused myself.

Before I reached the table, I glanced back and caught sight of them. Maria stepped forward, but Francisco didn't wait for her to come to him. He reached out and wrapped his arms around her. From my position it appeared that they were both weeping.

34

21 April 1910

Contreras Farm, Menorca, Spain

Francisco

"Miguel, Anita? May we come in?" I stuck my head in through the front door as a flurry of activity met my ears.

"Yes, oh yes, Cisco," Miguel hollered on his way towards me. "Please, please come in." He opened the door wide. The tantalizing smell of fermented meat and spices met us from within.

Anita appeared in her bright red apron. A dot of flour graced her cheek. Clapping her hands together, she giggled at the sight of me and Susana, and this stranger dressed as though he was a guest at the royal palace in Madrid.

Monsieur Fabron had not quite grown used to the country in the three days he had lodged with us. His lofty suits were perfectly pressed, and he changed every time the smallest hint of dirt appeared on any part of him. Although, to his defense, I had not yet explained the process in which we handwashed our clothing. It might slow down his constant wardrobe changes.

I was not thrilled with the overnight arrangements for the last ten days of the harvest, but I complied. When the *Delgado Familia* declined even before their visit, this left me with Monsieur Fabron as our only likely option. Our season depended on his partnership.

From our brief interactions, it seemed as though our rustic accommodations were beneath Fabron's customary comforts. Though we employed a cook and a maid, we don't have personal valets and he was forced to see to his own private needs each day. I was also not pleased with the notion of having an unattached man under the same roof as my sister. Thankfully, Susana's nursing duties kept her away quite often, but she returned tonight for dinner with the Contreras'.

While I had no solid reason to distrust my new partner, the way he gawked at her irritated me so. And much to my surprise, the nuisance ended with me. Susana appeared to enjoy the outlandish flattery. Fortunately, that is as far as it went. I knew her to be quite particular in her taste. She often voiced her lack of time for a courtship and Monsieur Fabron was no exception. Despite Susana being more than deserving of this man's excessive compliments, the adulation reached an unprecedented level in the short time they interacted, and he exhausted me.

Truthfully, I couldn't wait for tonight, a sort of respite from the trifle and to enjoy the company of our good friends, but most importantly, I longed to see Maria.

"Sr. and Sra. Contreras, may I introduce Monsieur Fabron."

"Please call me Luc." He reached for Anita's hand and lifted it slowly to his lips. I gaped as she giggled like a schoolgirl. Then walked away patting her cheeks as though she needed to cool them.

Miguel led us to the sitting room. "Supper is not quite prepared. May I interest you in a drink?"

"By all means." Monsieur Fabron's gracious manners filled the air. "You have a lovely home, Sr. Contreras. Thank you for inviting us to dine with you."

"Miguel, please call me Miguel."

"Miguel, how long has your family lived here?"

"I've lived here all my life. Anita and I acquired this home after we wed over fifty years ago."

"My goodness that's a long time. Congratulations on your long, happy marriage."

"What would you like to drink? Scotch, gin, wine, Pomada?"

"Pomada?" he asked, apparently unfamiliar with the island's favorite drink.

"A mixture of gin and lemonade. Though the concoction sounds harmless—" Miguel barked laughter, "—after only a couple of glasses, you forget yourself, and your wife and kids."

Luc joined him in his humor but waved off the alcohol easily. "Tea please, I'm not much of a drinker." My eyebrow tipped. That's an interesting response considering the alcohol in *my* own home was slowly dwindling and Susana doesn't touch it.

"Francisco, Susana? Anything to drink."

"Tea as well." Susana sat down. I nodded my agreement.

Luc turned to her. "You look breathtaking tonight, Susana." One of her brows rose under his stare. She chuckled lightly to herself.

I sat next to her. "That she does, Monsieur Fabron." I leaned forward to block his direct sight of her. "So, Monsieur, you spent a great deal of time outside today, did you enjoy yourself?"

He smiled, but it wasn't the same charming smile he flashed to Susana. "Of course. I love being on the land. It's refreshing to be a part of something as natural and free as farmland." He drew his attention away from me. "Miguel, do you and Anita live here alone?" He glanced between them both as Anita arrived. Her apron now removed.

"Oh, no, we have a relative staying with us."

"A relative?" He pursued. His interest stung.

"Sí, Maria. She's picking flowers for the table. It takes her quite some time in the garden. It's her favorite place."

"Maria?" Anita tapped a nearby windowpane. "Come," she called, "our guests are here." Anita flashed a big smile my direction.

Just hearing Maria's name sent chills down my back. The last time we spoke was at the memorial the previous week. I held her for an unusually long time. Though few words were spoken, the grief we shared was enough to break even the strongest of wills and weighed heavily on our hearts.

Since then, the work at the ranch had kept me quite busy, but I reflected on her every day. I missed everything about her. Then the reminder came—the unpleasant truth of our separation. I couldn't shake the questions. Why would she go to such great lengths to keep the shipwreck from me? Why did she hide her real identity? Was it possible for me to trust her again?

A blast of color and sunshine flashed through the doorway. "I'm here," she said without stopping. "I need to retrieve a vase." Her arms filled with a variety of blooms. When she finally made it to the sitting room, I fought my desire to go to her, hold her, and kiss her. She wore a light green cotton dress with embroidered daisies on the front. Every inch of her was perfect—her wavy hair, her wide eyes, the jet-black eyelashes I adored, her pink lips, and the way she carried herself with an unusual balance between coyness and poise.

My heart caved, completely mesmerized. Unfortunately, to my astonishment, I wasn't the only one.

Instantly, Luc was on his feet and at her side. She lowered her head, her cheeks turned rosy with her lovely bashful blush. A jealous nerve flared. I glanced at Susana. Her brows furrowed at the overt response of our guest. With no intent to let go of Maria's hand, Luc seemed to forget there were any other souls in the room.

"Milady." The way he smothered her and kissed her fingers, maddened me.

I mouthed the word towards Susana. *Milady?* Does he think he's amongst nobility? I wrung my hands together and fumed silently. Susana nudged her head my direction and pushed me upward. I stood next to him though he was hardly aware.

"Maria, this is our new business partner and guest, Monsieur Fabron."

Her focus should have remained on him. His perfectly chiseled jaw and slick curve of his mouth were sure to draw many women to him, but not her.

She only had eyes for me.

My heart thundered in my chest. I smiled at her. The softness in her face begged for something—forgiveness maybe, but it was I who should be asking it of her. She returned my smile gracefully. I wanted to whisk her out the door and into the privacy of the garden, take her in my arms and never let go.

"It's good to see you again, Maria." I reached for her other hand, the one not poisoned by my competition. She easily gave it. I kissed it tenderly but kept it simple. No drivel or poppycock. Much was said in this small interchange, we undoubtedly missed each other. I retrieved a small book from my pocket and placed it in her hand.

"Anna Karenina!" She cried and pulled her hand from Fabron's hold to cradle the book. The way her eyes thanked me I could've kissed her right then.

From the corner of my eye, Luc stiffened. His stare went from her to me. His expression turned taut and he took several steps backward.

Then as if she suddenly awoke, she shook her head. "Um, wait, did you say Monsieur?" A small tremor escaped her lips.

Luc launched forward again. "Yes, Mademoiselle."

"Y—you are French?" The stammer in her words was not mistaken. I glanced towards her, but her gaze found the floor. "May I please have your name once more, Monsieur?"

Luc puffed his chest out like an ostrich. "Monsieur Fabron. I come from Algiers, but my family is from Paris."

"A—Algiers?" Maria's face drained pasty white. I moved forward to touch her when Anita clapped her hands.

"What luck, Maria. Someone to speak French with."

"You speak French?" Luc renewed his enthusiasm.

Maria quickly smoothed the lines from her countenance and smiled up at Luc. "Yes, I—I do." Then she quickly excused herself and fled the room.

"Don't be long, dear," Anita called out. "Supper is ready."

Miguel slapped his knee when he stood and pointed to the kitchen. Everyone seemed fine, but Maria's reaction troubled me. There was much I had yet to learn about her, but there was no doubt she was unsettled with something surrounding our guest.

When Maria returned, she deliberately sat next to me and far from Fabron who was placed at the other end—much to his obvious disappointment. Though Luc seemed to carry his gentlemanly appearance well, he exhibited bouts of solemn contemplation throughout the meal. It was difficult to pinpoint exactly what bothered me the most about him.

"Maria?" He finally spoke up. "The Contreras' say you are visiting. Where do you call home?"

Maria nervously glanced from me to Anita and Miguel before she reached Luc's face again. We were all aware of the false stories she told and waited to hear which one she would share with this stranger. Her lips parted with a faint grin. "My family is from the mainland."

"I visit often, what part?" His enquiry was persistent.

"Barcelona."

I glanced from Anita to Susana. Unsure whether lying had become comfortable for her or if she saw a reason to deceive. I didn't trust him, maybe she didn't either. I grinned, pleased she didn't tell the truth this time. The less he knew of her the better.

"Ah, the pearl of Spain. Such a beautiful and romantic city. When do you plan to return?"

"Hopefully never," Miguel piped in. "She's quite happy here and we're happy to have her."

I watched this interchange with fascination, but Luc was not finished.

"Well you must miss your family, your parents."

"Yes, I do." She answered with confidence, then turned to Susana. "Did Sra. Hernández have her baby yet? She was quite heavy when we conversed in the market a week ago."

Susana laughed. "No, not yet, but every time I visit her, she curses her husband, again and again." Susana shared her next bit of news with all of us. "This will be her seventh child and her oldest is only eleven. Can you imagine it?"

Luc's complexion flared ruddy. Then with a brief exhale it returned to its normal color again. When he glanced up and caught me watching him, his smile came curtly. Though he stared at me, he addressed Miguel. "Sr. Contreras, Francisco informed me that you have offered to sell your property."

Startled, I quickly jumped in. "Only in the past and only to my father."

Miguel glanced between us both. A long wrinkle appeared across his forehead. My chest tightened at the course of this conversation. I had not prepared him of the possibility this might arise. "Sí," he cleared his throat. "I proposed the possibility to the elder Sr. Carrasco several years ago."

"Are you still offering?" Luc now eyed Miguel boldly.

Miguel met his gaze, rubbing his chin carefully. I almost saw his mind spinning.

Luc leaned forward with what appeared to be impatience and somehow ignored the mounting tension in the room. I wiped the growing sweat off my upper lip. I couldn't believe anyone to be this impertinent.

Luc continued, "I find that my business with the Carrasco's is contingent on growth. Their acreage is fair but could use another five or ten to increase their profits."

I lowered my head unable to look Miguel, Anita, Maria, or even Susana in the eyes. I should've known this was Luc's intention for accepting their kind invitation to supper.

"Is this what you want Francisco?" Miguel asked.

"I—"

"Of course, this is what he wants," Luc chimed in.

I lifted my head to his brashness, shocked he had the audacity to speak for me or to Sr. Contreras in this manner in his home of all places. I forced a series of slow exhales—anything to calm the fire he ignited in my chest. When I peered back in Luc's direction, his black eyes sent a silent warning my direction.

I softened my expression when I faced Miguel. "Only if you want to senyor, but how insensitive of us to speak of business in front of the ladies and at the behest of your kind invitation. Forgive us, Sr. and Sra. Contreras, we have forgotten our place and won't speak of it again tonight."

An awkward silence followed until Maria once again drew attention to the village and the topic of our neighbors. I could've embraced her right there for her mindful distraction.

At the end of the night, I struggled to face anyone directly, humiliated at what I had allowed to happen. "Thank you, Anita. The *Sobrasada* and *Tombet* were delicious. Your aubergines are unmatched." I kissed her on the cheek. Miguel had excused himself early before I had a chance to apologize privately, for which I will amend tomorrow.

I waited for Luc to say his goodbyes, once again, pouring nauseous sweetness all over the women. Once he replaced his hat and stepped outside, I went to Maria. For the first time tonight, I breathed freely.

"It's really good to see you, Maria. It's been too long." My smile came forth genuinely.

One of her hands moved up to my face. Her touch against my skin made me want to close my eyes and fall headfirst into her arms. When her finger poked my dimple, she laughed. "I have missed this." My heart warmed. There was still a great deal we needed to talk about, and even more I needed to learn, but one thing was for certain, I was smitten.

35

24 April 1910

Contreras Farm, Menorca, Spain

Isabel

"Maria?"

"Yes, Anita?"

"Would you mind helping me make *Perol* today dear?"

"Oh, yes, I would love that. But you know I never have before, are you sure you want me to help?"

"Every woman needs to know how to cook. I'm afraid part of being a good wife is making your husband's belly just as happy as his heart."

"I'm ready and willing to learn how to cook—" I chuckled. "But I have no husband."

"Not for long . . ." Anita chortled and handed me an apron.

I smiled coyly. Tying the apron on, I took my place behind a large bowl and a handful of ingredients on the table—small round potatoes, juicy tomatoes fresh from her garden, and the striped fresh mullet that Miguel caught yesterday in the cove.

Anita has been very patient in my studies. Besides the potato tortillas which have gotten considerably better tasting, she has taught me how to make *Kaldereta*, the lobster stew, *Macarrones* with gravy, and *crespelis* for dessert. The flower shaped cookies with a jam center were a favorite of Miguel's. Come to think of it, everything was his favorite . . . but not at first. I aspired early on to make him something he would eat before he fed it to the pigs. It took quite some time, but now my presence in the kitchen was no longer feared.

Anita's lessons didn't end in the kitchen. She taught me how to retrieve water from the well, milk the cow—that one took multiple attempts to get anything more than a drop in the bucket—gather eggs from the chickens, beat the rugs, launder clothes, sweep the floors, wash the windows, and Henry taught me how to exercise and groom the horses. One would have assumed I never lived a life of luxury or that of an over indulged miss. And yet, I didn't lack joy in my newfound life.

"What did you think of the Carrasco's guest?" Anita sliced the potatoes into thin wedges.

"Well, he was an interesting fellow."

"He seemed quite taken with you, then turned all his attention to Susana by the time supper had ended. Like he couldn't make up his mind which fair maiden he should be drawn to."

"No, I believe he was being polite to me. He does show an interest in Susana. It is well deserved."

"There's no question who Francisco has eyes for." Anita laughed aloud and slammed her fists into the bowl pounding the fish flat.

My cheeks heated. "I don't know, Anita . . ." My insecurity mounted. I was sure something rekindled with Francisco until the awkward conversation about the property arose. After that he seemed distracted and distant. I did get him to smile before he departed, but it was brief.

"Oh, I have known Francisco his entire life, I think I would know when he cares for someone." She winked and layered the bottom of the clay pan with the potatoes. "He's weighed down with the farm. He's afraid to lose it, and now he's agreed to a partnership with this toff."

"Do you think Susana likes Monsieur Fabron?" I added salt, pepper, and paprika.

"It's hard to say with Susana. She is quite selective, but maybe."

"That's true. For as long as I've known her, she's been headstrong and confident." I recalled how happy she was at the dinner several nights before. The way the stranger fawned all over her must be part of that.

"Well, she has worked quite hard at her studies and now her medical practice. It's good for her to enjoy the attentions of a man. A very handsome man."

"Are you and Miguel really thinking about selling? I mean, I've never heard this mentioned."

Anita clapped her hands and tomato juice sprayed across her cheeks. I laughed at the sight of her.

"Maria . . . oh dear, does it bother you I still call you that?" She reached for my hands and now I was covered with tomato juice and fish entrails. "I know Isabel is your given name but to me you are Maria."

"I don't mind at all. I wish to be called Maria."

"We're getting older, Miguel and I, and one day, yes we will need to sell. We don't have children to pass this on to and it would please me if Francisco were to be the caretaker."

"I'm sure he would manage it nicely."

"Yes, no doubt he would. The offer had been made years ago to Cisco's father. I think its sudden emergence following the loss of Basilio and Cristina may have upset Miguel."

"He did seem rather quiet after that. I believe Francisco handled it well."

"He did. He is quite aware of us. And though Monsieur Fabron seems like a gentleman, his manners that night discussing business at supper were rather offensive. If we are to have him over again, he must not engage in it."

"While I do admit seeing Francisco again was wonderful . . ." I grinned. "I would be okay if we waited until after his guest departed before we host them again."

Anita chuckled, nodding in full agreement.

Hours later, after a lovely bath to get the vegetable oil off my skin and the rank smell of raw fish out from under my fingernails, I took a walk.

Today, however, rather than staying in the Contreras' garden, I ventured farther out. I walked to the creek. If I couldn't see Francisco, the best alternative was the very place he kissed me. I sat down on the same rock and recalled every move he made in that one cherished moment. My fingers grazed my lips, and I couldn't stop the smile that spread as I savored the emotion.

"Srta. Maria?"

36

24 April 1910

Carrasco Ranch, Menorca, Spain

Thomas

Six days I wandered the property since my arrival. Now it's been three days since the dinner at the Contreras', yet nothing to see but the sweaty peasants who worked the fields. *Doesn't she ever leave their home?* The irritations were piling. Francisco's ever watchful eye in the house nettled me, though he didn't know I left my room twice in the middle of the night and entered Susana's room. Tempted to wake her, I resisted. My primary reasons for being here were greater than simple pleasures of the night. Isabel is the reason I must behave. With only three days left to entice her. I had yet to find her alone. Until now . . .

"Srta. Maria?" My prayers had been answered. I galloped to her side. Conveniently hidden under the boughs of a giant oak, she appeared quite at ease in her privacy. I slid off my horse and into her presence. Her beauty stunned me the moment she entered the room at the Contreras' and undoubtedly confounded me now.

"Monsieur Fabron." She stood quickly to her feet. "H—how may I help you?"

Her blonde hair blew in the light breeze across her open neck. The white cotton dress she wore hugged her figure. I fought my desire to follow her curves. *Charm* I reminded myself. *She must find me charming!*

"Milady, *bonne journée*." I reached out to kiss her hand as I wished her a good day. Her hand slid slowly to meet mine.

"I am far from a lady, Monsieur but your French is excellent."

"Oui. I spent some time in different parts of France, mostly Paris and of course, you must know Algiers is French occupied."

"Yes, I am aware of that and Paris is a lovely place to visit." She smiled faintly.

I kissed her fingers lightly, they hinted of lavender blossoms. "The Eiffel Tower, Notre Dame, they speak to my soul."

"Oh, and the Sienne." Her countenance lightened at the talk of France. "Have you ever taken a riverboat on the Sienne?" She took a few steps backward.

"Why yes. May I—walk with you?"

Her eyelashes flickered before she nodded her acquiescence. We silently fell into a slow saunter. I gripped the reins of my horse and trailed next to her. Hypnotized by the sway of her hips, and the slight glisten of sweat beneath her neck. My desire reached unyielding peaks. I tried to inhale her scent as she moved. I pictured her once again on our wedding night. Only this time, the tangible form greatly surpassed the photograph.

"Have you, Monsieur?"

"Uh, forgive me," I stumbled clamoring to recall her question. "My mind has been caught up in business, it forgets to enjoy a moment of freedom. What was your inquiry?"

"Marseille, did you ever have the pleasure of visiting Marseille?"

"Oh yes, and I must say it was the epitome of pleasure." I beamed, offering her the deepest most sincere look a man can surrender. I relished the hint of pink that rose in her cheeks.

"What did you like most about Marseille?"

"Too many things to name only one." I had never been there, and though I was born in Paris, we left when I was two years of age, but she would never know this. My proficiency in French came from my mother and my visits to a red-haired vixen in Madame Salazar's bordello. "What about you? What is your favorite?" We had reached the Contreras' grape vines and remained splendidly hidden in the brush.

"Chateau d'if, I believe. Did you see it, the island prison?"

"Naturally, one cannot miss the Chateau d'if," I concurred.

"I often times took a pleasure cruise around the island and back to Calanque for a picnic."

I found myself admiring the way her eyes lit up with her memories. "Beautiful place, Marseille. How often did you go, you sound quite fond of it?"

"Many times." She glanced down when she answered.

Her ability to lie impressed me, and *Maria* . . . how clever to go by her middle name. She had this family quite fooled as to who she really was. I wonder what she would trade to keep her secret safe.

My eyes dropped to the scooped bodice of her dress which barely reached above her breasts. As she moved, the beginnings of her cleavage peeked out. I glanced around. Would she resist me if I lured her into the vines and kissed her? Would she refuse me if I coaxed her to lie with me under the covering of the grapes?

"I'm sorry, Monsieur." Isabel's eyebrows curved inward. She caught me watching her chest. She carefully clasped her hands in front of her, shielding herself.

"What must you apologize for?" I shook off my stupor and smiled again, but she didn't smile back this time.

"I have leisured too long. I must return."

"Let me escort you home."

"Oh, no, that is quite unnecessary." Her pace picked up and she pivoted quickly to reach the center path.

"I insist." I grabbed her hand a little rougher than planned. She let out a small cry and yanked her hand back.

"I take your leave, Monsieur Fabron." And she ran swiftly out of sight. I could've hopped on my horse and overtaken her with little effort, but this was not how I pictured the allurement to ensue.

I rubbed the back of my neck and paced. Spurts of ire inched up my spine the more I considered my circumstances. I have invested too much time and energy to turn my back on this now. If I can't convince her to leave with me in three days, I will resort to more forceful means. I won't let this charade and my miserable visit go to waste. By Wednesday, there was no doubt in my mind I will leave this dismal country life with Isabel at my side, willing or not.

37

26 April 1910

Carrasco Ranch, Menorca, Spain

Francisco

"Susana?" I stepped inside the house after seeing Charles prep a horse for her departure.

"In here, Cisco." Her voice rose from her bedroom.

"What are you doing?" I entered to find her packing an overnight bag. Her medical kit laid out on her bed.

"Senyora Hernández has gone into labor, but during my last visit the child was positioned wrong in the womb. I'm afraid it's going to be a long night, possibly several if one or both are in danger."

"I'm sorry. That sounds serious. Is there anything I can do to help you?"

"No, I just don't know when I'll return."

"Don't worry about us. We are wrapping up the final reap, and the season is practically over. The salutary work you do is much more important than being here."

"Do you plan on having the traditional dinner?" She paused with a garment in her hand.

"I don't know," I mumbled. I didn't feel much like having the customary celebratory meal this time. Especially without our parent's here. "I'm not sure it's a good idea this year."

"We must. You know they would want us to."

"Then I'll wait for your return. I doubt I will feel much like celebrating alone."

"But you aren't alone, dear brother." Her gaze softened. "When will you give Maria the item you found?"

After we retrieved our parent's belongings, Susana and I searched the papers for Maria—or Isabel's—personal effects as well. Nothing was found of hers, but something of her parents. "I want to soon, but privately . . ."

"It's time you admit how you feel about her."

"How I feel?"

Her eyes rolled dramatically. "It's quite apparent to all of us how much she means to you. It's time you told her."

I frowned. "I don't know how to explain my feelings. I'm all caught up in the moment when I'm with her but I still have questions."

"What questions? She cares for you, I see it." The clock in the hallway chimed and forced Susana to finish stuffing in a rush. "I must go, can we speak of this when I return?"

"Yes, yes, of course. But please allow me to have someone take you so you don't have to balance your bags on a horse."

"No, I know you need the wagon for town. I can't let you be without it."

"I'm not leaving until tomorrow. If Guillermo drove the team for you, they'd be back by tonight."

She chuckled, no doubt knowing Guillermo's skill at being steady and swift. "That would be most helpful, Cisco." She closed her bag. "Oh, and please say adéu to Monsieur Fabron for me. I tried looking for him, but he must be out on the property. I understand he will be leaving us soon."

Heat trickled up my neck and settled into my cheeks. The very mention of his name put me on edge. Susana found his complimentary nature flattering, but it gnawed gratingly at me. Everything about him seemed off—the way he dressed, his knowing expressions, vanishing for hours at a time, even the bottles of liquor that have somehow walked away—the list could've very well continued on, but I realized my sister had stopped moving and stared at me quizzically.

"You don't like him, do you?" The right side of her mouth lifted partway.

I huffed. "No, I don't, and I can't pinpoint exactly why. I know it's probably nothing, but his whole presence feels fraudulent. He tries too hard to please everyone... everyone but me, of course."

"I think you're being unreasonable."

"You saw what happened at the Contreras' and the way he insisted on discussing business... at their home during supper!"

"He's ambitious."

"He's cunning, Susana. I had already mentioned to him before that night that we didn't need to speak of it this year, that we could discuss it at a later date, yet he still persisted for heaven's sake."

Susana remained attentive but said nothing.

"And I hear him at night. I know it's not Javier because he would never enter our home after dark without knocking. I don't know why he's moving about late at night, but he is. Even alcohol in father's cabinet is missing. The good wines he and mother enjoyed before bed. Several bottles are missing. What would be the reason for that? You don't drink. And just last night—" I stopped and realized I was keeping her. "Never mind, you must go."

"No, tell me." Her expression turned serious.

"Last night when Henry dropped off Anita's tortillas for the men, he pulled me aside. He said that Maria and Fabron were seen talking in the fields the day before. Then only moments later, Maria rushed back to the house in a frenzy. Henry added that she appeared visibly upset, but when he tried to talk to her, she told him not to worry." I took a breath for the first time since I rattled off my list of crimes against him. "Susana, I know he's been kind to you. He's been amiable and flirty, and I suppose any woman would be thrilled to receive his attention, but you are better than this."

"Francisco!" Susana's face swung from stunned to angry. "What is going on in that head of yours?" Her cheeks turned bright red. I had not seen her this mad in quite some time. "I only asked you to say goodbye for me. I have no unrealistic forethoughts of Monsieur Fabron and myself. Yes, he's charming but for goodness sake, Cisco, you know me better than that. I am not some capricious adolescent who flings herself at the slightest attention. I know what I want and it's not Monsieur Fabron!"

While I was thoroughly grateful for her words, I frowned with regret. "I'm sorry, sister. I did not mean to offend." I placed my hand on her shoulder and squeezed. "My mind is not in the right place and I find this man insufferable. The sooner he leaves, the better."

Susana backed up. "I'm not cross with you." She exhaled. "I appreciate your concern, but I hope you have more belief in me than that."

"I do. You are one of the strongest women I know." Then I grinned wickedly. "God help the man you do fall in love with."

Susana stepped over to me and clasped my hands. "You can be pretty insufferable yourself." She smiled. "But I know that you have done your very best to fill father's shoes."

My eyes dropped to my boots. "I haven't come remotely close to father's capabilities."

"Oh, but you have Francisco." She let go and moved both her hands to my cheeks. "You have protected this farm and all that you love exceptionally well. Do not worry about me, dear brother, I can take care of myself. However, I do believe there is a young woman who would benefit greatly from a knight in shining armor. Don't wait. Tell her now."

I smiled and brought her hands to my lips. "I love you Susana."

"I love you too, brother."

38

26 April 1910

Contreras Farm, Menorca, Spain

Thomas

Crack! A twig broke under my boot, I froze. I must be careful. I took another step forward. Darkness shrouded my approach as I peeked through one window. *Nothing.* I moved to a second window and waited. A sole candlestick glowed in the corner. The nearly empty bottle of gin in my hand was like drinking sweet juice, but it was better than nothing at all. I resigned to leave when she suddenly entered the room.

Though slightly blurred, my sight followed Isabel's every move—slow and measured. She sat on a stool near her wash basin, her poise rendered as graceful as *Venus de Milo*. Photographs of the famed marble statue extended beyond the walls of the Louvre and here, it was if the goddess herself descended to earth.

Surely Isabel was unaware of my presence but teased when her dress dropped off her shoulders. I held my breath. A simple chemise remained, but I hoped not for long. She reached for a cloth and dipped it into the basin. Tugging at the lace, she let her cover slip to her waist. Her bare back faced me. I let out a disappointed groan. With another gentle dip, she squeezed the excess water out of the cloth and smoothed it over her arms, her shoulders, and her chest. I'd seen naked women before, why did this one make me pine, and yearn and work for her attention?

I stepped closer. *Crack!* Another twig. *Merde!* My cuss came out significantly louder than planned. Her head whipped back, and I dropped to my knees. Movement sounded as though she approached the window. I wanted to look, but by the time I did, the curtains were drawn tight.

Slamming my fist against the ground, I fumed for several minutes before I left the Contreras'. It has never been this hard for me to get a woman. *And this one belongs to me!*

After our brief visit at the creek, I tried two additional times to appeal to her in a gentlemanly manner. Once, I brought her and Anita fresh bouquets of lilies though Isabel had fallen ill and was unable to leave her room. The second time, I found her in the garden alone, but again, she graciously excused herself and vanished inside the house. Tomorrow—tomorrow is the day I must convince Isabel that her future lies with me and me alone.

I withdrew to my horse, which I left in the fields. Once on top, I rode back towards the Carrasco's but did not enter. I needed to formulate a better plan. Isabel has not made this easy. With the contract her father signed, this was my one and only option to improved prosperity. It had been over a year since this endeavor had been pursued, and the whole affair has taken much more time than anticipated. *It ends tomorrow.*

I went to the porch and sat down on a step. The more I allowed my predicament to fog my mind the more aggravated I became. No matter what the consequence, I was determined to not let a simple farm life, or an olive farmer stand in my way of my future. *I will get my due reward.*

Later that night, in the quietness of my guest room, I retrieved ink and a quarter sheet of foolscap from the desk. By sole candlelight I began to write.

Dearest Isabel,

I crinkled the draft in my fist and threw it in the hearth. *You idiot.* I chided myself. They don't know her as Isabel. I retrieved another sheet.

Dearest Maria,

My jaw grew rigid. In order to make my deceptions real, I had to recognize that there were feelings between Francisco and Isabel. The more I contemplated this, the more I wanted to drive a sword through him. Jacque's wise words arose from the darker corners of my mind. Before he returned to Algiers, he convinced me that it would be prudent to avoid mayhem or violence to enjoy the fruits of my labors. He, of course, also convinced me I had the skill to deviate Isabel from her life here. Something that has proven to be impossible. Until now . . .

It has been far too long without you. I yearn to spend time together. Please meet me at sunset at the creek.
Yours truly
F.

Though I penned the *F* to lead her to believe it was Francisco. I was distinctly aware that Francisco intended to make a supply trip to town tomorrow and Srta. Carrasco departed earlier today to assist Sra. Hernández in her delivery.

With brother and sister out of the way, their absence would allow my designs to fall into place quite easily. By this time tomorrow night, Isabel will be gone, and they will be led to believe she left on her own accord. I sealed the letter with a satisfactory grin and set it aside to have it delivered by a stable hand in the morning.

I penned one last letter for Arthur, alerting him to my return and to ready the house for a guest. I didn't relish in the possibility of Isabel's coercion, but would no longer play these games. If only she allowed me the time, she would see that I have superior qualities for a mate. I could give her everything she wanted, much more than a rancher for a husband. I only needed the chance to prove it.

At dusk the next day, I waited behind the trunk of the thickest tree near the creek. If she came, it confirmed her attachment to Francisco. Something that I would have to accept or ignore but mattered little at the moment.

Horse's hooves thumped proportionally against the ground and suggested a rapid approach. A lump caught in my throat at the sight of her. Her very appearance took my breath away. Even without the silks and parasols, her beauty shone as if she was the daughter of Aphrodite herself.

Once again, I criticized the behavior that I'd been reduced to. If only things had proceeded as planned, I would've never had to stoop to such childish deception. Yet in the end, I justified my actions. She is my intended, bartered and sold by her own father. And nothing, nothing at all will stop me from getting what is rightfully mine.

A glimpse of the descending sun soothed me. I did not fear anything, nor did I expect any further complications, but I had always found comfort in the shroud of night. The whisky I had taken from the Contreras' the day I entertained Anita was gripped tightly in my palm. I pressed the rim to my lips and let the cool liquid tickle my tongue before it slithered down my throat. *Yes, this is going to be a good night.*

I watched as she slowed to a trot then stopped. She scanned around until she apprehensively slid off the saddle. The reins remained tight in her hands. She was a vision of near perfection. Her hair was braided and draped down one side of her neck, though errant strands framed her porcelain complexion. Her dress was a delicate shade of yellow and the ease in which she moved enticed me to run to her, though I waited.

Even from my distance I saw the color of her eyes and the shade of her lips. It was apparent to me she had preened for this encounter with *Francisco*. I rubbed the scruff on my chin slowly as I studied her and fought to keep the fiery sting of jealousy buried. She might believe that Francisco is right for her . . . she will learn that is not the case.

"Francisco?" she whispered, "are you here?"

I took another long swig before I straightened my tie. This would be our first visit based on truths.

"Francisco, is that you?" Doubt rose in her voice.

I inhaled long and hard then stepped into her light.

She gasped.

Her lantern fell to the ground as she whirled on her heels to run. This time she would not get far. She tried to wriggle free when I grabbed her wrist. The fading light expounded her terrified expression. I reached for her other wrist and held both with an unyielding grip.

"Please, stop," she screamed and twisted. I pulled her close, close enough for me to feel the heat emanating off her skin.

"That's enough, Isabel."

Her eyes magnified. She froze. "I—I'm not Isabel."

I smiled. She glanced down as I leaned forward. My lips enunciated every word slowly. "Isabel Marie Fontaine."

Her breathing elevated. Her cries came out as whimpers. "No, no you have the wrong person."

"I know who you are." My upper lip curled. "I can't say the same for your *family* here. Does your beau know you are betrothed?"

"I'm not—"

"Stop!" I yelled loud enough to stun her. "Stop it," I said through gritted teeth. "The game is over."

Her body stilled under my touch. "Thomas," she relented weakly. "Thomas Chastain." Tears slid from her lashes. I bowed my head in acknowledgement. My lips pressed faintly against her cheek and brushed her tears away. The salt tingled on my tongue. Even now she tempted me.

"H—how did you find me?"

"Were you trying *not* to be found?"

She flinched but the hold on her arms gave her little freedom. I inhaled deeply taking her sweet scent through my cavities and emphasized, "you will complete the contract your father arranged before his . . . untimely death."

"No, please, please don't make me," she whimpered. My jaw tightened then released. *Her fright will pass.*

I gripped harder. "I can make you happy, Isabel. I will take you back to Marseille, your home. You will have all the pleasures of your childhood and more. You will want for nothing."

"I *want* to stay here."

"Why?"

"This is my home now."

"What can that foolish farm boy offer you?"

She turned her head. Her insubordination irritated me. "These people are good and kind. They care for me."

"I had every intention of being good to you." My mouth bowed into a frown. "You never gave me the occasion." She kept her face turned. I leaned in again and brushed my lips against the skin in the nape of her neck. She stiffened. I tipped back as my temper smoldered. Then I cautioned, "you will learn to love me."

Her eyes met mine and though there was no softness in them, the endless blue drew me in with her pleas. "There must be other means. Please don't force me marry you."

I considered her words. I didn't much enjoy having to force someone to be with me. I'd never had trouble in the past. Though Isabel would be a tantalizing treat, I wanted what she came with more.

"Well, I am a businessman." I jutted out my chin. "I can be open to negotiation."

A flicker of light reached her countenance. Irritated at how quickly she jumped at the prospect, I wanted to slap that flicker away, but I held tight. "Yes," she asked, "what, what can I offer you in place of marriage?"

"Well, the contract positioned me for a great deal of money, an estate, and a business. What else would be comparable?"

"I will contact my grand-mère in France. She will arrange for you to receive my inheritance. If you leave me be, I will give you everything."

I laughed aloud. My eyes washed over her innocence. "You are a naïve little thing aren't you."

Her nose wrinkled to her glower, but she remained silent.

"Now that would normally be enough, but in this arrangement. I only get your inheritance if you marry me first. That's the law."

She held her breath. "I will give it to you willingly. Please don't make me marry you."

"I have no assurances from a liar." I scowled. "You've deceived everyone and now suddenly I'm expected to believe you, trust you?"

Tears spilled onto her perfect cheeks once more. If she'd been more compliant, this could've been a deeply romantic moment.

"I have a different proposal."

She waited.

"You willingly return with me back to Algeria, marry me, we take control of your inheritance and within a short amount of time you can return to this quagmire never to see me again."

She frowned. She did not seem to find my offer appealing. "How much time?"

"A few months. Long enough to make sure the transactions are complete. Then you can leave."

Anger appeared on her brow and her skin sparked a rosy pink. "Why did you create this elaborate scheme to deceive us? Why did you have to bring the others in to this and pretend to be a businessman?"

"I didn't pretend. I am a businessman. I fully intend to take the Carrasco olives. However, I don't intend to pay for them."

"That will destroy them," she cried. "They have done nothing to you."

"On the contrary, Mademoiselle. It is apparent Francisco has done much harm."

"You're an evil man." She spit in my face. "If you were going to force me to marry you, why didn't you take me at the first available moment?"

I gripped her arm tighter as she let out a cry. "I've never had to steal anything, much less a woman!" Her assumptions riled me. Reaching into my suit pocket I retrieved a handkerchief and wiped my chin.

"You can't compel me to marry you."

"I can. Within the peripheries of the law, the contract your father signed with me is legally binding. He *gave* you to me."

Her next words came out weakly. "What if I refuse?"

My laugh began as a chortle but grew into a full-blown laugh. She did not share my humor. "Then . . ." My eyes pierced hers. "I will destroy *everything* you love."

Her sobs came fast.

"Enough!" My patience wore thin. I was exasperated with this place and these games. "I tried to make this easy, Isabel. You, you were the one who brought us to this. Only you are to blame."

Her body trembled. Her skin whitened where my fingers held tight. I released her. She didn't move. "Do we have an understanding?"

Her nod was slight but sure.

"Wise decision . . . milady." I tipped my hat. "I need to wrap up my business with the ranch. Be ready to leave within the hour and Isabel—" I thrust her back up on the horse. "Don't test me."

39

27 April 1910

Contreras Farm, Menorca, Spain

Isabel

Thankfully, Penelope knew the path home. Tears blurred my sight and the cries which stifled my throat yearned for freedom. Thomas' foul liqueured scent fixed to me like a hot linen. I tried unsuccessfully to shake free of his touch and his horrid threats.

As I approached the Contreras' farm, I slowed. Glancing behind me, I sighed with relief that Thomas did not follow. I looked to my wrists where red lines marked my skin from his clutch. How could my father have ever believed Thomas Chastain was a good man? How could I have been this foolish or this naïve to believe I could hide from such a man?

And now, my friends will suffer for it.

I trotted past the porch. Through the window I caught sight of Miguel and Anita in the kitchen. They were dancing. Tears pooled in my eyes with my last image of them. A beautiful memory contrary to the profound sadness in my heart.

Since that first time Miguel taught me to ride, I had been on Penelope a dozen times and came to love this mare's gentleness, but this also gave me the confidence I needed for what I was about to do next. I leaned down and patted her neck. "Alright Penelope," I whispered, "take me away sweet horse. We can't let anyone hurt them, right?" She neighed as if she understood. I kicked Penelope to a slightly faster speed and steered her down the road that led away from their farm. From the droplets on my hands, I knew I was crying, but didn't stop to brush them away. I needed to get as far away as possible—as quickly as possible.

On the road, I spied the Carrasco Ranch to the right, and the ache in my chest amplified. Francisco's image stirred my soul. Even if I married Thomas for a short time and tried to return, Francisco might not take me back. I would be a used piece of property. He might never understand why I would've chosen to go with Thomas in the first place, and never look at me the same way. I shook my head and tried to think of another way.

"What if I found my way to Mahón?" I reasoned. "It might take me all night, but once there, I could send a telegram to Grand-mère." Buoyed by the idea, I lifted my head and let the breeze of the jaunt fill my lungs and strengthen my limbs.

Grand-mère would've received my post by now and was most likely aware of my survival. Would she allow me to return to Marseille? Or would she think I was a silly girl and lecture me on my responsibilities? My confidence wavered. There was still a possibility she could insist I do the right thing and fulfill the contract with the man Papa had chosen. Or would Thomas only follow me to France and threaten to hurt her like he threatened here?

I cannot let that happen!

It seemed that the only true option was to disappear. I couldn't live with myself if anyone suffered because of me.

I pulled Penelope's reins to a stop at the fork in the road. I peered to the right. I soaked in the memory of the man who lived at the end of that dirt road. Francisco's name slipped off my tongue with agonizing finality. If only we had met under different circumstances or a different time. Wishing I could be more to him at this moment was hopeless. The quicker I created separation, the safer he would be.

I turned back towards the main road but stopped. Everything around me had stilled but the terrifying sound of approaching hooves. My head twisted around at the very moment a fist slammed the side of my head. The force hurled me off Penelope and easily to the ground on my weak shoulder. I cried out in pain. Attempting to push myself upward, I faltered as the world spun around me.

Darkness loomed in the form of a man.

My assailant's coarse touch chilled me to the bone. I squinted to find the same cruel eyes that threatened me only moments ago, spearing through me. A warm liquid trickled down my face. When I wiped it, bright red blood smeared across my fingers. When Thomas shook me, my head rolled with the quake.

"Isabel!"

I caught my name.

"Isabel!"

His lips curled and spit at lightning speed. I hardly kept up.

"Do you think I'm foolish?" He raged, then lifted me up to a horse, I fell forward until he secured himself behind me. It was his horse.

His deep voice growled in my ear. "I warned you. Now you don't get to say goodbye."

Within seconds we launched down the road at a rapid pace. My woozy head fell back against Thomas' chest while my throat fought to keep my stomach from erupting. Suddenly, his body tightened behind me and his arm around my waist constricted with additional force.

"Dammit!" Thomas scowled.

The sound of wheels had reached my ears. I lifted my eyes to see an oncoming wagon. My lips parted at sight of the driver.

"Luc!" The cry came out in a panic as the team came to an abrupt stop. "What happened? Is that Maria?" Francisco's voice sailed to my ears as he sputtered out a string of questions. "Where are you taking her?"

"She's injured." Thomas spoke with less urgency. "She fell off her horse."

"Take her to Susana!" Francisco demanded standing up in the wagon.

My comprehension improved the longer we remained still. I peered towards Francisco.

Thomas' grip around my waist tightened. "Isn't Susana at a birth? I'm taking Isabel to Es Mercadal."

And he called me a proficient liar. Everything that came out of his mouth was a fib. He had no intention of taking me to town except to put me on a ship. My breaths came quick—he also called me Isabel. Did Francisco notice?

"The closest doctor is hours away," Francisco jumped from his seat. "Anita can help. Hand her to me, I'll put her in the wagon."

Thomas remained stiff behind me. For a moment I feared he would set off again. He could easily outrun a wagon filled with supplies, but if Francisco unhitched one of his stout horses,

Thomas' horse would be easily surpassed. I held my breath, sure that Thomas was calculating this.

"Your wagon is full," Thomas yelled. "I can take her faster by horse."

"I will make it comfortable for her." Francisco moved to the back of his wagon. Thomas took advantage of the moment and pulled me solidly against him. Through my hair, his hot breath lingered on my ear. The stale odor of liqueur and tobacco curled my toes. "If you say anything, Isabel," he threatened. "I will kill everyone, starting with him."

My throat constricted and he released his grip. Francisco stepped up to the horse and reached out for me. The tenderness in his arms as he carried me to the wagon, ripped me in two. I let my head fall against his chest and felt the rapid thump of his heart before he laid me down across two bags of flour. Once I was settled, he cupped my cheek tenderly. "We will be there shortly."

He jumped back up to the bench and grabbed the reins. With a swift flick we were off and headed back towards the Contreras'. The air that swirled above me helped refresh my mind and as we traveled, my dizziness faded. Piecing the event together, I gained a more stable composure and realized Thomas had attacked me. He must've seen me fleeing and followed me from the Contreras'.

Panic seized my chest. *If he is willing to strike me, a woman, what will he do next?*

A horse neighed from behind the wagon. Believing it to be Thomas, I never dared look up until I heard Francisco's voice.

"Anita? Miguel?" He yelled as we rounded the bend to the front of the house. Francisco scooped me into his arms and rushed up the porch steps by the time Anita appeared. Breezing past her, he went straight to my bed and laid me down.

"Oh, my goodness," Anita said as she flew into the room followed closely by Miguel. "What happened?"

"She fell off her horse." A commanding voice claimed.

I didn't fall of my horse. My mind whirled. But the moment I glanced at the others, I caught sight of Thomas hovering in the doorway. Gooseflesh rippled my arms. "Yes, I fell."

Francisco removed my shoes as Anita checked my head. "You're bleeding. Where else does it hurt, love?"

I stared into her sweet eyes, wishing I could tell her the truth of what really happened. "M—my shoulder." I swallowed hard.

"I found her on the ground." Thomas stepped forward. "The horse must've bucked her off."

"I told you it was too soon to let her go off on her own." Anita wagged an angry finger at Miguel.

"What horse, Maria?" Miguel quizzed.

"P—Penelope."

"Penelope?" He rubbed his chin. "No, that can't be right."

"It's true." Thomas insisted. "I witnessed it from afar." He stared at me and though no words were exchanged between us, his earlier threats rang clear.

Anita clasped his hands in hers. "Bless you, Monsieur Fabron, bless you for finding and helping her."

I shuddered. *He's not Luc Fabron. He's Thomas Chastain. The man who won't stop until he has what he wants.*

Anita knelt to my side. "My dear child..." She kissed my forehead. "I'm most grateful it was not worse. Miguel, get rags and warm water." She moved her hands all over me checking for breaks or bruises.

In the flurry of activity, a smirk emerged from the fiend himself. Then he bowed pretentiously. "I will be outside if you need anything."

"Do you want me to see if Susana has returned?" Francisco asked Anita.

"Yes, please."

With Thomas out of sight, I stretched forth my fingers to grasp Francisco's. He regarded me and smiled. "You will be fine, Maria, you're safe now." Tears sprung from my eyes. Francisco cupped my cheek and wiped the moisture away with his thumb. I leaned into his touch. "Everything will be okay," he declared and disappeared.

Anita went to remove my muddy dress when I grabbed her arm and stopped her movement. In that brief second, she gazed upon me with a fear I had not seen in a long time. *She is worried about me.* I wanted to tell her—explain what really happened, but at what consequence? Could this wicked man be stopped? Miguel owned a shotgun, but he was old, hardly able to defend us against a man like Thomas.

My touch softened. "It's alright, Anita," I assured but didn't look her in the eyes. Adjusting myself to a sitting position, I took quick breaths to regain my composure. My mind grew clearer by the second. "I'm fine."

"You're not fine!"

"It doesn't hurt much now."

"Well, let's let Susana confirm."

Miguel entered with a bowl of hot water and some rags.

Several minutes later Susana rushed in with Francisco at her side. "Are you okay?" She moved to my side and immediately into action. Francisco stood at the door. "What can I do?"

"Francisco, wait outside. I need space to work."

He stepped out. My face fell. I wanted to see him. I *needed* to see him.

It was just as I thought—only a cut on the head and a sore shoulder, no broken bones, and no serious damage. The dirt on my dress had come from the fall and led them to believe my condition was much worse than it really was.

Susana finished bandaging the cut. "Rest tonight and tomorrow, Maria. You'll be back to normal shortly, I promise." She kissed me on the cheek, stepped out, but paused in the doorway. "You can go in now Francisco, but only for a moment. Let her rest."

He anxiously moved to my side. "May I?" He pointed to the edge of my bed. I nodded. Every part of my heart ruptured as I tried to memorize the contours of his face for the last time.

"Why were you out riding so late?" His fingers brushed my hair from my face and his hand rested against my cheek.

"I—I, um," Movement next to my door silenced me. Thomas' intimidating form leaned against the frame. His stare blazed through me, but when his hate-filled eyes shifted to Francisco, my breath hitched.

Francisco's reaction grew dark at my behavior. He circled around to see what drew my attention. When his face returned to mine it displayed confusion.

"I w—wanted to ride t—tonight," I stuttered, desperate to recapture the compassion Francisco entered with, but it was one more thing Thomas stole from me. My nose stung. Tears simmered hot and threatened to break.

Francisco relaxed with a gentle smile. His fingers trailed my jaw then tugged at my chin. When our eyes met, his lips curved further, and his dimple deepened. "Are you sure there's nothing else troubling you?"

"Susana says she must rest," Thomas called from the door.

"One moment." The muscles in Francisco's jaw tightened but softened when he gazed at me once more. "I will return in the morning, Maria."

Oh, how I wished for him to stay.

"Francisco, Susana is waiting for us." Thomas interrupted again, his tone sharp and penetrating. Francisco released a slight exhale before he pulled my hand to his lips. The gentleness in his touch both pleased and terrified me. I refused to look at Thomas' reaction.

"I hope you recover quickly." Thomas' insincere words fell on deaf ears. I only beheld the beautiful man I'd grown to cherish.

I hesitated under Francisco's touch, undoubtedly knowing whatever I did would be witnessed by Thomas. *If I'm being forced to leave, I will not allow him to pilfer my goodbye.* I tugged Francisco towards me and wrapped my arms around his neck. Settling my mouth against the tender skin below his ear, I rested my head on his shoulder and drank in his earthy scent. His arms wound around my lower back and squeezed.

When I opened my eyes, Thomas' black eyes pierced me with a glower I had never seen, but I ignored him. Shifting my sights to the angles of Francisco's face, this embrace became more than just a farewell, it was a bequest—for half of my heart would remain here with him.

When we released and my gaze drifted to the doorway once more, Thomas was gone. A knot formed in my chest. Not that I wanted him to still be there, but a slight nagging reminded me of how malicious his schemes could be. He had shown that his motivations reached far above reason.

"I will see you in the morning." Francisco kissed my hand once more and winked his goodbye. When he left the room, all warmth departed with him.

40

28 April 1910

Contreras Farm, Menorca, Spain

Miguel

"Anita! Quick wake up!" I ran through the house frantically trying to light a match for the lantern. "Anita!" I bellowed again.

Maria rushed out from her bedroom.

"Child, go back to bed, you're injured." I scrambled to put my boots on.

"What's wrong. What's happening?" Terror filled Maria's tired eyes.

"The barn!" Anita's screams ripped through the house.

Maria flew to her side and the two of them ran to the window. Their cries multiplied.

I'd already seen it. The barn was fully engulfed in flames.

"Anita, find Henry."

"Let me help!" Maria scrambled to put a robe on.

"No!" I insisted, but my growl melted under her stare.

"Please, Miguel. You're my family."

I succumbed. "Help me with the animals."

As we stepped outside Francisco's horse came flying up the path. He hopped off before it came to a stop. "Quick, the buckets."

I placed my hand on his shoulder. "It's too late, we can't stop it now. Help me with the animals."

The animals had the good sense to flee the barn but were scattered across the yard. The heat of the blaze kept us back and the dark smoke that swirled above cast a gloomy shadow against the budding dawn.

I'm too damn old for this. Maybe I should've sold to Francisco or Monsieur Fabron when talk of it came up.

"Maria, the chickens. They're hiding in the garden. Close the gate and we can keep them in there."

"Okay." She pulled her robe tight and rushed to the side of the house.

"Francisco, can you help me round up the horses? We can tie them up on the far side, away from the smoke."

Susana came down the road in the wagon. Luc followed behind her on his horse. *Good more hands.*

"Miguel!" Anita shrieked at the top of her lungs. "Miguel!"

"What in God's name are you screaming for, woman?"

"Henry! I can't find Henry!"

I exchanged looks with Francisco. It took him only a second to sprint from my side and towards the barn.

"No! Francisco!" I couldn't get my old legs to follow at that speed and hobbled after him. Flames leapt angrily upward below the billows of thick black smoke. By the time I reached the front of the barn, the searing crack of wood collapsing, reverberated before me. I jumped backward. To my horror the roof disappeared, and Cisco was nowhere to be found.

"Where is he?" Maria ran to my side.

I rubbed my forehead. Black soot covered my face and hands. "I—I don't know."

Her eyes tore from mine and scanned the scene. Ash fluttered down from above as if it were snowing, something I had only seen in pictures. Maria wrung her hands anxiously and paced. I suspected Francisco had entered the barn but didn't say this out loud. Additional cracking confirmed one side had now buckled. I reached for Maria just as she leaped forward and held her back.

"Francisco!" Maria's cries soared above the scorching timber.

Anita arrived a moment later, attempting to drag her away, but she refused to go anywhere.

Susana rushed to our side. "Where's Francisco?" Her expression matched the tormented realization. "No!" she shrieked. "Please, no." Doubling over, she gripped her chest. With Anita struggling to keep Maria back, I moved to comfort Susana.

Within seconds, a bulky form appeared from the back of the barn. It was difficult to make out who it was in the darkness but with a surety it was a person. As I ran towards the figure, the outline of one man carrying another one emerged. The heat from the flames fought to distance everyone, but the further the form stumbled from the barn, the closer we could get.

In the glow of the flames, Francisco's familiar silhouette held a lifeless Henry over his shoulder. They collapsed to the ground.

"We need help!" I peered around. Three women rushed behind me to where the men fell. "Where's Monsieur Fabron?" I shouted. I knew he arrived with Susana but was nowhere to be seen. Maybe he's rounding up the animals.

"Quick, help me move them." I directed the women forward. "We are too close to the barn." I grabbed Henry's arms and pulled. My back throbbed in pain, but a surge of energy kicked in. I needed to get this boy away from the structure. The remaining walls were close to coming down. Susana and Maria each grabbed one of Francisco's arms but barely budged him. He was too much for their petite forms. Anita stepped in and between the three women they drug him a couple of meters. Once Henry was down near the trees, I went back to help.

"Susana, see to Henry. He's not breathing." Tears flowed down her cheeks. "It's okay," I placed a hand on her shoulder. "I will take care of your brother. I will get him to safety, please go."

Every muscle in my body screamed as I bent down once more for Cisco. "Maria, Anita, you take his legs." Each woman moved swiftly on my command and we were able to get him to where Susana was treating Henry.

"Tell me what to do!" Maria cried, rushing over. She tenderly moved Francisco's unresponsive head to her lap. As she brushed her fingers through his hair, parts of his singed tips fell off in her hands.

I remembered in my military days; we could get a man's heart to beat by pushing on it. "Lay him flat, Maria."

She did. I knelt next to him and curled my fist into a ball and pounded. Opening his mouth for air, I pounded again then pressed my ear to his chest. His heartbeat was faint. I continued until it strengthened, and he coughed. Maria kissed his forehead. Her tears trickled to his cheeks.

I took a deep breath and met Susana's eyes, they were red and swollen. She shook her head subtly and drew my sight to the lifeless body at her side. A lump caught in my throat. Her attention shifted to Francisco.

"No!" Anita cried, and knelt next to Henry. "Oh, please no."

It had been a long time since my eyes stung with tears. I put my arms around my sweet wife and let her sob into my shoulder. The realization that swiftly registered pricked at my chest. Henry was gone—and at sixteen. A gamut of emotion built. Henry had a loving family, but I still considered him one of my own.

Maria's flushed cheeks drained of color. Her eyes shifted from us and Henry to Francisco, then something beyond. They were filled with fear. Her whole body trembled when I came to hold her.

"This is all my fault." She sobbed. "This is all because of me."

"No, Maria." I drew her to my chest. "It was an accident. Henry probably fell asleep with a lantern on."

My shirt became drenched with her tears.

Susana peered over to us. "Francisco will be okay, let's get him into the house." The four of us lifted him up and carried him inside. Maria led us to her bed. The same one she herself was brought back from the dead after the shipwreck. We laid him down while Anita and Susana prepared to tend to his injuries. Two significant burns appeared on one arm and a smaller one on his cheek.

I reached for Maria's hand. It shook fiercely under my own. "Will you help me attend to Henry?"

She assented and we quietly slipped out.

The twinge in my chest grew as I scanned the damage. The fire had taken the whole barn but when nothing else fueled it, only embers remained. Black wood and black smoke surrounded us. When I caught sight of Henry, I no longer cared about the barn. Tears fell once more as I stood over him. He was strapping for a young man but right now his form curled like a baby. His face, smooth and calm as though he slumbered like one too.

Maria wrapped her arm around my waist. Her sniffles multiplied. "He was too young."

Words caught in my throat. "H—his mother will be devastated. He was her eldest."

"What should we do?"

"His mother will understand the need to bury him quickly. Even if we sent word this morning, I doubt she could be here before tomorrow." I wiped my brows. Black soot settled into the creases of my palms. I glanced around. "If we leave him outside much longer, the pests will get to him."

"There." Maria pointed to the largest almond tree. Her voice trembled as she spoke. "He loved to sit under that tree when his work was complete."

"Sí, I believe he would like that." I took a deep breath, peeked down at Henry, then back up to Maria. I wasn't sure we could move him without help. "Have you seen Monsieur Fabron?"

Maria's form stiffened. A look of panic skirted her face. My brows furrowed. "Something wrong?"

She shook her head. "I thought he arrived with Susana."

"Yes, me too. Maybe he's still rounding up the animals. We could really use his help."

Maria stood to her full height and cupped my jaw. When she leaned in and kissed my cheek, she spoke with confidence. "I will help you. I will try my best."

I retrieved two shovels from the shed and we began to dig beneath Henry's tree. I had to show Maria how to hold the tool, but she used every bit of energy she had to dig a grave . . . a grave, no less. Two hours into it, Anita arrived with water. "Francisco woke up," she said. "He wants to see you both."

"You go Maria, I will finish up here, we're almost done. It won't be as deep as a normal grave but decent enough to keep him safe."

Maria stood up and squeezed my arm. "I'm sorry about Henry." She bit her bottom lip. "And I want you to know how much I love you. I've never told you that."

My hand covered hers. "I love you too."

As she slipped away, I finished the hole. Leaning on my shovel I studied the blanket that covered our dear Henry and I couldn't recall a more tragic night in my entire life.

41

28 April 1910

Contreras Farm, Menorca, Spain

Isabel

I knocked on the door before I entered even though it was my own room. Susana moved away from the bed. Her expression alarmed me.

"Oh, Maria, your head is bleeding again. What happened?"

My hand flew to my forehead. A moistness leaked below the bandage. "I probably hit it by accident. We were, um, we were digging."

"Digging?" Susana gasped. Her hand flew to her mouth. She must've remembered why.

"I'm sorry." I glanced her way, tears pricking my eyes, "I shouldn't have said anything."

"For Henry?" An exasperated voice spoke from behind Susana. She moved out of the way to reveal Francisco.

I nodded. How could I even look upon him? Everything that has happened to these families came about because of me. There was no doubt in my mind, Thomas was behind this. I, alone, have brought this tragedy upon them.

Susana reached for my hand and tugged me forward to Francisco's side, then quickly vanished. Francisco's arms were bound with linen and there was a smaller bandage covering his right cheek. Black soot appeared along his hairline, most likely the remnants from when they washed his face. He forced his tired eyes open on my account. Less than 12 hours ago, our positions had been reversed. He had been sitting at this very edge while I lay injured. I reached for his hand. His fingers curled through mine.

"Maria?" His whisper broke the silence. "Are you okay?"

I couldn't stop my cry, it slipped out without control. My head lowered to his shoulder and I sobbed. This time, it really was goodbye. I just didn't know how to face it. His other hand went to my hair. He rubbed it soothingly as I inhaled the smoke and eucalyptus that emanated from his skin.

"Maria, I'm sorry I didn't amend things sooner. I was occupied with business and lost sight of what was right. I let pride—"

I placed one finger gently over his mouth to silence him, then moved my tip tenderly across his dry and cracked lips. I leaned in and kissed him. A simple last kiss for the man I loved.

"Rest now," I whispered.

I stood up and went to the corner, retrieving my shell box from the desk then blew out the candle before stopping at the door. His gaze never wavered.

"Sleep well, Francisco."

He smiled and my heart collapsed.

I placed my box on the rocking chair in the kitchen and retrieved a book from the counter. Grabbing a shawl, I wrapped it around me as I stepped outside and back to the tree. The sun had moved directly above us now. Miguel had laid Henry and the blanket in the grave. Anita and Susana held each other tightly at the edge. I leaned down and placed *Don Quixote* atop the form and fought to keep from weeping. When I stepped back, Anita reached for me with her other arm. She was humming and Miguel bowed his head.

"God, receive this soul into your care. He was young, too young to die. Ease his mother's pain and bring a swift recovery to Francisco. Amen."

"Amen," we uttered in unison.

When Miguel reached for his shovel, I did the same. He held up his hand. "You don't need to do this, Maria."

"I know." I stuck it deep into the pile of dirt next to the grave and tossed it onto the blanket. Each time I did, another tear ripped my soul. *I will never forgive Thomas.*

Once the grave was filled, we went inside. Susana went to her brother's side while he rested. In the parlor, Miguel took a swig of whisky. This was the first time I had seen him drink the harder liqueur, though no judgement passed from me. We sat in silence for hours as the skies darkened around us. When the light of the growing moon shone through, Miguel stood up and kissed me on the cheek. Then I was alone. From where I sat I had full view of the garden. The silhouette of a man leaning against a tree materialized. The red glow of a cigar flared from the dark. I knew it was Thomas, and he was waiting for me.

I opened the small shell box that held my only possessions; my bracelet, my earring, and the flower Francisco had placed in my hair on a walk through the orchards—it was limp and dry now but remained intact. There was also a small red and blue doily. It was the first item Anita had taught me how to knit. Its stitches were uneven and flawed but brought a great deal of happiness to me upon completion. I wrapped it around the flower and placed it in my pocket. I reached for Anita's paper, quill, and ink, and by the firelight, wrote two letters.

> *Miguel and Anita,*
> *I will never be able to repay you for the kindness you have bestowed. You are more of a family than any I have ever known. Your love has been my saving grace. I'm sorry to depart at such a difficult time, I have some duties I must see to. I pray in time I may be welcomed here once more. Please accept my bracelet. I want you to use it to pay for your barn to be repaired. I know you may try to refuse, but it would mean everything to me.*
> *With all my love, Maria*

And ...

> *Francisco,*
> *Thank you for all you have given me, shown me, and shared from your life. I'm a better person having known you and Susana. I will always remember you and carry a piece of you in my heart. My earring is for you. There is only one, but it was in my ear the night you saved my life. May you forgive me for leaving.*
> *I will always love you.*
> *Maria.*

I placed each jewel with the corresponding letter. I knew they would both be found when I wasn't. Closing the box, I returned it to my desk. Susana had fallen asleep in the chair next to Francisco's bed. They appeared quite peaceful. I stared at him, etching his features in my mind. I reached for a clean dress and stepped out of the room to change.

Moving the doily and the flower to my new pocket, I studied the house in its eerie quietness. The screams and horrors of the day were put to bed. I glanced about, absorbing the memory of the places that brought more happiness to me in a few months than the eighteen years before.

With the shawl wrapped tightly around my shoulders, I stepped outside. The fresh mound of dirt under the almond tree rose dauntingly in the shadows. My throat constricted. Turning, I shuddered.

Thomas stepped forward and blew smoke casually into the air. "I warned you not to test me."

My eyes speared daggers into his heart. I had never wished death upon anyone until this very moment.

He extinguished his cigar and motioned to his horse. "Your chariot awaits, *milady*."

My jaw tightened. I hated this man with every ounce of my being but would never . . . never allow additional harm to come to those I loved.

I stepped forward.

"Your belongings?"

My stare was unyielding. "Everything I love remains here."

"So be it." He pointed to the saddle.

I climbed on the horse myself, determined to keep his touch far from me as long as possible. It was an unladylike effort in a dress, but something snapped within me and the moment we turned away from the house, I became someone else. Someone who abandoned all feelings of love and compassion. If marrying this man was the only way to keep my loved ones safe, I will do it, but not without the promise of vengeance for the one responsible.

42

29 April 1910

Algiers, Algeria

Thomas

"Welcome to your quarters." I guided Isabel into the boudoir that had been prepared for her back in February. Aside from a little dusting, nothing further was required to make her stay any more comfortable. The green and gold décor was my mother's choice for the suite that connected to her bedchamber back when she was matron of the house. It was the closest anyone had come to residing in the apartments my mother occupied before her death. "Felicia will see to your needs. Tomorrow we begin the arrangements to wed and pen the telegram to your family estate."

Felicia followed us in and placed some night clothes on the bed. She glanced at Isabel who stood in the center of the room with her shoulders curved and her head lowered. My housekeeper sighed and shook her head. Reaching for Isabel she held her hands and spoke within earshot. "Tomorrow I will have some dresses for you, if you have need for anything else, please let me know." When Isabel didn't look up, Felicia tipped her chin and passed a look of forlorn onto my guest.

I watched the exchange with frustration. I was tired of Isabel's lowly martyr performance. "Felicia, leave us," I demanded. When she hesitated, I bellowed louder, "Now!" I refused to allow my staff to believe that I was the aggressor. My hand was forced.

When the door closed and we were alone, I confronted Isabel. "You may think I'm a monster now . . ."

She looked at me for the first time since we left the Contreras'. Even on the ship she evaded every greeting, every interaction, or conversation. I convinced myself that her silence was surely due to being on a ship for the first time since the Chanzy wreck. Though it was apparent she was unhappy, the rigidity in her form confirmed her anger as well.

I continued, "but you will thank me one day when you realize I have saved you from a tragically inferior life." Her blue eyes narrowed and turned dark. I chuckled. Even in rage, her beauty compounded.

I stared until she drew her face downward again. She smoothed out her dress and attempted to bring some confidence to her voice. "How much time, Thomas?" *Her first words.*

"Time?"

"How much time do you require? I will give you everything. The entire inheritance that is owed to me, but when can I leave?"

"Leave? You've only just arrived." I tittered with a tease. "Maybe you will find pleasure in it."

The revulsion in her expression spoke volumes. "I will *never* find pleasure in it."

A scorching prickle crept up the back of my neck and I slammed my fist against the wardrobe. She jumped at my outburst, but her stance never softened. She provokes me so! *I should take her now.* My own will clashed with her resistance. Forget the wedding, the planning, the charm, I justified. She doesn't deserve it. She's heartless and ungrateful. I allowed my eyes to scan her silhouette wondering if I'd enjoy the fight.

"Get some rest." I made sure she glanced up before I departed. "You will need it for your wedding night." I slammed the door behind me. As I walked away, the sound of glass crashing against the door startled me. I stopped and tempered my anger. She's tired, I conceded. With a good night's rest, she will come to her senses.

Grumbling on the way to my bedchamber, I reiterated the fact that it should've never come to coercion. I'm an amiable man. A man who has never imposed upon a woman against her will. I glanced back at her door. She's a spoiled child and must learn her place quickly.

I reached for the handle of my bedchamber and paused, but tonight…tonight I needed something else. Something to release the pent-up energy from recent events, beginning with the fire. Though I had not intended on killing the stable hand, his loss was an acceptable cost to prove my seriousness. The memory of Isabel's complacent embrace with Francisco the night before unleashed a scorching fervor within. She *must* be held accountable.

I circled around and descended the stairs two at a time. When I reached the bottom, I took a quick swig of the nightcap Arthur prepared and slipped my long coat on.

"I'm leaving." I motioned to the old man. "Have Calypso saddled. I will be gone for the night."

"But Monsieur, you've only just arrived."

"I have matters to attend to." Grabbing a full bottle of vodka off the sideboard, I grumbled his direction, "and know this, both of you." I pointed purposely to Felicia. "Isabel is not to leave her bedchamber, is that understood?"

I stepped outside the manor and into the stable. Studying the bottle, I uncorked it and took a satisfying swig. Finally, something solid, none of that prudish brandy from the island. The liqueur sizzled down my throat and burned my belly, competing with another searing drive. Being next to Isabel for the entire journey brought forth all sorts of emotion, though she remained as cold and distant as possible. I bolstered my resolve—it won't be long before I melt her glacier, but tonight my need was urgent.

I rode to town. While the brothel was quick and easy with no questions asked, I desired something longer, more substantial. Something that would last hours and be repeated as often as requested. It had been over a month since my privations had been satisfied.

I arrived at Charlotte's door. How many times had I convinced her this was the last? Weeks extended to months, months to years. She would never be my equal, but I could never resist her. The way she loved me was the way every man dreamed of being pleased.

I knocked.

No answer.

I knocked again.

Nothing.

By the third time, I pounded.

Footsteps finally approached, but the door remained closed. "Charlotte," I muttered against the wood. "I know you're there. Open up."

"I can't," she whispered back.

"Why not?" I demanded.

She remained silent.

I leaned against the door. "I've missed you."

She clicked it open. Her auburn locks slid off her shoulder. "Please?" I begged.

"I believed you had left . . . for good."

"I had business on Menorca, but I have returned."

She sighed as I nudged the door open and reached around, pulling her next to me. The sweet scent of vanilla emanated from her hair. My other hand carefully unlaced her nightdress where we stood. My lips went to her neck, caressing as they moved.

"I can never refuse you," she moaned.

"I'm leaving for Marseille soon," I mumbled across her curves.

She stilled in my arms.

My breath blew heavy. "Come with me."

43

29 April 1910

Contreras Farm, Menorca, Spain

Francisco

"Both gone? What do you mean gone?" I sat up. Everyone was in the room. Anita was crying. I could see her handkerchief soaked through even from my distance. Miguel frowned and Susana steamed.

"Where did they go?"

"I should've known he was a cul," Susana cussed. I'd never heard her call anyone an ass before.

"Luc, yes. But Maria? I just don't understand, why would she leave? Are you sure she left with him?"

"She left us notes," Miguel confirmed. "Drat it all to hell, a note for heaven's sake!"

"Hush, Marit," Anita scolded, but the gentleness in her touch expressed sympathy for their shared frustration.

"A note that said she left with him?" I had been asleep in recovery, long past daybreak, and now struggled to awaken my senses.

"We don't know." Susana glowered. "Javier informed us this morning that Monsieur Fabron hadn't returned last night. His horse and belongings are gone."

"She would never . . ." I reasoned. "There's no way she would go with him." Even as I said it, I recalled his striking good looks, his charm, and above all, the qualities that a gentleman of means would possess. I knew so little of her previous life, perhaps I was mistaken and she could be swayed by such things. "When? When did Maria leave?"

"Last night as well," Susana confirmed.

"Why didn't you wake me?"

"We only found the letters this morning." Anita sat at the end of the bed. She handed me a note inscribed with my name then asked me to open my hand, gently placing one pearl earring in my palm. I unfolded the letter to reveal her perfect handwriting and in her perfect, simple words Maria said goodbye. *But she also said she loved me!* My hand went to my forehead. Small beads of sweat formed under my fingers. Even after reading the message a dozen more times, it still didn't seem real.

"Nothing in here infers she left with that man." My nose and eyes stung when I glanced to my audience.

"They left the same night," Susana insisted. "I'm sorry, Cisco, that can't be a coincidence."

"No, Susana. I won't believe it."

"Well, aren't we the fools." She snapped and stormed out. Confused at her reaction, I glanced at the Contreras'. "What could possibly have upset her so?"

Miguel followed her out. Anita pulled her lips into a tight line. "I suspect our Monsieur Fabron used his charms on your sister as he did all of us women." She exhaled. "He was quite captivating."

"Yes, but I confronted Susana. She didn't like him, not that way." I ran my finger over my cracked and dry lips and read it again. "Have I been that naïve?" My stomach churned from emptiness or nausea, I couldn't tell which. The only thing I'd consumed was the mint tea Anita gave me yesterday afternoon. "Do you believe Maria went back to France?"

"I know she sent a letter to her grandmother weeks ago informing her of her survival. Maybe there was contact after all."

Miguel stood at the doorway. "I'll go get her!" He stomped out, only to return with his shotgun.

"Put that thing away, old man!" Anita cried. "You'll only end up shooting yourself. If Maria left, she left on her own accord and we have to accept that."

"No." My breath sputtered. "No. Every time she regarded Fabron, she feared him. I know it. I saw it. Wait—" I placed a hand to my forehead. *It may be nothing, but* . . . "The night she fell off the horse, Fabron referred to Maria as Isabel. How would he know that name?"

Anita frowned. "Maybe she told him."

I shook my head. Nothing made sense.

"He was very, very convincing, Cisco," Anita continued. "Maybe he persuaded her into believing that he would be a better option than her intended."

"Intended?" I launched forward with intensity. "What are you speaking of?"

Anita sat down at the end of the bed. "She tried to tell you."

"Tell me what?"

"How she came to be here."

"I already know," I barked unfairly. "The shipwreck, the same one that claimed my parents. I know all this!"

"No!" she yelled.

I froze. She'd never raised her voice to me before.

She sighed heavily then softened her tone. "She tried to tell you why she lied about her name, her circumstances."

"Forgive me, senyora. Please tell me."

"She was betrothed."

"Betrothed?" My head spun. "She was promised to another man?"

"Sí. From Algiers."

"Why didn't she tell me? Why did she lead me to believe she cared for me?"

"Because she does care for you." Anita patted my hand. "She didn't know the man who her father promised her to. She was frightened."

"Do you suppose that's where she went?"

"I don't believe that." Anita's head now shook with resolve. "That's why she stayed here. She hid. She changed her identity because she *didn't* want to marry him. She fell in love with someone else."

"Luc Fabron." My voice faltered.

"No!" She hollered and slapped my hand. "You, Francisco. She fell in love with you."

"You really believe that?"

"Without a doubt," Anita whimpered. "Which makes her departure all the more confusing . . . and painful."

"Why didn't she tell me last night?"

"I'm not sure, Francisco. I know she felt guilty about many things, maybe she thought she let us down or maybe she believed she let her own family down."

"But now she's gone." Weakness tingled all over my body. "Do you suppose she went to the man she was supposed to marry out of obligation or guilt?"

"Thomas was his name," Anita confirmed. "Thomas Chastain."

"Chastain?" I challenged. "As in Chastain L'entreprise?" I remembered the paperwork Luc provided with the name Thomas Chastain on it. I stood up too quickly and lost my balance.

Anita reached for me and guided me back down on the bed. "I don't know anything about that, but I do know you need more rest."

I closed my eyes. This all seemed too coincidental and strange. "Are you certain his name was Thomas Chastain?" I opened them again.

"Yes," Anita recounted. "I remember her telling me his name and that she had never met him and knew nothing about him. Above all she didn't want to marry someone she didn't love. That's why she hesitated to notify her grandmother of her survival. She feared her grandmother in Marseille would require her to fulfill the contract."

"Do you believe she would have?"

"I can't answer that. I do know she respected and loved her grandmother."

"Susana?" I called, then turned to Anita. "I have to confirm something."

Susana appeared in the doorway.

"Would you please go back to the ranch and retrieve the product papers from father's desk? The ones that listed Chastain as the distributing company."

Susana's face was taut but relaxed once I told her why. Her response reflected kindness from the sister I knew. "If you truly believe Maria left against her will, we need to find her, Cisco, and I will do anything I can to help." She grabbed her shawl and rushed out to the wagon.

"I wonder if we could locate her grandmother."

"In France?" A light reached Anita's swollen eyes.

"Sí." I allowed my mind to start formulating a plan. "She would know if Maria was on her way home. She would have had to provide passage and expenses."

"Maybe—" Anita jumped to her feet. "I wonder—" She went to the desk and retrieved the box Maria left behind. A pang of frustration reminded me I had seen Maria herself pick it up—after she kissed me. She kissed me goodbye, though I didn't know it was goodbye at the time.

"Look inside, did she leave anything there that might lead us to her grandmother?"

Anita opened it. She pulled out the bracelet. "This is all that's inside." Anita sniffled as her fingers wound around the jewelry. "She left this so we can rebuild the barn."

From my distance, something sparkled from the sun's reflection through the window.

"This could pay for many barns," Anita murmured. "She came from vast wealth."

"Did she tell you that?"

"She mentioned she had means in her past, but I suspect her family is still prosperous." She handed me the jewelry. "This was hers."

It spoke for itself. My fingers grazed the exquisite detail of a diamond bracelet far above the one I gave her. I peered back over to Anita and relented. "Are you saying I shouldn't try?"

"I'm suggesting the possibility that she really did leave on purpose."

I fumed. I couldn't give her the life that included fine jewels, fancy clothing, or lavish estates . . . the only thing I could offer her was me! And every bit of my heart.

"Sometimes love isn't enough." Anita's eyes seemed to read my mind. An aggravating stir started deep within the pit of my stomach, though this time I was positive it wasn't from hunger. "No." I spoke with confidence. "I need to hear it for myself."

Anita's lips curved in curiosity.

I reached for her hand. "Did she mention if her grandmother is the only living relative?"

"Yes, she is."

"That's it!" I jumped up again and steadied myself against the bedpost. "I'm going to find her." It didn't matter that I hurt in every possible place. My arms and face stung, and my lungs grappled for more air. "First, I must go to Ciutadella, the Procurators who managed the shipwreck would know how to locate the grandmother."

"Do you think they will divulge that information to you?"

"Possibly, I'm the son of victims too. They might take pity on me. I have to try."

Susana returned with the stack of papers. I scrambled through them and there in very clear, black writing was the name Thomas Chastain, and next to that appeared *Chastain L'entreprise, Algiers, Algeria*. "Susana," I leaned forward. "Hand me some paper."

"Tell me what to pen, brother, I will do it."

"We need to send word to Chastain L'entreprise on how to reach their associate Luc Fabron. I can't shake the feeling, he's somehow involved."

"And Thomas Chastain?"

Just thinking that this man was the one who Maria was assumed to marry completely vexed me. "If we know Maria didn't go back to France, I will go Algiers and find Monsieur Chastain in person."

Anita's face lit up. "How can I help?"

"Be here in case she returns." I pulled the bandage off my cheek and winced in the looking glass. Black streaks materialized over raw flesh. It was only the circumference of a coin but stung with ferocity. "Miguel!" I shouted his given name for the first time ever.

He came running in with the gun once more.

"Let's saddle the horses, we're going to town."

44

29 April 1910

Contreras Farm, Menorca, Spain

Miguel

Pulling my boots on, I stepped off the porch in line with Francisco. "Now explain to me what is happening and speak slower. I missed half of it the last time."

"You knew Maria was on the Chanzy, right? The shipwreck?" Francisco asked, but didn't stop moving, and marched to the side of the house as we conversed. With the barn in shambles, Francisco assigned his ranch hands to build a temporary structure for the animals until we had time to construct something more permanent.

"Sí, I'm aware."

"Did you know that Maria was betrothed to a man in Algiers?"

"Yes, but she didn't want to marry him."

"That's what I'm learning." Francisco sighed with significant relief.

We reached the horses in a swift second. Diego and Paco neighed restlessly upon our approach in their unusual quarters. This morning Javier had found Penelope down the road wandering in a field. That must've been near where Maria fell off her.

Francisco double checked the horses' condition before securing the saddles. For someone who had been recently injured in a tragic fire, his intensity surged forward like the bulls from Pamplona. His arms remained bandaged though covered by long sleeves and he had removed the linen from his cheek, but for any lack of energy he may have had earlier, his resolve more than made up for it now. He seemed hell bent on one mission—find and bring Maria home.

"Why Ciutadella?" I questioned, placing a knapsack of food in my side pouch.

"The Procuradors are our only hope of finding her grandmother, senyor."

"So it seems." I paused. "Then what do we do? Bring Maria back from France?"

Francisco froze next to his horse. "If she will have us."

"Francisco," I placed a hand on his shoulder. "I know Maria well. She's been under my roof for three months. Granted, she wasn't exactly truthful, but she had her reasons and if she wanted to marry that man, she would've told us from the beginning."

His exhale took effort.

"She chose not to be that person." I contended. "It's also why she prefers the name Maria over Isabel."

He tilted his head towards me, his eyes reflected deep contemplation. "Do you believe she departed willingly, Miguel?"

"No." My head shook vehemently. "I don't."

"Then we must move swiftly."

I pulled my hat off my head and wiped the sweat from my brow. The sun grew hotter the longer it took to prepare. With the lateness of the hour, we would arrive in town long after dark. "But Cisco," I didn't want to say it, yet it needed to be said. "If she did . . . if she made up her mind to leave, son, out of our love for her—"

Francisco cut me off "—she may not believe she has a choice. We are giving her a chance to make a choice."

"Then maybe we should find Fabron first or that man who set up the meeting to begin with, Jacque Roman." I rubbed my scratchy jaw. "It seems odd to me that Fabron and Maria vanished the same time. Or maybe we should seek her intended, Thomas Chastain."

"First we will locate her grandmother and determine whether or not she's in France. Then we will go to Algiers. If she's with Luc, or Thomas, we will find her and convince her that her home is truly with us."

I had one foot in the stirrup when the sound of horses pulled my attention away from my steed and towards the rapid advance of a coach. "Who in the blazes is this?" I griped, eyeing the two men who sat atop the fine carriage, the likes of which I'd never seen.

Francisco moved next to me. "I've never set eyes on anything like this." He gaped. "Not even in Ciutadella."

It came to a stop before us and both men, dressed in extravagant uniforms, eagerly jumped to the ground. One approached us while the other went to the door and waited.

The man nearest us bowed deeply. His suit, though wrinkled from travel, was made of a fine material. "We are looking for the home with the family name of Contreras."

I closed my mouth and stood a little straighter while all eyes fell upon me. "I'm Sr. Contreras." I extended my hand, but the man kept his arms clasped behind him and bowed lower this time. Why he put on all this pomp and circumstance confounded me. His voice was deep and steady. "My Madame wishes to address you."

My eyebrows lifted. I glanced towards Francisco. His mouth curled tight as a handsome elderly woman was escorted out of the carriage and drew near. Her feathered hat was nearly as round as the entirety of the carriage door. With one hand, she held up the skirt of her ruffled black dress to reveal shoes unaccustomed to dirt and with the other, flicked a painted fan feverishly before her face. When she stood only a meter away, she gazed evenly at us both.

"Bonne journée, Monsieur. I am Madame Clarice Fontaine, and I am here to see my granddaughter, Isabel Marie."

45

30 April 1910

Algiers, Algeria

Isabel

I paced the room. The dresses that were brought to me this morning were exquisite, much like the gowns I wore what seemed to be a lifetime ago. I had no desire to put them on. They no longer brought the pleasure I once felt for such things.

"You mustn't wear your nightdress all day, Mademoiselle." Felicia, the woman I was introduced to the night before, attempted to coax me into dressing. "Please don't give the master reason to be cross."

My eyes flashed over to her, simmering with fury. "I don't give a damn about the master and his emotions."

Felicia winced at my outburst. I suddenly regretted the fact that she was the one who took the brunt of it. She most likely incurred her own daily criticisms from Thomas.

"Forgive me," I muttered. "You are not the one who deserves my wrath."

After assisting me into a morning gown, Felicia encouraged me to sit while she brushed my hair. Images of Ines doing this very thing brought tears to my eyes. It seemed like ages ago I was a young woman from France, living a life of abundance. But now all I longed for was the simple life of a farmer's wife.

"Who is this man who keeps me captive?"

Felicia paused. Her wrinkled hands trembled slightly as she peered towards the door. *She must know something I do not.* "He's a man with a great deal of pain. A man who was once good."

I shook my head. I didn't want a reason to pity him. He may have had the world crash down on him, but regardless of whatever he had been through, he certainly had the ability to control his actions. Much like myself, I assumed. Then I shuddered at the idea we were aligned in any way. One can choose *not* to react to sorrow with hatred.

Once she had finished placing combs in my hair, she helped me dress. I peered out the window. The property was vast with no sign of another structure in any direction, other than the stables. Even if I found a way to run, he would either chase me down and drag me back or finish the job he had started at the Contreras'. "May I go downstairs or outside for fresh air?"

"I'm sorry Isabel, but you must remain in here until the Master comes for you."

I stewed silently. There would be no benefit to making Felicia feel worse. She was kind to me, after all. I did question how someone of her demeanor could continue to be employed for such a man, but he did force me here, he may have done the same with his staff.

Horrified with my circumstances, I let my mind wander. If I must wed and go along with his twisted plan, what else would he take from me? I curled my hands into fists. He was calculating and cruel and wasn't beyond stealing more than just my freedom—my innocence was sure to be next.

Just then the door flew open. Thomas never knocked. Dressed like he was attending a dinner party, he bowed low. "You look . . . breathtaking, my love."

My lips pulled tight at his liberal use of endearments.

"Felicia, take your leave."

She peered at me and lowered her head as she scampered out of the room. His eyes scanned my figure starkly as if he already claimed ownership. I spun away from him.

He scoffed, "only a matter of time." Then spoke much louder. "Time to write your missive, my dear . . . and try not to be too clever, you have already learned what happens when you do."

I wheeled around and faced him once more but kept my chilling thoughts to myself. As long as he held Francisco and the Contreras' over me, I was at his mercy. At least until I contrived a more permanent solution.

I sat down at the desk and penned a letter to Grand-mère. It would be less descriptive than my first post. Clear and concise and, though I did not deliberately try to trick him, if she read through it, she might conclude on her own that I was not myself.

Grand-mère,
I have had a change of heart and wish to proceed with Papa's original plan for me. I am to wed Thomas Chastain in Algiers shortly. I'm writing to begin the process of allocating the estate and all the matters

of business into his name as my lawful husband. Please see to the particulars in Marseille. We shall be in touch.
Isabel

Even though Thomas stood over my shoulder the entire time I composed the post, he retrieved it swiftly and scanned it. "This will do." He gloated. "I will have this transposed into a telegram and delivered immediately. Until then, your happiness is at my disposal. Anything you wish in order to make your upcoming wedding more suitable, it is yours."

"I wish to not be wed," I mumbled.

Certain my words were equally heard and ignored, I flinched at his next move. Starting at the crown of my head, he ran his fingers down the length of my hair. The longest strands fell against my lower back. When his hands reached the ends, his breath caught next to my ear. I remained motionless at the desk.

"If you require anything," he whispered, "let my man know. He's outside your chamber."

I swung around so quickly that Thomas startled. "You have a guard at my door?"

He stood to his full height and tugged on his suit coat. "It's for your safety, my love."

"Or yours?"

He licked his lips and allowed them to curve into a sly smile. "Our bed won't lack excitement, that's for certain."

I sneered and turned my back on him once more.

It wasn't until the door sealed shut that I allowed myself to fall into a sea of tears. Through my continuous cries, the only words that seemed to materialize in my desolation were the ones from Francisco's mother—ironically on the ship that was bringing me here— "you might not be able to command your world, but you can *always* own your response."

I sat up and took a deep breath . . . the kind that cleanses your lungs and reaches your toes. I wiped my face free of moisture and viewed my appearance in the looking glass. Despite Thomas's stranglehold on me, I will not allow him access to my heart or my soul. I will *own my response,* and he will not break me.

46

1 May 1910

Algiers, Algeria

Francisco

"This is the street," I said, stepping out of the coach. "I should approach the door alone."

"No, son," Miguel insisted. "If he's armed, it's best I'm there as well." He gripped his gun tight against the length of his leg.

I knew there would be no arguing with Miguel. The fire in his eyes had been lit the moment we learned Maria was not with her grandmother nor had she returned to France, something Madame Fontaine confirmed with her household. Thankfully, the wealthy had means of swifter communication as new inventions came forth.

"Fine, but we need to be cautious." I circled back to the wide-eyed woman in the carriage. "Madame Fontaine, please stay here with the coachman." She conceded. An unusual mixture of fear and anger seeped from every line on her face. Since the moment we were acquainted two days ago, a design was set in motion to locate Maria and bring her home.

Having only arrived in Algiers this morning, we began searching for a Monsieur Luc Fabron straightaway. Despite our best efforts, our resolute attempt had led us to nothing more than blank faces and dead ends. The man was a ghost. Fortunately for us, Monsieur Jacque Roman, the gentleman who came to our properties to arrange the meeting for Monsieur Fabron was quite real and much easier to unearth.

Our information directed us to the docks and a Moorish coffee shop wherein a man of his height could hardly remain unseen. To say that Monsieur Roman was surprised to see us or acknowledge us was indisputable and severely underestimated. His quick attempt to run was thwarted with Miguel's handy shotgun and after some firm prodding, the man admitted the chilling revelation that nearly brought me to my knees—

Monsieur Fabron and Monsieur Chastain were, in fact, the same man.

Visions of the tragic events that unfolded back home conjured up the probability that this deceptive man—who I allowed into our home—may have, in truth, been the cause of all the harm. I cringed at my role in it but had little time for guilt.

Our next move was to find the only person who must answer for his actions—Luc Fabron, also known as Thomas Chastain.

I double checked my pistol that was stuffed into the waistband of my trousers, the handle easily accessible in a moment's notice. The only reason I didn't raise it eye level was because there was a sliver of doubt it would be Thomas himself who answered the door, yet I kept one hand on it as we approached.

My loud knock went unanswered. I glanced at Miguel who had a substantial amount of sweat building on his nose. He motioned to repeat it. "Harder."

I knocked again. The hour was late, but I would not wait another second to find Maria. She had been gone now for three days. Anything could have happened to her.

A muffled voice answered from behind the door. "Who is calling?"

The voice was not that of the smoothly deceptive Luc that I remembered in my head, but instead shrewd and severe sounding. Perhaps Jacque had somehow gotten a word of warning to him.

"Open the door, Thomas," I demanded, fully prepared to break it down in a moment's notice.

The door cracked an inch. The whisps of a mustache appeared when rage engulfed me. I heaved the door open with blazing force, propelling the man a couple of meters backward and onto his tile floor. In an instant, I leaped over him and thrust my pistol into his chin. Waves of fear flooded the man's eyes and I gasped. My mind whirled nearly out of control as I tried to make sense of the moment.

Miguel's hands tugged my arm. "Back off, Cisco."

I fell to the side. All the emotion I had repressed since the night of the fire exploded in vengeance. "Who the hell are you?"

The man scrambled towards a wall and curled in the limited light of his candelabra. His features were familiar . . . but different. He owned the same facial structure and thinly trimmed moustache I burned into my memory, but everything else was new. If this was Thomas Chastain, he not only changed his features to some degree, but he had also shrunk. This man must be a good half head shorter and much thinner.

"Who are you?" I charged with the same vehemence as before.

The man's cheeks drained of color. He truly feared for his life at this moment.

"M—my name is Thomas Chastain."

"Oh Lord." Miguel appeared as though he might faint. He hastened to sit on a nearby chair.

I moved the aim of my pistol away from the man and slid my own body against the nearest wall. My heart thumped rapidly as I took my first real breath since we arrived.

"Another lie. Another impasse," I mumbled with exasperation. "Are you really Thomas Chastain?"

The man grew more confident without a weapon leveled upon him. He stood from his cower. "I am." Then moved over to his sideboard. With a loud exhale, he continued, "I don't know what this is regarding, but it looks as though you both need a drink."

Miguel was quick to answer. "Hell, yes."

My mind spun for answers.

After the man handed us each a glass of whisky, he sat at the nearby table.

I downed the contents with one quick swallow. "Are you the owner of Chastain L'Industrie?"

"Yes, with my brother. My father started the company twenty years ago."

"You import and export goods?"

"Yes." The man's eyes narrowed. "Might you explain what this is all about?"

I exhaled and moved to a chair at the table. "I don't even know how to explain."

"Try," he said, refilling my glass.

"From the beginning, son." Miguel urged.

"I'm Francisco Carrasco. This is Miguel Contreras. We are from Menorca. I own an olive farm on the Northern side, midway between Mahón and Ciutadella."

"I'm familiar with Menorca. We do business there." The man added.

"Last February a ship called the Général Chanzy sank near Ciutadella."

"I recall that disaster. I lost acquaintances aboard that ship."

"A young woman by the name of Maria—Isabel. I mean, Isabel Fontaine . . ."

Thomas instantly shot forward. I jumped in place at his exertion. "Did you say Fontaine?"

"Yes."

The man paced wildly. "From Marseille?"

"Yes, and she survived."

"Survived? This cannot be true. Her family all perished on that ship."

"She did not, I can assure you." I hid my growing agitation, realizing that this was a secret few were aware of. "But how do you know of her or her family?"

"Forgive me, Francisco, I mean you no harm. I'm only shocked by this news." He sat back down. "I knew of her father. Our companies had a business relationship, but it was one of the accounts my brother insisted on handling. He normally did so little to help I allowed him to have full control."

"Your brother?" I questioned in a way that alerted us all to what might be transpiring.

Thomas averted my gaze. "I need you to explain the whole story to me."

"Miguel here found Isabel—who we know as Maria—the day after the wreck. She nearly died, but he and his wife Anita cared for her. Now, looking back," I mumbled, "she had this

349

determination to keep parts of her life private. However, during this time, I was involved in the changes of my own ranch. I was looking for a new distributor and managing my business when a man came to our house offering his services as a representative of Chastain L'Industrie. Through others, I learned that your company was reputable to work with, so I agreed."

"What is your business, Francisco?"

"Carrasco Olives." I watched his mouth purse into a thin frown. "You've never heard of us, have you?"

"No, I'm afraid I have not."

I drew another big inhale and continued. "I allowed a man named Luc Fabron into my home for eight days."

"Did you say Fabron?"

"Yes."

"That's my grandmother's family name."

"Is she from Paris?"

"She is."

My fists clenched as this mystery unfolded. "This man had similar features to you, but he was taller, stronger. No offense."

"None taken." Thomas waved his hand for me to proceed.

"Luc was smooth and most amiable. Full of compliments and charm. He convinced me that my olives were in good hands."

I watched as Thomas' countenance cringed with familiarity. He knew something.

"We don't understand why he targeted us, but he brought misery, destroying much of my season since the olives were delivered but never paid for. We also believe he torched Miguel's barn and . . ."

Miguel interrupted. "The fire killed my farm hand, Henry."

Thomas' face bled a darker shade. It seemed as though the fury had finally reached him. "Is that the end of the story?" he asked curtly.

"No." I narrowed in on his face. "Maria . . . I mean Isabel is missing."

"Missing? What do you mean?"

"She was betrothed to a Thomas Chastain by her father as a means of uniting their companies, but disappeared from our home the same night Luc did."

Thomas' cheeks now drained of all color. "Betrothed to me... or a man who *claimed* he was me." His hands covered his face.

I continued to relay all the information Anita had told me. "Mr. Fontaine was a wealthy man with a beautiful daughter. She was to wed shortly after their arrival to Algiers on the Chanzy. Then Thomas would be the heir of that vast fortune."

He lowered his hands. He appeared ill when he whispered, "There's nothing for me here. Greater opportunities are coming."

"What are you saying?" I couldn't follow Thomas' statement.

"That is what my brother told me back in February. I suspected he had a scheme brewing, that he had some plan in the works."

"Do you have a photograph of your brother?"

"Not a photograph, a painting. My mother had it done shortly before she died. He was seventeen years old."

"May we see it?"

"Follow me."

Only moments after entering a sitting room, an icy chill ran the length of my form. The portrait carved a hole through my chest. The eyes that faced me back were those of who we believed to be Luc Fabron. "That's him."

"I have more to tell you." He led us back to the table. I wasn't sure if there was more of this sordid tale I could handle. With additional pieces coming together, we needed to find Maria soon. Her safety was at risk, now more than ever before.

"A month ago, my brother had notified me that he was going on holiday to Menorca and needed use of our employee, Jacque Roman, as his valet."

"We are quite familiar with Jacque," I scowled.

Thomas proceeded cautiously. I had given him more than enough reason to fear an outburst, but I controlled my temper as he continued. "I encouraged him to see to some business while there and he easily agreed. I was pleased in his acquiescence. He had been less than enthused about the business for years, so I believed this might be the beginning of change." He rubbed his chin. "While he was gone, however, I was contacted by a Maître Bureau in regard to the Antoine Fontaine estate. I deflected it and told the man the Fontaine association was handled by my brother. The man insisted that the person he needed to speak with was Thomas Chastain. I agreed to meet, but when he spoke of a marriage contract involving Isabel Marie Fontaine, her death on the ship, and the subsequent allocation of her estate, I excused him. I insisted he had incorrect information. I was *not* betrothed to her. He left and I've heard nothing more."

"So, your brother used *your* name to create a contract of marriage with her father. Why would he do that?"

Thomas shifted uncomfortably in his seat. His eyes immediately diverted any direction but mine.

"Why would he do that?" I slammed my fist down on table.

Thomas finally faced me. "Because he has a reputation."

"A reputation for what?" I stood to my feet and leaned closer. I was fairly certain this man was only guilty of being related to a bastard, but my anger fueled me. "For what?"

"For everything."

My eyes flew to Miguel, my hands immediately went to my pistol. Aiming it at Thomas I cried. "Where do I find your brother? Where is he?"

"Calm down, Francisco." Thomas stood to meet me and pushed the pistol downward. "I can help you, but you must remain calm."

Miguel moved to me and grabbed the pistol. My hands raked through my hair while my thoughts flew faster than I could breathe. "He had to have taken her. Dammit! I know he took her against her will . . . for the money!"

"Yes, quite possibly," Thomas said but with an eerie calm. "I won't lie to you. He can be singularly minded when it comes to finance."

This only charged me further.

"But," he continued, "we can get her back. Lucien, I'm certain, only wants the money. He is driven by power and money."

"Lucien?" I muttered hotly.

"Don't agonize. I will help you."

I steamed over the unraveled deception. "We are wasting our time here. Where is he? Tell me where Lucien is. He could've already harmed her by now."

Thomas' expression revealed little. "Francisco, we must be smart about this, he could kill you given the chance."

"That's if I don't kill him first."

"And if you go in there and take Isabel, he will only continue to plot or strike. He has the means and the ambition to destroy. All I'm asking is that we work together and plan this sufficiently. It's been years since I've been to the estate, it's possible he has a strategy in motion . . . so must we." Thomas paced thoughtfully around the room. "I will request his presence at the office tomorrow. He will come, and I will furtively discern his intentions." Thomas stared hard my direction. "You have my word, Francisco. I will do everything in my power to help you find her. You love her, don't you?"

I glanced at his odd question then conceded. "Yes, she is everything to me."

"Then let's make sure you are alive to enjoy a future with her."

"Very well, what do we do?"

47

2 May 1910

Algiers, Algeria

Isabel

"Good morning, my love." Thomas' sickly voice dripped with sarcasm. He held his hat against his chest as he bowed low my direction. I glanced away. Looking at him made me want to wretch. "Why so forlorn this morning? Are the accommodations not to your liking?"

"It is not the accommodations that are vile." I hissed and kept my back an affront to him.

"And bitter." His laugh grew louder as he narrowed the distance between us. One tug of my arm and he whirled me around to face him directly. I wrestled my desire to spit in his face, afraid his reaction would result in more violence. His hand lifted to my cheek and he allowed his fingers access without permission. I brushed his hand away, but he caught mine immediately. "I would be cautious if I were you." His tone grew dark. "It almost appears as though you are ungrateful."

I glared at him. Though many hateful retorts came to mind, I still feared him. My hand trembled under his hold. He pulled my hand down and glided his fingers over mine. "Delicate," he whispered. "Perfect." I peered up to see a snakelike smile emerge. "And all mine." My jaw grew rigid. "Felicia is bringing up your wedding dress."

My body stiffened and the words caught in my throat, nearly suffocating me. He can't be serious. *Today?* He lifted my fingers to his mouth and kissed them individually allowing his lips to linger longer than any gentleman ever would. He stopped short. When my eyes followed to where his froze, my breath cut short. He stared at the bracelet Francisco had given me. Though I was certain he couldn't possibly know its origin, in one swift move he had it off my wrist and in his hands.

"No, please," I begged. "That's mine."

He studied it. The simple make and design pressed within his cold fingers. "Who is this from?"

I lowered my eyes.

"Well, it must not mean that much to you then." And slipped it into his pocket.

I launched forward with both hands on his sleeve. "Please, please give it back to me." My heart pounded in my throat. The bracelet had not left my wrist since the day I received it.

He glanced at my hands touching his coat and I quickly removed them. "You have no need for plain trinkets any longer." He adjusted his cuffs. "Make sure you are wearing the dress upon my return to the house."

The quiet knowledge that he was leaving the grounds lightened my countenance. He must've noticed. "Oh, don't worry, love, you will be safe here. The room is well guarded and with my newly acquired wealth, we won't be here for long." I peered up, beseeching elaboration. He smirked deviously. "We are booked on a ship for Marseille tomorrow. We will be traveling as husband and wife by then, so naturally . . . one stateroom." I circled away from him. His laugh echoed in the large bedchamber. "And be sure to bathe, milady." The door clicked closed.

I stormed to the window, once again assessing the damage I would suffer if I fell from its height. *I can't go with him!* Though I had forbidden myself to shed another tear due to this man, my heart wilted at the news. How did it all come to this? How could my father have allowed me to be given to such a frightful man?

I watched the grounds. Thomas paraded from the entrance as primped as a peacock and retrieved his horse from his groom. With the arrogance of a man who never backed down, he glanced up. Our eyes met—his danced with joy at the sight of me, mine wanted to slash him to pieces. A broad smile appeared before he bounded atop his horse and broke into a fast run.

Vexed, my body dropped to the window bench. There must be another way. Could there possibly be a way to protect those I loved and not be forced to endure another minute with this loathsome creature?

The door unlocked once again and Felicia entered. Relief flooded my face as I met her reassuring smile. Her frail arms were overcome with a bountiful pile of white laced fabric, waning under the weight. I took it from her and threw it on top of the bed. Stepping back, I withdrew from it as if it brimmed with disease.

"I'm here to prepare you for your wedding."

Though I was certain she meant no harm in her words, they caught me off guard and I struggled to respond. "I, uh, I don't know if I can do this."

She came to me and offered a sincere embrace. The top of her head barely reached my shoulders despite my own size being considered petite, but her meaningful hug meant everything to me at this moment. "I wish I could do more."

I watched her. She grasped my hands and glanced towards the door. A very large, intimidating man stood within the frame. "She will need complete privacy for two hours. Don't open the door or allow anyone to enter."

The man grunted but consented with his disappearance and a sure click of the handle. I took a deep breath while Felicia led me to the tub that had been filled for my bath. "Take as long as you need, dear." She helped me undress. It had been quite some time since that happened. Once inside the warm rose water, I relaxed.

"Felicia," I inquired as she picked at the hem of the dress. "Will you be traveling to Marseille?"

"No. Monsieur no longer requires our services after tomorrow."

"Our?"

"My dear husband is the butler. We served the elder Chastain's for thirty-five years. We came with them from France."

"Were they good people?"

"Oh, very."

"What happened to their son?"

"Two sons, actually."

"Two?"

"Yes, but two very different men." She sighed. "It wasn't always this way. The brothers were quite close, and the parents loved them dearly."

I wasn't sure what to think of her story, but it did make me curious. "What happened?"

Her eyes filled with tears. She sat down at the dressing table and pulled out a handkerchief. "Madame Chastain died of Cholera in 1902. She was a lovely woman with a kind heart. It was only six months later that the elder Monsieur Chastain took his own life, unable to overcome the grief."

My nose wrinkled. Thomas was a horrible man, but what a devastating thing to live with. A parent who *chooses* to leave you.

"Felicia, why do you stay?"

She held a silk robe out for me, indicating it was time for me to leave the comfort of my warm bath. "I promised his mother on her deathbed that I would always look out for him."

"I'm sure it would never be her intention for you to be subjected to such cruelty."

She pointed to the chair and gestured for me to sit. "We must ready you before Monsieur returns." This signaled that the conversation was over.

As Felicia arranged my hair, I didn't even bother to check my reflection in the looking glass. It didn't matter how I appeared, it was the furthest thing from the wedding of my dreams, or the man of my heart. Once she secured the gown in place, a loud knock reverberated through the room. The large man entered once more and cleared his throat.

"Please don't leave me," I pleaded when Felicia did one last glance over.

She reached for both of my hands. Her smile widened though I saw sadness spill out. Another grunt from the protector caused her to jump. "Forgive me, dear, I must leave." She reached into her pocket and placed something in my hand. "Be strong." She quickly departed.

I opened my hand to find Francisco's bracelet. Warmth enveloped me as I recognized the kind, sympathetic risk she took to return it. How she became aware of its connection to me I did not know, only that it was truly in my grasp. "Be strong." I repeated to myself as I moved to the window. The trees swayed under a light breeze and the way the sun shone on the nearby pond created an ambiance of peace. The complete opposite of what I actually felt.

I glanced down at the wedding gown and back to the bracelet. A fleeting image of Francisco emerged. I smiled, remembering all that I had memorized of him that final night and tucked away in a special place. "Yes, I will be resilient." Slipping the bracelet inside a fold of my chemise and against my breast, I labored to remove the wedding dress.

48

2 May 1910

Algiers, Algeria

Lucien Chastain

"Brother, why have you called me here? Your message said it was urgent."

"It is, Lucien." Thomas' countenance appeared controlled though a bit of disdain leaked from his eyes.

"What is it? What do you detest about me now?" I sat at his table waiting for his lecture.

He sighed deeply. "I am concerned for you."

"Indeed," I growled. Then watched his lips bow. "Your disposition reveals all, Thomas." I brushed my lapels and motioned to stand. "Just know, I no longer adhere to your demands, your reprimands, or anything to do with this company. I wash my hands of it."

"What do you mean?"

"I'm done. Father's inheritance and his crumbling ruin are superfluous. I am free of it all."

"How so?"

"Not to worry brother, I haven't stolen from you."

"Well then share with me your good news. What fortune has smiled upon you?"

My lips curled. Though I haven't cared for the man for years, having the upper hand brought some satisfaction. "I'm taking a wife."

"You are? When?"

"Tonight."

"Tonight?" His face showed more surprise than I would have expected. "Why so sudden?"

"It's not sudden," I snapped. "It's been in preparation for over a year."

"Why have I not heard of this? Am I not your closest relation? What of my invitation?"

"No guests." I responded curtly. "My bride prefers privacy."

"And who is this charming maiden who has captured your attentions?" When I hesitated, he continued, "is it Charlotte?"

"No!" I barked.

"But she loves you." Then he swiftly added, "And I believe you love her, too."

An aggravating pulse throbbed at the back of my neck. I had spent far too many nights wishing Charlotte's inferior circumstances were altered. It was a squandered hope and, though my feelings for her had grown over the years, I knew it to be an impractical match.

"It will never be Charlotte." The muscles in my jaw tightened. "The woman I wed is the daughter of a well-positioned acquaintance."

Thomas' brow furrowed before he smoothed his countenance. "May I send a gift in my place?" He sounded genuine. "I'm much inclined to send my well wishes in the form of a gift for you and your lucky bride."

I eyed him carefully. Nothing seemed amiss other than his typical displeasure in me. Thomas had always been the more thoughtful one of us both. I laughed out loud. "If you insist. Send it to the house. I will receive it after the ceremony."

"Where is the union to take place?"

I glanced warily his direction. "Why? Why do you need to know? I've asked you to leave us to our privacy."

"I only presume you might use the same chapel mother and father attended . . . that's all." His voice tapered off.

"Do not burden yourself. Mother's memory is justifiably considered. Now, what do you need from me, I must attend to my preparations."

"Well if you are to discharge your portion of the company, I must have the papers arranged. It might take some time."

"Send them to me."

"Where are you going?"

"To France. Tomorrow."

His mouth fell open. "So soon?"

"This should bring you joy, brother. You are no longer obligated to trouble yourself with me and will reap the full rewards of the family inheritance. Does this not make you happy?"

"Well, not entirely, Lucien. Father gave this company to both of us. You are a part of this family. I don't want to see you go."

"Rubbish!" I cried. "I don't know what games you are playing but I know that is an outright lie. You've hounded me for half of my life for all the inappropriate choices I've made. I'm giving you a chance to be rid of me and you are dancing around it, but no heed. Whether you send the papers of not, I have washed myself of this. Good day." I stormed out.

"Implausible!" I cried as I exited the house. "Brought in here for nothing." Yet I made myself clear, that much was accomplished. I jumped up on Calypso and patted her mane. She neighed under my touch. I pulled my pocket watch from my waist coat and peeked at the time. In a mere three hours, I will take lawful possession of Isabel, her estate, and all of her family holdings; but did I have time for something else? I steered Calypso towards her usual path, the one I often took when I came to town.

As I neared Charlotte's street, I paused. Isabel would never do the things that Charlotte willingly did to me. If only Charlotte had been born to privilege, been fortunate to have a wealthy father, or anything but a pauper's life. I promised her I would take her to Marseille. I wanted to, but I would not have time for both a wife and a mistress in Marseille. Well, at least not a permanent mistress. My ties to Algiers will end the moment I step off its land and onto the ship tomorrow.

I stopped at her door. I considered the time it would take for her to gratify me one last time, then envisioned my wedding night to come. Isabel would never be as agreeable or as loving, but as long as I held everything she loved over her, she would learn to be obedient. She knew what I was capable of. She had witnessed it firsthand and all I had to do was remind her of it every time I came to her bed.

"No." I kicked Calypso forward and trotted away. "My new life awaits me far from here."

49

Algiers, Algeria

Francisco

"Francisco!" The real Thomas showed up at our Inn. "We need to speak, it's urgent."

Miguel's cheeks drained of color. On Thomas' counsel, we had waited in the courtyard most of the day. Our fifth round of tea in hand. The strain in Thomas' voice put me on high alert.

"What's happened?" I pressed.

He scanned over each of us but stopped at the elderly woman seated at our table. They had not yet been introduced.

"Thomas, this is Madame Fontaine, Isabel's grandmother. We met in Menorca and she insisted on accompanying us here. She's anxious to be reunited with her granddaughter."

"Pleased to meet you, Madame." He peeked over to me, his eyes scrunched like saucers. "I need to speak to you."

"Whatever you have to say," Madame Fontaine interjected with a firmness, "you can say it in front of me. I have been informed of the circumstances and Isabel is *my* granddaughter."

He looked to me for help. I nodded. "She stays."

"Very well." He cleared his voice. "I arranged for my brother to meet me at the office today and managed to elicit his plans." He removed his hat and wiped his brow with his sleeve. "It is worse than I feared."

I stood up and my chair hit the floor. "Tell me."

"Please sit, Francisco." He waved me down. Then while he waited for me to right my chair and sit, he tugged on his tie as if he were suffocating.

"Continue," I said eagerly.

"They are to marry tonight and leave for Marseille on a ship tomorrow."

"Tonight?" I flew to my feet again. My fists clenched tightly at my side. "Where are they? Has he harmed her?"

"I don't believe so." He nervously glanced to the only woman present. "My brother is quite experienced with women, but rarely finds one who is disagreeable to him. I don't know how far he'll go."

"Where is the house?" I grabbed the sleeve of his coat. "Where is he?"

He held me back as if he expected a repeat from when we first met. "Calm down, we need to keep our heads clear."

"There is nothing about your brother or this situation that is worth being calm about.

Thomas rubbed his chin. "Is there any way Isabel would willingly agree to being his wife?"

Miguel reached out and held me back before I strangled the man. Then he stepped in front of me and faced Thomas. "If she's with Luc, we are certain it is coerced."

I paced behind the group. My mind rotated in a jumbled mass of fears. "Jacque did not want to betray your brother's confidences, but we managed to induce their plot. From the subterfuge involving my olives and ranch to . . ." I couldn't say it. Miguel finished my sentence. "Your brother planned to force Isabel to marry him if she didn't fall for his charms."

"Would he negotiate for my granddaughter?" Madame's voice chimed in, clear and direct.

We all turned towards her, stunned.

"What do you mean?" Thomas asked.

Her steely eyes met his directly. "You said your brother wants the money. Will he negotiate?"

"Yes!" I placed my hand to my forehead. *Why didn't I think of this earlier!* "Yes. I will offer my ranch, my olives, everything. If he will give Maria back to us, I will give it all."

Madame Fontaine studied me in the silence that followed. A hint of sympathy entered then departed her deep blue eyes, the same shade I missed when gazing upon Maria. She lifted her head stalwartly. "No, Francisco. I will offer him my own allotment." Her lips curled into a tight bow.

"Yours on top of what he's receiving through marriage?" Thomas shook his head. "Don't succumb to his intimidation."

"He believes he's acquiring everything now—the estate, the wealth and the business, but by marrying Isabel, he gets nothing."

I choked. "Pardon?" *Not only is he trying to destroy us, but he's also doing it for no return?* "Please, explain."

"Antoine and I co-owned the assets. Everything. He was always careful, that boy."

My mouth parted in awe. "So when he perished, you became the sole proprietor? And by marrying Maria, Lucien actually receives nothing?" Displaced anger coursed through my veins. "He wasn't made aware of this?"

"Please," Madame Fontaine nearly whispered, "please call her by her given name. You may know her as Maria, but she is Isabel to me."

I nodded. "Of course, I will do my best."

She continued, "there would've been no purpose in Antoine disclosing the arrangement he had with me to his daughter's husband before the wedding. The new son's procurement of the holdings would have likely taken years. Antoine viewed the union as a partnership, not an acquisition."

"How would Lucien have come to believe he gained it posthaste?"

She shook her head. "Greed, I assume."

"I still don't understand, Madame." I stood before her, stunned. "Why would Monsieur Fontaine agree to give Isabel away to a man like Lucien?"

"That's the point. My son must have agreed to the contract because he believed the unification of the two competing companies was a brilliant match. He verified the company's strength." She looked to Thomas. "And he verified *you*." She pointed at him. "You, Thomas Chastain. Your character made you a probable candidate, not Lucien Chastain. I don't believe for a moment my son had any knowledge of the deception."

Glancing around, our expressions shared similar bewilderment.

"Though it might not appear so, my son loved his daughter very much. He wanted to secure her future if anything were to happen to him." She pulled a handkerchief from her lap and dabbed her eyes. This was the first I'd seen any emotion from her.

I moved next to her and placed a hand on her shoulder. "I don't believe I ever told you how sorry I am for your loss. Here you are fighting a battle against a madman while grief is still fresh in your heart. I'm truly sorry."

She placed her weathered hand over mine. "You must know, I never agreed to the arrangement, Francisco. I believed giving away your daughter to a man you'd never met was a mistake, but I never told him so. It's as much my fault as it was his. I should've stopped it."

"But." Miguel tapped his finger against his lips as he processed the conversation. "Time is working against us. Whether he finds out today or tomorrow that Isabel doesn't come with a financial boon, she's in danger."

"I will go see this man straight away." Madame Fontaine reached for her reticule and fan on the table.

"Not alone, Madame." I squeezed her hand. "I've seen this man's handiwork. He's dangerous."

"But if you three come with me, there is too much emotion involved. A fight could ensue and someone, like Isabel, could be harmed."

She was correct. If I saw the man, I would tear him to pieces. This newfound fervor surprised me but was warranted. "How can your safety be assured?"

Thomas held out his hands. "Allow me. I have two very trustworthy men. They could accompany her to Lucien's estate."

"Won't he recognize them and know you are involved?"

"Lucien knows little of my life. He's too absorbed with his own. I assure you he won't know them. They will see to her and Isabel's safe return to us . . . but Madame, are you sure about this?"

"Sure about what?"

"You are giving up everything you own, everything your son built."

"For my granddaughter."

He bowed his head with reverence. None of us had grandchildren, in fact none of us even had children of our own, but in that moment, the unwavering power of a grandmother's heart abounded.

"I will make the arrangements." Thomas jumped to his feet. "The ceremony is in two hours. We must proceed quickly." Thomas shook our hands, then reached for Madame Fontaine's hand. "I'm deeply sorry for the pain and injury my brother has caused you and your family. If there is one thing I can promise, it is that it will never happen again."

When Thomas departed, Madame Fontaine, as stoic as she'd been, let out a sorrowful sigh. Slivers of tears teetered in the corners of her eyes.

"Madame . . ." I took the seat nearest to her. "May I ask you something before you depart?"

She paused.

I stole a quick breath. "I would like to ask Maria...Isabel to marry me. Would you give me permission in her father's stead?"

She remained silent for an uncomfortable amount of time. When she finally met my eyes, she smiled and reached for my hand. "You're a good man, Francisco—" She paused, then her smile waned.

The thundering in my chest seemed to amplify in my ears while I waited for her to continue.

The tears that lingered now slid easily down her cheeks. She patted my hand gently. "But the decision is hers and hers alone. I would be pleased to know she has a home to return to, but I will not take that choice from her ever again."

My smile grew. "If she will have me, Madame, I would have it no other way than for you to join us in Menorca as well."

Her smile reached her eyes this time. "Then let's hope Lucien accepts my proposal."

She stood to leave, and I let go of her hand. "Good luck Madame. We'll be waiting for you here; both of you."

She excused herself and I found the emptiness to be smothering. Striding the perimeter of the garden again, I wrung my hands together tightly and groaned, "Oh, Miguel."

"I know." His eyes dropped to his knees where they bounced nervously up and down.

"Miguel, I can't let him leave with her. She is my life."

He regarded me then called for the serviteur. "We need something stronger than tea here."

As the sun lowered, all the guests went inside. Only Miguel and I remained. My heart pounded with every tormented step I took.

"Son, you will wear a path in the tile. Come and sit, there is nothing else we can do right now."

I cringed at the suggestion of leaving tonight in the hands of a diplomatic solution. Lucien was not a good man. He had proven that much in the short time we were acquainted, and now Maria was his bargaining chip.

"Miguel, I can't sit here and do nothing!"

"We must, son. Madame's right. If we storm the castle, someone could get hurt. Someone you love." He sighed heavily, "Here, drink some whisky."

"No, thank you, Miguel. Tonight, I need my mind to be quite clear."

50

Algiers, Algeria

Lucien

"Isabel, we leave for the church in one hour. I thought Felicia dressed you."

My bride to be sat at the bench near the window, a robe wrapped around her small frame. She had been washed and cleaned of any Menorcan filth and should be ready, though she didn't even acknowledge me when I spoke. A fire lit in the pit of my stomach. I walked over to her, but she still didn't look up. The way her blonde hair framed her porcelain skin and cascaded down her back was breathtaking even without the gown.

I reached for her jaw and gripped firmly. Angry blue eyes flashed towards me. A twinge of fear emerged behind her obvious resentment. I chuckled. "This behavior is not befitting of a bride on her wedding day."

Her lips, her dusty pink lips, pulled firm as she tried to yank free of my hold, though she said nothing.

"Might I remind you I have men assigned to Menorca."

Her eyes glazed over and she stopped struggling.

"They are positioned in two intentional places." My smile lifted as I leaned in. My nose touched the skin on her cheek and I inhaled to the fresh scent of roses. "It won't take long to get a telegram to them, and when I do, they move on my command."

Tears bubbled on her lashes; it was quite tender actually, and I wanted to kiss them away. "Everything that happens will be on you." I reminded her. "Obey as a proper wife should or live with the consequences and I will still get what I want in the end. The choice is yours."

"Monsieur Chastain?" Arthur was at the door.

"I told you never to bother me up here. For heaven's sake, man, I'm with my *wife*."

Her jaw went rigid under my touch.

"I understand, Monsieur, but we have a visitor."

"Who?" I ripped around so quickly it nearly knocked Isabel backward. She scooted farther along the window bench. "Who is it?" I demanded.

"A Madame Clarice Fontaine."

I swung around to Isabel. With wide eyes she was quick to her feet. I grabbed her wrist. "Sit," I ordered. "Arthur, we will be down shortly. Show her into the parlor."

When he left, I whipped back to the woman before me. My hold was still very much attached to her arm as she tried to squirm free. "It's my grandmother, please let me see her."

"On one condition, Isabel." I moved in again. The yearning desire to touch her immaculate skin rekindled. "You remember yourself." I let my lips run across her cheek towards her ear. "You must remember that your behavior decides the fate of your friends."

Her cry came quickly. Pulling her hand away, she whirled her back towards me.

"Now get dressed. I will send Felicia back up to help. You will meet grandmama as a happy, blushing bride." I opened the door briskly and pointed to the man in the hall. "Escort her down in fifteen minutes. Dressed or not." Then I stepped into the hall. *I need a drink.*

I slipped into the master suite to check my appearance and went straight to the sideboard. My nerves needed something strong tonight—something that would help me get through all this scheming. *It's exhausting!*

After pouring my glass, I went to the mirror and retied my ascot. *How in the world did grandmother find us this quickly?* The telegram was only sent yesterday, which means she had to have already been here. *Merde!* Any delays on the acquisition of the estate will be most inconvenient. Though Isabel seemed to believe I would make good on my threats, I didn't trust her, or anyone related to her. I stared at my image reflected in the glass. *Could she be here to take Isabel from me?* If so, she will learn quickly she has made the journey in vain. Of course, she's welcome to return with us to Marseille, but I will waste no time in putting the old bird away. I shall not spend another day with the elderly.

I emptied the glass. Its contents both burned and soothed as I swallowed. Pouring another, I gulped it swiftly before I stepped into the hall. I glanced towards Isabel's bedchamber; the presence of my man outside her door told me she was still inside. I grinned as I headed for the stairs. *I think I will have a tête à tête with granny first.*

I entered the parlor. "Madame Fontaine, how fortunate we are for your . . . unexpected arrival. What brings you to my home?"

"Monsieur Chastain." She sat like a peacock on my settee. Two men near the back of the room guarded her. *As if I were a threat to her chastity.* "Monsieur Lucien Chastain." She spit out with little ability to hide the contempt in her voice.

I smiled. *So, she knows.*

I bowed deeply. "At your service, Madame." When I peered up again, our eyes locked in a battle of wills. She was not a frail woman, and the bitterness in her expression told me she came prepared to fight. "May I get you some tea? Or do you prefer something with a little more kick?"

"Nothing."

"Again, I ask, Madame Fontaine... what is the purpose of your visit?"

"The contract."

"Oui, the contract your son signed offering me his daughter Isabel."

"Offering Isabel to *Thomas* Chastain." She snipped back.

"Yes, yes, that is true." I snickered.

"Does she know?" Madame asked.

"The detail that means nothing?"

"That detail means that the contract is null and void." Her chin lifted.

"It's irrelevant." I stepped closer and whispered, "Because she's marrying me of her own free will."

"Liar," she retorted. Her mouth pulled into a tight arch.

"Oh," Isabel gasped in the doorway.

Standing in my mother's wedding gown, she was stunning. The white lace flowed from the bodice to the floor. I nearly lost my breath.

"Grand-mère!" She cried and ran as fast as the garment allowed. Falling to her grandmother's knees, she hugged her tightly. It would have been a moving moment had I been one for sentiment.

"Well now," I went to the bar and found my *Old Forester* bourbon. Uncorked, the single malt filled my nostrils with a fresh scent of caramel. I glanced up before I swallowed the contents. "Isn't this lovely."

Isabel continued to kiss the old woman's hands.

"So, Isabel." I ambled over to her and lifted her to her feet. *No wife of mine will be groveling on the floor.* "Your grandmother doesn't believe that you are marrying me of your own accord." I stared hard at her with what was perfected as a silent threat, which was mostly unnecessary since I had already planted additional seeds of fear in her mind. *She knows I'm capable of murder. She could hardly doubt me now.*

Her head hung low. She spoke with a timid voice, barely above a whisper. "I am marrying Thomas—"

"No, dear." Her grandmother cut her off.

I chuckled and refilled my glass. *It's as good as time as any to learn the truth.*

"He is *not* Thomas. We have all been deceived. His brother is Thomas Chastain. This is Lucien. Your father chose a good man by the name of Thomas as your husband, not his brother."

Isabel's countenance turned dark. Her cheeks flashed a cherry red though it only made me chuckle more. "Continue, Isabel. Your grandmother needs to hear your answer."

She sent a sizzling stare towards me before she picked up her grandmother's hands. "I'm marrying him," she mumbled.

"Speak up, my love."

"I'm marrying this man willingly." Her voice rose an octave, though her eyes cast downward.

Grandmother squeezed Isabel's hands back. I could almost see the steam rising from the elderly woman's ears.

"What is he holding over you?"

Isabel's head remained lowered, and she stood in silence.

Madame shook Isabel's hands with haste. "Are you certain?"

Isabel nodded.

"Look at me." She pressed. "Are you certain?" As she repeated her inquiry. The alcohol I had just consumed roused a burning flame that ignited my temper.

"She's certain!" I shouted. Both women jumped. "Now we must depart for the church. Arthur will show you out."

Madame put her hand up and raised one finger. She seemed moderately cool and collected after my outburst. "One last thing to consider before you leave."

My patience grew thin. I reached over and grabbed Isabel's wrist and brought her close to me. "Pray tell?"

She smiled. "I have my own contract to show you." She waved one of her men over. I sized him up quickly. I was taller, but he was broader. It would be quite a tussle if we wrestled. The man opened his coat and brought out a parchment.

I let go of Isabel and reached for the vellum. As I unraveled it, I immediately detected the Fontaine seal and Antoine's signature at the bottom. I read swiftly, sure that I had missed some words along the way, but it didn't matter. The words multiplied and grew hands that choked me the farther I went. This was a letter confirming the ownership of the Fontaine property belonged to—Madame Clarice Fontaine.

My head spun. My stomach threatened to expel all the alcohol I had consumed at any moment. I tugged at my collar. The need for air clawed at me. When I peered up, a wicked curve had formed on the hag's lips. Maddened, I screamed, "It's not possible!" One hand clenched my hair, the other let the document fall to the floor. I moved to a chair afraid that I would collapse.

"Oh, I can assure you, Monsieur, this is quite authentic. With an additional copy kept in Marseille."

I wanted to retch the filth of this woman's lies away. In the corner of my eye, Isabel, herself, grinned like a Cheshire cat. Infuriated I moved towards her. The man who had presented the contract to me quickly moved in front of her.

"She is my wife, you ass!" I shouted.

"No," Madame insisted. "She will never be your wife if I have anything to do with it."

I backed up and peered around him. My stare thrust daggers her direction. "Remember, Isabel, whatever happens is on you."

Her smile quickly faded. "Grand-mère, please go. Please, go back to Marseille." Her pleas came out strained. Tears burst from her eyes as I took quiet satisfaction in the control I wielded—even when everything seemed to topple backwards.

"We are late!" I grumbled. "We are going to be married." My mind calculated the time in which it would take to dispose of this wretched woman and Isabel and myself would be the benefactors. *The plan can be salvaged.*

"Wait!" The woman held her hand up again. "Hear me out. I believe I have a proposal you cannot refuse."

I stopped.

"If you will release Isabel from this obligation—"

"Obligation!" I scoffed. "Many women would vie for this arrangement."

She ignored me. "If you will, I will turn this inheritance over to you. In full."

"Grand-mère!" Isabel cried out and flung herself at her feet once more. "No! You can't! I won't let you."

Madame patted her head, but her glare never veered from me. "Do we have an agreement, Monsieur?"

I searched for any sign of trickery in her face, but there was none. "All of it? The estate, the business, the fortune?"

"Oui." The woman assured.

Isabel's sobs came loud. "Please, please don't do this."

Madame Fontaine held her chin. "I would give anything for you, my love."

"Done!" I picked up another decanter and poured a fresh glass. "But the legalities must be completed here, tomorrow, with my solicitor."

"I would expect nothing less."

"And Isabel stays with me until it's sure."

"No!" This brought the Madame to her feet. "She leaves with me."

I stood my ground. "She is my assurance that you won't flee with my property."

"I am a woman of honor."

"And I won't let her out of my sight until everything is properly assigned."

Silence filled the room. Piercing eyes dueled between me and the woman.

"It's alright . . ." Isabel soothed. "It's only one day."

"No marriage!" Her grandmother shook her fist at me. This was the most energy I had seen come from her thin frame. "And your promise we will never see you again."

I lifted my glass to cheer the decision. "I promise." Then emptied its contents and traipsed loosely to my desk. Now that the tension had passed, a sense of numbness spread throughout my limbs. I labored over the words as I wrote down the name and location of my solicitor's office. It took longer than expected, but the missive could still be read. I handed the paper to one of her brutes and walked over to the two women linked together excessively long and broke them apart. "Women whispering, now that is not to be trusted." I pulled Isabel over to me, pledging nothing untoward would happen. "Arthur will show you, and your . . . friends, the way out."

After their departure, I turned my gaze from the closed door and let my eyes settle on Isabel. Though her cheeks were puffy and pink, she resembled an angel. The pure white of the gown glowed in the lamps that were lit all around me. "That dress looks beautiful on you."

Her mouth parted as if she was going to speak, but nothing came out. Temptation to fill that gap with my own lips surged. *She would've been mine tonight.* As fiery as our wedding night would have been, I imagined it would have been equally pleasurable.

"Are we finished?" Her tone surfaced flat.

"For now," I snarled and waved her away. She was a means to an end. Tomorrow, I will be wealthy and on a ship to Marseille. I snickered and took another swig but by the time I turned around, Isabel had vanished.

I found comfort in the nearest wingback chair and reflected on the night as a growing fire lapped wildly in the hearth. The orange flames hypnotized me and released my heightened vexation. I would have been a fool to marry Isabel and risk not receiving the rightful inheritance. The old woman presumed she was clever coming here, but it is I who would have the last laugh. *I hold the ace of spades now.*

I glanced at the empty doorway. The memory of Isabel in that dress could not be erased. I gulped my drink and mused. "I believe a wedding night is still in order, with or without the vows." I poured another drink and walked out with it and an additional bottle in my hand.

51

Algiers, Algeria

Miguel

"Sit down, Cisco," Miguel pleaded. "Your pacing won't do anything but wear out perfectly good boots."

"Miguel, I can't. I can't think of anything else."

"Madame Fontaine will manage this fine."

"How do you know?" Francisco stopped and stared at me. "She is strong. That, I have no doubt, but she doesn't know Luc like we do. We know how capable he is of manipulation and deceit."

"Yes, he definitely had us all fooled, that's for certain." I glanced towards the water. The glow of the lanterns shimmered across the glassy stillness. If it weren't for our circumstances or reasons for being here, this would be a lovely place to bring Anita on holiday. "I have complete faith in Madame Fontaine. Isabel is her only remaining relative. She will do what she can for her granddaughter, I have no hesitation."

"She's an interesting lady." Francisco stopped moving for a brief moment. "I get the sense she has had to overcome great suffering in her long life."

I paused. "She did just lose her entire family. It must've been a delightful moment when she learned of Isabel's survival."

"Yes, I can imagine."

"Francisco," I took a sip of my drink. "Might I ask what your plans are once we leave here?"

He smiled. It was the first time I had seen his dimple since we arrived. "Whatever it is, it must include Isabel."

I grinned back. "Well for goodness sake, about time you admitted it, son!"

His head dipped. "But do you think she'll have me, Miguel? My foolish behavior back home might prevent her from trusting me. Will she forgive me?"

"You're too hard on yourself, Cisco. You didn't know her secret. You didn't know why she lied. Anyone would be hurt by that."

"But you and Anita didn't know either and still loved her. I questioned everything."

"You don't question how you feel about her when you're with her."

"No." When Francisco's mouth curved upward, his eyes shone. "No, I don't."

"Love does funny things to us, doesn't it?"

He beamed. "I can't imagine a future without her. She's everything to me."

"She is certainly beautiful, Cisco."

"Yes, but . . ." He stared into the water. "She is much more than that. She is kind and compassionate, Miguel."

I chuckled at the memories of watching her play with Hugo, cooking with Anita, or fishing with me. I could not recall a time I had ever seen her *unkind*. "Despite her secrets, son, which we now know to be justified, she truly is an exceptional woman."

Francisco rubbed his forehead. "She's the only woman—"

"They're here!" Thomas suddenly appeared at the gate of the courtyard. "Come, quickly."

Francisco tore off. I hardly had the stamina to keep up with him but hustled to the front as swiftly as possible. I caught sight of the carriage coming to a stop.

By the time we arrived, Thomas had already reached the door to help the Madame down. Francisco didn't wait and joined him, hoping to retrieve Isabel.

"Where is she?" Cisco glanced inside and spun around in a panic. "She's not in here." Madame Fontaine's lips pulled into a frown. Thomas led her to the closest chair.

"Where's Isabel?" I questioned. My heart thumped in my throat and even though Francisco confirmed her absence from the carriage, I still looked inside. "What happened? Isn't she coming home?"

Francisco moved over to where Madame Fontaine took her seat. From the way she was breathing, she needed a few seconds before she spoke, but Francisco's fretting wouldn't allow for it. Alarm clearly surfaced in everything he did. From the agitated pumping of his fists to the grimace that filled his face.

"Francisco." I reached for his arm. "Let the Madame catch her breath."

"I need to know what happened," Cisco bellowed.

"You will." I grabbed his arms and forced him to a nearby chair. "Sit," I demanded. He complied but watched Isabel's grandmother intently.

She retrieved her fan from her reticule and cooled herself down. When she seemed relieved, she reached for Francisco's hand. "I know you are upset. You must know, she means the world to me too."

He nodded and stilled himself.

The two men who accompanied Madame Fontaine rode up on horseback. Once they tied up their horses, they joined the rest of us in a circle around the elderly woman.

"Pardon me," she cried. "This has been a dreadful ordeal, but I will explain." When she removed her fan, I noticed she'd been crying. My heart ached for this woman who recently learned of her granddaughter's existence only to lose her again so suddenly. "I was successful at the negotiation." She took a long breath. "I informed Monsieur Chastain of the arrangement my son had with me. That it was I who have control over his accounts, not Isabel. He was obviously disgruntled but allowed me to make the proposition. Especially since he realized he would remain penniless without my help."

"But why is she not here then?" Francisco's question was well warranted if this negotiation was to be deemed a success.

"He made a condition of his own." She tilted her head towards Francisco and once again tears glossed her eyes.

"What?" Francisco interrupted. "What condition?" I threw him a look to be patient.

Madam's countenance collapsed. "He insisted that Isabel remain with him until the new contract is complete."

"No!" Francisco flew to his feet. His hand rubbed the back of his neck. "That's unacceptable."

I grabbed his shoulders. "Please, Francisco. This is not helping."

"But he could still marry her. He could—" Francisco's voice went weak and his body seemed to have lost all strength. I kept my grip on his arms as he looked to me for help. "He could do any number of things to her."

Madame's face shot to Cisco with a fury. "He assured me he would not."

"And how can we trust him?" Francisco questioned. "After all the deception we have witnessed, how can we truly trust him?"

An immediate flash of terror filled her eyes. We all understood what kind of man we were dealing with.

"Thomas?" I turned to the only genuine source. "Can he be trusted to keep his word?" I rubbed my cheek contemplating the severity of the situation.

Thomas took a long time to process the situation. Then looked at his men. "Had he been drinking?"

The men exchanged looks. One spoke up. "At least three or four glasses while they conversed, but his behavior indicated he had been drinking well before we arrived."

"What does that mean?" I asked Thomas, but it was Francisco who answered.

"That he *can't* be trusted." He stood up and looked to Thomas. "I'm right, aren't I?"

Thomas' mouth pulled into a deep frown.

"We have to go get her," Francisco said with the most amount of calm thus far.

"Yes," Thomas relented, "yes, we do."

52

Algiers, Algeria
Isabel

Once I returned to my room, I allowed myself to finally breathe, *really breathe* for the first time in days. I had hoped to leave with my grand-mère but even just seeing her brought an enormous reprieve. She fought for me. She was willing to sacrifice everything for *me*. I can only pray that tomorrow will come quickly and we can leave this awful place, never to return.

Although unanswered questions still lingered in the dark corners of my mind, I tried not to worry. Questions about *where we will go* or *how we will live* would be something to think about after today—nothing I had the strength to contemplate at this moment. If Thomas, I mean, Lucien will be in Marseille, I will remain far from there and far from him.

With a certainty, Miguel and Anita would welcome my return but I discerned little of Francisco's state. I caused him pain. By now he may have believed I left with the man he knew to be Luc Fabron. He may even believe I left willingly. If I returned, would I be able to convince him otherwise? Would he allow me the chance to tell him everything—most of all that my heart belonged to no one other than him?

Luc Fabron. Thomas Chastain. Lucien Chastain. The names used by *one* man. The man who had deceived my father into a wedding contract, destroyed people's lives . . .and killed Henry! My heart ached as the image of Henry's silent form resurfaced in my mind.

Through all Lucien's dastardly deeds, he had the distorted belief that I would somehow embrace his "charm" and be inclined to be his wife. How could anyone find happiness with such a man? How did he so effectively mislead my Papa? And how did my grandmother learn of his deceit and know to come to Algiers?

The door's hinges creaked. A brief flash of panic crossed my face until Felicia entered. Though we spoke little, her kindness and care always came through the sincerity of her touch. When she helped to dress and groom me, it was always with a gentle hand. Quite contradictory to everything else in this place.

She approached me. Her palm cupped my cheek as she whispered, "I'm happy you get to leave with your grandmother." Her lips pulled tight as if she dared not say much else. That was seen in the brief times Lucien was in here with us. His treatment of her must make her fear for her life. Now with Lucien leaving for Marseille, she too must be anticipating her own freedom. "Turn around love, I will help you ready for bed."

I smiled and did as she asked. The bridal gown I'd been compelled to wear fit adequately for the most part but had many buttons down the back, many that were difficult to reach on my own. This I already knew from my earlier disrobe. The tug of each release multiplied as I gazed out the window, grateful tonight's events took a wonderful turn.

"Merci, Felicia."

"Of course, dear. I'm sorry it has been—"

The door slammed open. We both flinched at the sudden noise. Felicia's hands froze in place halfway down my back as I turned to see Lucien had entered. He had a glass of liqueur in one hand and a bottle in the other. His movements were loose and uncoordinated as he attempted to lean against the frame of the doorway, only he slipped, and nearly fell to the floor.

My body quivered under his gaze, but I pulled my chin forward and spoke with authority. "You have no right to be here, Monsieur. Take your leave."

His lips twisted to a sly smile before he guzzled the contents in his tumbler.

"I said leave, Monsieur."

He licked his lips slowly. A lump rose quickly in my throat. Felica's fingers flew swiftly in an attempt to button the dress back up.

"You..." Lucien slurred his words, "Felicia, y—you a—are exxcusssed."

She ignored him and buttoned as fast as her aged hands would go.

"I sssaid, leave, woman!" Lucien's eyes narrowed. They appeared blacker than night. His cheeks, however, were flushed and ruddy.

Felicia patted my hand, but when she moved away from me, it wasn't far. Her thin, frail form stood firmly in front of me like a warrior ready for battle. Her hands curled into fists at her side. "You will not harm this girl, Monsieur."

A spark of surprise crossed his face but did little to dissuade him. He chortled as he filled another glass and set his bottle down on the desk. "N—now this is most ennndearing." He chuckled, but Felicia didn't falter. Fear filled my eyes. I knew how strong he was from the time he struck me. One such blow could possibly kill the woman.

I touched her shoulder and begged, "Please Felicia, please do as he asks." She peered back up at me. Tears formed in the corners of her eyes though her hands remained balled. "Please," I repeated, "I cannot bear to see you hurt."

She shook her head. "And I too, Mademoiselle. I cannot allow him access to you."

But when she turned back to face Lucien, he had already moved before her. My breath caught the moment his hand struck. The poor woman crumpled to the floor from the force.

"What have you done?" I screamed. She didn't move. I reached for her when Lucien grabbed my wrist. Like before, his grip paralyzed me. Yanking me away from her, he pulled me against his chest. He moved awkwardly, but no less commandeering.

When his face leaned towards mine, a rank mixture of liqueur and sweat seized me and the moment he opened his mouth, I cringed. "It's a woman's dutyy to obeyy. She—" With his glass still gripped in his other hand, he pointed Felicia's direction. Her body completely still. "—Sheee did not obeyyy."

I whipped my head away from him.

He threw the glass into the fireplace and with his free hand gripped my chin and pulled it back to face him. His clasp sent piercing pain throughout my jaw. "It'sss your turn." With only a moment's hesitation, he brought his mouth fully upon mine. I tried to stop it, but my lack of mobility allowed his tongue to move freely inside. I punched his chest in an attempt to push him off. It was like hitting stone, nearly impossible to breach, but I refused to let him have his way without a fight. He threw me backward atop the bed. I landed on the edge and slipped to the floor. Glancing at the door, still ajar, I considered the risk of running.

Lucien stood boldly before me. He removed his coat. I inhaled sharply. My heart thundered in my chest as he moved on to unfolding his tie.

"You won't get your money if you do this," I hissed in desperation, hoping logic would somehow reach his ears and make him stop.

"Nobodyy is going to even sseee you until after I have my mmoney." He chuckled darkly. "Nobody wwill know."

"I *won't* let you."

Thomas unbuttoned his shirt, taking his time as he eyed me like prey. The moment he started to undo his trousers, I made a break for the door, but underestimated his agility and the weight of the dress. He clutched it from behind and slung me roughly back. I hit the ground in a thud and instantly he was on top of me. Both of his hands pinned me down, while his legs straddled across me. Tears blurred my sight. I peered over to Felicia who remained unmoved a short distance away.

My cries graduated into screams the moment Lucien leaned down and kissed my neck. His lips slid sloppily across my skin. "No! Please no!"

Bam! A loud ruckus surfaced. *Whoosh!* A blur flew above me and toppled Lucien to the floor. I threw my arms over my face. Violent crashing and thumping emerged nearby. Two arms reached beneath me and slid me across the floor away from the unidentifiable horror. Miguel's face appeared before me with an outstretched hand. "Isabel, come."

"Miguel?" I mumbled, hardly able to comprehend what was happening or if I was somehow dreaming. A tangle of bodies slammed against the armoire. I shook to the crash and trembled long after the wardrobe clattered to the floor.

"Quick, take Isabel out." A man I had never seen before swiftly scooped Felicia up in his arms while Miguel grasped both of my hands and lifted me upward. He then swiftly placed an arm around me for balance.

When we reached the doorway, Miguel's worried expression softened when he faced the strange man and spoke, "Thank you, Thomas. Thank you for helping."

Thomas? "Wait." I cried out to Miguel. "What's happening and—who, who is that?" I pointed to the skirmish that continued behind me.

He tugged me to move into the hallway, but I fought to see. Familiar features flashed before me. Rugged, beautiful features. *Oh no.* My heart seized. *It's Francisco!*

I struggled to go towards the men, but Miguel held me back. "No," he insisted. "Let Cisco finish this."

Even as Miguel quickly ushered me out, I peered back around as the fierce sounds continued. Once in the hallway, I spied the strange man who had brought Felicia out. He gingerly laid her down on the mezzanine. "Please, Isabel," he pleaded, "will you see to Felicia."

How does he know me? And Felicia? I peered up at his face. Similar features to Lucien appeared, but with a gentleness that was far removed from my attacker. "Thomas," I hinted. "You're the brother."

He nodded. His mouth bent into a frown as he quickly stood up and moved back to the bedchamber door. He entered and cast me one last look before he closed the door behind him.

Panic seized my chest. I gripped Miguel's arm. "Francisco. H—he's in there."

Miguel patted my hand. "Thomas will help. They can manage." He pointed to the unconscious woman in front of us. "We need to help her for now."

I knelt down to Felicia and pressed my ear to her chest like Susana would've done. I spoke with a lift in my voice. "She's still breathing." I peered up. "Miguel, you need to get the butler. He's her husband."

Miguel stood up but eyed me sternly. "Don't go into that room, Isabel." I glanced to the door and took an extra breath. A wrinkle emerged between his brows. "Promise me you'll stay here."

"I promise." Every part of me fought that promise. The man I loved was behind that door; and with a monster, no less. I took brief reprieve in the knowledge that Thomas was with him and it was two against one. The way he cared for Felicia led me to believe he would not let Lucien continue his brutalities.

I placed Felicia's head on my lap and brushed her hair off her flushed cheeks. She was quite brave to stand up to her employer for me. *What a courageous thing to do.* I held her hand and spoke to her as if she could hear me, and maybe she could. After all, I experienced that—back when I was unconscious.

At last, the sounds stilled behind the door. I held my breath and listened. Loud panting and exasperated breaths were taken between mumbled words. Nothing I understood. I stared at the door, willing it to open. My temptation to enter consumed me. A moment later the butler arrived, his face looked drawn and sullen.

"How is she?" He stooped down. He was as aged and small as she, but reached for her, kissing her cheek.

"She's breathing but hasn't awoken yet," I confirmed as he called her name.

"Please," he looked to Miguel. "Help me get her downstairs. I must retrieve a doctor."

Miguel studied me and then the unconscious woman. He reached for one of her arms while her husband held the other.

"You should come downstairs with us."

I shook my head. "No," I mumbled, regarding the quiet door once more. "I'm going to stay here."

He nodded and helped the butler with his wife. My hands wrung nervously in my lap. *What if Francisco doesn't walk out of there?* My chest heaved at the very thought. Additional "what ifs" haunted my mind until the door swung open.

Francisco's face appeared. I gasped and jumped to my feet. When I threw my arms around his neck, he wobbled slightly then placed his hands at my waist for balance. When he pulled me in, his face buried into my shoulder. I felt his moist body through his clothes. His breath labored for relief.

I moved my hands to his cheeks. His flushed skin bore battle wounds. Scrapes and cuts and a lengthy blood trail trickled down his left eyebrow. I leaned closer, the scent of blood and tears practically on my tongue. "You're here."

I closed my eyes and inhaled his breath, savoring his proximity when his lips pressed against mine. The gentle pressure deepened as if this was the very source of life. Francisco's hands went from my waist to tangling his fingers in the back of my hair, pulling me closer than one could believe was possible. I shared the desperation in his touch. Every emotion amplified since I had left his side.

When Francisco pulled away, his hand cupped my cheek. "Did he hurt you?" He scanned my torso then halted when he caught sight of the condition of my dress. It was torn at the neckline, and practically separated at the waist seam of the skirt, but I was uninjured. He caressed my cheeks, my neck, and my shoulders. "Isabel, are you hurt?" He begged for an answer.

"No." I fought back tears. "No, you arrived in time."

"I'm sorry." His voice trembled.

Mystified, I choked, "For what?"

"For not protecting you better." He seized another deep breath. "For not listening to you. For everything."

I wrapped my arms around his neck again and held tight. Tears filled my eyes as my love for this man nearly burst out of my skin. "You're not to blame, Francisco," I whispered in his ear. "Lucien is the only one at fault here." I stopped short. My sight darted to inside the bedchamber. Thomas, the brother, bent over a motionless Lucien sprawled on the floor. Blood pooled beneath his head. I gasped. Francisco held me away from him and turned his sight to where mine was frozen. Thomas' back shuddered as if he wept.

"Is," I mumbled, "is he dead?"

Francisco's arm kept me close to him. His chest still rose irregularly. "He can no longer harm you or anyone else."

A sharpness stung in my chest. My emotions teetered between elation and grief. I was grateful to be released and free of him, but the moment saddened me. Something I couldn't quite put my finger on, possibly the suffering of his brother—and because the raw emotion of losing a loved one remained fresh.

"Come, Isabel, let's go down." Francisco placed an arm around my waist and led me towards the stairs.

"How did you know to come here, and with Thomas?"

"There is much to explain, but you should know Lucien took on his brother, Thomas' identity for your betrothal."

My mind spun trying to make sense of this. "Why? Why would he do that?"

"I believe you already know why." Francisco's hold tightened. "He was not a good man."

"He was dreadful," I muttered.

Francisco stopped in place midway down the stairs and faced me. "Why did you leave with him? Why did you leave me?" The pain in his countenance nearly crushed me.

I lifted one hand and brushed a wild strand off his forehead. His eyes closed to my touch as I traced his cheekbone, along his jaw, then across his lips. "Oh, Francisco, please know, I would have never left you willingly." A small sigh escaped his lips as I continued, "He said he would harm you all if I didn't. He killed Henry so I believed him."

His exhale warmed my fingers. Placing his hand over mine he pressed it against his mouth and kissed. "I thought I lost you, Isabel."

My heart melted to his words. When he let my hand go, his arm reached around my waist and pulled me against him. His sheltering hold confirmed his poignant emotion—and exposed the depth of his fear. Then as if he melded to my bones, a deep wave of security embraced me. A connection, if ignored, would be an offense to human essence—we belonged as one.

Mesmerized by his tender strength, I marveled at my growing clarity—this man searched for me, fought for me, and now surrendered to me.

"She's waking up!" Miguel's cry pulled our attentions to the settee below where Felicia lay. Her husband knelt lovingly beside her. The doctor leaned over her on the opposite side, a miniature bottle gripped in his fingertips was waved back and forth under her nose.

Francisco released his embrace but kept his arm at my waist while he escorted me down the remaining stairs. Yet the moment I reached the ground floor, I ran to Miguel and threw my arms around his neck. "Thank you, Miguel." I squeezed. "Gràcies for coming for me."

He patted me on the back and cleared his throat. "It's what I would've done for my own daughter." His eyes glossed over as I leaned back to kiss him on the cheek.

"Any girl would be fortunate to call you *Papa*." He pulled me in tight once more and I could hear his labored breath begin to slow. Surely, we both recognized how vastly different tonight could have gone.

"We owe Thomas our thanks," he continued. "It was he who directed your grandmother here and upon her return without you, he showed me and Francisco the way."

"Grand-mère is here?" I scanned the room.

Francisco came up behind us. "No, she's waiting for you at the Inn. She's safe."

I glanced up to the room once more where the mezzanine remained empty. I did not want to think of what might've happened if they didn't arrive in time. "Where is the man who guarded my door? Did you see a man when you arrived?"

"A large burly fellow?" Miguel quipped.

"Uh, huh."

"He didn't stick around for long." Francisco's lip lifted part way. "As soon as he caught sight of Miguel's shotgun aimed at his chest, he dashed out of the house. I knew that gun would come in handy at some point." The men chuckled lightly while I grinned at the thought of Anita scolding Miguel for such an exploit.

I moved towards Felica as the doctor stood up and spoke to her husband. "Aside from the unsightly contusion, her injuries are slight. With rest, she will make a full recovery."

The butler reached out and shook his hand then leaned in to kiss his wife. His nose gently nuzzled hers. My eyes filled with tears at the sight of such fond affection.

"Doctor," a calm voice floated from the floor above us. "Would you please come upstairs." My eyes met his—the man I now knew to be Thomas. His ruffled black hair framed apparent sorrow as he clutched the iron railing. Though striking similarities to him and Lucien caused my breath to hitch, a warmth, far from his brother's callous demeanor, was easily conveyed.

"Thank you," I spoke near silence, but loud enough for all to hear. He nodded my direction and only shifted his attention when the doctor arrived on the second floor.

Turning back towards Felicia, I stepped closer.

"Oh!" she gasped and attempted to sit up but her sweet husband encouraged her to lie still. I came to her. "Oh, my sweet girl," she continued. Her frail hands cupped my cheeks. "Are you alright?"

"Yes," I smiled. "Thanks to you."

"I never believed he would harm me . . . or you." She sniffled. "I . . .I did nothing to stop him."

"Oh, no," I reached for her hands and brought them to my heart, "but you did. You delayed him long enough for my rescuers to arrive." I kissed her hands. "You are very brave."

"As are you." She smiled again and looked to Francisco and back to her husband. "Where is Lucien?"

Francisco stepped forward placing both his hands on my shoulders. "Thomas is with him, upstairs."

"Thomas?" Her eyelashes fluttered. Her weakness still apparent. "I have missed that boy."

"We must go," Francisco said. "Isabel's grandmother awaits her."

"Yes, of course." She faced me and smiled.

I kissed her on the cheek. "Thank you, Felicia."

Once Francisco and I joined Miguel and turned to leave, I stared back for a moment. "Do you think she'll be alright?"

Miguel wiped his eyes. The weariness of the night appeared on his face. "I hope so," he mumbled and added, "I believe they both will be better off now." His intimation of Lucien's absence being a good thing was not missed.

Inside the carriage, I took a long, cleansing breath. Miguel sat across from us and pulled his hat low over his eyes. His snores thundered before the driver even shook the reins. This whole ordeal, leaving Menorca, facing the unknown in Algiers, and rescuing me must've taken a toll on him. It very well could've been the hardest thing he had done in decades and he did it all for me.

Francisco wrapped one steady arm around me, his other hand comforted mine in my lap. My head fell lightly against his shoulder. Relief finally made its way through my aching limbs and for the first time in days, I felt truly safe.

"Thank you, Francisco," I whispered. "Thank you for saving me . . .again."

His breath slowed. Its warmth tickled my skin as his lips brushed my forehead. With a quiver in his voice, he repeated his sentiment. "If I had lost you, Isabel. I—"

Placing my fingers over his mouth to stop him, I cut him off and gripped his hand once more. "You didn't." I assured. *Tonight will not haunt us with 'what ifs'*. It was a dangerous path to roam and the fact that we were all leaving together, *alive*, brought the only comfort I needed.

His hand released long enough to retrieve a small pouch from the seat cushion next to him. Tugging the small opening apart, he pulled a long rusted chain out and placed the dangling object into my palm. The raised relief of a woman's profile faced me. I gasped at the sight of the cameo that had been worn around my mother's neck for as long as I could remember. Its surface was tarnished, and the coral had chipped off her hair and face, but I recognized it nonetheless. I slipped my fingernail to the grooves on the side and cracked the locket open to reveal the damaged photographs within. Had they been preserved; they would've revealed both Papa and me. Turning it over to the backside, the simple engraving "from Antoine to Harriet" remained intact. I hardly believed its existence. "Where did you find this?"

Francisco smiled, his deep dimple beaming through his injuries. "When Susana and I retrieved my parent's possessions, I searched for yours as well. This was the only item they had listed under the name Fontaine. The Procurador said it was found tangled in the hinge of a porthole that washed ashore."

I curled my fingers around it and held tight. "This is the most wonderful gift you could ever give me."

Francisco reached for my hand and brought it to his pounding heart. "Please," the plea in his voice was filled with emotion. "Please don't ever leave me again."

My spirit soared with his touch, his words, and his very presence. I lifted my head and let my eyes behold him. His hair was tousled, a bruise formed on his jaw below the previous burn, and a jagged cut trailed blood, yet he was the most handsome man I'd ever known.

My lips parted in awe. My body quivered. "You *want* me to stay with you?"

"No." He shook his head and leaned forward as his lips brushed mine. The sweetness of the kiss kept short, but his mouth remained near. "I *want* you to marry me."

EPILOGUE

10 February 1911

Isabel Maria

"Take my hand, Isabel, the terrain is rather rough." I glanced at Francisco's outstretched arm then ahead, past the century old stones etched with loving epitaphs. A small crowd gathered, adorned in mostly black attire, and though this was a commemoration of sorts, a grim mood hovered around us.

"Cisco . . ." I pulled his clasped hand to my chest, hoping his touch would soothe my rapid heartbeat.

He drew me in and wrapped his arms around me. His lips brushed past my cheek and settled next to my ear. "We can do this together, love."

I knew he had as much of a reason to feel as disheartened as I. Both he and Susana suffered greatly with the loss of their parents. Their absence carved a hole in all aspects of their lives. Nothing could replace Basilio and Cristina's zest for life.

Leaning back, I glanced into Francisco's eyes and allowed his strength to ease into me. The sun's rays overhead forced the gold in his pupils to burst with intensity. A longing stirred deep within and the love that I had for this man consumed every part of me. He had been my anchor this past year; very rock I stood upon.

Today was the first anniversary of the Général Chanzy sinking. This fateful day's approach had lingered in the hazy corners of my mind, yet ached to come forth and be done with. Standing in the Ciutadella cemetery, the angelic sculpture fashioned by the famous artist, Logroño Indalecio Rodriguez, loomed dauntingly high above and cast an eerie shadow across the tombstones. It was meant to bring peace and comfort to the families of the deceased, but to someone who had survived, its reminder of my near drowning came much more forceful.

Francisco knew this look all too well. Leaning in, he kissed me, long and lovingly—the one sure way to shift my thoughts back to him. It never failed. "I love you." His lips shuddered against mine as he spoke. "And I will always be here for you."

In truth, he had hardly left my side since our return from Algeria and, with no hesitation, made true on his promises. He asked me properly for my hand and opened his home and life to my sweet Grand-mère. Though she insisted on remaining in Marseille most of the time to manage the compagnie affairs, she insisted we visit every summer, after the olive harvest.

When Francisco leaned back, my eyes followed the outline of his face. He no longer bore the scars of that dreadful night when he, Miguel, and Thomas came to my rescue. I let my finger graze his jaw, slide up across his cheekbone, and brush his hair off his forehead. He smiled at my touch and when his dimple intensified, it never failed to take my breath away. "You look handsome." My heart continued to thump in quickened beats as one of his eyebrows rose in playful response. He reached for my hand and lifted it to his lips. The caress came light and sincere. His mouth stopped at the ring which grazed my third finger and kissed the silver band twice before he released.

Our wedding the past July had been a joyous occasion. The garden at the Contreras' had been prepared for a beautiful, intimate ceremony. Grayish purple orchids burst in full bloom, jasmine blossoms thrived, and long-stemmed lavender fringed the pathway to the vicari. Grand-mère offered me to Francisco through a trail of laurel leaves and Miguel stood as his man of honor.

In my simple ivory gown, and Francisco in his new dark suit, we shared our vows. Watching the man I adored promise to love and cherish me forever, I couldn't help but show gratitude for the treacherous path that brought me here. Though my journey was filled with enormous pain, uniting with Francisco in the end was worth every part of it.

Anita and Susana prepared the wedding feast with a desire to honor my French traditions. This included the customary *la roste*, a roasted bread soaked in sweet wine, as well as a *croquembouche*. The crème filled pastry puff drizzled with caramel glaze was the wedding dessert served at my own parent's nuptials. I was touched by Anita's kindness to include their memory.

Only a handful of friends attended, including Javier and Lupe. Thomas Chastain graciously answered our invitation and brought Arthur and Felicia from Algiers and, though his brother Lucien's memory hovered nearby, Thomas had effectively restored his family name making every effort to undo his brother's misdeeds—even a renewed business arrangement to distribute the Carrasco olives.

Though there was little admission from either party, it was hard to miss the energy that came from Thomas and Susana's first introduction. Thomas' attractive looks were magnified through the gentleness of his words. The arrogance and pride Lucien had perfected was not to be found in Thomas' delightful nature. He was every bit the opposite of his brother, honest and honorable. And to Susana's great benefit, Thomas showed genuine admiration for her intelligence and determination. Even today as we maneuvered the coastal landscape near the Nati Headlands, I peered up to see Susana's arm draped comfortably through the sleeve of Thomas' stylish long coat, their heads leaning near one another in quiet whisperings.

Being Francisco's bride these last eight months has made me the happiest woman in the world. He doted on me at every turn, showered me with love, and assured me, without question, all of it was real. Lies and untruths no longer wedged between us, cleared entirely by love and devotion.

"Wait." I stopped in place. The heavenly wings of the angelic creature sheltered merely a step away. Francisco moved his hands to my waist and faced me. Even now his touch tingled. When his eyes caught the sunlight, they showered me with kindness. "Are you well?"

I peered over to the monument which had brought us all together again.

"It's this place." I pointed across the sea as it rolled in waves then crested ardently along the coast. The mild weather and slow breeze contradicted the turmoil from my memory. My chest raised and lowered to uneven breaths several times before I found the right words "The weight of the loss of your parents, my parents, Ines, and Remý, in addition to many other's loved ones plagues me. I struggle to understand why the sea spared *me*. What did I do to afford a life of true happiness?"

Francisco's eyes warmed over me, sending shivers down both of my arms. "Because God knew, *amor meu*, I could not live without you." There was no humor in his words and the seriousness in his countenance confirmed the depth of his devotion.

Pulling one of his hands to my belly, I laid my hand over his. "I want this place to be a joyful memory. I don't want to be overwhelmed with grief every time I visit. When I look out to the sea here, I want to embrace peace, love, and affection.

"We can . . . remember?" His lips curled into a soft smile. "We are the ones who *own our response*." Francisco quoted the words from his mother. The very words that imprinted on my soul the day we departed from Marseille on the Chanzy.

"I'm expecting, Cisco."

It only took a second for the news to register before he let out the breath he'd been holding. He wound his arms tight around me as if there was a sudden need to protect me.

"Truly?" he whispered.

I nodded.

His breath increased as he looked upward and when his eyes returned to mine, they were filled with tears. "Thank you," he said and kissed my cheek. "Thank you for making me exceedingly happy." His dimple deepened. Its appearance always stirred me in mischievous ways.

I returned his smile and he kissed me again. Once separated, he glanced around. "Can we . . .can we tell them?"

"Yes.".

He gently swung me around to the loving faces before us. They had stopped moving when we did. Anita's arm draped through Miguel's, Susana's through Thomas'. Arthur's arm clutched Felicia's shoulders, and my Grand-mère stood stately between them all.

Francisco took one last sweep across my face and flashed the biggest grin. Emotion fringed on his tongue. "We are going to have a baby!"

A joyous hurrah erupted and I immediately found myself embraced by loved ones—most of which I was not acquainted with a year ago. Yet as my eyes fell upon each one, a simple affirmation stirred within . . . regardless of the way our peculiar family came together, there was no doubt, we were meant to find each other.

Author's Note

In 2018, as part of an archaeological dig, I became familiar with the Balearic island of Menorca (*Menorca* is the Spanish/Catalan spelling. *Minorca* is the English/Latin spelling), the town of Ciutadella (aka Ciudadela) and the areas known as Sanisera and Sanitja Port. I have always been fascinated with centuries old churches and convents and spent some time in the *Convento de San Agustin* (convent) in Ciutadella. While there, I discovered a room with various shipwreck stories and artifacts (there were many!) and stumbled upon a French newspaper clipping of the Général Chanzy shipwreck. I was immediately drawn to the story. I remember being fascinated with the idea that there was only **one** survivor. Then of course, my mind began to spin. *What if there was a second survivor?* One who did not want to be found. From that point on, every afternoon after being in the field, I walked to the coast which was only a few streets from my flat and sat on the rocks and penned my story.

Since the shipwreck took place in February, I had to stretch the timeline for the olive harvest in Menorca which actually takes place in November, December, and January. Depending on the type of olive or its purpose, it can begin as early as September and October, but for the rationale of this novel, I made the harvest dates March to May.

The names of the Général Chanzy passengers listed in the book, were retrieved directly off the ship's manifest, however just like the story, it initially did not have a complete listing. There are also varying numbers for the deceased, anywhere from 150-180. Most of the specific details I used in the novel of the shipwreck came from both a Welsh and French press including the name of the sole survivor, Marcel Badez. He too, was found to have various spellings of his family name- Badez and Bodez. I used the one from the French article printed on 12 February 1910 (in the novel the date of the article is 16 February 1910). Marcel Badez was traveling to Algiers to his new employment as a customs clerk. He was not a serviteur that we know of as created in the story. He did, however, cling to rocks, then swam to shore and took refuge in a cave for a day before he climbed the jagged coastline to get help. Due to the language barrier from French to Spanish, Marcel drew a picture of the shipwreck using charcoal. It is true nobody in Ciutadella knew of the Chanzy shipwreck until Marcel arrived in town and notified authorities two days later.

In a book by Alfonso Buenaventura called, "*Naufragios y siniestros en la costa de Menorca*", he includes Monsieur Badez' belief as to why he survived.

> "*...In his explanations he would attribute the catastrophe to the invasion of the water of the sea to the room of boilers producing immediately afterwards an explosion. «What saved me is that I had the presence of sufficient spirit to get a life jacket and of throwing myself firmly to the sea»...*"

Any conversations between Marcel Badez and fictional characters in the novel were created for the purpose of storytelling. There is no record of his interactions or behavior with others.

It is presumed that the reason there were no other survivors was because the incident happened around 4 am when most passengers were asleep and the crash, explosion and sinking occurred under 3 minutes. The bodies which were retrieved were mostly found in the channel between Menorca and the neighboring island of Majorca and quite unidentifiable. Many of the items recovered from the sea contained scorched evidence of the explosion.

The actual site of the Général Chanzy sinking (The Punta Nati Headland) would not technically allow for Isabel's body to float to the Sanitja Port, but possibly the coast near the British Defense Tower that Miguel speaks of in the story. On the east side of the tower in the cove you find *Sanisera*. It's the location of the archaeological dig, which includes a Roman city, basilica, and port, and across the bay you see the Cavalleria Lighthouse. Departing Es Mercadal on the way to the Sanitja Port, we enter a lush and hilly tract of land where numerous estates are seen immersed with olive trees and grape vines. I fell in love with this area and for that reason I chose this as the location for both the Contreras' and Carrasco's properties.

There are three known memorials for the Général Chanzy in Menorca. An elaborate sculpture of an angel designed by Logroño Indalecio Rodriguez is found in the Ciutadella cemetery completed in January 1911. On 16 June 1917, 12 unidentified bodies were transferred from their initial burial ground and interred there. The English translation of the inscription is as follows-

In Paradise
"Let the angels take you to paradise, let the martyrs greet you on your arrival, and let them guide you to the holy city, Jerusalem. Let the choirs of angels welcome you and with Lazaro, the poor old man, you reach eternal rest…"

Antiphon/ Requiem by Gabriel Faure

Another memorial is a concrete cross found near the Punta Nati Lighthouse. Completed in one year, the lighthouse became operational in 1913 at the demand of French authorities, specifically in response to the Chanzy shipwreck.

The third memorial is a stone block placed on the grounds of Chateau Danem and designed by Georges Wybo. It honors the loss of the many French cabaret artists (including acrobats and comedians) who perished in the wreck on their way to perform in Algiers.

(In the Epilogue, the angel statue is fictitiously portrayed at the Punta Nati Headland for storytelling purposes but is found at the Ciutadella Cemetery.)

Though Isabel quotes Pio Baroja's novel *"Las Inquietudes de Shanti Andía"* at Cala Morell, the book itself was not published until 1911. The "El Mar" series of seven books were written by Pio Baroja over several decades covering adventures on the sea and eventually brought to Spanish Cinema. I found this concluding excerpt to be hauntingly true.

> *"We want to understand the sea, and do not understand it, we want to find reason, and we do not find it. It is a monster, an incomprehensible sphinx, dead is the laboratory of the life, inert is the representation of the constant worry. Often we suspect if there would be hidden something as a lesson in it, some moments one supposes to have deciphered her mystery, in others, her education escapes from us and gets lost in the reflection of the waves and in the hiss of the wind. All without knowing why, we suppose to the sea woman, we all provide her with an instinctive and changeable enigmatic and perfidious personality."*
>
> -Pio Baroja *"La Inquietudes de Shanti Andía"*

Thank you for reading *Second Survivor*. My hope is that the facts surrounding the tragedy of the Général Chanz, have moved you as much as it did me. Though there is no obligation, I would love for you to review your experience on Amazon, Goodreads, or Bookbub. I also invite you to join my mailing list at www.leahmoyes.com. I send a newsletter once a month and guard your privacy fiercely. Once on the website take a moment to view the gallery, read my blog or discover the other historical fiction novels I've written. Thank you again for choosing to read *Second Survivor*.

Notes: The Général Chanzy's story can be further researched at http://www.generalchanzy.com/historia_en.html and the SS Général Chanzy at https://www.wrecksite.eu/wreck.aspx?142689 with a copy of the French press document at https://www.wrecksite.eu/docBrowser.aspx?7175?5?1

Language glossary (Alphabetical order)

Adéu- **Goodbye** (Catalan)
Adhhab- **Go** (Arabic)
Aidez-moi- **Help me** (French)
Aigua, si—us plau- **Water, please** (Catalan)
Aix-Marseille 1- **One of the locations for the University of Provence** (French)
Arroz caldos amb peix con langosta si us plau- **Rice broth with lobster, please** (Catalan)
Arroz de la Tierra- **Rice from the earth** (Catalan)
Ascot- **Tie-** (French)
Au pair- **A nanny or helper** (French)
Bé- **Good** (Catalan)
Benvingut- **Your welcome** (Catalan)
Bergère- **An upholstered armchair** (French)
Bienvenue en Espagne mon ami- **Welcome to Spain my friend** (French)
Boisson- **Drink** (French)
Bona Tarda- **Good afternoon** (Catalan)
Bon dia- **Good day** (Catalan)
Bonne journée- **Good day** (French)
Bourak- **Middle Eastern egg rolls** (Arabic)
Brasseries- **Breweries** (French)
Chemise- **Undershirt** (French)
Chignon du cou- **Neck bun** (French)
Compagnie- **Company** (French)
Confit de canard- **Duck breast and leg** (French)
Crespelis- **Flower shaped cookies, stuffed with jam or lemon/cottage cheese and covered in fine sugar** (Catalan)
Cul- **Ass** (French)
Décolletage- **A woman's cleavage** (French)
D'équipage- **Crew** (French)
Dona- **Wife** (Catalan)
Elixir d'Amorique- **French whisky** (French)
Estable- **Stable** (Catalan)
Et- **And** (French)
État irve- **Drunken state** (French)
Faux- **False** (French)

Femme- **Woman** (French)
Fêtes- **Celebrations/Festivities** (French)
Fleques- **Bakeries** (Catalan)
Germà- **Brother** (Catalan)
Gràcies- **Thank you** (Catalan)
Grand-mère- **Grandmother**
Ho sento, amor- **I'm sorry, love** (Catalan)
Hola- **Hello** (Catalan)
Hola, si us plau- **Hello, please** (Catalan)
House of Worth- **Charles Worth fashion** (French)
Infirmière- **Nurse** (French)
Kabyle- **Berber people and customs in Northeast Algeria** (Arabic)
Kaldereta- **Lobster stew** (Catalan)
Kun hadiana- **Be quiet** (Arabic)
L'amour- **Love** (French)
Le peinture apparaiser- **Painting (Fine art) Appraiser** (French)
L'homme d'affaires- **Man of business** (French)
Limonade- **Lemonade** (French)
L'Industrie- **Industry** (French)
Liqueur- **Liquor** (French)
Macarrones- **Menorcan dish of pasta and meat** (Catalan)
Maisîr- **Gambling forbidden by Islamic law** (Arabic)
Maman- **Mother** (French)
Maria. El meu nom és Maria.-**Maria. My name is Maria** (Catalan)
Marit- **Husband** (Catalan)
Mélange- **Mixed** (French)
Meravellós- **Wonderful** (Catalan)
Merci- **Thank you** (French)
Merda- **Shit** (Catalan) *Merde*- **Shit** (French)
Mesdames- **Ladies** (French)
Migdiada- **Nap** (Catalan)
Mon frère- **My brother** (French)
Monsieur- **Mr.** (French) *Madame*- **Mrs.** *Mademoiselle*- **Miss**
Négligé- **Nightgown** (French)
No ho sé- **I don't know** (Catalan)
Non- **No**- (French)
Oh, doux- Saint Laziosi- **Oh, Sweet, Saint Laziosi** (French)

Oliaigua soup- **Oil soup mixed with mushrooms, asparagus, or figs** (Catalan)
Oli de romani i all- **Garlic and Rosemary olive oil** (Catalan)
On sóc?- **Where am I?** (Catalan)
Oudh/Oud- **An ancient perfume/ a woodsy balsamic scent typical to Arabs** (Arabic)
Oui- **Yes** (French)
Pares- **Parents** (Catalan)
Passagers- **Passengers** (French)
Père- **Father** (French)
Perol- **Menorcan dish that layers fish, potatoes, tomatoes, and bread** (Catalan)
Personnes- **People** (French)
Petite fille- **little girl** (French)
Pettis- **Underskirt** (French)
Plaça d'es Born- **Square in Ciutadella** (Catalan)-
Plaza del Mercat- **Market Square** (Catalan)
Procuradors- **Solicitors**-(Catalan)
Profiteroles- **Crème puffs typically with custard filling** (French)
Què?- **What** (Catalan)
Senyor- **Mr.** (Catalan) *Senyora-* **Mrs** (Catalan) Senyoreta- **Miss**
Serviteur- **Servant** (French)
Sí-**Yes**- (Catalan)
Sobrasada- **Raw, cured sausage a food known to the Balearic Islands** (Catalan)
Soldados- **Soldiers** (Catalan)
Subteniente- **Second Lieutenant** (Catalan)
Sûreté- **French civilian police** (French)
The Salon de Vente- **A high-end dress shop** (French)
Ton frère- **Your brother** (French)
Tombet- **Traditional vegetable dish of the Balearic Islands** (Catalan)
Un vàter- **A toilet** (Catalan)
Vicari- **Vicar/Priest** (Catalan)
Voile drawers- **Sheer linen for clothing** (French)
Whisky- **European spelling of the alcoholic drink** (French)
Ya lbn el sharmouta- **You son of a bitch** (Arabic)

About the Author

Leah Moyes is from the sunny state of Arizona. She is a wife and a mother, a former teacher, and a coach with a background in Archaeology. She loves popcorn and seafood (though not together) and is slowly checking off her very long bucket list.

<u>Current Titles</u>
The Berlin Butterfly Series-
Historical Fiction Novels about the Berlin Wall
Ensnare (Book 1)- Amazon #1 Bestseller
Deception (Book 2)
Release (Book 3)
Charlock's Secret- Historical Romance /Time Travel 19th century England
Return to Charlock- Book 2

<u>Upcoming Releases</u>
Berlin Butterfly Novellas- Anton and Stefan- (2021)
Susana and Thomas Novella (2021)

Printed in Great Britain
by Amazon